ORANGE [MINT AND HONEY]

An Essen[...]

"*Orange Mint and Honey* . . . wil[...] [...]sence

"Poignant." —*Ebony*

"[An] accomplished debut . . . Brice's straightforward prose is dead-on in describing the challenges Shay and her mother face as they reconnect."
—*Publishers Weekly*

"Carleen Brice is a fine writer. I have recommended and will continue to recommend *Orange Mint and Honey* to others."
—TERRY McMILLAN, author of *The Interruption of Everything*

"A wonderful, jazzy, exciting read. The marriage of historical confidence with creativity brings forth the first novel by Carleen Brice. *Orange Mint and Honey* makes use of the oldest of relationships: mothers and daughters. Looking at the plights of love, forgiveness, understanding, and redemption brings to this first novel a fresh and unique feel."
—NIKKI GIOVANNI, author of *Acolytes*

"A keeper . . . an open, sweet, realistic novel about a woman's journey to find her own heart and home."
—KRIS RADISH, author of *The Sunday List of Dreams*

"Mothers and daughters—the closest of bonds, the most loaded of relationships. Carleen Brice mixes in alcohol, abandonment, and anger for a potent cocktail and a penetrating read."
—VIRGINIA DEBERRY and DONNA GRANT, authors of *Better Than I Know Myself*

"In *Orange Mint and Honey*, Brice deftly shows the importance and joy of understanding our past and not only forgiving those who hurt us, but loving them in spite of that hurt. We see Shay on her journey to discovering who she is and all that she can be—even when she's not sure she's ready to meet the person she's about to become."
—JUDY MERRILL LARSEN, author of *All the Numbers*

"*Orange Mint and Honey* is sweet fun—yet also a socially conscious page-turner about accountability and forgiveness. In this memorable story of a once-derelict mother and a profoundly wounded daughter, rage, sadness, and humor jump off the page and grip us until the end."
—ELYSE SINGLETON, author of *This Side of the Sky*

"After several praised works of nonfiction, Colorado author Carleen Brice sucessfully moves to fiction with this bittersweet story featuring an engagingly wry, spirited narrator. Grade A–."
—*Rocky Mountain News*

ALSO BY CARLEEN BRICE

Orange Mint and Honey

Children of the Waters

CARLEEN BRICE

Children of the Waters

~~~ A NOVEL ~~~

Carleen Brice

ONE WORLD

BALLANTINE BOOKS | NEW YORK

A One World Books Trade Paperback Original

Published in the United States by One World Books, an imprint of The Random House Publishing Group, a division of Random House, Inc., New York.

ISBN 978-0-345-49907-3

Printed in the United States of America

www.oneworldbooks.net

www.randomhousereaderscircle.com

2 4 6 8 9 7 5 3 1

Book design by Laurie Jewell

TO DIANE DONALDSON,
WHO'S LIKE A SISTER TO ME

AND TO WUANDA WALLS,
WHO WILL NEVER BE FORGOTTEN

"Not everything that is faced can be changed.
But nothing can be changed until it is faced."

— JAMES BALDWIN

"You didn't come into this world.
You came out of it, like a wave from the ocean.
You are not a stranger here."

— ALAN WATTS

A NOTE TO READERS

The hoodoo rituals in this book, while based on actual concepts, are fictional. I am not a roots worker, nor did I feel that it was responsible to reproduce real spells or magic in the pages of a novel. If you're interested in real African and African American spiritual practices, I recommend *Sticks, Stones, Roots & Bones* by Stephanie Rose Bird, *Tapping the Power Within* by Iyanla Vanzant, and *The Way of the Orisa* by Philip John Neimark.

PROLOGUE

~~~~~~~~~~~~

Nineteen years ago

Time was short. Maxine Kuepper was starting to say things she didn't mean. Yesterday, she told her granddaughter to *move my dish,* when she wanted to ask her to bend her leg. Trish stared, stumped and afraid, yet all Maxine could do was yell the word "dish" over and over, knowing that she wasn't making any sense.

Cell by cell, bone by bone, Maxine was floating away. She didn't know if it was the cancer or the medication that made her say such things. She was wearing a patch that released heavy doses of relief into her bloodstream, and still the littlest weight on her, like a sheet or the cotton nightgowns they dressed her in, hurt. The nurse promised that when the time came Maxine wouldn't have any pain. "We'll snow you out," the nurse assured her. "Don't worry."

Maxine would die the way her daughter did, like a mermaid swimming at the bottom of an ocean of drugs. It was small comfort after all these years to believe that Jocelyn hadn't been in any pain when she died. *Jocelyn*. Such a cultivated name for a daughter who would not be tamed.

They were coming for her, Jocelyn and John, her husband, both dead. She dreamed of them so much now that sometimes she could swear they were really here in this room, whispering their secrets to her. They were coming for her. If they weren't already here, she knew they were just over the other side waiting. And even though she was only sixty years old and her granddaughter Trish was only seventeen, she was ready to join them. But she had one last thing she had to do. She had secrets of her own to tell.

She looked at the Polaroid picture she'd kept hidden for thirteen years. Not even John knew she had proof of this moment. There was Jocelyn, blond and movie-star gorgeous even after just giving birth, holding the baby, only hours old with a cap of thick dark hair. And Trish, smiling wide, skin, teeth, *and* hair white as cream, on the hospital bed next to them. Both girls marked with a stain that couldn't be washed away.

Maxine wished she had done things differently. But wishes are for the living. She sighed and pain rippled through her as her lungs pushed up against the battlefield of her ribs and the space where her left breast used to be. She raised the pen with the same amount of exertion that it used to take to lift a gallon of milk and began to write.

The nurse said don't worry. But how could she not? What would they think of her? Would they hate her or would they be glad to know the truth? Probably both. But she would do this one last thing for them. She would make things right. As soon as Trish came home, Maxine would give her the letter.

I should have told you this a long time ago, she wrote to her granddaughter, putting everything that was in her battered heart onto the page so that when the time came cowardice wouldn't seal her lips. Each word, a lifetime.

Just as she finished, she heard the front door open and close. Or she thought she did. Lately it was hard to tell what sounds were real and what sounds were memories sweeping over her like ocean waves. But if it was Trish coming in, Maxine knew she did not have the strength to see the look on her granddaughter's face after she read this letter. She didn't have the strength to answer the question she knew would come no matter how hard she tried to explain: *How could you?*

She opened the box, put the letter and photo inside, and replaced the lid. After she was gone, Trish would find everything she needed to know. When Maxine was buried, her lies would be unearthed. It wouldn't be long now. She was sipping life from a glass that was neither half empty nor half full, a glass emptying so rapidly she could see it in the eyes of the hospice nurses and the few friends who came to visit her at home.

The bedroom door opened, and Trish poked her head in. "Nana, you awake?"

Maxine nodded, thinking *For now,* and, *Please, God, let them forgive me.*

PRESENT DAY

CHAPTER 1

~~~~~~~~

Trish

Since Trish Taylor came back home to Aurora, Colorado, she had found ten jigsaw puzzle pieces. They seemed to be everywhere: on the sidewalk near her house, in the parking lot at the grocery store, in the park where she walked her dogs.

Trish's grandmother used to put jigsaws together. Now, a different type of woman would have started to think something funny was going on, that all these puzzle pieces were some kind of sign. But Trish wasn't the kind who believed in symbols or signs from above. No gods, ghosts, afterlives, religion, or anything that couldn't be studied and quantified.

She believed in a life force. She had felt it when she was pregnant, and had seen it in animals in the different clinics where she had worked. So natural? Yes. But supernatural? No way, José. She'd known there wasn't a god since she was four years old, when her mother and baby sister were killed in a car accident.

She'd been on her way to work this morning at Friendly's Animal Hospital when she'd found the eleventh puzzle piece on the sidewalk right in front of the doors. She picked it up and bounced it in her left hand, the small pasteboard piece making a soft clicking sound against the peridot mother's ring she wore where her wedding ring used to be. The question that came to her when she found the first puzzle piece tickled the back of her mind, but again she dismissed it. One of her coworkers must have dropped it on the way in. Or maybe a client's child had lost it yesterday.

"Don't be silly," she said to herself, blowing blond bangs out of her eyes. She slid the jigsaw piece into the pocket of her scrubs and went inside to stock the treatment rooms with supplies before the first clients arrived. She set the puzzle piece on the front counter while she reached for her key to the supply room and pharmacy.

"*Qué es?*" Alicia Alemán asked.

Alicia, the practice manager, was the closest thing to a friend Trish had since she returned to Colorado. Friendly's was a three-doctor practice. All the vets were male and over forty. The rest of the staff was female, and most were so young Trish and Alicia secretly called them fetuses. Half-Mexican and half-Cuban, Alicia was even shorter than Trish (who was only five foot one) and reminded her of a beautiful tabby cat. Fat and sleek at the same time, caramel-skinned, with lush black hair. The definition of the word feminine. No matter the weather, she was always in heels and a skirt. One evening they went for drinks after work and Trish watched a man jab his chin with a fork full of food, missing his own mouth, because he was staring at Alicia.

"Nothing. I found it. I keep finding pieces of puzzles."

"*Cómo que . . . ?*"

"I've found eleven puzzle pieces in the last month."

"*Here?*"

"All over town."

Alicia scrunched up her face, creating charming little wrinkles around her eyes. "To the same puzzle?"

"No. Different parts of different puzzles."

"Why would you be finding puzzle pieces?"

"I have no idea."

"Do you do puzzles?"

"No." Trish hesitated. If she said the ridiculous idea she couldn't seem to shake, the conversation was going to veer in a direction she was pretty sure she didn't want it to go. "My grand-mother liked to do puzzles."

"Your *abuela* who's dead?"

Alicia was very close to her family. A semi-lapsed Catholic, she was divorced and only went to mass on Easter and Christmas Eve, but she still crossed herself before she ate and lit a candle to St. Francis of Assisi, patron saint of animals, every time they lost a patient.

"Don't get all weird on me," Trish said. "It's just a coinci-dence."

"Believing in ghosts isn't weird."

"Uh, I don't know about on your planet, but on my planet it is."

"Hey, my people invented a whole day to celebrate those who have passed on. On *El Día de los Muertos* we decorate and play music and put out food as offerings for our dead relatives."

"But that's totally symbolic. You don't really think they come back to eat the food."

"*Mira,* your *abuela* could be trying to talk to you."

Though she wasn't ready to admit it, this was the question that was swirling around in her mind: Were the puzzle pieces from Nana? "To say what? The woman barely spoke to me when she was alive. Why would she start talking to me now?"

"*Se las da de sabihonda.*" Alicia said to herself with frustration,

tucking a few strands of hair that had the audacity to go astray behind her ear. The rest of the female staff wore jewelry with little
dogs or cats on it. No critter earrings for Alicia though. Today, she
had small gold hoops in her ears. Trish would have bet money that
Alicia slid out of her mother's womb wearing pearls. Simple and
elegant even at birth. "She's not my grandmother. How should I
know?"

"The only advice she ever gave me was 'Keep your legs crossed
until you graduate.' "

Alicia laughed. "That's not the worst advice I ever heard."

"And why is it that when the dead 'speak' they don't come out
and say what they mean? Why do they always use mysterious hints
and clues? I mean really, fuck. Nana, if you've got something to
say, just say it already."

"This is how you speak to your grandma?"

Trish rolled her eyes. "That's my point. She can't hear me."

"That's *my* point. You're so *fresca,* cynical. You think life is supposed to always make sense. Not everything about life and death
is so reasonable and rational. You watch, once you figure out what
she's trying to tell you, you'll stop finding puzzle pieces."

She got a fun-size chocolate bar out of the bowl on the counter.
"Here. I know you think chocolate makes sense."

"Sadly, this is true," Trish said, opening the foil and popping
the candy into her mouth. Chocolate, doughnuts, cookies, and
pizza were Trish's four food groups. The sweetness melting on her
tongue now was almost enough to make her forget the fact that
she had gone up another dress size since her separation and divorce. She'd always been chunky, but now about the only thing she
felt comfortable in were her drawstring scrubs.

Back when things were good, Tommy, her ex, who was black,
used to tease her about her curves, saying things like, "How'd a
white girl end up with a big juicy booty like this?" But a few years

after having Will she went from having a luscious ass to being fat and boring, and by the time Will was four, Tommy was cheating on her.

"I totally have to go on a diet," she said.

Alicia rubbed her chin theatrically. "Hmmm. Where have I heard that one before?"

Trish frowned. It was all Tommy's fault. So she gained a little weight after getting married and having a baby. Who didn't? But the real weight didn't start to pile on until after she started finding condoms in his pocket and strange phone numbers on his cell.

"I mean it this time. I've got to do something. I've got to change something." And not only her weight. Trish had ostensibly come back to Colorado from North Carolina to escape the heat and humidity, but there was more to it than that. She was also hoping she'd be able to figure some things out. She was thirty-six and divorced, and her only son would leave the nest in a couple of years. If she wasn't going to be a wife and a mom, what was she going to be? Somehow she thought that if she came back to the place where she and Tommy had started, and where her family had started and disintegrated, she'd be able to figure out who she was again. If there was anything left for her, it had to be here.

But the last eight months had been taken up finding a house and a job and enrolling Will in school. She worked four days a week for at least ten hours, often eleven or twelve. And between her job, Will, and her dogs, she found herself just as lost here as she had been back in North Carolina.

"Maybe your *abuela* is trying to give you some clues about how to change."

Trish nearly choked on her candy. Nana giving anybody clues about changing their life was totally crazy. She looked at the clock. "I better get started. It's almost time to open the madhouse."

Over the course of the day, they saw a Lab that had swallowed six rocks, several vomiting cats, a cat that had killed a squirrel (a serious concern, since some squirrels in the area had tested positive for the plague), a dog that had been hit by a car, and lots of dogs and cats being treated for diseases like kidney failure, cancer, and diabetes. Trish barely had time to go to the bathroom, let alone think about puzzles and her dead grandmother.

At the end of the day, Shelli Pierce, one of their regular clients, brought in a Boston terrier she'd found.

"Left at Chatfield Reservoir like so much garbage," Shelli said furiously in a clipped accent still reminiscent of a childhood spent in England, her bushy ginger hair quivering with indignation. She was a compact woman with tiny round eyes and a sharp, cunning face like a Pomeranian.

The Boston terrier's ribs were showing, his breath was bad, and he had no tags or ID chip.

"I'd put him about a year old, and he hasn't been neutered," Dr. Pat muttered as he examined him.

That was how *friendly* Friendly's was: Clients were encouraged to call the vets by doctor and their first names.

Tall, skinny, hawk nosed, Patrick Volt was from the old days of vet med, when it was a man's game. Trish had hated Patrick since she started working there. Today, most veterinarians and technicians were women, but Dr. Pat treated everybody but the other doctors like servants. Well, except for Alicia. Nobody fucked with Alicia.

"Definitely mange," Dr. Pat said authoritatively, parting the dog's matted fur to look at his skin.

Trish mentally rolled her eyes. It didn't take six years of schooling to know that.

"He keeps dragging his bum," Shelli volunteered. "So I brought in a fresh sample."

"I'm sure we'll find worms."

We as in me, Trish thought, accepting the plastic bag of dog poop Shelli held up.

"Look at those big beautiful eyes," Shelli cooed to the scared dog. "Don't worry, puppy. I'll take you home soon. Yes I will. Yes I will."

Trish knew this was coming. Their records showed that Shelli had five dogs and six cats, more animals than the city allowed, and the staff was almost certain Shelli had other pets that she took to another clinic. "Just how many dogs do you have now?" Trish asked.

"What are you implying? I'm the good guy here! I saved this dog's life!" Shelli snapped. "Are you saying I don't take care of my animals? Because I take care of my animals! You should know that, considering you people have made a small fortune off me. I do not have to take this!"

She held her head high as if suddenly the animal smell of the clinic was disturbing her fine senses. But her overreaction only confirmed Trish's suspicions.

Dr. Pat's dark bushy eyebrows flew up. It always freaked Trish out that his eyebrows were black, but his hair had gone gray.

"That is not how we converse with our clients. Please apologize right now!"

Grrr. "I'm just looking out for you and the welfare of all your animals. That's all."

"That's what I'm trying to do too."

Well, at least she knows that someone around here has an eye on her. "Good. Then I apologize and I'm glad we agree." Trish turned to go to the lab with the bag of feces.

"Apology accepted," Shelli said grudgingly. "I'll be back to pick up Jigsaw tomorrow."

Trish spun around. "Excuse me? What did you call him?"

Dr. Pat glared down at Trish over his bifocals. "Jigsaw's a great name! Very unique," he said.

Shelli beamed. "I thought of it because he'll fit so well with the rest of the family. All my dogs are little ones, so they don't scare the cats. He'll fit right in."

The tickling in the back of her mind got a little stronger, but Trish still didn't believe that Nana was somehow communicating from beyond the grave. Trish was sure as shit that she wasn't supposed to let this dog go home with a hoarder.

After she went to the lab, she walked Shelli out to the front door. Just before she opened it, she leaned in close and whispered forcefully, "You're not taking that dog home. You have enough, *more* than enough animals."

Shelli gasped, but Trish held up one hand to stop her. "And I'm prepared to call animal control and file a report to prove it if I have to."

The tiny woman cringed. "You wouldn't."

Trish opened the door. "Try me."

Shelli drew all fifty-some inches of herself up straight and puffed her chest out. "I've been thinking I should look for another veterinarian. Now I'm sure of it," she said with a huff and marched out.

Trish closed the door behind her. It was time to lock up. She went into her pocket for the keys and the curves of the puzzle piece she had found that morning scratched a question she struggled to ignore against her fingertips. *No way am I calling that poor dog Jigsaw,* she thought. She turned the sign over so it read "Sorry, We're Closed" and locked the door behind her.

CHAPTER 2

~~~~~~~~~~

Billie

Billie Cousins shook exactly seven drops of sunflower oil mixed with lavender and rose essential oils into the palms of her hands. Then she bowed her head.

"Grandmothers and grandfathers,

Please watch over me.

Please watch over my man.

Please watch over the child growing inside me, who is of him and of me.

Thank you for your wisdom.

Thank you for your strength.

Thank you for your protection.

Ase!"

We'll name our baby Ambata, she thought. "To connect" in Kiswahili. She said it out loud, "Ambata," and anointed a pink candle with the blessing oil. Pink, the color of health and spiritual and familial love. She lit the candle and placed it on the low white-cloth-covered table next to the stick that showed the word "pregnant" in its little window. Also on the makeshift altar were a glass of fresh water (purification), a cobalt blue bowl filled with cornmeal (to feed the ancestors' spirits), a scallop shell (representing the Great Mother from which we all come), a few copper pennies (an offering to the ancestors), and photos of her deceased grandparents and great-aunts and -uncles. Because Billie didn't have an actual photo of her great-grandmother—the Cheyenne Indian who had passed down her long nose, narrow eyes, and wide cheekbones to her—she had framed a picture of a Cheyenne girl taken by the famous Western photographer Edward S. Curtis.

She lit a smudge stick, then left the bedroom and went to the living room. Starting at the front door, she waved the bundle of sage in the air. Even with the windows opened, the pungent aroma—reminiscent of marijuana, only sweeter—filled her nose. She was clearing the house with smoke, opening windows so that any negative energy could escape, just as she had done five weeks ago, the night this baby had been conceived. She knew now that what she was doing that night was opening the way for conception. Deep inside her there had been a secret wish to have a baby.

After she was diagnosed with lupus nine years ago, she had stopped taking birth control pills (she no longer wanted to put hormones and chemicals into her body) and switched to a diaphragm, closely tracking her cycle. The night with the sage had been far enough after she ovulated that she should have been safe, so she had left her diaphragm in the medicine cabinet. At least that's what she had told herself then. But now she had to admit that she had been hoping to tilt her world toward a change. A change she had once thought she'd never want to make.

Her sweetie Nick didn't want kids, and Billie wanted Nick. So when they got together she told herself that teaching Head Start, spending four long days a week with preschoolers, would fill any need for children. But she had been only twenty-six then, and had no idea that only six years later a wind would sweep through her empty womb and set off so many bells inside her that it would seem as if every wind chime in the neighborhood was ringing.

She wafted smoke over Nick's baby grand piano, the most expensive thing they owned. She kept it polished to a high sheen, and she could see her reflection in the dark wood.

Nick was in Oakland at his father's funeral. Billie had wanted to go with him, but he wouldn't let her. He never told her why he left California or why he didn't stay in touch with his family. He hadn't seen his father in fifteen years. The only thing he would say was that they put the funk in dysfunctional. Then he'd try to laugh it off, but she could tell he was hurt in some profound way.

She smiled wanly at herself and brushed a tuft of cat hair off the piano. Even though most of their stuff came from flea markets, garage sales, and thrift stores, their home pleased her. She had selected every stick of furniture, rug, plate, dish towel, woven basket, and piece of art with great care. She felt happy whenever she opened a drawer and everything was in its place. Sure, she was a little OCD (she and Nick had their first fight when he set the table with mismatched napkins), but she didn't understand people who didn't care about their living space. You could tell a lot about people by the way they lived. For example, if she went into someone's home and they didn't have any real art, not even one small piece by a local artist, if they had only framed posters or stuff that looked like it had come from cheap motels, she knew these were people she didn't want to associate with. Bourgie-boho, Nick called her.

And proud of it, she thought, moving one of the sofa pillows over just an inch, before she went through the dining room, kitchen, and to the small second bedroom.

Though there was an extra bed, they mostly used this room for storage. It was filled with their out-of-season clothes, the vacuum cleaner, bookcases with her old textbooks and books she'd read as a girl, and miscellaneous boxes of stuff. They'd have to move all the junk to the basement to make space for a crib. She'd make new curtains, sea-foam green for Ambata.

She returned to their bedroom and opened a window. She was starting to feel light-headed, as if the sage really *was* weed. She smiled at the ways in which her body was already changing. She looked up at the full moon, the Frog Moon, some Native American tribes called April's moon. Then she waved the burning herbs over the bed, remembering Nick's long brown body underneath hers, the desire for her in his eyes, how he smelled like almond oil from the massage she had given him, how he called out her name, his voice so deep, so hoarse, it made her honey-colored skin flush now to think of it.

She extinguished the smudge stick, pulled her hair into a ponytail (Billie had what her mother called "Indian hair," meaning that compared to most black folks, the texture was fine, and since it curled more than it kinked, it was considered straight), and knelt before her altar, excitement and anxiety rising in her.

She had started speaking to the ancestors when she was twenty-one and her body turned on itself—her immune system attacking her own body's cells—causing fevers and unbelievable fatigue and making her joints ache like those of an elderly woman. At first she thought she had a terrible flu, but the symptoms hung on longer than any flu. When a strange rash broke out on her face so that her nose and right cheek were almost as red as the port-wine stain on her left cheek, she went to the doctor.

Her parents had taken her to church every Sunday until she was seventeen, but religion never meant to her what it did to them. However, when the doctor told her she had an incurable disease, she felt so scared and alone that she needed someone, something, outside of herself and fast. Getting dressed in the exam room after the doctor left, the only thought that made her feel even a little better was *Mommy and Daddy*. Knowing they were in the waiting room comforted her so deeply that she started to imagine everyone in her family surrounding her with love until they became as present as her own heartbeat. She could feel their energy in the room, feel them connected to her by a thick red cord unbroken by death, space, or time. And the more folks she added, the stronger she felt.

Just as she was about to leave the exam room and go out to her parents, she felt a warmth swell through her up from her feet as if coming through the floor, flowing up through her body all the way through her head. Then she felt a voice—*felt* was the only way to describe it—say *Fear not, daughter of our daughters. We are with you.* And she knew that her ancestors were there.

Over the years, she imagined a chain that stretched all the way back to Africa to the first mother. She pictured a veritable world of strong, proud, loving, wise black people behind her. And she found that if she spoke to them and listened very carefully, they offered guidance and direction.

Right now, she wanted comfort, assurance that the ancestors would be with her during this pregnancy, but she was far from sure they were going to give it. They would have something to say about Nick.

She couldn't imagine that Nick would be unhappy about the baby once reality set in, but at first, well, at first it was going to be rough. He'd been in such a funk after losing his only regular gig. The Nick Campbell Quartet had been playing every Friday and Saturday night at Bronco Bill's for a year. It was a dive and didn't pay a whole lot, but it was a steady gig when steady gigs were hard to come by. But two weeks ago the band showed up and the place was closed. No warning, just a note on the door for the bartenders, waitstaff, kitchen workers, and Nick's band. He was still absorbing that blow when his father died. He would be doubly likely to take the news about the baby badly.

Hopefully he was wearing the silver and turquoise ring she'd given him. It would protect him, as would the burdock root she'd hidden in his bag.

She took a small bottle and spritzed herself with lavender water to soothe her nerves. She tried to concentrate on praising and honoring her ancestors, feeling the connection between them and her and between them and her baby, but the more she thought about how moody Nick had been lately, the harder it was to keep calm. She could sense that the ancestors were telling her not to wait to tell him about the baby. Sooner was better than later for this kind of news, but she was starting to think that now wasn't the right time.

She tried to exhale negativity, fear, and doubt, and inhale peace and love, tried to let divine energy flow through her. For double good luck, she crossed her eyes and snapped her fingers three times. Then laughed at her silliness. Her older brother had taught her to do that when she was little. It had never brought her any luck, but it never failed to make her smile. Which was its own kind of luck.

Her condition increased her risk of miscarrying. But she hadn't had a lupus flare-up in three years, and all without Western drugs, thank you very much. The acupuncture, herbs, diet, exercise, and meditation the ancestors had guided her toward were working. She was healthy. This baby was healthy. Nick loved her, and once he got used to the idea, he would love their child too. And the ancestors would be with her through this pregnancy just as they had been since that dark day in the exam room nine years ago.

She sat on the floor cross-legged, limber from yoga and African dance, her joints loose in remission, closed her eyes and breathed, inhaling and exhaling loudly through her nose in deep ocean breaths. Juju, her cat, rubbed against her legs and purred.

They say when ghosts come around, the room goes cold. It was the opposite with the ancestors. When they were near, Billie felt the air around her and the blood in her veins warm. Then she would get a message. The ancestors would speak in one voice, neither male nor female. It was a voice without sound, more like a thought that entered her mind but wasn't her own.

Today she felt the familiar warmth spread through her. *Trying to control life is like trying to hold water in your hands* was the message she received today. *Daughter, tell your man the truth and the healing will continue. Wait too long and healing will slip through your fingers.*

She knew they were right, but still she worried about what would happen when she told Nick. She prayed for his ancestors, including his father, to help him through his depression, help him see that building a family with her would be a wonderful adventure. When he came home she would run a warm bath with sandalwood oil and rose petals and they would bathe by candlelight and make love under the fat moon. Then, the next morning she would tell him. After a breakfast of eggs, turkey bacon, strawberries, and wheat toast.

In the meantime, she ignored her fears, ignored the ancestors' urgings, and gave attention only to the knowledge that the thick red cord that ran through her would continue. She stood and turned in a circle, lifting her arms and legs, waving her hands in the air in a West African dance. The only drumming she needed was that of Ambata's heart.

CHAPTER 3

~~~~~~~~~

Trish

Skipper, Little Buddy, and Daisy were in the backyard when Trish got home from work with the Boston terrier she had decided to call Lucky. She left him in the car for a minute with the window halfway down to go greet the other pooches and let them know she loved them too. Skipper and Little Buddy were cattle dogs with speckled black-and-white coats. They looked alike except that Little Buddy, a boy, had only one eye, was three years younger, and weighed a good fifteen pounds more than Skipper, a girl. She'd had them for five years. Daisy was a cheerful, three-legged German shepherd–chow mix who had just come to live with them a month ago.

The dogs leapt at her when she opened the gate. "Down! Down!"

They sat and sniffed her scrubs. You'd think they'd be used to her coming home smelling like other dogs and cats, but they always got excited. She gave each of them a treat and a scratch behind the ears. "Now, listen everybody. There's a new guy in town. I want you to be nice to him, okay?" She went back through the gate and let Lucky out of the car. They entered the house through the garage. "Will?"

He was in the family room. Her handsome beige boy. Redbone, his dad's family, the black side, called him. The white side of the family was made up only of her, and she just thought of him as her baby.

Trish had grown up without a father and had desperately wanted her child to have one, which is why she stayed with Tommy far longer than she should have. Her grandfather had been a good provider. She never worried about food, always got three new outfits and a pair of new shoes every school year. But he was cold and mean, certainly not what she had fantasized about. Not a father, a *dad*. Someone who would read her bedtime stories, dance her around the living room on his feet when she was little, and teach her to drive and tease her about boys when she was a teen.

She wondered what Will would miss now. Tommy had been gone so much when Will was little that Trish had called herself and her son the Two Musketeers, which Will had pronounced "the Two Muckateers." But still, Tommy was better than no father at all. Would Will blame her one day for taking him away from his father?

The TV was blaring and he was on the computer, sitting next to his girlfriend Jessica. The room, as usual, was a mess, with several pairs of stinky sneakers all over.

"Hi, Jessica," Trish said, as usual a little taken aback by the girl's eyes. One was hazel and the other blue. Trish saw it occasionally in white cats. It was called heterochromia. But Jessica was the first person she'd met with the condition.

She was white, not that it mattered. Trish was proud that her son had friends of all colors. She wanted her son to see not race but people, to see beyond skin color to what was on the inside. She made sure that his new high school and their suburban neighborhood were totally integrated.

"Hey, Trish."

"Who's up for a walk?"

"Now?" Will asked. "We're getting ready to go to a movie."

"I could really use your help."

Will noticed Lucky sniffing around. "Another dog?" he grumbled.

Jessica popped up and went over to the little dog. "Come here, puppy. What's your name?"

That Jessica liked dogs was only one of the reasons Trish liked her. "I'm thinking Lucky?"

"Seriously, Dude, that's fuckin' crazy," Will said.

"Language!" Trish cussed like a trucker herself, but even she couldn't believe the foul things she heard coming out of kids' mouths these days. Will's friends called each other bitches, pussies, and motherfuckers—even the girls talked like that! And now that Will wasn't around his dad, he had developed a totally foul mouth.

"Look who's talking!"

"When you're grown you can talk however you want, but until then please do not use the f-word in front of your mother! Now come on, get up off your lazy butt."

"Dude, you know I ran, like, five miles this morning."

"Did you do poop patrol today?" It was supposed to be Will's job to clean up the backyard after the dogs, but somehow Trish always ended up doing it.

He smiled sheepishly, making the exact face he had made when he was three and tried to flush a toy car down the toilet.

If Tommy was here, no way would Will shirk his chores this way. Of course, if Tommy was here, Will's life wouldn't be turned upside down either. She sighed, knowing she was letting him get away with too much lately.

"We'll help you walk the dogs," Jessica said with girlfriendly authority.

The influence Jessica had on Will made Trish pretty sure they were sleeping together. Trish knew she could count on Jessica, who was always eager to be in her good graces. But she was starting to feel both grateful and uncomfortable having this girl count so much in Will's life. *Maybe I should get Jessica to tell Will to do poop patrol too.*

"Whatever, man," Will said, but he got up and put on his sneakers.

She was going to ask him later if he was using the Odor Eaters she'd bought him. She'd think he had a condition except that Tommy, once a teenaged boy himself, had assured her that it was normal. Not even the dog kennels were as smelly as her son's sneakers. Corn chips didn't even begin to describe it. They smelled more like a skunk that ate poisoned corn chips and died in the family room. Or maybe she was just more used to cat-and-dog stink than she was to growing-man stink. If he *was* sleeping with Jess, she hoped he left his shoes on. Otherwise, the poor girl would be traumatized for life.

"When we come home, I want you to leave those outside to air out before you bring them back in. Matter of fact, put all of them outside now."

"Dag, Mom!"

Jessica looked away, unsuccessfully trying to stifle a giggle.

While Will collected his shoes, she gathered plastic bags for poop. Then she put Skipper, who would be the easiest, on a leash. Skipper was fat, slow, and easygoing, like the ladies who worked in See's Candies, Trish's favorite place on earth. Little Buddy, mister alpha dog, would be introduced last.

Trish held Lucky while Will took Skipper's leash. The two dogs sniffed each other hesitantly. Tails wagged slowly. Treats were gobbled. So they took off.

Will cupped his crotch with his left hand as he walked. She remembered when he was a baby and he had discovered his penis. As soon as he found it, he didn't want to let it go. *Leave it. Leave it,* she thought, willing him to move his hand. It was the same command she used on Little Buddy when he tried to charge strange dogs. Will moved his hand away, and Trish smiled to herself. Will had lived in her body. She had nursed him for almost two years. But proof of their connection was growing rarer each day, so this made her happy.

So did walking in the chilly twilight with her son, his girlfriend, and the dogs. They were her only family now. They walked a couple of blocks and circled back to get Daisy. Daisy was a bit more curious about Lucky, and since she didn't let the lack of a back leg get in her way and she was three times his size, she scared him. But with lots of sweet talk and doggie chews they made it okay.

They did the same thing with Little Buddy, who miraculously behaved well.

After all the dogs were walked, Will dismissed himself. "All right. We gotta bounce."

"Why don't you guys watch a movie over here?"

"Yeah, right, we wanna hang with my mom on a Friday night." He rolled his eyes.

Jessica didn't rescue her this time. Clearly, she too was ready to ditch the old lady.

Trish walked them to the front door. She had hoped something in her life would change when she moved back home, but she was unprepared for what was changing. *This,* her son and her relationship with him.

"Bye, Trish." Jessica headed out to her car.

Trish tugged on Will's sleeve. "Wait a second."

"What?"

She hugged him. He was thin and lithe as a greyhound. It was hard to believe any body as beautiful as this one had come out of her chubby self. He was taller than she, with thick curls he smashed into waves by wearing a do-rag to bed (and sometimes out in public, which she hated). In the last year he had sprouted more than a few hairs above his lip.

She had been to his MySpace page. If he was drinking or drugging, he was smart enough not to put it on his page. But with all the girls who "friended" him, and all the talk about "ballers," "pimps," "hos," "hoochies," and "hooking up," she had to believe that he was probably no longer a virgin. He would be leaving to go to college in two short years and after that?

She flashed on the first time she had left him with a babysitter. He was ten weeks old, and the cries he made sliced through her. Hours later at work she could swear she still heard him wailing. But what was worse was the first time he cried for the babysitter, Barbara, when Trish picked him up to take him home. Trish had run out of the house holding him while he held his little arms out and screamed "Baba!" By the next week she had him in a day-care center where he had to share the "teachers" with a dozen other kids. She had lost everyone else in her life. She wasn't going to lose her son. Her head told her he wasn't her baby anymore, but her heart still didn't want to believe it. Still, her head told her it was time to ask the question. "Are you using condoms?"

Will turned a shade of red that his father's side of the family didn't get. "No you didn't just ask me that!"

Tommy had had "the talk" with Will before they left Charlotte, but still Trish felt it was important to reinforce the message. "Yes, I did. Are you?"

"Yeah."

"Every time?"

"Damn!"

"Language!" is what she said, but what she wanted to say was, *You think this is embarrassing for you?* "Well?"

"Yeah, yeah, and Jess is on the pill, okay?" he whispered. "Dag, nobody wants a kid, all right?"

"Or an STD," she reminded him. "Honey. . . ." She had so much else she wanted to say: *Be in love, but don't think this is it. First loves don't last. Don't do what your father and I did.* But she made herself stop. First of all, she tried not to say anything negative about Tommy to Will. And second, what would her warnings matter? People had told her and Tommy it was crazy to get married the year they graduated from high school, but they didn't listen. What teenagers in love ever did? "Be careful."

"Don't worry, okay?" Will kissed her on the forehead before hustling out as fast as he could.

She went into the kitchen and fed the dogs, filling the bowls according to pack order: Little Buddy, Daisy, Skipper, then Lucky.

"What should we do tonight, guys? Bowling? Putt-putt golf? Scrabble?"

Not surprisingly, the dogs were too busy gobbling their food to answer. Besides, they were on to her. They knew the only thing she'd do was pop in some movie starring Julia Roberts, Meg Ryan, or Reese Witherspoon and plop down in her easy chair. Who needed a husband or kids or a life when she had her dogs, her movies, and her La-Z-Boy?

She pulled some leftover Canadian bacon and pineapple pizza out of the fridge—there were only leftovers because Will claimed it "tasted like ass"—and nuked it in the microwave. She ate standing in the kitchen, giving each dog a piece of ham except for Daisy, who preferred pineapple, and washed the pizza down with Diet Coke and a few extra-strength antacids.

She pulled her latest find from the pocket of her scrubs. This new piece—with protuberances on either end and alcoves on each side—was large and bright yellow with sky blue on one tip and bubble gum pink on the other. Most likely from a kid's puzzle. She was about to toss it into the junk drawer in the family room computer desk with the rest of her collection, but changed her mind and took the other pieces out and laid them on the desk to see if any of them fit together. Of course they didn't. Why should they? Nothing in her life seemed to fit anymore. She threw all the pieces back in the drawer and turned on the TV.

"Should we synchronize our watches?" Trish asked. She and Will were at the mall the next day preparing to go their separate ways.

He laughed. "You're so gay."

"Hey!" she smacked his arm. "What'd I tell you about that?" His father, forever a Marine, encouraged macho homophobic behavior, but Trish didn't approve.

"It just means loser."

"Gay does not mean loser. I mean it. Don't talk like that."

"Yeah, yeah."

"And do you really have to wear that in public?" Trish asked of his do-rag.

"You know the ladies like how it makes my hair wave," he teased.

She rolled her eyes.

"So can I get some of that paper?"

"You know, when I was your age I had a job to earn *my* paper."

"Yeah, yeah and you had to walk a mile in the snow to school."

"What happened to the money your dad just sent you?"

"Dude, that's my savings for my car!"

She sighed and pressed a ten into his hand. "Right here in two hours. Don't make me track you down." She hugged him, then watched him walk away, crotch in hand, his boxers hanging out the back of his jeans, in search of his buddies.

Leave it, she thought as he disappeared into the crowds.

The kid had no idea how good he had it. Trish's teenage days at the mall were spent behind a counter saying, "May I take your order?" Not that she minded. It was better than being home in prison with the wardens.

Her grandparents had treated her like a criminal, tried and convicted of some crime she didn't understand until she was grown. Her transgression? Being her mother's daughter. Nana and Pawpaw were so scared that Trish would turn out like Jocelyn that they monitored her every move. They mistook discipline for love. They were determined not to make the same mistake twice. Except—why did they think Jocelyn was so wild in the first place? Like a cat, the harder they tried to control her, the more she fought.

They didn't learn from their mistake. Trish's schedule was just as strict as her mother's had been. Every morning, she had to make her bed tight enough that you could bounce a quarter on it. She was never, *ever* to leave her shoes anywhere in the house except her closet or under her bed. When she was seven she left her tennis shoes in the bathroom and Pawpaw peed in them. On Saturday mornings, she dusted and vacuumed. Monday–Friday, she washed the dinner dishes. The kitchen had to be spotless. If she so much as left a crumb on the counter, she'd hear about it. She once went to bed with a dirty plate on the counter after having a couple of chocolate chip cookies before bed. Pawpaw woke her up in the middle of the night, took her into the kitchen, and made her wash all the dishes in the house. He took every plate, cup, glass, and bowl out of the cabinets. Every pot and every pan. She was up till three a.m. on a school night. She was eleven years old, and it was the last time she left a dirty dish in the kitchen.

But housework was nothing compared to how strict they were about boys. Boys were the enemy. Boys were evil. Boys were the end of all good things. Her grandmother even read her horror stories from the morning newspaper about abusive boyfriends and husbands. "Here's another one: Man killed his girlfriend in front of a King Soopers," she'd point out almost happily.

Nana was strict, but Pawpaw was just mean, with a slab of concrete where his heart should have been. Trish's first rebellious act had been bringing home a mutt. Pawpaw was dead by the time she committed her second rebellious act, bringing home Tommy. A boy—and not just a boy—a black boy.

You would have thought her grandparents were from the deep south the way they talked about black, Hispanic, and Asian people, but they were both born and raised in Colorado. When Trish was a girl, they moved to the west side of Denver to avoid "the coloreds" who were at the time heading east to the Aurora suburb. But they were no happier on the west side because around the same time, after the Vietnam War, Vietnamese people started moving into Colorado, settling in west Denver. Trish's grandfather ranted about "slant eyes" taking over every time a new Vietnamese restaurant or shop opened on south Federal Blvd.

But, oddly, when Nana came home one day and caught Tommy in the house with Trish, she didn't have a stroke. She welcomed him like a long-lost son. She fed him smothered steak dinners and tuna noodle casseroles and baked a cake for him every week. Before she died she told Trish she was grateful Tommy would always be there to take care of her.

But now Tommy was nowhere around, and Trish had to take care of herself. She sighed and headed for Macy's. After two hours wandering through the mall, she had two pairs of jeans (size sixteen, grrr!), a book called *Divorced Doesn't Mean Desperate*, a half-eaten bag of caramel popcorn, and, on a whim, a jigsaw puzzle. She was on her way back to meet Will when she saw a crowd of people and a couple of security guards in their faux park-ranger uniforms. As she got closer, she saw that one of the people the security guards were talking to was Will. And he had his arms behind his back like he was handcuffed! She raced ahead. "What's going on?"

"Lady, this is none of your business," a chubby, pink-faced security guard said, holding one of Will's arms with one hand and pulling at his own waistband with the other. "Everybody, move along."

"That's my son!" She grabbed Will and pulled him to her. "What the hell happened?"

"Oh," said the security guard, the pink deepening to red. "Oh."

"Ma, I didn't do nothing!" Will looked scared, angry, and humiliated.

"Ma'am, I simply asked if he would come with me to our office. He tried to run."

"I didn't run! I told him I didn't do anything and walked away," Will said. "We all did."

Will's friends Josh and Eric, both white, looked at the ground.

The other security guard, much older and even fatter, spoke up. "We got a report of a boy running suspiciously away from Shade Land. This young man fit the description. All we was doing was trying to ask if he took anything. If he would have cooperated, it wouldn't have gone this far."

She saw then what the security guards saw, a brown teenage boy in a do-rag with jeans sagging, probably holding his dick. It startled her and wounded her, this view of her son. *But he's not like that,* she thought. He still let her hug him in public and slept with a six-foot-long stuffed snake called Henrietta his father won for him at Six Flags years ago. The *ma'ams* and *sirs* weren't as quick from his lips now that he was older and Tommy wasn't around, but he was still a good child; a sweet, tender boy. *He's not like that.*

"What was the description?" she demanded.

"Well, he was, he was . . . a black . . . Afro-American . . . person of color," the first security guard sputtered, even more befuddled.

"Height? Weight? What kind of clothes was he wearing?"

"The sales associate only told us what she could remember," the older guy replied, trying to smooth things over. "Look, we had cause to believe this young man was the one. Nobody meant any offense.

"The Denver PD are on the way. If you'll come with me to the office and wait, we can clear all this up."

"Oh, man," Will groaned.

"What? But he just told you he didn't take anything!"

"We can talk about this in our office."

An older, well-dressed black woman walked up to Trish. "Lady, get that boy out of here. These guards don't have any legal right to hold him. You don't have to get the police involved."

Neither guard said anything. Trish saw that the handcuffs were plastic, almost like the twist ties that came with trash bags. She hesitated. Wouldn't they be admitting guilt if they left before the police came? Would she be teaching Will a bad lesson? But what if they hurt him? What if he got in trouble even though he hadn't done anything? She had entered a weird place in which she was no longer sure of the rules or who to trust.

"Go!" the woman hissed. "Now!"

In the end her maternal instinct told her to listen to the woman. "Come on," Trish said, taking Will by one of his arms and walking away fast.

They rushed through the mall. Will's hands still clasped behind his back. People stared, and she wondered what they thought about a white woman tugging along a brown-looking kid with his hands behind his back. What assumptions were they making?

When they were in the car, she searched through the glove box and found an old pair of surgical scissors. The scissors were a bit dull, but she was able to cut the so-called handcuffs off.

"Are you okay?" she asked.

He rubbed his wrists. "White motherfucker!"

A tiny fissure started in Trish's heart. "What did you just say?"

"I called him an MF. Sorry."

Yes, but why not *fat bastard* MF? Or *Canadian Mountie–looking* MF? But she was afraid she knew the answer. She had always taught Will that race didn't matter. That she didn't see black or white or brown skin and neither should he. But would that change now?

She wouldn't let skin color come between her and the person she loved more than her own life. "Will, don't let this . . . They were assholes! But don't let them get to you, okay?"

"How come they didn't say nothing to Josh or Eric? They were in the store too. We all left at the same time. Why was *I* the one who had to be stealing?"

Trish knew the answer as surely as Will did. "I'm sorry. I'm really sorry this happened." Sorry didn't begin to cover how she felt. Add in embarrassed to be white and pissed beyond words at those racist fat fucks and that would be a start.

"Yeah, well . . ." Will looked out the window.

"What?"

"Nothing," he said without turning back around. He didn't look at her again the rest of the drive home.

CHAPTER 4

~~~~~~~~~~~

Billie

Billie could tell right away that there wasn't going to be any candlelight bathing. And she was going to be lucky if she'd see any lovemaking in the moonlight. Nick returned home more sour than when he left.

She tried to improve his mood, though. "How's your mother holding up?" she asked tenderly.

"She's her usual self. Huddled up with her pastor, bitching about my father."

"Even now?"

"What? You thought death would stop her from dogging him?"

"How was the funeral?"

Nick shook his head and slumped on the couch. He rarely spoke about his family. The little bit he just gave her was all she was going to get.

"You hungry?"

"I ate on the road." He had driven straight through from California.

"I'm sorry, sweetie. What can I do?"

"I'm gonna take a shower and hit the bed."

Billie nodded, tired too. But since they could always connect on the level of their bodies, she was still hoping they'd make love. She climbed naked into bed and waited for Nick to come out of the bathroom.

Twenty minutes later he arrived with a bowl. He sat next to her and scooped a big bite of vanilla ice cream into his mouth.

"Sweetie, I know you're sad, but junk food isn't the answer. And you know I don't like you to eat in bed."

He sighed and stood.

"I'm sorry. Come on. I got something sweeter for you than ice cream."

"I'll eat in the other room."

Should have kept my big mouth shut, she thought after he left. Why couldn't she for once just let the man eat in bed?

In the middle of the night she woke and rolled over. Nick was sitting up against the pillows, wide awake.

"Can't sleep?" she asked.

"Billie . . . I . . ." He had tears in his dark eyes.

"Oh, sweetie." She tried to hug him, but he pulled away from her.

"What is it? What's wrong?"

"You mean besides going to my father's funeral and spending a week with my crazy-ass family?" he snapped, wiping his eyes with the heel of his hand.

"I wish you would have let me come with you."

He rubbed her bare shoulder. "I'm sorry. Baby, I'm so tired I can't even see straight."

"What were you going to say?"

"Nothing."

"Tell me."

"It's nothing. Like I said, I'm tired. And, you know, kinda jacked up."

Now was definitely *not* the time to tell him about the baby.

She sat up and started to knead the tight muscles in his shoulders. "Want one of my special back rubs?" she whispered.

He shook his head. "Go on back to sleep. I'm sorry I woke you up. I'm gonna go watch TV."

Nick left and Billie lay there thinking about their relationship.

They met six years ago at a restaurant in LoDo, lower downtown Denver, the former warehouse district that was now upscale bars, restaurants, and million-dollar lofts. It was right after she went into remission. She hadn't been out clubbing in years, and had promised her friends she'd go with them if they made it an early evening. Her girls were drinking, and they and Billie were laughing and talking a mile a minute. Then this stocky, dark-skinned guy went to the piano and started to play, and it was like something in a movie. She forgot about her cranberry juice and club soda. She no longer heard her friends chattering, the clinking of ice in glasses, or the clatter of forks against dinner plates. All she heard was piano. When the tune ended, she clapped like a maniac until she realized that everyone else had stopped applauding. Nick tipped his head at her and gave her a mysterious smile. When his set was over, he came over to her table and introduced himself to her and her friends.

"You don't sing?" she asked.

"Terrible pipes," he said.

She had been alone while she was sick. Something about Nick awakened a passion in her she had all but forgotten. They exchanged numbers, but he didn't linger. Every other table seemed to be filled with folks he knew. She watched him mingle as he headed to the bar for a drink. By the time he finished his second set, she was daydreaming what she'd cook for him for their first dinner together.

A typical Taurus, once she made up her mind there was no turning back. She had been the one to make the first move, seducing him with salmon and mango chutney (which she cooked in his kitchen because she was living with her parents), a massage with warmed almond oil, and a long night of sex.

Not that Nick seemed to mind how strongly she came on. He deejayed on KUVO, the local nonprofit jazz station, one night a week and the next night he dedicated a night of his radio program to her, playing all love songs. Over the next few weeks they spent all their time together or talking on the phone. He told a slew of corny musician jokes (What's the definition of an optimist? A trombone player with a pager. How can you tell when a guitar player is at your door? He says, "Here's your pizza. That'll be $12.98.").

He confessed that the reason his smile was so mysterious was because he had six missing teeth on the sides of his mouth, and didn't like to show the gaps. When he was growing up, there wasn't money to take care of cavities. Nick said he thought the port-wine stain on her cheek gave her character. She told him about her lupus and how much she felt she had missed in life while she was sick.

"What's your favorite thing?" he asked after they had been seeing each other a couple of months.

"A long bath with lots of bubbles and candles," she replied.

"Now *you're* a sister a broke musician can appreciate."

The next night, they went for a long stroll and then went back to his studio apartment. Nick drew a bath for her with dish-soap bubbles and lighted white votive candles and placed them on the back of the toilet and sink. After she lowered herself into the steaming-hot water, he went to the piano in the next room and started to sing Stevie Wonder's bouncy song, "Ebony Eyes." His singing voice was lovely, deep, and sexy.

She was surprised. "Thought you couldn't sing?" she called.

"Only for you."

By the time he got to the line "She's a girl that can't be beat, born and raised on ghetto streets," Billie had fallen hard.

Her mother had warned her about dating a musician. Zenobia thought Nick would be running around with groupies, but he wasn't what anyone expected. Billie saw him be polite, but direct, with women who came on to him in bars. And when she wasn't there, he came home right after his gigs with no lipstick or perfume on him. He didn't have any unexplained, mysterious blank spaces when she didn't know where he was or what he was up to. Sure, he smoked a little weed, but he wasn't an addict or an alcoholic. He worked hard at his day job mowing lawns, had decent credit, and was a stand-up brother.

The ancestors approved, and Billie believed she had hit the jackpot. She moved in with him and they bought their house (the down payment a gift from her parents) soon after that.

She shifted in the bed, wondering what to do. She wished she could reach him. But even before his father's death, he seemed to be slipping away. As the economy worsened and fewer club owners and wedding couples booked live bands, his mood had darkened. To her it didn't matter how much he made or didn't make, whether he had steady gigs or not. She was proud of him and his music. And she was eager to make a family with him. Unfortunately, she feared he wouldn't be so eager to do the same.

In Head Start any activity could be made into a song. "Stop what you're doing. It's time to pick up the toys," Billie sang to her students. "Iiiii . . . like the way Micah is helping. He's picking up the big blocks. Iiiii . . . like the way Darleetha's helping. She's putting away the animals."

"Miss Billie, George hit me!" Shannelle pulled on Billie's smock.

"She wouldn't give me the block!" George said.

"George, that's not how we treat our friends. We don't hit. Use your words to ask for something if you want it. Shannelle, tell George you don't like it when he hits you."

"Miss Billie, my mom got a thing on her face like that," A'Lexus said of the port-wine stain on Billie's left cheek. "She just got it."

Billie inhaled deeply. The kids were always telling their families' business.

"I was born with mine," Billie said.

As a girl, she had been terribly insecure about her birthmark. Nobody else in her family had one, and kids used to tease her, calling her Spotty Face and Sore Head. A group of especially snotty white girls at St. Theresa's, her private high school, nicknamed her "Gorbitchoff," after the Soviet president Mikhail Gorbachev with the port-wine stain on his forehead. How she had wished hers was on her forehead, where she could hide it under bangs! But by the time she was sixteen she realized that to most people light skin and fine hair compensated for the permanent bruise on her face, the way being located in a good school district could make up for a home not having a basement. To most, though it wasn't right, light skin equaled pretty.

"Can I touch it?" A'Lexus was jumping up and down.

They were all wound up. The kids had so much energy, it was unbelievable.

Billie bent down and let the girl touch her birthmark.

Teaching Head Start was one of the ways she tried to honor the ancestors. Just as they had laid a foundation for her, she wanted to lay a foundation for these kids. If the ancestors were her roots, then her students were their fruit . . . at least until Ambata came.

The Fuller Head Start Center sat on a ten-acre campus at the nexus of Denver's low-income black and brown neighborhoods. The campus had been built for orphans in the early 1900s. Rumor had it that old man Fuller stipulated in his will that the land continue to be used for the education of unfortunate children, as long as they were white, but the Fuller Foundation's trustees had changed those rules in the sixties before the Foundation got sued. Now, ninety-five percent of the kids at the center were children of color, American-born and immigrants from Mexico, Guatemala, Sudan, Myanmar, Ethiopia, Eritrea, and Somalia.

The non-English speakers would show up too frightened to participate in class, but by the end of the semester they'd be playing (and fighting and throwing tantrums) the same as the other kids. After seven years of teaching, she was still amazed at how quickly three- and four-year-olds learned.

A'Lexus grimaced as she traced the mark on Billie's face. She seemed to be using her fingertips to try to understand what had happened to her mother.

"Does it hurt?" she asked.

"No, sweetie. It doesn't hurt."

A'Lexus was upset, while the rest of the kids were bouncing off the walls.

"Come on, let's do some yoga before lunch and naptime."

Billie and Katie gathered the kids in a circle on the rug.

"Okay, everybody inhale," Billie said, dramatically breathing in so they would know what inhale meant and lifting her arms.

Her young students threw their little brown arms in the air. Katie, a young white girl who was her assistant teacher, did as well, saying *aspirar,* for Alejandro and Miguel, who didn't quite speak English yet.

Billie liked Katie. Tall, tattooed, bespectacled, with short hair that she dyed often (these days it was extreme black with a shock of electric blue in the front, which the kids really enjoyed), she was the real deal. She cared about the kids. And she wasn't condescending like some of Billie's older colleagues. Maybe they were only jaded from too many years of working with parents who often seemed too tired or too beat down to be very interested in their kids' education, but sometimes Billie would catch a hint of "us" and "them" in their voices when they discussed their students. Sometimes their expressions betrayed a type of pity that bordered on disdain for students and their parents.

"Now exhale." Billie breathed out heavily and lowered her arms.

The kids dropped their arms and loudly blew air out their noses.

The kids weren't the only ones who needed to cool out. She had tried to tell Nick she was pregnant, but every time she opened her mouth the only thing that would come out was a sigh. She had been to her doctor to confirm the pregnancy. She was now six weeks along, and she knew that if she didn't tell Nick soon, her body would give her away. She was sleepy all the time and, while she hadn't thrown up yet, she was starting to feel queasy in the morning.

The poopy- and pissy-pants smell in her classroom didn't help. She had a couple of just-turned-three-year-olds who weren't quite hip to doing the toilet thing. You could change a child after an accident and seal his soiled pants in a plastic bag, but the scent lingered. She remembered how it had bothered her when she first started teaching. She had grown accustomed to it, but today it was nauseating. She made a mental note to fill a spritzer bottle with distilled water and peppermint oil and bring it to work so she could deodorize the room, and to bring a box of ginger tea to help settle her stomach.

"Okay, now put your right foot next to your left foot, like this." She placed her right foot against her left ankle, teaching balance and trying to reinforce left and right at the same time. Half the kids stood on their left side, and she had to correct them. "And when you're balanced . . ."

George tipped over, and once he went, Kavon, Jayden, Jordan, and Alejandro fell on the round rug like dominoes. Giggling, squirming dominoes.

"Come on guys. We're going to do tree pose. Tree pose is about balance. Let's see who can be like a tree."

Katie went to Alejandro and pulled him up, patiently whispering to him in Spanish.

"I like how Tybari and Cymfonee are standing," Billie said, pointing out the two girls who were closest to tree pose.

Eager for Billie's approval, the other girls quickly mimicked them, and the boys stood and tried again.

"When you're balanced, put your hands together like this." She put her hands in a devotional pose.

"You look like a prayer," Promise said. Promise was four going on forty. She had come to Head Start already knowing the alphabet, how to count to one hundred, and how to spell her first and last names. She was always very prettily dressed (today in head-to-toe pink), and her short hair was always skillfully braided. She was an only child, her mother's and grandmother's pride and joy, and used to getting her way. Promise worked Billie's nerves sometimes, but with a mother who evidently spent a lot of time with her, Billie felt that this little girl was going to make it.

Billie worried for most of the other kids. She worried about how they would do over the summer, when she knew most of them would end up at grandmothers' or neighbors' houses watching TV all day.

"Yes, it is like a prayer," Billie affirmed. "This is tree pose. We are solid and steady as trees—"

"Nuh-uh, this is not a tree, it's a prayer," Promise repeated stubbornly.

"Promise," Billie warned. "Use your listening ears. This is my time to talk and your time to follow along."

They switched sides, then she took them into downward dog (a big hit!), cat and cow, and child's pose, amazed, as always, at how easily they bent their little bodies into each pose.

Afterward, they ate and went down for a brief nap. Billie usually dimmed the lights, closed the blinds, and put on soothing music, but today she was afraid she would fall asleep too so she left the blinds open and skipped the music. Katie straightened up the room and Billie wrote notes to parents about the day's homework (making a shoe and bringing it in for show and tell) for the twenty minutes the kids napped.

Or she was supposed to be writing notes, but her thoughts kept drifting back to Nick. He was such a Pisces, inclined toward the blues, which she understood because as a Taurus, she herself had a tendency to be gloomy. But lupus had changed all that. It was absolutely necessary that she keep her head to the sky as often as possible. With her illness, negativity was a luxury she couldn't afford.

Tonight they were going to dinner at her parents' house, and she was hoping some down-home food would cheer him up. Maybe even bring him back to the lighthearted Nick she used to know.

"You ready for nap time to be over?"

Billie jumped a little as Katie's voice jolted her out of her reverie. She nodded.

Katie snapped the lights on and they both started singing the wake-up song:

"Are you sleeping?
Are you sleeping?

Classroom A.
Classroom A.
Morning bells are ringing.
Morning bells are ringing.
Wake up now. Wake up now."

"Is this all my mail?" Nick asked.

"You've been awfully worried about the mail lately. You looking for a check or something?"

"I'm not worried. I was just asking a question," he said quickly.

He was acting strangely. This was the third or fourth time he had grilled her about the mail. "Yes, that's all your mail."

Nick fell down on the couch and pulled off his grass-covered sweat socks. He had just gotten home from mowing lawns all day. His already dark skin took on a reddish glow that she found beautiful, but he was funky, reeking of sweat and both the grass you cut and the grass you smoke. He must have smoked a joint right before he came in the house. Since he'd returned from Oakland after his father's death, he'd been smoking more.

It dawned on her then. Maybe that's what he was looking for in the mail, an inheritance check. His family didn't have much money, but maybe his father had had a life insurance policy. She knew he was concerned about how the recession was going to affect his lawn-care business, and whether he'd get enough gigs to make it until next spring.

"You expecting something from your mom?"

"I told you I'm not expecting anything. It was just a question."

"Okay. Okay. You're gonna shower before we go to dinner, aren't you?"

He twisted the top off his bottle of beer and took a long pull. "You go on without me. I don't feel like it."

"Since when do you say no to fried chicken?" Billie asked, sitting next to him to stroke the roll of flesh where his bald skull met his neck.

Now she was really worried. A former sugar junkie, she kept what she called a "clean" kitchen, meaning no refined white sugar, white flour, white rice, dairy, beef, or pork. Nick had lost fifteen pounds since he'd hooked up with her. He still had a little belly (which he'd lose if he cut down on the beer and weed), but he looked twenty-eight instead of thirty-eight, and he used to say he had more energy. He appreciated her healthy cooking, but he had never before turned down a chance to go to her mother's house and get his soul-food grub on.

He slumped farther into the couch, his eyelids heavy. "I'm not up for all the chitchat, that's all. Bring me back a plate."

"What are you going to do here all by your lonesome? You gonna play?" Sometimes a few hours on the piano helped. But lately, those hours at the keys had become few and far between. Unless he was rehearsing with his band—they still had occasional gigs—he did what he was doing now: watch TV, drink beer, and smoke weed. She looked at the screen. Was he watching a *fishing* show?

Nick shrugged.

"Baby, I know you're grieving, but you've got to get out of this mood," she said. "Your father wouldn't want you to be this sad."

Nick snorted. "My father couldn't even get his own act together, let alone worry about me."

She knew grief didn't end overnight, but she was getting worried about Nick moping. She had to fight the urge to sing to him like she did her students. "Iiiii like the way Nick is helping. He's getting off his ass. . . ." At the thought of children, the ancestors pounced. *Now! Now, Billie, is the time to tell him about his child.* She ignored them, and even as she did it she knew it was a mistake, but she didn't want to tell him when he was so blah and blue. "You want me to rub your back before I go?"

"I'll be all right," Nick said.

She clicked off the TV, stood, and held out her hands to him. "Come on, sweetie. Get up and shower and come with me."

Nick took the remote from her and turned the TV back on. "I told you: I don't feel like it."

Billie nodded in defeat. "I'll bring you a plate."

"Hiya, Pumpkin." Her father, Herbert, stood and engulfed her in his arms. She barely reached his chest. Her father—with his graying hair, mustache, and beard, and deep booming voice—was the most handsome and distinguished man she knew. He reminded her of Ed Bradley, minus the earring and the friendship with Jimmy Buffett. Herbert was dean of the business school at the University of Colorado. He did *not* associate with rock stars.

They were in his large home office, where he was watching a baseball game. Herbert loved sports, especially baseball. He collected sports memorabilia and had packed every inch of wall space in his office with signed photos of African-American athletes, posters, team jerseys, and baseball cards. In addition to books and family photos, the shelves were lined with valuable autographed baseballs and footballs, alongside kitschy things like bobble-head statues of players. His prize possession was a baseball autographed by Jackie Robinson, who had integrated major-league baseball the year Herbert was born. Jackie Robinson and John Johnson, the founder of *Ebony* and *Jet,* were Herbert's biggest heroes.

In this way, Billie was like her father. She had inherited his veneration for those who came before.

"Where's Nick?"

"He's not feeling very well."

Herbert frowned. Nick wasn't what he'd had in mind for Billie. He'd planned on a blackademic just like himself. Herbert was the son of teachers who had instilled their deep love of education into him. And as a former banker, he had a true appreciation of capitalism, and was intent on the need for black communities to build wealth. Herbert, who thought art and the bohemian life were luxuries that only white folks could afford, had been on Nick's case about getting a master's degree since Billie had met him. After the economic downturn he was especially critical. "Maybe he'd feel better if he got a real job."

"Daddy, don't, please. Nick *has* a real job. He's a musician."

"There's nothing wrong with mowing lawns for a living if that's all you can do. But the man's got a college education. If he got a master's, he could teach. If he got his doctorate, he could get tenure. Now's a good time to go back to school and ride out the recession."

"Nick doesn't want to teach. He doesn't need to teach. He's doing fine. We're doing fine, really."

One of the players hit a pop fly, sending Herbert to the edge of his seat, before it was ruled a foul ball.

Billie saw her chance to change the subject. "Who's winning?"

"Two to one, Phillies in the top of the third."

She kissed her father on his scratchy cheek. "I'm gonna go help Mommy."

Billie made her escape and went down the hall to find her mother in the kitchen.

Not that Zenobia Bailey-Cousins was cooking exactly. A working woman all her life, she was an expert order-inner and heaterupper. On Sundays she always stopped by Joseph's Southern Food after church and got fried chicken, fried catfish, fried okra, collard greens, and mac and cheese.

"Hi, Mommy," Billie greeted her mother just as she was unpacking the sacks of food.

Zenobia was fashionable, as usual, in black slacks, a long-sleeved pale blue T-shirt, a denim apron, and the delicate gold necklace with the heart locket she always wore around her slim neck. Even on a Sunday in her kitchen Zenobia looked ready for a sit-down with the mayor. Like her husband, she was tall, five-ten. She had bright white teeth, immaculately coiffed hair, and the air of a woman who always knew exactly who she was, what she wanted, and how to get it. A strong black woman.

She had to be. In 1976, Zenobia was the first African-American woman to anchor a newscast in Colorado. It took five years after our nation's two hundredth birthday before the fan mail (*So articulate! Such a lovely smile! What an interesting name!*) outnumbered the hate mail (*Jungle bunny! Quota bitch! I'll never watch your station again until you get that nigger off the air!*). Even after somebody anonymously mailed in a headless black Barbie doll, Zenobia just smiled and shook her head at her white station manager, producers, and cameramen. A sad smile, as if she felt sorry for people so sick and lost. Not progressive and together like all of *us*, her smile said, making it okay for the white station manager, producers, and cameramen.

But at night she'd come home to the arms of her husband (who also worked all day long in a white world) and children and curse those so-and-sos out. On Sundays, in church when they prayed to love their enemies, Billie knew whom Zenobia was praying about.

Still, they couldn't keep her down. She served on the board of directors for Denver's Children's Hospital, the SafeHouse for Battered Women, the Food Bank of the Rockies, and the Foot on the Rock A.M.E. Church. Every year after Billie's diagnosis, she was emcee for the Lupus Foundation's fund-raising dinner. Ten years ago, at fifty, she had gone back to school (while still doing the 5 a.m., 6 a.m., and 11 a.m. morning news shows) and earned her master's in communications. After more than thirty years on the air, she was a beloved public figure with six Emmys and many other awards. But there wasn't much room in the business for women her age (there barely was for men her age). Her station manager had let her know they weren't renewing her contract when it ended in December. But instead of retiring to that anchor desk in the sky, she already had a job lined up to teach journalism, and was considering getting her doctorate.

Billie was more than a little in awe of her mother, whom she tried hard to emulate. In fact, she had inherited her aesthetic tastes from her mother, and was probably the only high school girl who ever tried to dress like her mother. But she didn't have Zenobia's height or her mellifluous voice. It wasn't just the height gene that had skipped her. She never had Zenobia's poise, her inherent *togetherness* either. Even though her mother never said so, Billie felt like she didn't live up to her mother's high standards.

"You always smell so good," Zenobia said when Billie stood on her tiptoes to kiss her on the warm cheek she offered. At five-three, Billie was the shrimp of the family.

"It's the same neroli oil and lavender I bought you. How come you don't wear it?"

"Doesn't work on me. I smell like an old grandma in lavender."

Grandma. The word made Billie smile.

"Pick out something else for me. No gardenias or roses, either. I do better with something citrusy or spicy. Did you say hi to your father?"

"Yeah, I stopped in his office."

"Did you see those walls? I swear he's going to start tacking stuff up on the ceiling next. What do you have there?"

Billie set her square tub of food on the counter. "A baked sweet potato, some brown rice, and a stir-fry of collards and tofu."

After she was diagnosed with lupus, she got very serious about nutrition, going back to the food of her roots (minus the fatback and bacon grease): whole grains, fruits, and vegetables, foods that reduced the inflammation in her joints and strengthened her health. That's when she got into yoga, meditation, and acupuncture. After two years, her lupus went into remission; these days her blood tests still showed the antibodies, but her symptoms were gone.

Everybody agreed it was a miracle, but they had different ideas about what or who should be credited for it. Herbert and Zenobia praised Jesus. Billie's rheumatologist chalked it up to luck. But Billie knew it was the ancestors. They had led her toward holistic healing. How they had laughed at her Western doctors' puzzlement! And if divine intervention *had* helped, it was done at the behest of the ancestors, as well as her parents.

"How are the virgins?" Billie asked.

Zenobia laughed. "The virgins" were a beautiful set of copper pots that she never used. Zenobia had an appreciation for the things that make a house a home. She was always buying new dish towels, kitchen utensils, small appliances, and whatnots, or "freshening" some room with new paint, rugs, or pictures on the walls, but she had no interest in cooking, cleaning, or anything else that black women had been forced to do for centuries. Zenobia and Herbert had a cleaning woman from Eritrea named Sashir who came in once a week and kept the house spotless.

"The virgins are fabulous," she said.

Billie started to set the dining room table, as she did every time she came for dinner. There was already a crisp white tablecloth on the table. It was new, and so were the square black dishes. When they remodeled a few years earlier, her parents put in granite countertops and replaced the almond-colored appliances with stainless steel. The effect was very modern, and Billie was still a little shocked when she walked into the kitchen, as if she'd made a wrong turn, with only the smell of soul food to convince her that she was home. Home was always how she would think of this house.

When she was done, she returned to the kitchen and sat down at the new breakfast bar while her mother brushed butter over a pan of raw white dinner rolls (the dough made by Miss Mae from Zenobia's church). They would taste like little bits of heaven, Billie knew, but in your body they'd turn into pure sugar.

"So where are the twins?" Billie asked about her joined-at-the-hip older brother and his wife.

Zenobia glanced at the clock. "James and Yolanda should have been here by now." Then she said the line she was famous for: "Don't tell him I told you—" which her children couldn't believe she hadn't figured out is exactly what they would always do "—he wants to tell you himself. But he got a big promotion."

Billie was suddenly thankful Nick wasn't there. This would just put more emphasis on the money he wasn't making.

"What's wrong with you?"

Billie must have been frowning. She forced a smile. "It's nothing."

Zenobia pursed her lips and waited. She sat on the stool next to Billie and swiveled to face her. "You can tell me anything."

It was true. Billie always felt like she could talk to her mother. Zenobia was the first person Billie told when she lost her virginity, when Kevin Wilbanks, her boyfriend in her freshman year at college had pushed her, when she knew she was in love with Nick. But was it right to tell her mother about the baby before she told Nick?

Zenobia clasped Billie's hands and leaned in so her forehead touched Billie's.

Billie smiled. It was what they used to do when she was little.

"Tell me," Zenobia urged.

"Well, it seems that I'm pregnant."

"Oh, Wilhelmina!" Zenobia's face glowed like the sun. She had given up on grandchildren. Billie allegedly didn't want any, and James and Yolanda seemed to be having trouble in that department.

"I haven't told Nick yet."

"Oh, Wilhelmina." The light went out as if Billie had flipped a switch. "You mean this wasn't planned?"

"Not exactly."

Zenobia clutched her locket. "Have you seen your doctor?"

Billie knew Zenobia was thinking about the statistics. Women with lupus had a slightly higher risk of miscarriage. "I'm fine, Mommy. *Really.*"

Billie was certain that her regime was going to help her through this pregnancy just as it had put her into remission. She might require more monitoring than other women, but her health always required her to be vigilant. Yes, pregnancy hormones could cause a flare. And if they did she'd get back on prednisone and take the other stupid drugs, but right now, even her ob-gyn said she was as healthy as a horse. "What should I do?" she asked.

Zenobia was playing with her locket and had a faraway look in her eyes. "I know it's hard, but you have to tell him," she said without looking at Billie.

"You know he hasn't been in the best of moods lately."

Zenobia seemed to shake off whatever was bothering her. She cupped Billie's chin in her hand and smiled determinedly at her. "Wilhelmina, my love. We're going to have a nice dinner and then you are going to go home and tell your . . ." She always stumbled over what to call Nick. She disapproved of common-law husband, lover, and boyfriend. ". . . significant other that you're going to have his child. All right?"

Billie nodded.

"How far along are you?"

"Six weeks."

"And you're really okay?"

"Just tired all the time, but my doctor says that's normal. And I'm starting to feel a little queasy sometimes." And craving beef, something she would not tell her mother, because Zenobia would serve her a whole brisket.

Zenobia grinned. "There was just a study out that said women are more likely to have morning sickness when they're carrying girls."

It dawned on Billie that Zenobia never talked much about her own pregnancies. "Were you sicker with me than with Jimmy?"

Zenobia stood abruptly and popped the rolls into the oven. "Oh, pregnancy didn't bother me too much. I was lucky."

Before Billie could ask more, Jimmy and Yolanda arrived, each carrying a homemade pie. Yolanda could, as they say, burn when it came to baking. She was especially renowned for her pineapple pies, a recipe her family had brought with them from Brownsville, Texas.

Jimmy set his pie down on the table and grabbed Zenobia in a great bear hug.

Billie marveled again at how much they resembled each other. He was over six feet tall and had the same features, dark rum-colored skin, and imperial bearing as their mother. Jimmy didn't look like Herbert was even in the room when he was conceived. Billie often wondered if Herbert felt shortchanged since she didn't look like him at all either.

He headed over to give Billie a squeeze. "Looking good, Billy Ray."

"Feeling good, Lewis." It was their standard greeting, from the Eddie Murphy movie *Trading Places.* They might not look alike, but she and her brother shared the same sense of humor. "So, what's new?"

"You know Mama done already told you," he whispered.

"I'm just playing the game," she whispered back.

"I got a promotion," he said louder. "I'm senior vice president of marketing for the Western region now."

"That's cool! Congrats, Big Bro." The whole family was well educated—all of them had advanced degrees—but her parents and brother were more ambitious than Billie. She was impressed that they all had big important jobs, but the business world wasn't her style. They all respected Billie's dedication to helping children, especially Herbert, who loved the idea that there was still a teacher in the family.

Billie had no idea what Jimmy's actual work was. Something to do with advertising? He worked for a division of a conglomerate that owned a bunch of fast-food franchises, and it was all really too corporate for her to keep up with. She was the bohemian in the family, content to have a little house and work with little people for little money. The white sheep. Every family has one.

"Where's Nick?" Yolanda asked, giving her a hug.

Billie and Zenobia shared a quick glance. "He's at home, too tired," Billie replied.

After they sat down and Herbert said the blessing, Billie looked around the dinner table, trying to imagine what her baby might look like. Would Ambata look like Jimmy and Zenobia? Daddy? Maybe Ambata would end up looking like some long-ago ancestor, like Billie did. Maybe the baby would resemble Nick, with his expressive eyes, his dark skin, and his long fingers, and Billie smiled to think of a tiny baby with Nick's jug ears. Or, perhaps, as the name Ambata suggested, he or she would look like a combination of them all.

When Billie got home at 9:30, she was surprised to find the house dark. She put Nick's food in the refrigerator, and made a quick request of courage to the ancestors. She went to the bedroom and found him in bed. She was tempted to let him sleep, but she knew Zenobia would be calling first thing in the morning to see how it had gone. "Nick, don't you want some dinner?" she asked into the darkness.

"Not hungry," came his muffled reply.

That meant he'd gotten takeout from M&D's, the barbecue

joint around the corner, again. He was more strung out on M&D's ribs lately than he was on weed. She rolled her eyes, went in, and opened the windows. The yellow street light shone through the blinds. "How come you have it so stuffy in here? It's a nice night."

"Didn't notice." He rolled over, facing away from her, dislodging Juju from his legs.

Billie sat on the bed and scratched the giant black-and-white fluffball, hoping some good juju would rub off on her. The cat started to knead the quilt, and Billie gently pushed him off the bed. Her grandmother Wilhelmina, Zenobia's mother, had given her this quilt when she first moved out on her own. It was made of brightly colored paisley, floral, and striped fabrics that shouldn't have worked together, but somehow did. The pieces were sewn in an asymmetrical pattern, an African tradition said to confuse and keep away evil spirits. Billie wanted to crawl under it and lie next to Nick. But first . . . "Can I talk to you about something?"

"It can't wait?"

I wish. "Not really."

He rolled back over on his back and looked at her.

She took a deep breath, smelling the dried lavender flowers coming from the small flannel bag inside her bra.

"I'm pregnant."

"What?"

She repeated herself.

"I thought lupus made it hard for you."

"Hard, but not impossible. I've been in remission long enough that it shouldn't be a problem."

Nick put his arm over his eyes. "Fuck."

Billie teared up. "That's not exactly what you want to hear when you tell the man you love you're having his child."

"You told the man you love you didn't want kids."

"Things change," she said softly.

"Or not." He chuckled mirthlessly. Of all his new habits—

watching bad TV, smoking too much herb, eating junk food—this callous laugh worried her the most. Nick used to have a laugh that streamed through her ears like bubbling water. Now it sounded more like a brittle gurgle.

"What's that supposed to mean?"

"It means that from the dawn of time women have been saying one thing and doing another when it comes to babies."

Where did that come from? "I know this is a surprise for you, but can you just think about it for a minute? It's our baby! Will you look at me?"

He took his arm away from his face. "What do you want me to say?"

"I thought . . . I used to think I didn't want kids, but now that I'm pregnant, I'm happy about it." *Please be happy too.*

"I can't believe you lied about birth control. I never thought you were the kind of woman who would create some drama like this."

"I didn't lie! I admit that I wanted it to happen, but I didn't lie. According to the calendar, it should have been safe."

"Shoulda, woulda, coulda. The story of my life." He rolled over, again facing the wall.

"Last time I checked it takes two people to make a baby."

Nothing.

"Nick, we need to talk."

"Ain't no more to say."

He was wrong about that. There was plenty that needed to be said, but maybe now wasn't the time. She went into the living room, closing the door softly behind her. She flopped on the couch, put her feet up on the coffee table, and dropped her head into her hands. All together the ancestors went: *Umph, umph, umph.*

CHAPTER 5

Trish

Trish pulled into Aspen Hill Cemetery, acid bubbling in her stomach, trying to convince herself that she wasn't there because of anything as crazy as finding a few puzzle pieces. She was simply ready to finally see the graves of her family. That was all. This visit was part of the closure she had come back for.

The cemetery office was in a gray stone building that looked like a chapel. *So stupid,* she thought, *how we have to re-ligionize everything related to death. We can't accept the idea that this is it; this is all we get. We'd rather make up stories about heaven and hell than face the truth about the here and now.*

She shivered. The early May morning was chilly, with even a dusting of snow on the ground like powdered sugar on a cake. Snow in May. She hadn't seen that since she'd left Colorado years ago. But the sun shone brightly, and it would melt before noon.

She sat in the car, not yet ready to go inside, and tried to picture her mom. But all she could call to mind was the long blond hair that she'd let Trish brush for hours. Jocelyn, her mom, hadn't been there much. Nana had raised her, and Jocelyn was more like an older cousin, who would show up from time to time to babysit. When she was home, they would sleep in the same bed, and her mom would tell stories about exotic, faraway places, like Chicago, St. Louis, and Galveston. The house would be full of laughter, singing, and chatter. Even the dogs seemed to bark more when Jocelyn was home. She never stayed long. It was never more than a week or two before she and Nana argued so much that it was clear that one of them would have to go. When she left, the house would go quiet.

Then when Trish was four, her mom came home with a swollen belly. That time Mom and Nana had fought worse than ever before. There was lots of yelling and door slamming. Trish was so scared. Mom was having another baby! Kids usually were upset when told that they were going to have to share their mom. But not Trish. She was delighted at the idea of being a big sister! She might not have a dad or a mom who stayed around very long, but she had a grandma and a grandpa and now, she hoped, a sister. She'd have someone to play with, someone to share her room with and play dolls with. Someone who would love her and stay with her forever.

She was lucky. At the hospital, her mother handed her a golden, dark-haired baby. "You have a sister," she said to Trish. "Her name is Lauren." Trish held Lauren and thought, *family,* her little heart swelling with excitement. But her grandparents weren't as happy. She didn't understand what was wrong, but whatever it was was big. They yelled and cussed, in front of the nurses even. Her mother and Nana both cried.

When she got home she picked up the spoon her mother had given her. It was her most precious possession. When Lauren came home, she would use it to feed her. But Lauren and Mom never came home.

"They died," Nana told her. "There was a car wreck. You know what that means?"

Trish knew, but still she asked, "Will they come back?"

"No," Nana said. "They can't."

Trish felt herself closing up, as if a million doors inside her were locking.

She didn't go to the funeral. Nana said she was too little. For years, until she was a mother herself, she regularly dreamed of cars smashing into each other, would wake with her eyes crusted over with tears and the sounds of squealing brakes and metal hitting metal in her ears.

But she couldn't talk to Nana about those dreams. Nana was always so upset about their deaths that Trish learned not to mention her mother and her sister. Learned that the cemetery was a bad place to go.

Life went on in the quiet house, but even though she had a grandpa and a grandma, like other people had a mom and a dad, they weren't a real family. Trish couldn't have articulated what was missing, but she knew in her bones that something was lacking.

After Mom and Lauren died, her grandparents were never the same. They had never been very affectionate to begin with, but after their daughter and granddaughter died, they turned even colder, acting as if a smile required too much of themselves. A few years after that, Pawpaw died of a heart attack. Nana seemed to have lost her heart too. After his death, she spent the bulk of her time putting puzzles together and watching TV.

Trish met Tommy in eleventh grade. Tommy, whose father had left his family, knew what it felt like to be lonelier in your own home than out in the world. His mother and sisters didn't appreciate him dating a white girl, and Trish expected Nana to have a fit if she knew she was seeing a black boy, so they sneaked around. It was before the age of cell phones and instant messaging, so they passed notes in school, cut class, and made out at each other's houses. They were each other's firsts.

When Trish was seventeen, Nana died of breast cancer. The tumor started in her left breast, directly above her heart, and spread to her ribs, then went to her spine and finally to her brain.

The funeral was small. Some of the parishioners from Nana's church, a couple of ladies she had worked with, and one of the neighbors came. There were no other relatives but Trish. The minister tried to put a shine on Nana's dreary life, but Trish knew the truth: Nana had died a sad, lonely woman. When it was time to go to the cemetery, Trish refused. Instead, Tommy took her to his house. "Promise me we'll be a family," Trish pleaded and Tommy promised. They married right after graduation, and Will was born two years later.

She shivered again and the movement brought her back to the present. She rubbed her arms, and not just because the air was cool. Abruptly, she realized she was afraid, and she wished she had brought the dogs with her. She hadn't brought Will because she didn't want to freak him out, but now, being here alone, she wasn't sure she was ready to see her grandparents, mother, and sister, laid out side by side. The whole family together except for her. But she went inside.

"I need to know where the Kuepper family is buried. Maxine, John, Jocelyn, and Lauren Kuepper, please," Trish asked the receptionist.

The woman tapped on her keyboard and stared at her computer screen. "I only see locations for three in the family plot, Maxine, John, and Jocelyn Kuepper. No Lauren."

"I'm sorry? What?"

"I don't find a reference for a Lauren Kuepper."

"She and my mother died the same day. She's got to be here." Trish spelled out her maiden name.

"No, I don't see a Lauren Kuepper in our files at all."

"There was a car wreck. She was a baby. Would she and our mother be buried together?"

"Oh, how sad. I'm terribly sorry. But if they were interred together, we'd have a record of it."

"What *do* your records show?"

"Who made the arrangements, the mortuary, birth date, death date, and location of the resting place. Would Lauren be listed under a different last name?"

Trish's chest started to hurt as the acid backed up into her esophagus. "Maybe. We were half sisters. I was just a kid. But I don't know her father's name."

The woman sighed. "Gee, I don't know what to tell you."

"But why wouldn't she be with my mother and grandparents, even if she was listed under a different name? Are you sure she couldn't be in the same casket with my mom? Is there a way that could have happened without registering it?"

"I guess it's *possible,* but it's really not likely."

"So my sister's body just disappeared?!" Trish rubbed her sternum, feeling like her chest was on fire.

"Of course not. But without any more information I don't know what to tell you. I'm really sorry. You might want to go to Vital Records and see if you can find a death certificate. That might help."

Fucking hell, even in death we can't get the family thing right. What losers. "Who made the arrangements for my mother, for Jocelyn?"

"Maxine Kuepper."

"And who made the arrangements for her?"

"Lucille Sturgis."

The lady who lived across the street. That's right. Mrs. Sturgis had stepped in to handle the funeral arrangements and had helped with the legal and financial stuff. Nana rented their house, and after paying off bills and probate taxes from her life insurance, there was only a little savings left. It's what she and Tommy used to start Will's college fund.

"Okay, will you please tell me where the other graves are?"

The receptionist marked the area on a map of the large cemetery and Trish left. She followed the map, curving through the cemetery slowly, passing giant headstones and mausoleums with, she had to admit, beautiful statues of angels and saints.

Unsurprisingly, her family's graves were not nearly so grand. Only three flat headstones side by side in the ground, names and dates of birth and death on each one. She had picked up three plastic vases on spikes at the office. She placed them in the hard earth next to each headstone and divided a bunch of tulips into each one.

She expected herself to cry and had brought a whole box of Kleenex with her in the car, but no tears came. All she felt was anger and confusion. She reached for the Tums in her purse.

"What the hell?" she asked out loud, chewing the chalky tablets. "Nana, did you have them buried together secretly? Did it save money or something? Did you let her father bury her somewhere else?" Trish's breath was like smoke in the cold air. She slumped to the ground, pulling her jacket down so her butt wouldn't touch the snow-wet grass.

She'd never mourned her mother and sister. They'd just appeared and disappeared, and she was never given the chance to know them or even to know how she felt about them. There was an ever-present sorrow that she never questioned. It had been there so long it was a part of her.

She kept speaking, though she didn't have any confidence anyone was listening. All these emotions were coming up, and she had to get them out. "I thought I was going to have a happy family, like you guys never did. But my marriage is over and my kid is a teenager, and pretty soon I'm going to be all by myself, just like you, Nana. How the hell did that happen?

"If I died today, there wouldn't even be any neighbors at my funeral. Alicia and the other folks from the clinic would come. Tommy would come to support Will. Will would miss me. He's sixteen, but he loves me. I did do that right. But other than him, there would be nobody. And I've got to do something about that. No offense, Nana, but I don't want to end up like you did with friggin' TV and puzzles."

A couple with a stroller and a leashed golden retriever puppy jogged by, glancing at her like she was crazy. She stopped talking. She supposed that some people would be offended by people jogging next to their loved ones' gravesites, but it didn't bother Trish. Aspen Hill was near several apartment complexes and housing developments. Why shouldn't those people take advantage of the neat paths, endless green lawn, and stands of aspen the cemetery was named after? She watched them go by. That's how she and Tommy had started out too. Minus the jogging. She hoped their marriage worked out better than hers had.

After they were safely out of hearing range, she realized she had run out of things to say anyway. She went back to her Subaru. She beeped the lock and was about to open the door, when she saw it on the ground by the driver's side front tire: another puzzle piece. It was painted with what looked like part of a human eye, a brown iris. She picked it up. *If you're trying to talk to me, old lady, just spit it out!* She waited, but the only reply was silence.

Okay, things were officially getting weird. Suddenly, she felt hot. She couldn't tell if it was because the temperature was rising or if it was from all the ranting she'd been doing. She tore off her coat and stuck the puzzle piece in her jeans. Too bad she couldn't shed this strange feeling as easily.

Later that evening, she had just ordered two large pizzas (not from the joint whose pies "tasted like ass") and hung up the phone when it rang again.

"Hi Trish," sniffed Jessica. "Is Will there?"

"Do you have a cold?"

"No. I'm okay."

"Will, Jessica's on the phone," Trish called into the family room.

Will shook his head. He hadn't worn the do-rag lately, so his hair was a mass of curls. "Don't wanna talk to her."

Trish frowned. "I'm sorry Jessica, but Will can't come to the phone right now."

Jessica started to cry.

"Honey, what's wrong?" Trish asked her.

"I don't know! He won't, like, talk to me! He broke up with me, and I don't know why!" Jessica wailed as dramatically as only a teenage girl can. "Will you talk to him?"

"Uh . . . um . . . Jess . . ."

"Please! Please!"

Trish didn't want Will getting all caught up like she and Tommy had, but she remembered what it was like to be a girl, and she felt sorry for Jessica. "All right."

She went into the family room. The puzzle pieces were in a drawer, and pieces from the puzzle she had bought were dumped on the coffee table. She had tried for three nights to actually make the pieces into the picture on the box, but they were still all separate parts.

"So what's up with you and Jessica?"

"We broke up."

"Why? What happened?"

"I don't wanna talk about it."

"She sounds really upset."

Will shrugged.

"Are you okay?" He had been distant since last week at the mall.

Will nodded. "Yeah. Fine."

"So you're home this evening?"

"Naw."

Oh, so that was it. "Do you have a new girlfriend?"

"No."

"Then what are you going to do tonight?"

"Meeting some friends."

Getting information out of this kid was getting harder than brushing a cat's teeth. "What friends? Josh and Eric?"

"No, some other guys."

"Where are you going?"

"Not the Grand Peaks Mall, that's for fuckin' sure," Will mumbled.

"Language. What time will you be home?"

"Like, ten or eleven."

"Call me if it's going to be later, okay? Pizza should be here in a few."

"Cool."

They ate dinner silently, Trish standing against the counter, slipping food to the dogs as usual (even though she knew better), and Will at the breakfast bar. After he slammed down four slices he grabbed his jacket and took off down the street.

Trish settled in Nana's chair in front of her new puzzle. It was of a photo of a litter of German shepherd puppies frolicking on green grass.

She could see Nana at the dining room table (where they never ate because it was always covered by puzzles in progress). Nana had a system. First she would separate the pieces by color.

Trish decided to try that. All the pieces with green connected to them would be part of the grass.

After she had the pieces together by color, then she would start trying to fit parts that looked alike together. That's where Trish got lost. She had no spatial-visual ability. Nana had had a knack. She could hold up a part, slide her eyes around the thousand other pieces, and, with only a little trial and error, find where it fit.

Trish picked up one piece after another with no clue where they went. She could tell they were different shapes and had different colors on them, but she still didn't see a rhyme or reason to how all the different pieces connected. They looked like a jumble of colors and shapes, instead of parts of a whole.

She sat back in her chair, giving up. All that she had left of Nana was this chair, her china cabinet, and a few boxes of junk. If she didn't do something, this was her future.

She thought again about the weirdness at the cemetery. What the hell had happened to her sister? *Okay, for argument's sake, let's say Alicia was right and Nana was really trying to communicate with me about something. What in the hell could it possibly be? And why now?*

She went down to the basement where she kept the boxes of her grandparents' and mother's papers. Lucky and Little Buddy stayed close at her heels. They had become great friends, chasing each other and wrestling. Lucky seemed to enjoy having Little Buddy chew on him benignly. The only problem was that she was confusing the poor dog, half the time calling him Lucky and half the time calling him Jigsaw.

She turned on the light of the small storage room. The dogs sniffed eagerly, hoping for something good. "Move, you guys," she told them, but she was glad they were with her. She had a creepy feeling sitting with these boxes that she hadn't opened in years. Little Buddy grew bored when he realized food wasn't involved, but Lucky stayed with her.

The first box was her mother's. Here was her mother's high school yearbook from 1972, the pages warped, all the pictures in black and white. The boys looked like bankers in their jackets and ties. The girls all had straight hair parted down the middle or great big bouffants, and were decked out in off-the-shoulder dresses, like singers in a girl group.

Trish turned to the junior class and found a picture of her mother. Jocelyn Nicole Kuepper. She touched the photo. Under all that big hair and eyeliner was the girl who was about to get pregnant with her.

She may not have missed her mother much when she was four, but she had missed her like crazy by high school. She missed all the things a mother is supposed to help you with.

These days it's common for girls as young as eight or nine to start wearing training bras. When Trish started developing little buds on her chest when she was twelve, it was her teacher who noticed that action needed to be taken. She sent a note home telling Trish's grandparents to buy Trish a bra.

Nana got so flustered when she read the note Trish almost felt sorry for her. But then Nana looked from the piece of paper to Trish's chest and she felt like it was the first time either of her grandparents had actually seen her in so long she only felt sorry for herself.

Nana blinked and coughed, then picked up her purse and marched Trish down to May D&F. They bought three bras, flat as eye masks, that made her feel like her chest was being gripped by tiny, white-gloved hands. "Over-the-shoulder boulder holders," the boys in her class called them.

In the changing room, Nana told Trish, "You keep your legs crossed until you graduate, you hear?" Later that year when she started her period, Nana handed her a box of Kotex and said the same thing.

To this day, Trish hated the things. She reached under her shirt and unhooked her bra. Then she opened the next box. It was full of papers. She still had the last year's worth of her grandmother's bank statements. As if she'd ever need a bank statement from 1990. But she couldn't bring herself to throw them away. Tommy used to get so pissed when she carted these boxes every time he got stationed in a new state. They're filled with shit you never even look at, he'd said, correctly.

She rifled through the dank, musty files, but found nothing helpful.

She was about to give up when she felt something metallic. She sucked in a deep breath of dusty air when she saw what it was. A small silver spoon. The handle had tiny red dice and the words "good luck" painted on it. It was a souvenir from Las Vegas. Her mother had given it to her. Now she could see what a piece of crap it was, but as a small girl she'd thought it was beautiful. She had imagined feeding her baby sister with it. She tucked the spoon into her pocket. It was tacky, but it was from her mother.

After Nana died, she and Mrs. Sturgis had packed up the house. Mrs. Sturgis had taken some small things—books, puzzles, costume jewelry, a few polyester scarves—to remember her friend by. Trish wondered if Mrs. Sturgis was even still alive. She put all the files and boxes away, went upstairs, and opened the phone book to "S." There she was: still alive and still in the same house. Trish closed the phone book. Maybe Mrs. Sturgis would remember when her mother and sister had died. Maybe she'd be able to solve the mystery about where her sister was buried.

CHAPTER 6

~~~~~~~~~

Billie

"Grandmothers and grandfathers,
   Please bring peace to my heart.
   Bring peace to my man's heart.
   Bring peace to my parents' hearts.
   Bring peace to our home.
   Bring peace to our community."

Billie thought about the seemingly never-ending wars that pitted brother against brother and nation against nation and added, "Bring peace to our country, and to our world. And, like the song says, 'let it begin with me.' Thank you. Ase."

She covered the dining room table with a turquoise cloth, and set six places with white plates and napkins made from the same fabric as the tablecloth. She then set two blue candles dressed with sandalwood and myrrh in the center of the table. Water colors would help bring calm and understanding. The sandalwood and myrrh were to instill some much-needed peace.

How Nick used to tease her about her need for order! Even as a little girl she had kept her room and herself neat and tidy. It was something she got from her mother. Zenobia could spot a piece of lint on someone's shoulder across the room. Billie's condition only made her more dedicated to keeping her life orderly and neat. She had to keep things structured to stay healthy, that's all there was to it. She had to take her herbs and vitamins. She had to do her exercises, keep stress in check, and watch her diet. No way you can do that haphazardly.

She sat at the table quietly until she felt the warmth that let her know the ancestors were about to speak. The message she received was: *Daughter, you told the truth. Though the waters may be rough, truth always flows to peace.*

"Always?" she questioned, not sure she believed the ancestors on this one. Since she'd dropped the "p bomb," life in the Cousins-Campbell household had been anything but peaceful.

Nick wasn't speaking to her. When he was home, he spent his time in front of the television with it turned up loudly, creating a wall of sound to keep her away. Even though she polished it every day, his piano seemed to collect more dust from lack of use.

They didn't talk to each other during the day, but she and Nick still turned to each other at night, letting their bodies say all the things they couldn't say to each other during the day: *I love you. I need you. Please don't end this.*

In the morning, she'd wake thinking, *He just needs time to absorb the news.* A baby was a big deal. Everything would change. He was right about that. But once he got over the shock, he would see what an opportunity this was for the two of them. The baby made her feel connected to life in a way she'd never felt before. Inside her, her ancestors and Nick's ancestors were mingling, creating a whole new strain of folks. The past was becoming the future. How could you not be excited about that?

Her parents and Jimmy and Yolanda were coming to dinner this evening, though she wasn't at all sure it was a good idea. Her family rotated dinners: Once a month, they ate at Zenobia's. Once a month at Jimmy's. Tonight was her turn. These dinners were sacrosanct. You didn't cancel unless you were missing a limb. Still, she called her parents to try to get out of it, but her mother had started asking so many questions that it was easier to just have the dinner. At least she had thought so when her mother was grilling her like a salmon on the phone. Now, she wished she had stood her ground. Even with all the soothing colors, the way Nick was acting, tonight could be a disaster.

She looked at the table, hoping to take a little of the calming blue energy inside her. She went into the bedroom. Nick was sitting on the side of the bed tying the laces on his sneakers.

"You're not going somewhere, are you?"

He stood and slipped his wallet into the back pocket of his jeans.

"Mommy and Daddy will be here in a few minutes," Billie said.

"Like you want me here."

"Of course I do!" But she *was* a little relieved.

"Yeah, right," he snorted. He knew she was lying.

"I tried to get out of it."

He turned to face her. "Should have tried harder."

Even though he was freshly showered, an angry scent like burnt toast seeped from his pores as he brushed by her through the doorway and out of the house.

As the front door clicked shut, she thought again about what the ancestors had told her. The waters were definitely going to be rough.

Zenobia proved that right away. "Wilhelmina, my love, what is going on?" she asked as soon as the spinach lasagna was served and the blessing was given.

"I told you Nick had a gig tonight," Billie said to her plate, though she knew her mother hadn't believed her the first time she'd said it.

Why did she even try? She was a pitiful liar, and lying to her mother never got you anywhere anyway. Ask the city manager who was forced to resign after Zenobia discovered he was turning in fake time sheets for temporary employees who did no work and splitting the paychecks with them. The poor fool was lying right into the camera when she pulled out a time sheet he had signed for a worker who happened to have spent that week in jail on domestic violence charges and, therefore, couldn't have worked. To add insult to injury? Zenobia and her cameraman cornered him in a strip club parking lot during the workday.

Of course, that was back in the day when Zenobia was on the evening news. Nowadays, she didn't do any investigative reporting.

If Zenobia was less refined, she would have sucked her teeth to show her disapproval, but instead she made a tiny ladylike noise in her throat. "I'm going to let that one go because you know I'm talking about more than this evening."

"He just needs some time to adjust," Billie told her. "Just let the dust settle for a minute."

"Let the dust settle! What a concept! Can you come over to campus and help me out?" Herbert jumped in, clearly trying to change the subject. A scandal was brewing at his university because a visiting professor in the business school had given a talk called "Capitalism Kills."

"These folks are about to make me hurt somebody," he continued. "You would have thought the man said Christ should have been aborted the way they're acting! We have a committee conducting a formal inquiry. I wish I knew what happened to the constitution!"

"I know what happened to it," Zenobia, a rabid Democrat, said. Zenobia had been a delegate when the Democratic National Convention was held in Denver. She said one of the proudest moments of her life was when she stood on the floor for Barack Obama.

One of the things Billie admired about her family was how passionate they all were about their beliefs. And how well-informed. They could argue a subject down to the ground. Iraq, Darfur, the recession, the pros and cons of universal health care, pine beetles killing forests across the state. You name it, they could fill you in on the latest.

She was different. She had quit reading the newspaper the last few years. Too much bad news. She wanted to change the world, but she was going to focus on her tiny little part of it: her students, her community. Change, like charity, begins at home.

The subject turned to a scandal involving a local businessman who was busted for having two families.

"Can you imagine finding out something like that?" Yolanda said. "What about his kids? How could he lie to them like that?"

Herbert scratched his chin. Zenobia played with her necklace.

Billie could tell something had been bothering her parents all evening. Herbert rubbed the hairs on his chin so much Billie expected him to be clean-shaven by the end of the night. Zenobia was working her locket back and forth on its chain, which she always did when she was nervous, and she about jumped out of her seat every time Herbert started to speak. Billie knew they were upset about how Nick was acting, but they approved of the pregnancy, right? Or were they too worried about Nick and her lupus to be happy?

"Listen, is something bothering you two?" Billie asked her father. "I hope you're not worried about me."

Herbert opened his mouth to speak.

Zenobia put her hand on his arm. "Poopsie . . ."

Billie was always amused that as formal as her parents were about most things they called each other Poopsie.

"We're fine. You don't need to worry about anything right now. Just rest your mind," she said.

"But we do have something we want to talk to you about," Herbert added. He reached into his suit jacket, got his wallet, and brought out a check. "We were thinking that with things the way they are right now it would be better for you to take the summer off, and we want to help with that." He handed the check to Billie.

It was for $25,000. She gasped. "Daddy!" That was way more than she'd make over a summer ringing up groceries at Sunshine Market! It'd take them through the summer and through a good maternity leave next spring. Tiny organic cotton baby sleepers and cloth diapers and jars of all-natural baby food danced in her mind. And now Nick couldn't worry about money.

"And if you need anything else, you let us know," Jimmy said.

"I'll babysit," Yolanda offered with a melancholy smile.

"I'll be looking forward to returning the favor too," Billie answered. She felt sorry that Yolanda and Jimmy were having problems conceiving.

Jimmy and Yolanda exchanged a special glance, and Jimmy nodded.

"Actually," Yolanda said shyly, "we're thinking of adopting."

Zenobia choked on her iced tea. Herbert patted her back.

"Mommy! Are you okay?" Billie asked.

"She's fine," Herbert said.

Zenobia stood up, still coughing, and Herbert escorted her to the bathroom.

"I take it they're not fond of the idea of us adopting," Yolanda said.

"No, Mommy wants us all to give her grandkids. She's dying for grandkids," Jimmy said.

"I think it's a great idea," Billie said. "Would it be soon?"

"Conversations have just started," Jimmy said. "Nothing's definite."

"But I'd like it to be soon," Yolanda added.

Jimmy smiled.

"Something's up with them," Billie said "Don't you think they've been acting kind of funny lately?"

Jimmy shook his head.

Zenobia and Herbert reentered the dining room.

"You okay?" Billie asked. "Is something bothering you?"

"I'm fine," Zenobia responded, but she looked drained.

"Tell them you don't have a problem if we decide to adopt a kid," Jimmy prompted.

"Of course we don't!" Herbert said.

"See," said Jimmy.

But Billie had never thought that was it. She knew her parents were upset about where Nick stood on the issue of this baby. And Nick not being here at dinner had probably only made things look more desperate to them.

Zenobia went to Yolanda and hugged her. "I'm thrilled for you," she said hoarsely to her daughter-in-law. "Absolutely, positively thrilled."

"It's getting late," Herbert said. "You know your mother has to be at the station early. Come on, Poopsie, we'd better get going."

"I'll walk you out," Billie said. Outside on the porch, Billie stopped them. "I want to try to explain something."

Her parents looked at each other anxiously.

"Nick is not himself since his father died. It did something to him."

"He was like this before his father passed," Herbert said quickly, confirming Billie's suspicions. "The man has had a chip on his shoulder the size of Pike's Peak since the day we met."

One of the first jokes Nick had told Billie went like this: What do you call a musician without a girlfriend? Homeless. After her parents gave them the money for the down payment on their house, he didn't think that was funny anymore.

"He's a little insecure," Billie agreed, suddenly more than a little scared of how Nick was going to take the news of their gift tonight.

"And it's your job to fix that?" Zenobia asked.

"It's my job to take care of my man, yes." It made Billie happy that Nick needed her so much. She loved taking care of him, comforting him, believing in him when he was unable to believe in himself. And she could take a lot. She was strong that way, but she did have a limit, and when her limit was hit, look out. Her Taurus-the-bull temper would come out in full force. "But if things get . . . you know I won't take a lot of mess."

Zenobia shook her head with dismay. "Oh, Wilhelmina, how could you have let things get this far? How are you going to raise a child by yourself with your condition?"

"By myself? It's just a rough patch. That's all."

"Hope so, Wilhelmina," Zenobia said, starting down the steps. "Hope so."

Nick crept into the house after midnight, but Billie was sitting up in bed still awake. Waiting. "Can we talk about this?" she asked.

No reply.

She felt a twinge of the bull coming to life. She'd had hours to herself to vacillate between feeling ashamed of herself and humiliated that her man couldn't even be in the same room with her family. By the time Nick got home, she had built up quite a case against him. The least he owed her was speaking to her. "The silent treatment is kinda childish, don't you think?"

"You don't want to hear what I have to say. You just want me to agree with you, and I don't, so what's there to say?"

Feeling at a disadvantage because he was standing, she got out of bed. "That's not true! I *want* to hear how you feel. I need to know how you feel. Tell me why you don't want this baby."

"I just don't."

"That's not a reason."

"You knew that. I was clear."

"But why not?"

"I can't believe you're hitting me with this now."

When would be a better time? "This could be a good thing, Nick."

"I'm no good for a baby. You know that. I'm selfish, all right? I don't have it in me."

"You don't know that."

"I'm almost forty years old. I'm broke. My career is in the toilet. What do you think I have to give a child?"

"Thirty-eight is hardly old. And your career . . ."

Nick sighed heavily, interrupting her. "What happens now if you get sick? If you get sick and can't take care of the kid, who's going to end up taking care of it?"

Her shoulders sagged with relief. *He's worried about me?* "But I'm fine. I'm healthy."

"Now."

"What do you want me to do, Nick? I wish I could promise you I'll never get sick again, but I can't. You know that. So what can I do? What can I say?"

"It's not too late to fix this. We can stop this before we end up too far down the wrong road."

She stumbled backward as if he had slapped her. She'd expected him to be shocked about the pregnancy, but she had never imagined that he'd ask her to end it. "No—you didn't just say that."

"It's your choice."

She moved back toward Nick. "This is *your* baby. How could I choose between you and a part of you?"

He ran a hand over his smooth scalp. "I can't be a father."

"Is it the money? Mommy and Daddy will help," Billie blurted desperately. "They gave me a check tonight for twenty-five thousand dollars. It was supposed to be for me to take the summer off, but I can work part-time. We can put this money away until after the baby comes."

This time it was Nick who stepped away, putting distance between them. "Mommy and Daddy to the rescue again."

"They want to help, and if it's money you were worried about, now you don't have to."

"You really think it's that easy?"

No, nothing was easy with Nick anymore. But she wouldn't say that. "It could be."

"That's your problem. You're used to getting everything you want. You're spoiled."

"*Spoiled?*"

He nodded, unfastening his watch and putting it on the dresser.

"I am a black woman in these here United States. I hardly think spoiled is an option."

He laughed his new hollow laugh. "Know this: Anybody who has a mommy and daddy ready to come to their rescue with a check for twenty-five grand at the drop of a hat can't cry about being oppressed."

"Yes, my family has a little money, but you don't think my parents take shit for what they earn? You know they work damn hard for every dime they have."

Nick didn't talk about his family much, but Billie knew they were poor. He had once told her that he had his first job when he was ten years old and had practically been on his own since then.

She knew money was a touchy subject, but she also couldn't stand there and let Nick insult her parents.

"And I don't?"

"I didn't say that."

"C'mon now. You know they think I'm just a triflin' brother who can't get a real job. And if I had a real job their precious daughter wouldn't have to work so hard. That's why they gave you that money."

Nick was sort of right about what her parents thought, so she tried to steer the conversation back on course. "We're not talking about them. We're talking about us."

"See. You even want to dictate this conversation! Everything is all about you. What you want to talk about. What *you* can eat. What *you* can't do. We can never just eat a damn hamburger. I can't smoke in my own house. I can't eat in my own bed."

Billie knew she was hard to live with. Living with an illness that could kill you made you obsessive and controlling. It affected every decision she made, every action she took. She accepted that, and she had thought Nick did too. He used to say he was proud of her for how hard she worked to stay healthy. So this little tirade of his was bullshit. She knew she should stick to the subject at hand, but she felt like ramming her horns into something. "All about me, huh? When's the last time we took a vacation? Never. We're always broke. And you always work on the weekends. And summer is your busiest time. You always put your work, your capital A Art, before anything else, including our relationship, and I never get up in your face about it ever! I know you're not trying to jump down my throat because I take care of my health!"

"You can't even admit it. Well, I tell you what, you're not going to get your way this time." He grabbed a pillow off the bed. "I said what I had to say. You knew from jump I didn't want kids. The next move is yours." He stormed out of the room.

The next move. As if this was a game of chess. Billie climbed back in bed. *We never had any agreement,* she thought. Nick had said he didn't want kids, and they had both assumed that's the way it would be. Sure, the subject had come up a few times. Once she mentioned that Jimmy and Yolanda were trying to get pregnant and Nick had said "Better them than us." Sometimes Nick would make sarcastic comments about the parents of Billie's students. But never had they sat down and said *We're not having children. Let's shake on it.* There had been no promises made, no contracts signed.

She looked down and saw that she was clutching the sheets in her fists and realized she was still arguing even though she was alone. It wasn't very rewarding to win an argument when you're the only one bothering to fight.

Billie was a born teacher. In addition to Head Start, every Tuesday evening she taught West African dance at the Five Points Recreation Center. She had hoped to motivate some of the black women in the neighborhood to get fit, but there was only one older sister, Jackie, in the class. The rest of the students were white. Billie had been disappointed that more of her own people weren't interested enough in their culture to take her class.

Too often her dance students reminded her of the girls she went to St. Theresa's with: without a care in the world. Oh, she knew they considered themselves cool because they lived in or near a black neighborhood, watched the multiculti characters on *The Backyardigans* with their kids, took African dance, and had Barack Obama bumper stickers on their cars. The 2008 election, especially since Obama had won predominantly white states in the primary, made her believe that the country might be starting to shift, but she was waiting for more proof before she completely trusted white liberals any more than she did white conservatives. After all, death threats had also been made against Obama. One election did not a different country make.

One election couldn't overturn hard feelings she still held about how back in high school her opinion would be desperately needed anytime the topic was rap music or black celebrities. She could recite all the "harmless" questions they had asked her the first year she was there:

"My babysitter is black. Do you know her?"

"Is that Crisco in your hair?"

"My dad said you have a tail. Can I see it?"

"Is it true what they say about once you go black . . . ?"

She knew her parents sent her and Jimmy to private school because they wanted them to have the best education, but it came at the incredibly high price of always being the odd one out. When she'd complain, Zenobia and Herbert would just say "Better get used to it. It's going to be the same way when you enter the workforce."

To some degree they were right.

Then there were the white women who threw themselves at Nick in nightclubs. That's one of the reasons Billie stopped going to his gigs. She hated how they fawned over him, so obviously excited by his dark skin and fantasies of a good lay. Nick said just as many black women hit on him as white women, but a sister never had the nerve to get up in his face when Billie was around. Only white girls disrespected her that way. Black women might want to steal her man, but white women acted like they had a *right* to him. That's what she couldn't stomach. She trusted Nick not to mess with another woman, but the sense of entitlement that even drunk-off-their-asses white chicks saw the world with drove her crazy.

Billie wasn't proud that she felt this way, but white people were just different, culturally from another place, and she hadn't seen much evidence that the gap would be or could be closed. She had hoped the dance class would be a cultural refuge for her, but instead, it presented more of a challenge.

Today, she was in no mood for challenges. All day, Nick's ultimatum from the night before had weighed on her shoulders like a wet wool blanket. She was stuck between the slight swell of her belly and the hard line of Nick's threat. She wouldn't, couldn't abort this baby, but she couldn't let Nick go either. She'd have to find a way to get him to understand.

"Oh, Billie, I'm so excited!" Cecilia, one of her students, shrieked when Billie entered the dance studio. "I've been dying to see you!" Cecilia rushed over to her, chattering as they walked to the front of the room.

Billie sighed. To say Cecilia worked her last nerve was an understatement. She seemed to have great reservoirs of money—there were two dead husbands in the picture—and vast empty spaces inside her. She was the kind of rich white person who was in love, love, love with all things "ethnic." The kind for whom Botox and Buddhism easily coexist. She always wore colorful sarongs and kente cloth headwraps to class, presumably to show that she was "down" with colored folks, but they only made it harder for Billie to see anything but the long line of oppressors in her background.

Zenobia would say Cecilia was the kind of person who makes you have to call on Jesus. While Billie wasn't a churchgoer, she did try to think of Cecilia as the ancestors told her to think of everyone: as a beloved child of God. But Cecilia made it difficult.

"You know how they have these DNA analysis tests now?" Cecilia asked breathlessly. "I'd always been curious about my ancestry, way back to the whole 'Roots' thing. My family is mostly Scottish and British, of course, but you never know. So I thought, why not? I swabbed my cheek and sent off the test and you'll never guess what I found out?"

Billie forced a polite smile. The flannel bag inside her bra was filled with lavender for calming and rose petals for peace. She wished she'd added some pennyroyal for strength. "What?"

"I'm black!"

Billie looked at the moon-white, skim-milk-white, almost-blue-she-was-so-white white woman and forgot all about calm and peace and children of God. "Excuse me?"

"I'm fourteen percent African!" She held her hand up for a high five, which she dropped when Billie ignored it.

"Incredible."

"I know! Actually, I'm triracial. I'm also three percent Native American." Cecilia undulated her midsection and swung her chunky hips. "No wonder I felt the need to get in touch with those sides of myself."

You need to get in touch with something, all right, Billie thought, putting her hands on her hips.

The rest of the class watched uncomfortably. Jackie, the black student, had her eyebrows raised in a *no-she-didn't* kind of way. Both the drummers were shaking their heads and smiling. Billie could tell they had recognized the international sign for a sister about to go off.

"Who do you think you are?"

"I . . . I . . . ," Cecilia stammered, blinking rapidly.

"How could you even form your lips to say something as ignorant as that?"

"What did I say that was so wrong? Whatever it was, I take it back!"

This girl is not who you want to be fighting with, the ancestors said. *She's a crazy heifer, for sure, but she's not the one on your mind, and allowing her to distract you from your purpose here only diminishes you.*

Billie took her hands off her hips. She could see that the ancestors were right. Her mood had nothing to do with Cecilia. And Cecilia was a child of God, *at all times,* not just when it was easy for Billie to see it. "You should know that to a black person it feels insulting when a white person speaks like that."

"I didn't mean any insult. I'm very sorry."

Billie nodded her acceptance of Cecilia's apology. She knew the rest of the women were congratulating themselves on not being as crass and unhip as Cecilia, and just the idea of them mentally patting themselves on the back made her more tired. This was one time she didn't wish to be like her mother. She would explain things to Cecilia, but she wouldn't roll her eyes with the other women, colluding with them to reassure them. "Let's get started," she said.

The drummers started slapping the congas and Billie led the class in some warm-up stretches, losing herself in rhythm.

When she got home, after the sun had started to set, before she went into the house, she deadheaded her rose bushes. Lupus made her sensitive to sunlight, so, like the neighborhood foxes, she was a creature of the evening and early morning. Nick used to walk with her on nights when he wasn't gigging. They would stroll through the dark city for hours, talking about everything and nothing at the same time.

Tonight, Nick was at the public jazz station deejaying his weekly show. It didn't pay anything, but it gave him a chance to promote the Nick Campbell Quartet and to play CDs by his friends.

Billie kept a swept dirt yard in front of the house. Between the semi-arid climate and global warming, she had decided that lawns were destructive luxuries, and in Denver, where it rarely rained in the summer, mud wasn't a problem. She remembered hearing about how ancestors from West Africa had kept swept yards in Georgia, where the soil was clay, as it often is in Denver. Nothing appealed more to Billie than picking up a dying tradition of her ancestors. So when they moved in, she dug up the weedy grass and surrounded the dirt with river rocks so the soil wouldn't erode and wind wouldn't blow dirt all over. Most of the neighbors hated it at first. Billie had even overheard a woman driving by comment on "all that ugly-ass dirt." But she swept the dirt every day with a bamboo broom, keeping it tidy and free of weeds, and eventually the clay compacted and was now almost as smooth and glossy as the rocks. These days, people stopped to admire their yard and asked her how she did it. As she answered their questions, she smiled along with the ancestors.

Tonight, she swept the dirt, then she went to the backyard, which was completely different from the front. Where the front was all smooth stone, the backyard was wild with life. A large old crabapple tree shaded much of it. On the other side, Billie and Nick had put in a pond just big enough to hold three orange koi and two water lilies. Next to the pond, Billie grew herbs, vegetables, and roses.

She stooped down next to the water, waving away a tiny tornado of gnats. The fish swam to the water's surface whenever she appeared. Some would say they were conditioned to do this because they expected food. But Billie had found that fish were actually quite social creatures. "Hello," she said to them, putting her hand to the water so they could kiss her fingertips.

Next she went to the roses and gathered satiny yellow, coral, pink, and red petals. She went back to the front yard and scattered them on the porch and down the sidewalk ahead of her as she walked, speaking softly to those who had come before her.

"What am I going to do?" she asked. "How can I pick between two impossible choices?"

At least the choice was hers. How many ancestors had given birth to children who were then sold away from them? How many had loved a man or a woman they weren't allowed to marry and raise children with?

"What can I do to make Nick see that he can be a father, that this is a good thing for both of us?"

Who died and left you in charge of Nick? she felt the ancestors say.

"I hate when y'all get all sarcastic."

Nothing can be gained by trying to force this situation. You made your choice. It's up to Nick to make a choice now, and it's his to make.

Stand in love and stand in the truth and you'll be fine.

She was afraid to hear the answer, but she summoned the courage to ask, "Does that mean Nick will stay with me?"

Before they could answer, an old guy rocking a silver Al Sharpton hairdo pulled a dark Buick in front of the house across the street and blew on his horn, breaking her connection.

Once every couple of weeks he showed up and did the same thing. Billie and Nick called him Honking Harry. She glared at him, fuming. He honked a dozen more times before their neighbor, Fletcher, hobbled out of his house using an old golf club as a cane and gave him his package, and he drove away.

"Hey, Billie," Fletcher called across to her.

"Hey, Fletcher." As much as Honking Harry bugged her, the sight of Fletcher calmed her down. He was dark-skinned with wavy white hair and today, as always, was dressed in both the girls, Poly and Ester. She walked across the street, picking up an empty forty-ounce beer bottle to recycle. "How're your knees?"

"Fair to middlin'. Cain't complain, and if I did it wouldn't do me no good. Talking to the ancestors?"

"Always. Next time I'm going to ask them if they can get your friend to not honk so much."

Fletcher laughed. "Sorry 'bout that. I wish he'd save some of his stash to smoke a little 'fore he came over so he could calm down. Man's over seventy years old and still actin' in a hurry like the young fools."

Fletcher sold herb, or reefer as he called it, to other seniors (and to Nick) to supplement his Social Security. Billie and Nick got a big kick out of him, giving a whole new meaning to the phrase "respect your elders." He had the wide-shouldered build of someone who had been a larger man but was shrinking down into himself, and though his knees were shot, his grip was still strong. When he was young, he ran a craps house in Five Points and had a few other hustles, including something to do with selling supplies on the black market when he was a quartermaster in Europe during World War II. Billie and Nick knew he kept a loaded pistol in his home, and believed him when he said he'd use it if his golf club wasn't enough. Nick called him an OOG, an *original* original gangster.

Fletcher was one of the many things Billie loved about her grungy, incompletely gentrified City Park West neighborhood. Thanks to his clientele, they didn't have to worry about knuckleheads trafficking the block (though the idea of a slow-motion, oldster drive-by tickled her). Really, the only trouble from his line of work was Honking Harry, and even he wasn't that bad because he always came to score before it got too late. None of Fletcher's customers drove after dark.

"Next time Nick comes over, I'll send him with some more Tiger Balm for you."

"We'll trade," Fletcher said with a wink.

The wink got her. The wink made her want to tell someone else who'd be happy for her. "Fletcher, guess what? I'm pregnant."

"Hey now, that's beautiful! Congratulations. I bet Nick is a happy man!"

Her eyes filled, and she found herself divulging the whole pitiful story.

To her surprise, Fletcher just laughed. "Sometimes men don't know what we want until y'all women tell us."

She felt even guiltier. She liked to think of herself as a modern woman, a feminist even, but she had acted just like a woman from Fletcher's generation. She could hear Nick saying, "From the dawn of time . . ." "I don't think Nick sees it that way."

"Don't worry 'bout it. He'll come 'round. The good ones always do, and he's a good one, right?"

She thought about Nick telling her to abort the baby, and wondered if she could still think of him as one of the good ones. But she nodded. She had to. No matter what the ancestors said, there had to be a way to keep Nick and this baby.

"Well then." Fletcher turned and went back into his house, turning on the porch light behind him.

When Nick came home, Billie went to him. She was wearing the necklace of jade beads and cowrie shells he had given her for Christmas last year. "You are everything to me, *everything*," she said.

Hope brightened his eyes.

"So I have to choose you *and* your baby." She smiled tenderly. "The two of you are inseparable to me."

The light went out of his eyes.

"Please. We can do this."

"I can't," was all he croaked, as if the words were slicing his vocal cords.

Billie nodded, unable to speak, the smile frozen on her lips, but gone from her eyes.

"I guess you win. Until I get my money together, I'll stay in the basement if that's okay with you?"

She nodded again. She wouldn't ask him for child support. Would he ever want to see the baby? She'd never imagined that Nick would really disavow his own child.

He went downstairs and she stood in the living room alone. If she won, how come it felt like they had both lost?

CHAPTER 7

~~~~~~~~~~

Trish

Mrs. Sturgis, older, smaller, wearing an oxygen tank, but still familiar to Trish, answered her front door. "I've been waiting for you for twenty years," she wheezed.

Trish hadn't expected to be recognized. "You know who I am?"

"You're Max's granddaughter, aren't you?"

"Yeah."

"Well, then. Don't just stand there. Come on. We got lots to take care of."

Lots to take care of? The hell? They hadn't seen each other in about twenty years and she was acting like they were in the middle of a conversation. Trish followed her into the house.

It had the same layout as the house she had grown up in. Instantly, she was transported to her childhood. She heard the shepherds barking out in the kennels. Smelled her grandfather's cigars. Expected to see Nana in the corner working a puzzle and watching Channel 5 News.

She forced herself back to the present.

Mrs. Sturgis sank down into a recliner and Trish sat on a brown plaid sofa.

"How did you remember me?" Trish asked. "Please tell me I've changed since high school."

"Your birthmark."

Trish touched the splotch on her left cheek. Pawpaw had said when she was six, "Could never sell a pup with foul coloring like that. That's your grandma's family for you." Until she had Will she was self-conscious about her port-wine stain, hiding it under concealer and thick foundation. But he used to trace it with his little fingers while she nursed him, healing her bad feelings about it. She rarely thought about it anymore.

"And you still got the pretty blond hair, just like a baby doll," Mrs. Sturgis added.

"So why have you been waiting for me?"

"The folks over at Aspen Hill sent you, right?"

Trish felt like crying and she didn't know why. It was as if her heart understood before her brain that her life was about to change. "No, they didn't."

"Why, I left a note. They were supposed to put it in their computer. When you showed up, you were to come see me."

Grrr. "They didn't tell me."

"All these years and they never mentioned it?"

Trish was too embarrassed to say that this year was the first time she'd been to her grandmother's grave.

"I guess we're lucky I'm still alive." Mrs. Sturgis hacked her way through a vile coughing fit. "Though just barely."

"Are you okay? Can I get you some water?"

Mrs. Sturgis pulled a paper towel from the roll on the table and spat phlegm into it. "Takin' care of me is not what you came here for. Go on in the back bedroom. There's a desk. In the top drawer is a letter for you from your grandma. I didn't find it until you had already moved. It was in one of her puzzle boxes you gave me when she died."

Trish's eyes welled, adrenaline coursed through her, and acid bubbled in her stomach. She let out a gurgle that was half laugh and half sob. "A letter? With her puzzles?"

"Guess those were meant for you and not for me. Woulda helped if she woulda told somebody."

"Did you read it?" She rubbed her breastbone. Why hadn't she taken an acid-reducer before she left home?

"No, but I'm pretty sure I know the gist of what it says. You go on and read it and we can talk when you're done. It's in a yellow envelope."

"Yellow envelope," Trish repeated, then stood and pointed in the hallway.

"Yep, right back there with the gold carpet and bedspread."

When Trish turned toward the hall, Mrs. Sturgis called behind her, "Be sure to sit down first."

The bedroom was in the same location as her bedroom was in her childhood home. Nobody had slept here for decades. The bed was neatly made, but there was a layer of dust on the dresser and desk and a musty smell in the air. Trish retrieved the envelope and, following Mrs. Sturgis's advice, sat on the bed, her hands trembling as she opened it.

Inside was a Polaroid picture of a young woman and a little girl holding a sleeping infant. She imagined the screech of brakes and crash of metal that had taken her mother and sister. The picture was dated September 1977. Trish had never seen it before, hadn't even known a picture of her sister existed. They were in a hospital room. Her mother didn't smile, but looked defiantly into the camera, as if daring the photographer to snap the photo. Trish ran her fingers over the picture. The colors were faded. She could barely tell her mother was wearing a yellow housecoat. The baby was wrapped in pink. Trish wore a green dress. *We were a family.* She stared at the three of them until her sight was blurred by tears. She turned the picture over. It said "Me, Trish, and Lauren."

She wiped her eyes and started to read the letter, expecting to learn where her sister was buried, her whole body trembling.

Dear Trish,

I should have told you this a long time ago. I'm sorry that I didn't, but I'm ashamed. I couldn't bear for you to know what I've done. What kind of person I am.

I'm only sixty years old, but I feel like I'm a hundred. And it's not just because of the cancer. The guilt weighs on me something terrible. I tell myself I cannot burden you with any more at such a young age. You've lost your mother, your grandfather, and now me. But the truth is that I cannot stand to know that you could hate me. I am not strong enough. Please forgive me for the lies I have told you. Here is the truth:

Your mother didn't die in a car accident. She died from drugs, an overdose of heroin. I wanted to shelter you from the truth of what your mother was. I have to say I wasn't very understanding about it then. She just couldn't quit! She ripped my heart out over and over again, but still it's one of my greatest sorrows that I didn't do more for her. I will die with a hole in my soul because I wasn't able to help her.

That is the first thing I have to tell you and I know it's a shock.

The second thing I need to tell you will be an even bigger shock. Your baby sister did not die with your mother. She was put up for adoption. We wouldn't take another one of Jocelyn's babies. Your Pawpaw and I were so mad at Jocelyn! And hurt and embarrassed that she had yet another baby out of wedlock. The seventies weren't as permissive as everyone nowadays likes to think. Or maybe it was just us. Even worse, I have to confess that we didn't want to raise a black man's child. Just writing those words today makes me sick to my stomach, but they are the truth, and I will have to live and die with that knowledge.

I do not know for certain that she did it on purpose, but after we told her we wouldn't take that baby is when she died. Still, we put Lauren, that's what your mother named her second child, up for adoption. Lutheran Charities for Families and Children found a couple for Lauren. Their name is Cousins. Isn't that some poetic justice? Cousins. Like we are all related under the skin. I know their name because Lucy Sturgis worked for the Lutherans and she looked it up for me. The mother is someone you have seen before. Zenobia Cousins, the newswoman on Channel Five. I could hardly believe it when Lucy told me that's who was raising my grand-daughter! I watched Channel Five every day and you could see she was a fine, caring lady. It's a funny thing to watch some stranger and know she's raising your blood, the blood you turned your back on. But I would see this beautiful, articulate woman on the TV and tell myself that Lauren is in better hands. What would an old white lady like me do with a black baby? That's what I would tell myself, anyway.

But now it is my last wish that you and your sister be together. I wish I could see Lauren—she must be getting to be a beautiful young lady—and apologize to her, but just as I am not strong enough to say all this to you, I am not strong enough to face her.

I need you to go to her and explain, make it right. When you read this, please try not to hate me. When you meet your sister, please tell her I'm sorry. I'm so very sorry.

Love,
Nana

The news flooded through Trish as if a dam had broken. Her mother didn't die in a car wreck? Trish read the letter again. She was a junkie? She read it again. Lauren was alive? The horrific car accident she had imagined so many times had never happened? No, that part couldn't be right. Her grandparents wouldn't have done that to her. They wouldn't have taken away the only other relative she had in the world. Mrs. Sturgis was playing some kind of sick trick.

But she knew that wasn't true as soon as she thought it. This was Nana's handwriting. And there was no grave for Lauren. She was really alive. Trish had been all alone in that house with those two old people. How could they have lied to her all those years?

Her mind careened back and forth between the past and the present. *Zenobia Cousins. That's why Nana always watched Channel 5 News!* Her own sister was growing up in the same area and her grandparents knew it. Trish could have passed her on the street. Their schools could have played football and basketball against each other. Trish could have served her French fries at the mall without knowing it. All this time there was an emptiness in her life, a sister-shaped hole in her heart, that didn't need to be there.

No wonder Nana didn't want her at her mother's funeral! No wonder they clammed up every time she brought up her mother and her sister! She was trembling with outrage. She read the letter again, brushing the tears away to see the page, still not believing what she was reading. They didn't want their own granddaughter because her father was black.

Was that why Nana was so nice to Tommy? She felt guilty for what she had done to her granddaughter? What a load of crap! And now Trish was supposed to make up for their racism? How? *Hey Lauren, guess what? The reason they put you up for adoption was because of your skin color, but they felt really sorry for it. Or at least our grandmother did. She felt so sorry for it she was actually nice to my black boyfriend. See how that makes everything okay? Yeah, right.*

Trish marched back into the living room. Mrs. Sturgis had poured two cups of coffee.

"Why didn't anybody tell me?"

"It wasn't my place when you were younger. She always said she'd tell you one day, and when I saw that letter I figured she was finally doing it. I tried to find you."

Trish's scalp felt stretched tight across her head, and pain throbbed behind her eyes. Her chest ached, and she could feel more acid waves splashing up her esophagus.

"You don't look so good. How 'bout a little medicinal Irish cream in your coffee?"

Even though alcohol and coffee were bad for her acid reflux, Trish sat down and held up her mug. "Hit me."

Trish pushed the pieces of Nana's puzzle around on the kitchen counter and sipped her Sunday morning coffee. It was in a puzzle of the Egyptian pyramids that Nana had placed the letter for her to find. *How appropriate for the Queen of Denial,* she thought, then the same thoughts that had been running through her mind returned. *My sister is alive. My mother overdosed. My grandparents lied to me.*

And those weren't even the craziest parts of the situation. The craziest part was that Alicia seemed to be right: the puzzle pieces were meant to lead Trish to the truth about her sister. The idea was totally insane, but how could it be a coincidence that she had started finding pieces of jigsaws after she came back, and Nana had left her confession in a jigsaw puzzle box?

The letter said her mother had a drug problem. Trish could see now that's why her grandparents had raised her and why they had fought so much with her mother. Had she overdosed on purpose? Did she kill herself when they told her they wouldn't take her baby? Trish could imagine what kind of failure her mother would feel like not being able to raise her own children. But either way, accident or intentional, Trish blamed her grandparents for her mother's death, for not keeping Lauren, for keeping such secrets from her all her life.

She started to speculate about her sister. What kind of life had Lauren lived? What kind of person was she? She'd obviously grown up with some advantages—her mother was on TV, after all—but was she loved? Did she have a happy childhood? Had she grown up wondering about her family? Did she even know she had a sister? What if Lauren was out there searching for her birth family right now?

Trish hadn't slept all night, and was wired and tired at the same time. She sipped her coffee. One more cup and a long walk with the dogs and maybe she'd finally wake up.

Will ambled into the kitchen, text-messaging somebody, and poured himself a cup. She hadn't told him about her sister yet.

"What are you doing all dressed so early?" And the way he was dressed! He had on jeans that actually fit, that didn't show his boxers, and a button-down shirt and . . . *When did Will get a tie?*

"Getting ready to go to church," he said as casually as if he'd been going to church every Sunday of his life. Which he so had not.

"*Church*?!" Trish yelped, sputtering coffee.

"Yeah. Why you say it like that?" He added a ton of hazelnut creamer and a couple of spoons of sugar to his cup. They both liked cream and sugar with a little coffee in it.

"Because you haven't been to church since you were about five!" Tommy's mom had dragged them. *And what teenage boy in his right mind willingly gets up at nine on a Sunday morning?* But then Will hadn't been in his right mind since the mall incident.

"Maybe that's the problem," he mumbled, taking a sip of coffee.

"What problem?"

"Nothing."

"You can talk to me about it, you know? Whatever is going on with you."

"You wouldn't understand."

"It's about those dicks at the mall, right?"

He looked at his sneakers and spoke so softly it was almost a whisper. "They called me 'Little Barack' and 'O.J. Jr.' They said 'scum like you is what's wrong with this country.' Right in front of Josh and Eric."

She inhaled sharply. "I wish you would have told me."

"What would you have done?"

At the least, she wished she could get them fired. What she really wished was that she could tie raw meat to their bodies and sic a hundred big, mean dogs on them. But he was right. What could they have done? What was a teenage boy's word against two grown men?

"I understand," she said, feeling sick about how wrong the whole thing was. "Women get discriminated against too."

He looked up at her. "It's not the same. I went on the Internet. It happens all the time. They call it shopping while black, driving while black. Doing *anything* while black makes you, like, a suspect."

"Will, people made cracks about me being married to your dad. Gave me funny looks, mean looks."

"But that wasn't because of you, it was because of dad being black."

Trish wanted to tell Will that his own grandmother had disapproved of her marrying her son, but she had never spoken ill of Tommy's family to Will. But there were others she could tell him about. "Black *and* white people sometimes didn't like our relationship. Black women could be kind of mean about it actually. Mean to *me,* not your dad."

Will got a sick look on his face, and suddenly Trish felt that she was only reinforcing the differences he was beginning to feel, which was not what she wanted to do. The fissure that had started in her heart that day spread wider. She tried to backtrack. "But most of the time people were good about it, really. Try not to be too mad about those guys. It was a one-time thing. It doesn't mean everybody's going to treat you like that."

"Kids had said things before—" he said, almost as if he was talking to himself.

This was the first she'd ever heard about it. "What kind of things?"

"You know, the N-word and stuff."

Jesus, kids had called her son nigger?!

"But this is the first time I was really treated different than the other kids I was with by adults."

"Okay, you're still mad. I totally get that. I don't blame you at all. What they said, how they treated you was so unfair. But what does church have to do with it?"

"I just need some help with life now. Somebody's gotta help me with this stuff, and it can't be you."

Trish thought of the black woman who had told her to haul ass with Will out of the mall. Maybe he did need someone in his exact same shoes to talk to. "Call your dad and see what he has to say," she said, the words killing her. She hated that she had to put on a happy face to Will about Tommy.

But the good news was that Tommy wasn't radical about race either. He would tell Will to forget about those guys just as she had, that color didn't matter. Maybe he'd be able to accept from his dad what he couldn't accept from her.

Will shrugged, feigning indifference.

"He was a teenage boy once too. He's probably been through everything you're going through. You should talk to him about it. Really."

"Yeah, maybe."

She sipped her coffee while Will drained his cup and poured himself a bowl of cereal.

"So, what church are you going to?"

"Clear View. I know a couple people who go there."

"These new friends of yours?"

"You act like they just landed on the planet. They go to my school. I've known 'em since we moved here."

She knew lots of parents would thank their lucky stars. A kid going to church was much better than a kid joining a gang or taking steroids to make the team or all the other long list of damaging things a kid could do. But she was freaked. She thought it was weird. Thoughts of him proselytizing door to door and ranting about the end times on street corners ran through her head.

"And I met the youth minister, Reverend Eubanks. A black guy. He's cool."

Trish imagined some stranger luring Will in and taking advantage of him. "When? Have you been alone with him?"

"Dude, he's married," Will said, laughing. "His wife is a minister too. They have, like, three little kids. They do work with gangs and stuff. They a-ight."

Trish got it then, and pictured them: a happily married black couple saving black youth. What could be more attractive to Will right now? She recalled getting a crush on a couple that lived next door to her best friend in junior high. They were probably only in their twenties, but to her they seemed all grown up, and compared to her grandparents, young and pretty. They had beautiful curly-haired twins. Trish and her friend Susan used to babysit for them, and Trish half-wanted them to adopt her and half-wanted to marry the husband and raise the girls as her own.

"Will, morality doesn't have a color. Those assholes at the mall were white, but there are black and Hispanic assholes too. That's all I'm trying to say."

Then she remembered all over again: Her sister was alive. Trish quickly did the math in her head. Lauren would be thirty-two. She had a sister! And her sister might have kids! Trish might be an aunt, and Will might have cousins on her side of the family! *Biracial* cousins that he might be able to relate to. Biracial cousins who would help understand that he didn't have to choose between all the parts of himself. He could just be a person.

"Will . . ."

The doorbell rang.

"That's them. Gotta jet. Later."

Maybe it was better if she didn't tell him just yet. Lauren might not even live in Colorado anymore. The first thing she needed to do was contact Zenobia Bailey-Cousins.

She called Zenobia at the television station first thing the next morning. Of course, they wouldn't put her through. So she left a message. "Tell her we have someone in common that we need to talk about."

She kept her cell on and in her pocket all day, but Zenobia didn't return her call. She imagined that Zenobia probably thought she was some kind of weird stalker. But what could she say that was credible without revealing too much of Zenobia's personal affairs?

That night when Trish got home from work, Will dashed up to her as she walked into the kitchen.

"Don't you want to go change?" he said.

Trish looked down at her T-shirt and scrubs. "Why?" she asked.

"You been at work all day. I thought you'd want to freshen up."

She smirked. "Freshen up?"

A young girl walked up behind Will and waved at Trish. "Hi!"

Ah. The reason he wanted me dressed better, Trish thought.

Will jumped at the sound of the girl's voice and turned around to introduce her.

"Mama, this is Makeesha. Makeesha, this is my mother."

Trish's eyebrows made arcs over her eyes. *Mama?* Will hadn't called her that since he started kindergarten. Since they had left North Carolina, he usually called her Dude.

Makeesha had a gorgeous bright smile and dewy skin, the kind of skin that middle-aged women like Trish pay a fortune for fancy creams to try to get, but will never have again. Makeesha was dressed in jeans and a sleeveless smock top, similar to the other teens Trish saw at the high school. But Makeesha's jeans didn't seem to begin below her hips, her shirt only showed her collar-bone, and she had tiny gold studs in her ears and a chain with a cross on it around her neck.

"Nice to meet you," Trish said.

"Nice to meet you."

"Can I talk to you for a minute?" Will pulled Trish back out into the hallway.

"That T-shirt is blasphemous. Can you please take it off?"

Her T-shirt read "In Dog We Trust." "Will, Buddy, you gotta get a sense of humor. It's just a T-shirt."

"Can Makeesha have dinner with us?"

She was uneasy. He was replacing Jessica with Makeesha. Was that the only change he'd make? "Sure."

"Then please, please, please can you change your shirt?"

Trish rolled her eyes. "Fine. Call in some Chinese for us, okay?"

Will went back to the kitchen and Trish went upstairs, trying to convince herself that everything was all right. She showered and changed into an appropriately "nonblasphemous" shirt and jeans.

When the food came, they sat at the kitchen table, and Trish passed around the mu shu pork, sweet-and-sour chicken, and beef and broccoli. "So how did you two meet?" she asked once everybody had their food.

Makeesha held out her hands. "Aren't we going to say grace?"

"Yes," Will said, bowing his head and taking her hand.

Makeesha looked at Trish to take her other hand.

"Why don't you do it, since you're the guest?" Will said.

Makeesha closed her eyes and started to pray in a high, girlish voice, "Thank you for the world so sweet. Thank you for the food we eat. Thank you for the birds that sing. Thank you God for everything."

Believing they were done, Trish started to take her hand back, but Makeesha grasped it and continued.

"Lord God, Heavenly Father, bless us and these Thy gifts which we receive through Thy goodness, through Jesus Christ our Lord. Oh Father God, we thank you for bringing us together around this table and for giving us the opportunity to bring more people to your wisdom."

Trish's eyes widened. *The hell?*

"I know what your love has meant in my life, oh God, and I just ask if you would allow me to be an instrument of your will so I can help Will and Ms. Taylor know you the way that I know you."

Well, there was no way she was saying amen to that! But Makeesha wasn't done anyway. "Oh Father—"

"All right," Trish said, slipping her hand away.

"Amen," said Will, frowning at her.

"Amen," Makeesha murmured.

"So how did you two meet?" Trish asked again, her voice a little too high-pitched.

"Makeesha goes to my church," Will said.

Now, it was *his* church? Grrr.

"We got to talking after Bible study the other night," Makeesha said with a grin.

"Wait. *You* went to Bible study?"

"Yeah," Will said.

"You don't go to church, Ms. Taylor?" Makeesha asked innocently.

"No," Trish said, then watched the girl's face contort as she struggled to understand.

"Our church is very multicultural," Makeesha volunteered. "You should come and visit. I bet you'd like it."

"Uh," Trish stumbled. "Um." Who were these kids? What happened to smoking pot and sneaking into each other's bedrooms? She found herself longing to hear her son let lose a string of curse words that would make a sailor blush. It was bad enough that Will had switched to gospel hip-hop. She'd come home one day to the usual thumping bass line and gravelly voiced boys rhyming at each other. She almost didn't notice at first that instead of liquor and women and guns, they were talking about righteousness and getting to heaven. She almost missed the rap crap he used to play. Now this?

Will watched, alarmed. Trish couldn't tell if it was because he was afraid she wouldn't accept or afraid she would.

"We'll see."

Fortunately, Makeesha left right after dinner. As soon as he closed the door behind her, Will was asking, "So did you like her?"

Be diplomatic, she thought. "She seems like a nice girl."

"She is. She ain't a skank like Jessica."

"Excuse me?"

"Jess was always up in somebody's grill trying to get attention. Makeesha is pure, and staying that way 'til she gets married."

If Trish did nothing else, one of her jobs as a mother was to get her son to treat women respectfully. No way was he going to get away with turning Jessica into a whore for doing the same things he did! "Last time I checked it takes two to tango, if you know what I mean. If Jessica was a skank, what does that make you?"

"Probably a skank too. Though, you're right. I shouldn't be using that word. That's why I'm not having sex again 'til I get married."

Trish's mouth fell open. It wasn't the first time Will had ever said anything that she didn't know the answer to, but it was the first time in his life that she was totally speechless. But what were you supposed to say when a sixteen-year-old boy was talking about celibacy?

She should be glad, right? And she *was*. She was glad that her son was being responsible and thinking about values and stuff, but come on! No sex until he was married?! What normal teenage boy says shit like that? None. Normal teenage boys don't talk about being pure and saving themselves for marriage. Normal teenage boys think about getting laid like they think about getting their next meal. But how could she be upset about it? Nobody ever wrote to Dear Abby saying, "Help! My son's taking a vow of celibacy until marriage!" She stood there gaping at him, eyes blinking, trying to make some sense of the craziest situation she had ever heard of, waiting for words to come to her. That was when she noticed the gold cross glinting against his shirt. All she could think of was something she couldn't say out loud: *Some crazy-ass church is not going to get my son!*

She took a deep breath. "Sit."

Will sat at the breakfast bar.

"This is a big change, don't you think?"

"No, I gave it a lot of thought."

Gave it a lot of thought! You've barely known about this church five minutes! "Where is this coming from?"

He answered her question with one of his own. "What exactly bothers you about me being a Christian?"

"I just don't buy it. I don't buy an old guy with a long white beard living in the sky controlling everything that happens. If there's a God, if there's somebody who really controls everything, how can there be rape and child abuse and genocide? How come whole countries starve to death? And the things people do to each other in God's name?! What kind of God lets that happen?"

Trish shook her head. "I'm like John Lennon. I think it'd be better if everybody in every religion quit thinking they had a direct line to God. If there wasn't any religion maybe people would stop blowing shit up—"

"Language."

Trish was too busy talking to notice Will correct her. "And bombing people and going to war over their beliefs in something that just . . ."

"Don't blame God for evil! That's the devil. People who do that stuff need to get right with God. That's when there won't be no wars and stuff."

The devil made me do it. She rubbed her breastbone, which, as usual lately, was aflame. She reached for her Tums on the counter. Is this really what they had come to? Next thing you know Will was going to be telling her that God created man and dinosaurs in six days, and then laid in his hammock drinking beer on the seventh. "Wait. You still believe in evolution, right?"

"Yes, Mother, I believe in evolution," Will said, smiling condescendingly.

She wanted to grab him and shake the loose marbles in his head back into their rightful places. But at least he hadn't completely lost them. "Well, thank—" Trish almost said God and caught herself, but not before Will grinned. "Good," she said primly. "But I still don't like this."

"You can't seriously be trying to stop me from believing in God, something that, like, most of the world believes in."

She shouldn't have been so surprised. She had looked at Will's

MySpace page and found it completely redesigned. No more pictures of athletes and rappers with tattoos and gold teeth, no more pictures of scantily clad girls. Now there were Bible verses and poems about faith. In his profile, where his answer to "Name your favorite book" used to be "What's a book?" it now said the holy Bible. She shouldn't have been, but she was overwhelmed by all the changes in her boy. "I just want you to be smart about what you believe. Use your head. Think!"

"But Mama," he said, again with the condescending smile. "Faith isn't something you can know with your head. It's something you feel in your heart."

Trish sighed. She had a sinking feeling that this church already had Will's head *and* heart.

How desperate was Trish? She was so desperate she was calling her ex-husband to ask for his help. So desperate she was willing to hear his girlfriend, who was fucking him while he was still married to Trish, purr hello like a friggin' sex kitten. That's how desperate she was.

But Tommy wasn't getting it. "He's just rebelling. It's what kids do. You're not religious, so he's religious. If you did go to church, I bet you couldn't drag him to one."

"He's running around with a cross around his neck!" she told him. She was in her car on a quick break at work. "He's reading the Bible! I couldn't even get him to read Harry Potter and he's reading the friggin' Bible! He doesn't cuss anymore. And he says grace before he eats."

"Oh no, not grace! Is he saying 'please' and 'thank you' too? As usual, you're overreacting."

"He says he's not having sex again until he's married."

Tommy was shocked into silence.

"Uh-huh, not overreacting now, am I? It's like he's in a cult or something. He's brainwashed. And all this has something to do with those assholes at the mall. Can you please talk to him?"

"Don't panic. Yeah, I'll talk to him, and I'll see him in August, right? I'll have him back to being a heathen in no time."

"If anybody can, I know it's you," she said with saccharine on her tongue.

"Ahem. Goodbye, Trish."

She clicked the phone shut and mock-gagged, as she did every time she spoke to him now.

Would Tommy be able to get through to him over the phone? If he didn't, she'd have to wait until August for Will to go to North Carolina to be deprogrammed.

She opened her phone and dialed Zenobia Bailey-Cousins's number at the station again. She knew it by heart now. She'd left two messages, but Zenobia was ignoring her. Understandable. Why should she return a call to a total stranger? But Trish was getting desperate.

"Zenobia Bailey-Cousins please."

"I'm sorry, but she's unavailable. May I take a message?"

"Yes. Tell her. . . . Tell her that I'm related to her daughter. And please ask her to call me right away." Trish left her number. That ought to do it.

CHAPTER 8

Billie

Lemon and lavender filled Billie's nose. Since sage smoke made her nauseous, she was on her hands and knees scrubbing the hardwood floors, using a floor wash with water, baking soda, lemon juice, and lavender oil to clear the air between her and Nick.

He was staying in the basement, avoiding her as much as possible. Still she refused to accept the idea that he would leave, that she would have to raise this baby by herself. They loved each other. She had no doubts about that. He'd come around. Like Fletcher said, he was one of the good ones. And if he didn't come around of his own volition, well . . . there were ways.

At the store where she bought her oils, incense, and smudge sticks, they sold candles dressed with "Follow Me Boy Oil" and "Stay with Me Oil." They sold books of wiccan spells and hoodoo tricks you could use to attract and keep your beloved. Things like slipping urine or menstrual blood into a lover's drink, making dolls of mandrake root, sweeping up the dirt left from your man's foot tracks. The most heinous, but supposedly fail-safe, hoodoo trick was the black cat bone spell, which involved boiling a black cat alive to get one of its bones. Billie had never been tempted to use such magic before, but she was starting to understand how you could feel desperate enough to try it. Though not the black cat spell. She looked at her kitty, Juju, and shuddered.

The windows were open, and a fresh midmorning breeze carried the lemon and lavender through the house. She imagined the scents wafting down the stairs to Nick, who was most likely still sleeping, since he had worked last night, and it was Sunday, so he wouldn't be mowing lawns today. With each breath, *You love her,* the lemon and lavender would say. *How can you leave?*

She took her rubber gloves off and took the pail of murky water to the backyard to dump in the grass. Since she wasn't working and she wasn't taking care of Nick she didn't know what to do with her days. The house was spotless, but that didn't stop her from cleaning every day. When she scrubbed the tub and dusted the bookshelves, she was asking Nick to stay. It wasn't that she believed shiny floors could keep a man. She was reminding him of all they had together.

She woke up when she heard him come in last night. He had approached the bedroom door and she held her breath, willing him to come in. But he turned away. Every time she heard him pad through the kitchen and open the refrigerator, she wanted to run in and offer to fix him something to eat. The sight of fast-food wrappers in the kitchen trash pained her. She made herself ignore the fact that clothes were disappearing from his closet little by little.

Even with dark glasses on she blinked in the bright sunlight. Denver was a rough place for someone who should be avoiding the sun. Denver has more sunshiny days than San Diego. How she used to love to play outside in the summer. A dove in a family of swallows and crows, she loved that her skin would darken under the smile of the summer sun. At least she did until she was fourteen and Zenobia complained one day about the dearth of good makeup for dark-skinned women and told her wistfully that she was lucky to be so light.

She realized her mother envied her. Her mother was colorstruck; she had internalized the idea that lighter skin was better. People were always saying Billie looked different than her family. Women and girls on the block were always admiring her long, so-called "good" hair. It didn't bother her that much until her own mother pointed out the color line between them. She wanted to be on the same side of the line as her parents and her brother.

She started to notice otherwise sane and intelligent adults telling their children (especially daughters) to stay out of the sun, and making jokes like "coffee will make you black."

In high school, she read books like *The Bluest Eye* and *The Color Purple*. In college, she learned about things like the brown paper bag test that light-skinned Negroes in the early 1900s used to keep their dark-skinned brethren out of their social clubs: those darker than a brown paper bag, like Zenobia, weren't allowed. Billie wrote a paper on Spike Lee's movie *School Daze*, about the battle between dark and pale fraternities and sororities at a historically black college. She realized Zenobia was far from alone.

To this day, it hurt Billie to think a woman as beautiful as her mother was ever made to feel bad about her appearance. With her students she always made sure to tell *all* the kids, girls and boys, light and dark, they were beautiful inside and outside. But she was especially careful to compliment the darker, short-haired girls. Even in the twenty-first century, they would have it harder. And now she'd do all she could not to pass this self-hate on to her son or daughter.

She set the bucket down, went under the crabapple tree, and slipped off her sandals. The grass was cool and damp beneath her feet. The dryness of summer had yet to scorch everything. She did tree pose, warrior, cat and cow, and child pose. No big inversions, nothing too strenuous. Just ten minutes of movement to stretch her lower back, open her chest, and lubricate her joints. She marveled at how her body was already changing. Her yoga pants were a little bit snug, and for the first time in her life she had cleavage! Thank goodness she hadn't had any morning sickness. The biggest downside so far was having to pee all the time.

Every morning just before the sun came up she went for a walk. Every evening she did yoga. She meditated daily. But because she was pregnant she had to stop the hot baths that she loved. But switching to showers was a small price to pay.

She thought back to last spring, when the tree she was under blossomed and attracted an influx of butterflies. Billie and Nick sat on the back porch and watched hundreds of monarchs feed on the pink flowers. That Nick, the one she had fallen in love with, was still here. He had to be.

Just as she was lying back into corpse pose, he came out the back door. He didn't notice her or if he did, he didn't acknowledge her. He dashed down the porch steps and peeled away from the curb like a man running away from a crime.

She shook her head. She would not cry. She couldn't be heartsick. She had to keep going for Ambata's sake. She couldn't afford for her health to falter.

She looked at her watch. Noon. Nick was probably going out for breakfast. It was ridiculous, but she couldn't stop herself. She was drawn down to the basement, down to the pullout bed that he was using, as surely as if he had called her. The basement was divided in two, a small, concrete-floor laundry room and a family room that had been poorly renovated by the house's former owners, which is where Nick was living. The walls were covered in faux wood paneling that was starting to buckle and peel, and the floor was carpeted with brown shag. Nick stored his keyboard in here, and it served as a soundproof rehearsal space. It was furnished with a beat-up sofa with a pullout bed and an old TV.

She wasn't surprised to find the room was a mess, filled with towering piles of clothes, empty fast-food bags, and pizza boxes. The bed was out, and, of course, unmade. She fought the urge to make the bed, fold his clothes, and line his shoes in a row. Maybe if she put just a few drops of Stay With Me Oil on a washcloth and stuck it in the dryer with his bedsheets?

Oh, but she'd rather take his sheets and put them on the bed upstairs. The sheets on their bed had lost his fragrance. She sat on the edge of the bed, leaned into the pillowcases, and breathed in his scent, part smoke, part fresh-cut grass, and part something that was just Nick. The first time she was close enough to his skin to smell him, he smelled like home. She ran her hand over the wrinkled sheets where just moments ago his naked body had been. Tears welled in her eyes. *How did things get so bad so fast?*

She yawned and lay down, closing her eyes. She was often tired lately. But pregnancy tired was different than lupus tired. Before her disease went into remission, she had felt exhausted not just in her body, but in her mind and spirit too. Her thinking was fuzzy and her mood was low. She slept heavily and woke feeling drugged. Nowadays, she felt pleasantly fatigued, the way one does after exercising, sex, or a good massage. And she had the comfort of knowing she was fatigued for a good reason: her body was working hard to give shelter and food to the baby. Also, she would most likely gain more energy when she started her second trimester. Until then, thanks to school being out and the check from her parents that allowed her to skip a summer job, she had the luxury of resting when she felt tired.

The basement was peaceful and cool. She let herself relax into the comfort of being surrounded by Nick's things. It wasn't long before she was asleep. She dreamed she was strewing flowers and a woman came up to her to talk. It was her grandmother, Wilhelmina, but then she morphed into an older white woman. Then the woman, as Wilhelmina, embraced Billie. When she pulled back from the hug, she was the white woman again and she said, "I believe in Ambata too."

Then Billie woke with a start to find Nick standing in front of her holding empty liquor boxes. She sat up quickly.

"What are you doing?" he asked.

"I'm sorry. I just . . . I missed you. I guess I fell asleep."

He let the boxes drop to the floor. "Were you going through my stuff?"

"What? No. I . . . why would you ask me that?" *What did you think I was going to find?*

"You shouldn't be coming in here when I'm not around."

She looked at the boxes. "You're really moving out?"

His face softened. "I figure by the end of the month I'll have enough for a down payment and first month's rent on an apartment and for storage for my piano."

"You can leave the piano here as long as you want to."

"Thanks, but I don't want to hold you up."

She smiled ruefully. "Then don't leave."

"We been through this."

"You're not the runaway type."

"You don't know that."

Each word was a brick through the castle in the sky she had built. But Billie was tougher than that. She wouldn't give up now. "Yes I do. You don't mess around with groupies. You're kind to Juju. You even take spiders outside rather than kill them. You're too good a man to just walk away."

"I wish. . . ."

"What?"

"I wish that was true."

"Oh, baby—"

"I'm a fucking failure, and you and the baby are better off without me."

She stood up. "Don't say that!"

"Why not? It's the truth."

"Nick, I love you, and I know you love me."

"Love don't have nothing to do with it. This is something you don't understand and you could never understand."

"Explain it, then. Help me understand how we got here!"

"Just let me have a month to get myself together, all right? Please," he said hoarsely.

She'd never seen Nick like this before. Terrified. What was he afraid of? He gazed at her, his night-sky eyes filled with the wish for her to leave. She was scared he would run out of the house and never come back if she didn't, so she obliged, walking up the stairs thinking fast. One month. She had one month to figure something out before Nick left. She made herself a cup of chamomile tea and leaned against the sink, inhaling the vaguely minty scent, and looked down at her stomach. "Oh, Ambata, what am I going to do?"

That's when the dream replayed in her mind. She believed in the power of dreams, in their ability to illuminate herself to herself. They were a way of learning from her subconscious and possibly even the ancestors. Since she had gotten pregnant, her dreams had been even more vivid. She assumed it was typical. But what did this dream mean? Who was the white woman, and why were she and Billie's grandmother speaking about Ambata?

Billie sipped her tea, mulling over the dream. The two women were both elders. The crone! That's what they symbolized. The crone was the inner teacher. Billie had read somewhere that the word crone originated from the same word that meant crown, and had to do with the wisdom of the head. But why would the crone come to her in a dream now when she was pregnant? The three female archetypes were maiden, mother, and crone. Shouldn't it be the mother she was hearing from?

She went to one of the bookshelves in the living room and found a book about archetypes and symbols. She looked up crone. Crones symbolize wisdom, as she knew, but they are also symbols for being true to oneself, speaking up for one's wishes, and making truthful choices. She closed the book with a hopeful smile. Was her dream telling her she had been making a truthful choice to conceive Ambata? Because on a level deeper than her subconscious, her soul even, she wanted this baby. She had helped create this child, and now she needed to do everything she could to make sure Ambata's father stayed with them.

She and Nick didn't speak again the rest of the day. When he came upstairs to use the bathroom or get something from the kitchen, they stayed out of each other's way like polite strangers sharing the same house.

All day she wondered what was going on with him. He was so worried about his mail, and now he was suspicious that she was going through his things. What was he hiding? Could he have another woman? If he did, wouldn't he have moved out already to go live with her? Maybe it had something to do with his family back in Oakland. He was always so secretive about them. And it was after he got back from his father's funeral that he wasn't like himself anymore.

Maybe it was just a contract for a gig coming up that he was anxious to find in the mail. But why wouldn't he just say that? Was he afraid she'd try to take the money from him? No, he was acting funny about the mail even before he knew she was pregnant. By the evening she was worn out from the conspiracy theories rumbling through her mind. All that worrying wasn't good for her or the baby. She sat on the rug next to the piano to meditate, to release these crazy thoughts and calm her mind. When she was done it was getting dark outside. Rather than turn on the lamps, she lit candles on the coffee table and one on the windowsill. The light reflected in the window as if someone was standing outside holding another candle. She sat in the chair in front of the window and touched her fingers to the cool glass.

CHAPTER 9

~~~~~~~~~~

Trish

"You said you had proof?" Zenobia Bailey-Cousins asked, her voice sounding just like it did on the air except even more intimidating in person.

Her bearing was downright regal, like an Afghan hound. Trish had to fight the urge to curtsy. They were meeting in a small conference room at Zenobia's TV station.

Trish gulped and handed her the photo. She had planned to show Zenobia the letter, tell her everything, but suddenly that didn't seem like such a good idea. If her sister was anything like Zenobia, telling her how awful their grandmother was might make her never want to see her.

Zenobia inhaled ever so slightly when she looked at the picture, softly touching her necklace. "This could be any baby."

"But it's not. Lucille Sturgis was our neighbor. She worked at the agency. She looked in the files and told my grandmother. Your daughter is my sister." Trish thought that was a good way to go, throwing in "your daughter" to show Zenobia she wasn't trying to take her daughter away.

"And why did you believe your *half* sister was dead all these years?"

Zenobia had already asked that on the phone. She was trying to trip her up. Fire burned from Trish's belly to her throat, and perspiration collected under her arms and breasts. *Don't be such a scaredy-cat,* she scolded herself. "It's what my grandparents told me. I guess when my mother died it was easier to tell me they both died than to tell me they were putting the baby up for adoption. Maybe it made it easier for them too, to mourn their daughter and granddaughter at once. Can I ask you a question?"

Zenobia nodded.

"Does she look anything like me?"

Zenobia's spine curved just a little, giving Trish the answer even before she spoke. "You have the same cheekbones, the same mouth. The port-wine stain on your cheek."

Now Trish knew it was true. "Will you help me meet her? If she wants proof after that, I'll be happy to take a blood test."

"Nobody was supposed to be coming for her." Zenobia pulled the small locket back and forth over the chain, sounding like she was in shock. "Her mother was dead. Nobody even knew who her father was."

"Well, I'm here now."

Zenobia straightened her back and placed her hands on the table, as if to brace herself.

"Wait—she knows she's adopted, doesn't she?"

Zenobia didn't answer.

Trish wasn't nervous anymore. "Fucking hell! What is it with you people? You're the same as my grandparents! How could you lie about something like that? What right did you have to hide the truth from her?"

"We had intended to tell Wilhelmina, but there never seemed to be the right time."

"Wilhelmina?"

"We named her after my mother."

Shit in a handbag. Wilhelmina? No telling who their mother had named her baby after, if anyone, but they couldn't even let her have that. Besides, Lauren was much prettier. "I know this is hard for you, but can't you see you have to tell her? She has to know who she is."

"I can see that you're sincere. One day you and Wilhelmina will meet, but this is not the time."

Trish was done being intimidated. "It's never going to be the right time for you, is it? I'm sorry, but you don't get to decide that anymore. This is *my sister,* and for my whole life I thought she was dead. But she's not. Do you know what that feels like?"

"No, I don't. Let me ask you a question: Does lupus run in your family?"

"Not that I know of. Does Wilhelmina have it?" Her sister's name sounded strange and yet somehow familiar in her ears.

"Yes. And she's pregnant. This is a disaster. A shock like this. . . . This is her first child."

"Then she totally needs her sister."

"She *has* a family," Zenobia snapped, and Trish was reminded that Zenobia was far tougher than any Afghan hound. A friggin' rottweiler was more like it. But no problem. Trish could lift an eighty-pound rottie onto an exam table all by herself. She could handle this one too.

"I'm her family too. Look, tell her about me, and if she doesn't want to meet me I can live with that," Trish said even though she didn't believe for a second that her sister wouldn't want to see her or that she'd be able to accept that decision. "But I'm sorry. I can't be a part of keeping any more secrets from anybody. I can't do it."

Trish stared at Zenobia until Zenobia blinked. Trish: one. Rottie: zero.

Will and Trish were walking the dogs late in the evening. The sun had just gone down, and it was one of the first nights that was warm. The air held the scents of flowers and grass. The dogs were happy their humans were home. Trish should have been happy too, but all she could think about was her sister. She was as excited and nervous about meeting her sister as she imagined people were before a blind date.

But something told her not to tell Will yet about his aunt. When she did, she certainly wasn't going to tell him about the letter. The last thing she needed was for Will to know his own great-grandparents were racists. And what would Will make of the idea of Nana speaking from beyond the grave? If his own relative could communicate from the great beyond, would he start up about Christ rising from the dead?

"Mom, can I talk to you about something?" he asked. He had just started summer school. He was taking calculus, just to get a little ahead of the game, and English, because like most boys his age, reading and writing were equivalent to torture, so he needed to make up a class.

But school was not what Trish thought of. Her mind jumped to worse things. *Oh, shit. Makeesha's pregnant. Keeping pure, my ass! What if he's got AIDS? He's joining the Marines.* "What?"

"I'm worried about your soul."

That was one that hadn't crossed her mind. Now she wished Makeesha *was* pregnant. Teenage pregnancy was something she was prepared to handle; worrying about souls was not.

"You haven't accepted Jesus as your Lord and Savior, and unless you do you won't be saved."

"I'm the mother. You're the son. You're not supposed to worry about me. I'm supposed to worry about you."

"But don't you want us to be together in the afterlife?"

"You're sixteen years old. I don't think the afterlife is anything you need to be thinking about right now."

"Pastor Bob says we should always be thinking about eternal salvation. What's happening right here and right now in this life only counts because of how it's going to affect us in the afterlife. That's what's important."

She looked at his face. He really was worried. He used to get the same look when they found a worm drying out on the sidewalk or a baby bird fallen out of its nest. This church had too much of a hold on him. It was time for her to check out this Pastor Bob. "Would it make you feel better if I came to church with you this Sunday?"

Will smiled so broadly and with so much hope that she felt she had to add, "You're not converting me, okay? But I want to know what you see in all this."

"Good! That's all you have to do is visit. Just come see the joy and the spirit. Like, people's lives are changed, Mama. They stop drinking and smoking and doing bad things. It helps with everything. You'll see."

The boy acted like she had just given him the keys to the car for the first time. But she didn't think church was going to bring the happy ending Will hoped for.

Pastor Bob and Clear View Church were not what she had expected. First of all, the church wasn't located in east Denver like most other black churches. Clear View Church was in Thornton, a suburb on the northwest side of Denver. And just as Makeesha had promised, it wasn't really a black church. There were many, many black people driving around looking for parking and walking the long sidewalks up to the church, but the congregation *was* multicultural. In fact, it might have been the most diverse crowd Trish had ever seen, with blacks, whites, Latinos, Asians, old people and young people. Okay, so maybe they were a little right of wacko, but she couldn't think of anyplace she had seen so many people of different colors shaking hands and hugging each other. She even noticed more than a few interracial couples and lots of biracial kids. Nothing she could be mad about, she had to admit to herself, but she kept her guard up.

The church was a totally ginormous building surrounded by parking lots so big there were shuttles for the elderly and others who couldn't make the walk from their cars to the door. Walking in the doors was more like entering a small convention center or arena than any church Trish had ever seen. They passed a bookstore, a day-care center, a basketball court.

"An espresso bar?" Trish noted with surprise.

"Why not keep the money in the church instead of giving it to Starbucks?" Will answered.

Inside the large main chapel, there weren't pews. They sat in roomy, comfortable stadium-style seats like in a new movie theater. The huge choir and band onstage were deafening. Instead of using hymnals, song lyrics were shown on giant screens on both sides of the stage. That's what it was: a stage. Not an altar. This wasn't church. This was a show. Trish felt even more strongly that something fishy was going on.

She turned to look at Will, but he was standing, holding his hands palms up in the air. *To receive what?* Even in profile, she could see the peace on his face, and it scared her. He *liked* this?

After the song ended, Will's heroes, Reverend Eubanks and his wife, came out for announcements. He, with his head shaved clean, and she, with a wild, curly afro, emanated "black is beautiful" without even opening their mouths. And when they spoke, Will practically glowed. They talked about their work with gangbangers and homeless kids and the importance of community, and Trish understood how Will would get a crush on them. But still her intuition told her something was weird about the whole place. If she were a dog, the hackles on the back of her neck would be standing straight up.

Next, a female preacher, also black, in a classy pin-striped pantsuit, came onstage. Against her will, Trish was impressed. *A woman preacher. Maybe this won't be so bad after all.*

"Good morning. I'm glad to see y'all here this morning," the preacher said. "And it's not just because you look so good. Though you do. I can see everybody did their hair all nice, and greased your knees and your elbows. Ya look good, church!"

The congregation laughed.

"No, I'm happy to see you because I know you will receive favor from the Lord for coming out this morning. You see, God likes to reward his people, and when you give God praise, you get so much more back in return. Am I right?"

"Amen!"

"And we are gonna praise him this morning, right? God has been so good to us! But he's not done! God has new and higher plans for us. I'm here to tell you this morning that whatever we touch will prosper. Whether it's your family, your job, your finances, or your health. Scripture says our God knows what we need, and it's already coming to us. It's already preordained. It's already laid out for us. All the riches of Christ Jesus belong to us!"

Hmm, prosper, riches. Trish knew where this was going. So much for her hopes that a woman preacher would be any different.

" 'Job 36:11. If they obey and serve him, they will spend the rest of their days in prosperity and their years in pleasures.' God will give you back tenfold what you give to God," the woman said.

I knew it! It's all about "give us money." Trish was about to hurl.

"If you need a miracle this morning, hang on, because help is on the way! God has good things in store for you. In Jeremiah 29:11 God says he has plans to prosper you, plans to give you hope. For in giving, you will receive! Can I get an amen up in here?"

"Amen!" hundreds of voices called out.

"You heard about the work we're doing here with our youth, out in the community, with our homeless ministry. We can only continue to do that with your support and God's help. And now, let's get our praise on!"

The woman left and the choir and the band started to play again. Sure enough, a group of ushers walked up and down the aisles passing gold collection plates. The woman next to Trish dropped in a twenty. People acted excited to give. *For in giving you will receive.* Trish guessed there were at least a thousand people in the room. Did they all give so much? And where did the money go? When she received the plate, she dropped in a dollar.

She looked at her watch. They had been there over half an hour and the sermon was just now about to start.

Pastor Bob walked onstage and the crowd roared like he was a rock star. But Trish wouldn't have been more surprised if a Martian had walked onstage. Pastor Bob was white! Or orange actually, either spray-tanned or wearing makeup for the cameras. Or both.

She took an instant dislike to him. *Fuck a duck, the man wore a toupee!* Plus, he wore diamond rings so big that when the light hit them she was blinded.

He began his sermon. *Why did preachers all seem to have to have redneck southern accents?*

He spoke about how God could help you find what was lost, could help you heal at the broken places. "People are imperfect, and they will fail you. We don't mean to, but we all fail. That is the nature of man," he said. "Spouses, children, parents, friends, neighbors will all disappoint you, but Jesus will not fail. As a matter of fact, look to your neighbor and say, 'The Lord never fails.' "

People turned to each other and repeated what he said like sheep. An elderly black woman next to Trish turned and spoke, lightly touching Trish's hand.

"There's a blessing in your life, and it might be hidden right in plain sight and you can't see it. But God can. God knows where your blessing is. Can somebody say, 'God knows'?"

"God knows!"

No wonder Will followed this guy like a puppy. It was so easy. All you had to do was give to God and God would give to you. *If God is so powerful, why does he need our money?* Trish wished people would ask themselves that question. Will had no money to give to the church, but Trish could see he was giving something much more valuable: his heart.

"Hey, Will, I need to talk to you about something." Now that they had returned home and changed out of their church clothes, Trish was about to tell Will about her sister. If he was happy about having a black minister, think how he'd feel about having an aunt who was half black.

"I need to tell you about something too."

Oh, boy. She wasn't sure she was ready for any more talk about her soul. "What is it?"

"I'm going to get baptized."

"You were already baptized." At Tommy's mother's church, even though Trish didn't believe in it. Tommy's mom had insisted.

"When I was a baby. That's not the same thing."

"Will—"

"And there's something else."

Trish snapped her eyes shut. What else could there be?

"I have to tell you the truth about something I kinda like lied about."

Her eyelids flew up. "Makeesha's not pregnant, is she?"

"What? No! I told you we're not having sex. Look where your mind goes."

"Just tell me."

"That day at the mall?"

"Yes?"

"I took some sunglasses," Will murmured.

"What?"

"So did Josh and Eric. We each took a pair."

"You *what*?"

"I stole them."

Thoughts of talking about Billie left her mind. Trish hadn't wanted to hit Will so much since he was seven years old. "What in the hell were you thinking?"

"We were just like messing around and Josh was all like 'I dare you.' "

Everything she thought about that day was turned upside down. The security guards had been right. They were just doing their job.

"But they didn't go after Josh or Eric. Just me. Josh and Eric was just as guilty as me, but nobody said like squat to them. They was able to just walk away.

"That's why I was so mad. But I'm telling you the truth now because I know it was wrong. I shouldn't have let myself be influenced by Josh's madness. Reverend Eubanks told me it was the right thing to man up and tell you, so that's what I'm doing. And I won't ever do it again."

Trish was taking it all in. She had tried and tried to get him to talk to her and he wouldn't say a word, but this stranger tells him to tell the truth and he does. And now he's got it all worked out. Without her. She didn't know what upset her more, that her kid had shoplifted and lied about it or that her kid had turned to somebody else to talk about it with.

"Mama, are you gonna say something?"

"I'm glad you told me."

"Are you mad?"

Yes, but not for the reason you think, she thought. She was mad because she wasn't the one her son had turned to. Because the color of her skin made her one of the bad guys in the story, and yet were the bad guys even still the bad guys? "No."

"'Cause you're acting like you're mad."

Then Trish dealt the ultimate maternal blow. "I'm not mad. But I am extremely disappointed."

Will nodded. "I know. Reverend Eubanks said you would be. I'm sorry."

Grrrr! This Eubanks guy had even stolen her power to guilt-trip. She had felt Will turning away from her since that day at the mall. Pretty soon she would see nothing but his back . . . walking away from her.

"What?"

"Why didn't you tell me all this when it happened?"

"I guess I was scared."

Trish nodded. "You know you're grounded, right?"

It was Will's turn to nod. "I'm prepared to accept the consequences of my actions."

She could tell he was parroting exactly what Eubanks had told him to say, and even though it was right, it infuriated her. "No video games, no Internet except for homework, no MP3, and no texts or phone calls until you go to North Carolina to see your father."

"*What?*" Will said.

Trish had never been a big discipliner. The most she'd ever grounded him for before was a week, and even then she gave in after a few days.

"I don't care what Josh and Eric did. You embarrassed me, Will. And you embarrassed yourself. You let us both down."

"I know. But at least I told you the truth now!"

"And you're not going anywhere but school, either."

"What about church?"

Trish knew she was on dangerous ground. "Not until you come back from North Carolina."

"Mama! You can't do that!"

Lucky barked when Will raised his voice. And when he started, so did Daisy.

"Shush!" Trish told the dogs. "Oh, yes I can! You can take a month and think about all this on your own."

"But—"

"No buts, Will. I mean it. *This* is the consequence of your actions."

"Dude," he called her, for a second sounding like the old Will. "I ain't a kid anymore. I'm like sixteen years old. You can't stop me from going to church. After a month, I'll just go back."

"Be mad at yourself. You did this."

"Man. . . ." Will stomped up the stairs, Lucky following behind him, and slammed the door to his room.

Lucky trotted back down the stairs to the kitchen, sat next to Trish, and gazed up at her.

"Don't give me that look. He had it coming. It was a good thing for Reverend Eubanks to make him 'fess up. He lied to me. But I don't like that church, and I don't like it having so much influence over him. He goes from sticky-finger Josh and Eric to these church people. One bad extreme to the other."

But what was going to change in a month? How would she get through to him? She slumped down to the floor to pet Lucky. "What the hell am I gonna do with him?" she asked the dog. "Be glad we fixed you so you won't have kids. 'Cause it's a bitch, and I don't mean a girl dog."

Did she screw things up by moving Will away from Tommy? Is that why he was shoplifting in the first place? Would he have been so quick to try to show off for Josh and Eric if his parents were still together? Would he be so hung up on race if Tommy was still around?

All she had ever wanted was to have a family, and now the only family she had was like a stranger to her.

That's when she remembered what she had planned to tell Will. "Hey, Lucky, guess what? I have a little sister who I haven't seen since we were kids, and I'm going to meet her pretty soon."

Lucky's tail thumped, alerting Daisy to the fact that somebody else was getting some loving, so she ran into the room. Trish scratched her too.

She was cheered to think about her sister. Will would have an aunt. Their family would be more than just the two of them. Maybe for the Fourth of July she could have Wilhelmina and her family over for a barbecue! She imagined Wilhelmina and Wilhelmina's make-believe family, which just happened to include a boy near Will's age and a husband who could be a father figure for him.

"You guys want a treat?" she asked the dogs.

Their ears perked up. Trish stood and opened the drawer where she kept the doggie treats. At the sound, Skipper and Little Buddy came too.

She gave everybody a chew, glad she at least understood her dogs.

CHAPTER 10

~~~~~~~~~~

Billie

"I can't believe how pretty this yard is now," Zenobia said, as she and Billie settled on the porch. She had been one of those who hadn't approved of the swept yard. "Ugly and country," she had called it before it came into its simple glory.

Billie smiled at her mother's compliment, and waved at Fletcher across the street slipping a package to a customer.

"You not gonna put me on the TV, are you?" Fletcher called to Zenobia after the customer drove off.

"No, sir," Zenobia called back, playing with her locket as she had all afternoon. "Let's go in the back."

Billie followed her mother to the backyard. Both women seemed to be having an off day. Billie was still reeling from the idea that Nick might actually leave her. She hadn't come up with any bright ideas, and she had been tempted on more than one occasion to go into the basement and snoop around. So far she hadn't given in to temptation.

She was concerned about her mother. Zenobia had been acting strangely ever since Billie had told her she was pregnant, but her mother had never turned down an opportunity to lobby Fletcher for his story. Now Billie was sure something was wrong. "Usually, you're all over him for the story about senior drug buyers, promising to alter his voice and disguise his identity. What's up? You're about to wear a groove in your neck messing with your necklace like that."

"I don't . . . There's something that has been on your father's and my heart for a long time, but we didn't know how to tell you. I wish he was here right now instead of at his conference, but maybe it's for the best."

"Are you okay? You're not sick, are you? Is Daddy okay?"

"We're fine."

Were they getting divorced after all these years? She felt silly to be so scared, but even at the age of thirty-two the thought was devastating. "Then just say it." She held out her hands.

Zenobia let go of the locket, took Billie's hands in hers, and touched her forehead against Billie's. "You know we love you and we always have."

"Okay, now I'm really scared. *What*?"

For a few painful seconds there was only the sound of the water trickling through the koi pond. Billie's heart raced.

Then Zenobia spoke in a soft voice. "You . . . we adopted you."

Billie pulled back. "What?"

"We adopted you. Wilhelmina, you're adopted. I'm so sorry we didn't tell you before."

Why are you telling me now? Billie almost asked, but before she could form the words, she thought she had the answer. "The woman who had me—she contacted you?"

"No, Wilhelmina. She's passed on. She was dead when we

adopted you. But she had another daughter. She didn't know about you . . . well, she did, but she thought you had died too. She just found out about you, and she wants to meet you."

Billie shook her head, as if to knock her thoughts into order. She started to stand, then sank back down. "You knew about this all the time? All my life you knew I was adopted?" She knew it was a crazy question, but somehow she couldn't fathom the idea that her parents had kept such a monumental secret from her. Her parents? Now, they were her *adoptive* parents. "But Jimmy's not adopted. That's why he looks like you."

"I had three miscarriages after James. We couldn't take any more heartache."

Billie looked at the imposing figure she had stood in awe of her whole life, this woman she had admired and felt closer to than anybody in the world and thought, *You're not my mother*? "Why didn't you tell me this before?"

"We didn't know how. And it didn't seem like something we had to do. We never imagined you would find out. We never thought anyone would come for you."

Billie clenched her jaws, her shoulders and upper arms tense. "But Jesus, Mommy! I answer questions about my medical history based on your family and Daddy's family."

"I asked Trish about lupus and she doesn't think it runs in the family."

"Who's Trish?"

"Your half sister."

Half sister. The words burned across Billie's brain like a fire. She sat forward and put her head between her knees.

Zenobia rubbed her back. "Are you okay?"

"Why did she call you and not me?"

"She knew my name. Someone who worked for the adoption agency looked in our file and told her grandmother. She came to the station."

Billie sat back up. "You've met her?"

"Oh, Wilhelmina."

"Now what?"

"She's white."

"Well, this just keeps getting better." Billie started laughing hysterically.

"Wilhelmina, my love—"

"No wonder I never liked fried chicken." Billie cackled, the laughter like broken glass in her throat. Tears ran down her cheeks.

"That's not funny."

Billie wiped her eyes and sniffed, but she couldn't call back all the mucus. "No, it's not. My whole life is a lie."

Zenobia's eyes filled too. She whipped out a packet of Kleenex and handed one to Billie, and used one herself, carefully dabbing her tears to keep from smearing her mascara. "That's not true."

"You told me I was part Cheyenne Indian, like your grand-mother. That she had powerful genes. If that's not a lie, what is it?"

"The facts of how you came to us never made you any less our child."

"Does Jimmy know?"

Zenobia shook her head no.

Billie looked at the ground. She felt off balance, as if all the molecules in her body were rearranging themselves, listing to one side of her body. "I don't know what to say. I can't even talk to you right now."

"You need some time. I understand."

You do? Billie thought. *'Cause I sure as hell don't.*

"Here's her email address and phone number. Are you going to contact her?"

Am I going to contact her? Five minutes ago I didn't even know she existed.

"I know you don't need this now on top of everything else. I didn't want . . . she forced the issue. But I'll tell her you need some time to process all this," Zenobia said, standing to go. She kissed Billie on the top of her head. "I love you. You will always be my child. That doesn't change. Please don't let this wear on you too much." She turned to walk away.

"Does she look like me?" Billie called.

Zenobia gave a melancholy smile. "You have the same birthmark."

After her mother left, Billie went into the house and went straight to her altar. The sepia and black-and-white pictures of elders and color photos of her parents that usually greeted her when she walked up silently mocked her. They were strangers. Daddy wasn't Daddy. Mommy wasn't Mommy. The Cheyenne girl wasn't close to being her great-grandmother. Billie didn't look like *her*. She looked like some white girl. The people she prayed to and cried to and confessed to—the ones she had turned to about Nick and this baby—were not her ancestors. She'd been fooling herself, hearing them because she wanted to hear them.

She turned the photos on to their faces in a stack and shoved the stack into the bottom drawer with the ratty sweatshirts she wore around the house in winter.

They lied to her. And not just once. Her whole life, they lied. They lied to Jimmy. She wondered what they told him when he asked where babies come from. Zenobia told her she came from her stomach. Billie remembered the night at dinner when she had asked her what it was like when she was pregnant with her. How Zenobia had changed the subject so quickly. She remembered the evening when her father gave her the check, how they were both so jumpy. This was why they had been acting so odd.

When Billie was nine she had to make a family tree for school. She was going through old photo albums and noticed that there were no pictures of Zenobia pregnant with her. She had asked about it.

Zenobia had answered, "Do you see how fat I look in those pictures with Jimmy? Why would I want more of those?"

Billie threw the pink candle into the trash, and took the cobalt bowl and glass of water into the kitchen, where she emptied them both. She yanked the white cloth off the table, balled it up, and threw it into the dirty clothes basket. The small table she shoved into the closet and closed the door.

Everything was gone.

Her legs turned to jelly and she collapsed onto the bedroom floor. She heard Nick come in. She listened for his steps to go to the bathroom or down into the basement, but to her astonishment he came to the bedroom.

"I saw your mother outside," he said in the doorway.

"How did everything get so wrong?" she whispered.

"Hey, don't cry. Don't cry."

Nick sat on the floor next to her and she sank into his body like a key fitting into a lock, sobbing into his neck. The last time he had held her while she cried was when one of her students was beaten to death by her foster mother. White, wealthy JonBenet Ramsey's death still fascinated the world, but Billie's student's murder never even made the news. She had terrible nightmares for weeks after, and each time she woke up wet-faced and with a scream on her lips, Nick had pulled her into his arms and sung to her until his warm, rich voice lulled her back to sleep.

"Come on now. It's not that bad," she heard the same reassuring voice say.

"It's not?" she said into his chest. "They lied to me my whole life."

He ran his fingers through her wild tangles. "You know they love you. They didn't mean to do you harm. They did what they thought was best."

Nick was taking up for her parents? The world *had* turned upside down. "I don't know who I am anymore. Jesus, what kind of family am I going to give this baby? Full of secrets and absent parents. . . ."

She flinched as mention of the baby slipped out.

Nick too changed instantly. He lifted his hands and shifted over a foot as if Billie had suddenly become hot to the touch. "You'll be okay," he declared, as if trying to convince both of them. "You'll be fine." But he had such longing in his eyes that she knew he was fighting with himself.

She wanted him, too. They could go back to the way things were before and be there for each other. All she had to do was say the word. But right then she felt a shimmer in her uterus, as if a school of minnows swam through her. It was too soon for Ambata to be moving, she knew, but Billie knew it was also too late to go back. So instead of asking him to stay, instead of telling him she didn't know how she'd ever be fine again without him, she pretended that he was right.

Billie had talked to Zenobia at least once a day every day of her life. She had never gone this long without talking to her. Zenobia and Herbert each called several times to check on her, but she didn't call them back. What was there to say? At some point she would talk to them, she knew she would. But not yet. Not until it didn't sting so much. Not until she could think of them without thinking "liars," without seeing Zenobia working her locket back and forth on its chain. How long would that take? She had once read some marriage guru in a magazine saying that after a divorce it takes a year for every year you are together to get over the heartbreak. Would it be thirty-two more years before she could trust her parents again?

She swept the dirt front yard, each brush of the broom a reproach. Swish. *Whose ancestors had she been talking to, and who had answered back?* Swish. *Had she been fooling herself?* Swish. *Had she only been hearing what she wanted to hear?*

James's Lexus pulled up. "Looking good, Billy Ray," he said as he walked up the sidewalk.

She stopped sweeping. "Not feeling so good, Lewis."

He held a Tupperware container. "Yolanda baked these. Oatmeal, raisins, and walnuts, whole wheat flour, brown sugar. No white stuff, she told me to tell you."

She and James went up on the porch. She set the broom against the wall and sat down. "So I'm guessing you heard?"

James sat down next to her. "Yep. They're miserable, especially Mama. They miss you. You're having their first grandbaby."

"She told you about that too?"

Jimmy nudged her with his elbow. "Come on now, you know she told me that night at dinner."

Billie started to smile in spite of herself. But then she remembered. "The woman who can't keep a secret."

"Right?" He made a pinched face. "I guess when she wants to, she can."

When he frowned like that he looked so much like Zenobia that Billie wanted to cry. She saw now that it had helped that Jimmy looked like their mother and nothing like their father. It made it conceivable that you could look nothing like your parents. As different as she sometimes felt, she'd never doubted that they were her biological parents.

"So how're you feeling? Baby kicking or anything?"

"Too early for that. You didn't remember her not being pregnant and me just showing up one day?"

"I do remember when they brought you home. But over the years I guess hearing about babies coming home from the hospital made me remember it that way. I was barely four."

"Did they tell you the whole story?"

"Not that it matters, but yes."

"Not that it matters?"

"Your birth mother could have been a blue frog from Neptune. You are still my sister."

But am I still a sistah? she thought. "You and Yo have to tell your kid the truth."

"Definitely. We're looking at open adoption. Have it all up front from the start. You know a lot of black folks have taken in kids who weren't theirs from relatives and friends and 'June Bug down the street.' It just wasn't maybe an official open adoption but we have that legacy."

What would it have been like to know all along that she was adopted? To know who her birth family was?

Billie massaged the small rise in her stomach.

"Are you going to meet your sister?"

She shrugged.

"She's a stranger. She's my blood relative and a stranger. What am I supposed to do with that? Am I supposed to love her? I don't even know her. I feel like I don't even know myself anymore."

He looked deeply into her eyes. "I know you."

When she was six and he was ten, he convinced her that their dog could talk. He had told her a hobo lived in a field near their house and ate little kids. Still, she had adored him. He let her tag along with him and his friends, catching bugs, playing touch football, shooting hoops. And when she was in ninth grade and Kendrick Bryant dumped her and then spread nasty rumors about her, Jimmy kicked his butt all up and down the street, so the boys knew that if they messed with Billie, they'd answer to him.

She knew him too. "Nick's moving out," she said to change the subject. One way her brother was not like her mother: he could keep a secret.

"Now?! Motherfucker—"

"Don't. It's not his fault. He doesn't want kids."

"What, you tied him down and raped him? If the man didn't want kids so bad he should have gotten snipped."

She nodded. "That's true. But Nick's not a bad man. He just needs time to adjust." She could relate now with being hit with a surprise right between the eyes.

"Nick is a grown-up. It's about time he started acting like one and about time you stopped trying to take care of him."

She thought about it. It was the same thing her parents had said, but Fletcher's opinion was that men wanted women to tell them what to do. What had he said? *Sometimes men don't know what they want till y'all women tell us.* Who was right?

"You deserve better," Jimmy said.

Everybody but Billie seemed to think this was true, including Nick. "You never think anybody is good enough for me."

"'Cause they're not." Jimmy opened the plastic tub and offered it to her.

She *was* hungry, and there was Ambata to think of. "A cookie will make it all better?"

"With a glass of milk. You better believe it."

"Even soy milk?"

"For you, anything, even soy milk."

After Jimmy left, Billie went down into the basement. Something was going on with Nick. Something more than his father's death and more than this pregnancy. All the weird questions about the mail. His inability to tell her more than he "just couldn't" be a father. She stood around looking at the piles and boxes. What was she looking for? Money from a bank robbery? Gay porn? Women's clothing? There was a stack of mail on a chair next to the sleeper sofa. She rifled through the envelopes—nothing but bills and junk mail from what she could tell. No love letters. Nothing from a life insurance company or a lawyer. Nothing from his family. A couple pairs of jeans were slung over a chair. She looked through the pants pockets, and was deeply relieved when she didn't find any phone numbers or condoms.

She sat down on the bed. This was silly. She wasn't thinking right because of finding out she was adopted. She *knew* Nick. He wasn't a liar. He wasn't up to any nefarious plans. He was just a wounded, confused man.

But her parents and Jimmy were right to question whether Nick would allow whatever was hurting him to stand in his way forever or if he would take responsibility for fixing things. And what would she do if he didn't? One thing she knew was that she didn't want to be caught like Goldilocks sleeping on Nick's bed again. She put his stuff back the way she had found it and went upstairs.

Denver doesn't have a Chinatown. Dr. Wu's office was in a strip mall in Golden, a city in the foothills of the Rocky Mountains west of Denver mostly known for brewing beer. The building was old and dilapidated, but just the sound of the Chinese music and the scents of camphor, menthol, eucalyptus, and an indefinable herby smell as Billie walked in the door made her feel a little better.

"Hi, Billie. How are you?" Dr. Wu's husband and office manager asked, smiling.

Somehow, *My man is about to leave me and I just found out I'm adopted and half white. How are you?* didn't seem like an appropriate response. "I'm in desperate need of your wife."

Mr. Wu smiled. "That's what everybody say."

Dr. Wu had been an MD in China, but in the states she was a certified acupuncturist and Chinese Medicine specialist. Billie had had two different acupuncturists before she found Dr. Wu. They were good, but not great. Billie didn't know if Dr. Wu was better because she was also a medical doctor or if it was because she had trained in China, but whatever the reason she could work miracles with the needles.

Mr. Wu escorted Billie to a room and Dr. Wu came in. She was a short, round-faced, bespectacled woman in her early forties. She wore a crisp white lab coat over her blouse and slacks.

"How are you?"

Billie slipped her sandals off, and removed her jewelry. "Kind of stressed."

"Uh-oh, that's no good," Dr. Wu said cheerfully. "Let me see your tongue."

Billie went "ahh."

"Your pulse?" Dr. Wu took Billie's right wrist first and placed her fingers in several places. Then she took Billie's pulse on her left side. "I'll say, stressed. What's going on?"

Dr. Wu knew just about everything about Billie's life. Just by looking at her tongue and taking her pulse Dr. Wu could tell what kind of shape she was in. Billie trusted her. She had even told her that Nick wasn't sure he wanted the baby. But this latest news she wasn't ready to tell. "Family stuff," she said.

"Your husband? He need herbs. American men so stubborn."

"No, it's some things with my parents."

"Well, that happens. Just don't worry about it. Pregnancy takes a lot of kidney energy, and lupus makes kidney energy weak. Stress makes kidney energy weak. No good for baby. Up on the table."

Billie lay down and arranged her clothes so her abdomen, forearms, and shins were exposed. Dr. Wu started inserting the needles, although inserting wasn't the right word. It was more like she thumped the needles into Billie's skin. Half the time, Billie didn't even feel them. Sometimes, she felt a small electrical jolt, and every now and then, in a stress point, a pain like hitting your thumb with a hammer. Usually, as soon as the first needle pricked the crown of her head she began to relax. She didn't understand completely how it worked—something to do with balancing chi along the meridians and calming the central nervous system—all she knew was that it *did* work. The needles kept her immune system from going into overdrive.

"Dr. Wu, what do you think about adoption? You know, with all the Chinese girls being adopted by Americans."

"You want adopt Chinese baby?"

"No. I just wonder sometimes how they'll turn out. What'll it be like being Chinese with white parents. If they'll be confused about their identity."

"Nah. By time these kids grow up everybody will be all mixed up. They will be no different," Dr. Wu said.

Billie wondered if that was true. She knew things had changed since she had been conceived; interracial relationships were much more common. There were many mixed-race kids at her Head Start, but the world still tended to treat them as black even with white or Latino blood. She wasn't as optimistic as Dr. Wu that these babies from China would blend into their families so easily.

Dr. Wu dimmed the lights. "We'll leave you here for a while. Take a nap."

Billie breathed deeply. Acupuncture usually put her to sleep within minutes, but today her body fought rest. She couldn't turn off her mind. She looked at the needles along her arms and on her stomach, at the third chakra—circling Ambata—and wondered at herself. Who was that she was looking at? Who did she belong to? Where did she come from?

The disease the needles were fighting made her body not recognize itself as itself. She knew how it felt. She felt like her DNA was scrambled. She looked the same, but felt completely different. Now instead of merely seeing "light" skin she saw "mixed" skin. Instead of having "Indian" hair, she had white-girl hair.

She started growing more anxious instead of relaxing. With lupus, the body thinks its own cells are foreign enemies and attacks them. Billie couldn't afford to attack herself now. She knew she was going to have to do something to get this under control and fast. Dr. Wu was right. She was going to have to figure out a way to manage her stress, and if acupuncture wouldn't do it, she was in trouble.

The next day she turned on Channel Five for the 11 a.m. news. There was her mother. Warm, approachable, soothing, professional. Trustworthy. Thousands of folks along the Front Range invited her into their homes every day, depended on her to tell them what they needed to know.

Today, Zenobia, in a raspberry jacket and a white blouse gleaming next to her dark skin, was telling viewers about a man raping a mother, her son, and her daughter. It was horrific, but somehow, with Zenobia telling the story, you could bear it. You could feel her anger at the rapist, her compassion for the victims, and her belief that the man, who had been apprehended, would be punished, if not in this lifetime, then in the next. That's why people tuned in. Zenobia made you feel like it was all going to be okay.

Billie longed to go back to the time when *she* trusted that Zenobia would tell her everything she needed to know, when Zenobia made *her* feel like it was all going to be okay. Back to when Zenobia and Herbert were her parents and she was their daughter, their *black* daughter (mixed with a little Native American, sure, but black nonetheless).

Billie couldn't talk to Dr. Wu or Nick about the fact that she was adopted. Besides them, Zenobia, Herbert, and Jimmy were her closest friends, which now felt like a huge mistake because she couldn't talk to any of them about all the things she wanted to talk about.

A white girl. A white girl was her sister. And now she was supposed to, what, be family with this woman whom she didn't know and had nothing in common with except a dead woman? A dead white woman.

"Grandmothers and grandfathers, what do I do about this?" she whispered, but they were silent, as they had been since she found out. She didn't know who she was talking to anymore.

Billie got her purse and took out the slip of paper Zenobia had given her. Trish's email address was dnvrdogmom1173. Clearly, she liked dogs. Did she have human kids? What did she know of Billie's birth mother? And her father? And what the heck had happened that Trish had thought she was dead?

Trish didn't have lupus, which figured. Black women had a higher rate of the disease than white women. Billie probably inherited it from her father's side of the family. Her heart broke a little each time she thought of her birth parents. It made her feel more alone. Her birth parents *and* her adoptive parents were strangers.

No, she wouldn't be contacting this person. She threw the paper in the trash.

CHAPTER 11

~~~~~~~~~~

Trish

They had a packed morning of surgeries. Trish had set up the surgery suite with IV catheters, fluids, surgical tools, and other supplies, and had brought out their first patient, Shelby, a black Lab. Since the little scuffle with Shelli the hoarder, Alicia had usually been able to schedule her to work with one of the other two docs, but today she was stuck again with Patrick.

"Trish, if you'll hold Shelby, I can place the IV for surgery and induce her."

"Pat, I can do it." She intended to be helpful. She had promised Alicia she would be on her best behavior.

"*Dr.* Pat. The other doctors let you induce?"

Let me? "They prefer it actually. I've done a million of them. I can put in a catheter faster than any of the docs here."

He stared down at her over the tops of his bifocals. "Is that right?"

"It wasn't an insult. I'm just saying that it makes sense to let techs do what we do best and let the docs do what you do best. Keeps everything running smoothly, you know?"

"I've been doing this for over thirty years. I think I know how to run things. Now, hold her."

"You do realize I'm certified to do this? This is my job. Techs aren't just animal holders."

"Why must you always challenge me?"

"I—"

"The partners and I have discussed this, and they told me to talk to you about it."

"Did they?"

Patrick nodded. "It's insubordination and you can be fired for it."

This was crazy. She was being punished for making things more efficient? She wanted to yank his eyebrows off and shove them up his nose. But she needed the job. Tommy's child support and alimony covered only a little more than half her bills. And she had never been fired in her life. She wasn't about to let this asshole be the first to force her out of a job.

She took Shelby's haunches. "Okay. I'll hold her."

Three hours later, she walked out of the surgery suite and into the lobby to see what Alicia was going to do for lunch.

"I can't take that fucking Pat anymore. That patronizing prick Pat."

"Why don't you stand up to him?"

"I did, and he threatened to fire me!"

"He can't fire you."

"It doesn't work for me like it does for you. They don't listen to me like they do you."

"You think he doesn't pat me on the head and tell me not to worry my pretty little self?"

Trish was shocked. "I've never seen it."

"Manager's meetings. But the best revenge is a new plan, and my new plan is to open my own clinic."

"*What?*"

"I've been taking classes and networking. I was this close to doing it when the economy nosedived and credit froze up. I still have my business plan, and as soon as things turn around, I'm going for it. We could go in together. We could be partners."

"But you're a practice manager and I'm a tech. We'd need docs."

"We could hire them."

"Docs wouldn't work for us."

"Sure they would. *Mira,* I'm certified. You're certified. We've both been doing this forever. We have more experience than lots of people who open their own clinics. We could hire some mommies who want part-time work and don't want the hassle of running the place."

She *had* thought this through.

"Think about it. I'm hoping to make a move in the next twelve to eighteen months."

Where did Alicia get that confidence? How did she know that she could put together a business plan and hire people and manage a business? Trish was about to ask her those questions when Jessica walked in the door.

"Jess? What are you doing here?"

Jessica's thin dark hair was unwashed and pulled back into a tangled knot. Her different-colored irises looked even stranger surrounded by red. With the red eyes and pink nose she looked a bit like a sad bunny rabbit.

"He still, like, won't talk to me. He won't tell me why he broke up with me."

Trish ushered the weeping girl into the staff kitchen. "You need to let it go. It's not worth all this. *No* boy is worth all this."

She bought a Diet Coke from the vending machine and handed it to Jessica.

"Is it because I'm white?"

Trish tensed. "Why would you say that?"

Jess's eyes darkened. "I've heard he's hanging out with a black girl."

Trish could just imagine the cell phone minutes being used across Aurora discussing the tragedy of Will and Jessica. *They should put high school girls on Osama bin Laden's trail. They'd know where he was in a week.* She longed to chalk this up to normal teenage drama, but she was afraid that something deeper was also going on.

"But *he's* half white. Why should it matter if I'm white? Why should it matter what color I am?"

"It doesn't."

"Then why?" she wailed, hiccupping.

Her eyes were as big as a kid's in a Japanese manga.

Trish reached over and popped the soda can open. "I can't answer that, honey. I wish I could. Take a drink."

"What am I gonna do without him?"

Trish was slightly amused that her stinky-footed son was meriting this level of despair. "You're gonna keep going. You'll get over this and one day you'll wonder what you ever saw in him."

Jessica took a sip of her soda. "I'm gonna, like, miss you," she said, bottom lip trembling.

"We'll keep in touch. I promise you, pretty soon you'll be calling me about some boy who you like so much."

"But you married your high-school boyfriend."

"And look how that turned out," Trish joked weakly. But Jess was right. What did she know about relationships? "Go home and talk to your mom."

"She *so* totally does not get it."

"What about your sister? I would have killed to have a sister to talk to when I was your age."

"Mostly we just fight."

"Really?" Trish always envied people with siblings. Even the rivalry sounded better than being alone. "I bet if you told her sincerely that you needed her help, she'd give it to you. I bet if you told her just like you told me, she'd have lots of stories to tell you where she felt the same way."

"You think?"

"Absolutely." For many reasons Trish hoped what she was saying was true.

"What is up with you lately?" Alicia asked the next day. "Every chance you get, you're on the computer."

Trish looked up from the computer screen. Zero messages. She had been checking her email obsessively at home and at work, and kept her cell phone on, sure her sister would contact her. But it hadn't happened yet. One thing she knew from working with animals: you never gained trust by forcing it. You let the dog come to you. It must be the same with people. So she was waiting even though patience was so not her strong suit.

"*Qué es?*" Alicia prodded. "I know something's up. Tell me."

Trish hadn't told Alicia yet that she had been right about the puzzles. Somehow saying the words out loud would make the whole thing more real, and she still didn't know how she felt about it. "Well, you're going to love this," she said and proceeded to fill her in on the whole story. "Seems like you were right."

But Alicia didn't do an I-told-ya-so dance. She was just as stunned as Trish was. "*Dios mio!*"

"*Dios mio,*" Trish agreed. Why not call on God? Everything in her life was kooky. Her dead sister was alive, and her son was now a Christian. And not just any old Christian, but a Bible-thumping, cross-wearing, telling-everybody-else-they're-going-to-hell Christian.

Will had been doing his punishment like he was in solitary confinement. He came home from school, did his chores, walked the dogs, did his homework, and after dinner went to his room to read his Bible. Trish wondered if this monklike existence wasn't making him even more dedicated to the church. She was starting to waver, thinking it might be better for him to at least watch TV.

"Are you completely in shock?"

Trish nodded.

"You're doing the right thing, giving her time. She didn't even know she was adopted? Imagine how she must feel!"

"I know."

"And they didn't keep her because her father was black? *Dios mio.*"

Trish put her head down on the counter. "What if she hates me because of what they did?"

Alicia stroked Trish's hair. "*Mija,* she won't hate you. You're her sister."

Trish looked up. "Promise?"

Alicia, always so certain she was right, hesitated just long enough before she said "Promise" to let Trish know she was in trouble.

•

After two more weeks, Trish couldn't take it anymore. She'd hardly slept. Her chest was aching from reflux, and her tongue was constantly coated with Maalox. So she was sitting in front of her sister's house like a private detective or somebody on *Days of Our Lives*. She was even wearing sunglasses, as if sunglasses could hide her.

Wilhelmina's house. She could hardly believe she was here! Her sister was easy to find. Right in the phone book.

The house was a bungalow, with three old red metal chairs and Tibetan prayer flags on the front porch. On each stair up the porch was a pot of pansies. The yard in front was small and odd, with bare earth surrounded by rows of large river rocks. A rose bush climbed one side of the porch.

She didn't have little kids, or at least there were no toys or bikes in the yard. Trish fantasized about herself and Wilhelmina locking eyes across the yard and recognizing each other with a deep knowing, their souls' recognition of their relationship.

Go knock on the door, she told herself. This is what you came here for. This is where the trail leads. She sat, waiting, hoping for a glimpse of her sister or someone else in the house. But she couldn't will herself to do it. Will. *That* was why her sister's name seemed familiar. Will and Wilhelmina.

Then, just as the sun started to set, a willowy, light brown woman in a purple sarong, a long-sleeved T-shirt, big sunglasses, and a large straw hat came out of the house. Trish stared, the sound of her heartbeat loud in her ears. It was hard to tell what the woman looked like. With the hat and sunglasses, she looked like a beautiful spy, but she was acting like a flower girl in a wedding, pulling petals off roses and tossing them on the porch and then down the sidewalk. The effect was mesmerizing. Trish could imagine herself walking on the flowers, bruising the tender blossoms, releasing their sweet scent.

She got out of her car, clutching the last jigsaw puzzle piece she'd found in her left hand, and walked toward her sister's house. She knew she would hold this moment tight the rest of her life.

CHAPTER 12

Billie

After Billie scattered petals, she spooned dust from Nick's footprints on the sidewalk and put it into the small red flannel bag. Foot-track magic went back all the way to Africa. If she mixed this dirt with a piece of brown paper with Nick's name written on it nine times in red, a piece of penis-shaped mandrake root, and a lodestone fixed with Follow Me Boy Oil, he would have to stay with her. Or at least so said the women who worked in her herb and magic shop. She wasn't sure she really believed it. But she would take any chance if it would get Nick to stay.

Her stomach tumbled. She would like to think it was morning sickness, but because her neck, shoulders, and upper arms were tight with tension, she knew better. If she did this, if she used hoodoo on Nick, she would be crossing a line that up until a few days ago she'd never thought she'd consider crossing. What kind of example would this set for

Ambata? But wouldn't keeping Ambata's father close be the right thing? How could it be wrong to do everything in your power to keep the man you love and who loves you?

She closed her eyes and sent out a wish on the wind. *Grand-mothers and grandfathers, if you are out there, if there is any other way, please show me now.*

When she opened her eyes, the woman, the white woman from the dream was in front of her. But no, she wasn't the crone. This woman was younger, blonder, the same height as Billie, and she had a strawberry-colored mark on her left cheek.

"Surprise," the woman, Trish, Billie suddenly knew, said weakly. "I know this is probably totally the wrong way to do this, but I didn't know what else to do. Waiting isn't my strong suit, I guess. And I started to think maybe your mother didn't tell you about me. But I can tell by the look on your face that she told you."

"She told me."

A car horn blared and Trish jumped.

"I'm glad. I thought you had the right to know who you are, where you come from."

"I know where I come from," Billie said, unsure why because she no longer had a clue about where she came from.

"That's not what I meant. I'm not saying this right."

Honking Harry laid on the horn, drowning Trish out. "Rude," she said.

"He's old and in pain," Billie snapped.

"Sorry. You know him?"

"No, but he's an elder and *I* was taught to respect my elders." Why was she standing up for Honking Harry?

Just then Fletcher came out and gave his customer what he came for. Fletcher yelled across the street, "How y'all doin' over there?" his voice sounding like he was ready to take his golf club-slash-cane upside Trish's head if Billie said the word. Billie knew he'd ask her later who the white girl was and what she wanted. Always on the lookout for the police, Fletcher knew everybody's business on their block. When a stranger showed up, and a white stranger at that, he was going to want to know about it.

"Fine!" Billie yelled back. "You shouldn't have come here," she said to Trish.

Her face collapsed like that of one of Billie's preschoolers. "You're right. I shouldn't have surprised you like this. Can we set up a time or something and meet somewhere?"

"I don't know."

"You were never going to call me, were you?"

Billie looked away, the muscles in her arms and shoulders curling into tight fists.

"Look, I know this is a shock. It is to me too, but I'm your *sister.*"

"*Birth* sister."

"Okay, so doesn't that mean anything to you?"

"I have a family. I'm sorry. I don't feel . . . There's no gap. No hole where you fit. My life is complete."

"Wow." Trish blinked back tears. "I . . . Okay. . . ." She was walking backward toward her car as she spoke. "You think about it. Take some time and think about it."

Who did she think she was showing up uninvited like this? Billie thought. *She's just like Dick Cheney. Expecting the Iraqis to throw flowers at the soldiers' feet, but instead they got bombs.*

Billie noticed the rose petals on the sidewalk, and remembered the mojo bag in her hand and what she had been asking for when Trish had appeared out of the blue. Her stomach did a little flip. Could Trish somehow be the answer? "Wait."

Trish paused.

Billie tucked the mojo bag into her pocket. "Maybe we should talk."

Trish timidly followed Billie into the house. "You play piano?"

Billie frowned at Juju's dusty paw prints across the top of the piano. "Nick does."

She took off her hat and sunglasses and led Trish into the dining room. Billie liked this room. Instead of curtains, she'd covered the window with green muslin. A string of white Christmas lights hung loosely over the curtain rod and down the sides of the window, twinkling faintly over the fabric. Tea light candles and dried roses the color of black cherries ringed the center of the oak table, though it wasn't dark enough yet to get the full effect of their light.

They sat at the dining room table. "I love your house," Trish said, looking around. "It's so creative. And so neat! My house is really boring, and everything is covered in dog hair."

Billie pushed one of the dried roses into alignment with the others. "Thank you."

"We have four dogs. I'm a vet tech. You like animals? Oh, God. I'm babbling because I'm nervous and I'm trying not to stare, but your birthmark . . . it's just like mine. And you look so much like my son."

Billie had been trying not to stare too. Besides the port-wine stain, she didn't think Trish looked much like her. They were the same height, and if Trish lost a little weight, they'd probably have the same shape. But Trish was so different. *She had to be blond and blue-eyed? Being white wasn't enough?* "I guess I'm nervous too."

"I know this is a huge shock for you, finding out you were adopted and all. But for me it's a miracle." Trish's voice cracked. "All this time I thought you were dead."

Billie's heart softened. What must that have been like to lose her mother and her sister? "I'm sorry for you, really. But I'm not sure I'm ready for all this. I don't know if I'll ever be."

"I don't blame you. You couldn't remember me, but I remember you. I was four when you were born." Trish put her hand to her heart. "I remember you. I held you in my arms like a baby doll, Wilhelmina."

"It's Billie. Nobody but Mommy calls me Wilhelmina."

Trish sucked in her breath. "Holy shit!" She whipped a picture out of her wallet and handed it to Billie. "That's my son, Will. William. We used to call him Billy. Seriously, until he was like twelve and then he started making us call him Will. I think . . . I think I named him after you and didn't even know it. We had planned to name him Jason, but when the doctor handed him to me, I looked at him and said 'Hi, Little Billy.' " Trish's cornflower eyes were shiny with tears. "I didn't know where that came from. But look at him. Fuck a duck, girl, you could totally be his mom!"

He *did* look like her: same wavy hair, same eyes and features. There was no denying her connection to this boy. She felt a strange sensation as she looked at his photo. It couldn't be a coincidence. "And his name is really Will?"

Trish looked as astonished as Billie felt. "Yes, and we used to call him Billy when he was little."

The two women took a moment to absorb this news.

"How old is he?" Billie asked.

"That picture is from last year. He's sixteen now, and about a foot taller. He's kind of struggling. The divorce and moving back here . . ." Trish hesitated. "He's pretty lost. I think he's looking for a father figure."

A father figure. Billie's skin heated and her nerve endings buzzed the way they used to when the ancestors spoke. She needed a second alone. "Can I get you something to drink?"

Trish brightened. "Yeah. Thanks."

Billie went into the kitchen as Juju ran through the dining room. "Scaredy-cat," she heard Trish call behind him.

Billie took two glasses down from the cabinet, her mind racing. A father figure. A father figure for a kid who looked just like her. She had asked the ancestors if they knew of another way to show her. What if this was it? What if she hooked him up with Nick, like a big brother? Maybe they would get close. Maybe Nick would change his mind. But how would she convince Nick to hang out with a boy he didn't know?

Billie returned with two glasses of iced tea.

"You're a cat person, huh?"

Billie noticed Trish's dog-shaped earrings and remembered that her email address was something about dogs. However, animals were the last thing on Billie's mind. "That was Juju. He doesn't like strangers very much. But you were telling me about your son having some problems. . . ."

"He goes to this crazy church now." Trish froze. "Oh, God, I hope I didn't just totally insult you. Are you a church person?"

"Hardly. But what's so crazy about it?"

"It's really hard-core, totally fundamentalist. It scares the shit outta me. He's changed so much. He's worried about my soul. He quotes their pastor constantly. He's like a Stepford kid."

Billie hated proselytizing, and she could only imagine how obnoxious a teenager with a license to tell others how to live could be. But compared to what she saw at Head Start—the boys with no fathers, the fathers Will's age, the mothers whose baby daddies were dead or in jail—being brainwashed by a church, even a so-called crazy one, didn't seem so bad. A young black man could definitely make worse choices. "So the pastor is a surrogate father?"

"Yes, but it's really the youth minister he's bonded with." Trish shifted uneasily in her chair. "See, something happened about a month ago. Will shoplifted some sunglasses at the mall. The other kids he was with, white kids, took some too and goaded him into it, but the white kids didn't get in trouble. The security guards chased Will down."

Ah, so that's what this was about. Will was looking for somebody black to school him. He was smart enough to know he needed survival skills, and it sounds like he's not getting them from his mom. Sounded simple enough.

"At first he told me he didn't do it. Then the next thing I know he's going to this church and this minister told him to come clean."

"That sounds like a good thing."

"I'm glad he told me the truth, but the whole situation is just not like him. I grounded him for stealing and for lying to me. He's not even supposed to go to church."

"So all you're worried about is him taking some sunglasses and going to church?"

Trish sipped her tea. "I know it sounds like I'm overreacting, but a mother knows, and something is just not right. I went to the church and it weirded me out."

"Where's his father?"

"In North Carolina. He's supposed to stay with him in August." Trish's lips curled into a tiny smile. "My life has been such a mess lately. You're my one bright spot."

Light, bright, damn near white went through Billie's mind. That's what kids in her neighborhood used to say about light-skinned people like her. "Maybe I could ask Nick to talk to him."

"That'd be awesome! What's your husband do?"

Billie was grateful for the silver band she wore on her ring finger. She didn't want to tell Trish they weren't married. And she really didn't want to tell Trish that Nick was thinking about leaving her and the baby. She didn't want Trish to see her as a baby mama, instead of Nick's partner. She had never needed that validation before, but telling a white person she wasn't married to her baby's father felt different. "He's a musician." Billie nodded toward the living room. "A jazz pianist."

"Wow, that's so cool! Will plays guitar, or used to. He hasn't picked it up in a while."

Billie was tossing out the invitation before she even knew what she was saying. "You guys should come to one of Nick's gigs." *He wouldn't turn her away in public, would he?*

156 | CARLEEN BRICE

Trish beamed. "Totally."

"We'll try to do it sometime soon, okay?"

"Great."

Trish held up her hands, and Billie went to shake one of them, realizing too late that Trish seemed to think they were going to hug, so their goodbye got all bungled and Billie ended up shaking one of Trish's elbows.

They laughed a little at their awkwardness and Trish left.

Billie sat on the front porch. She didn't want to be mean, but she wasn't ready to hug this woman. She'd only just found out about her. They'd just met. They were sisters in name only. Billie couldn't deny that something was going on, though. Something she didn't understand and couldn't name, but something that she felt like she had to follow through with. For the first time since she had dismantled her ancestor altar, she had the feeling that she was connected to something greater than herself.

She pulled the red flannel bag out of her pocket. She had no need to cross the line now. She shook the dirt into the air, watched what she had almost come to enter the wind in a sepia cloud. It reminded her of when they had spread her grandmother Wilhelmina's ashes up in the mountains. But this time *ashes to ashes, dust to dust* marked a beginning, not an end.

CHAPTER 13

~~~~~~~~~~

Trish

Will was sulking.

"I thought you'd be happy to get out of the house," Trish said. They were in the parking lot at Pee Wee's Pizza.

He shrugged. "Should I call her Aunt Billie or what?"

"Yeah, sure, she's your aunt," Trish tried to sound confident, but she wasn't at all convinced Billie would react warmly to being called "aunt."

Trish didn't get her. One minute Billie was about to blow her off and the next she was inviting her to meet her husband. Of course, Trish had been so nervous she probably freaked Billie out even more than the situation would normally. She had relived the conversation in her mind a hundred times and each time she wanted to kick herself for not saying the right thing. Whatever that might be.

She checked herself in the rearview mirror. She was wearing a pair of her new jeans, a black tank top, and an oversize yellow linen shirt. She brushed dog hair off her jeans, which she had thought she had gotten all of before she left the house. "How do I look?"

"How you look isn't what you should be worrying about. The only thing that matters is your relationship with the Lord."

Trish sighed and ran her hand over Will's short curls until he pulled away.

"I thought you were supposed to honor thy mother?"

Will looked surprised, but Trish didn't feel the least bit guilty. If she was a hypocrite to use his religion against him, then fine. She couldn't bear her own son pulling away from her.

The band was setting up on a small stage in the back of the room. Trish looked for the piano player. He was so not what she expected. He had on Dockers and a polo shirt like a big old dork, not a hip jazz guy. Where was his ponytail? His fedora or beret? His goatee? His leather jacket? His earrings and tattoos? *Why am I thinking he should look like Aaron Neville?* she wondered.

None of the musicians looked like jazz guys. The young sax player was in a T-shirt, jeans, and sneakers. The bass player wore a suit and tie, looking like a banker. The drummer, a balding white guy, was in jeans and a Hawaiian shirt. They all looked so . . . regular. *I have got to get out of the house more.*

Billie came in behind Trish and Will. She was in a kimono-like red jacket with baggy black silk pants and turquoise jewelry. Even though Trish had dressed up for the occasion, she looked just like what she was: a boring mom. At least she had worn her silver kitty-cat earrings in Billie's honor.

"Didn't I tell you, you look just like your aunt?" Trish asked Will as they sat down.

Billie and Will smiled shyly at each other, both obviously amazed at the resemblance. Trish felt warmth spread through her. She wanted to hug both of them. She wanted them to hold hands and sing "Kumbayah." She imagined them all together at her house for Christmas. She'd buy one of those spiral-sliced honey hams with all the trimmings and put a stocking over the fireplace for each one of them, including the dogs.

"It's really something, isn't it?" Billie said to Will, who just nodded in reply.

"This is a nice place," Trish said.

Pee Wee's was a locally owned chain of pizza joints designed to look like it had been around forever. Someone had scoured flea markets for old Coca-Cola signs, vintage bikes, musical instruments, and black-and-white photos of Chevys for the walls, the furniture was fifties diner style, and the floor was black-and-white tiles.

"Feels kinda phony to me," Billie said. "Like a movie set. At least they don't make the staff wear fifties costumes."

"Well, the food smells good," Trish said, inhaling the scents of pepperoni, tomato sauce, and bread dough. She was glad her jeans had an elastic waist.

"Nick says it's okay, but I don't usually come out for his gigs much anymore, and even when I did I can't eat the food, so . . ."

"Why not?"

"Why did I stop going to his gigs or why don't I eat the food where he plays?"

"I guess both."

"Most of the time his sets start too late. I'm usually in bed by ten. And I used to hate the cigarette smoke, though that's changed since the smoking ban. But even when I used to go, I'd spend most of the night sitting by myself while he played. Even on his breaks he'd be talking to other people, working the crowd." She looked over at the bandstand and then back at Trish. "It was lonely."

Trish got the feeling Billie wasn't just talking about his gigs. She wondered if maybe Billie and Nick weren't so happy. Maybe she was carrying a save-the-marriage baby. "And the food?"

"Oh." Billie reached into a large straw tote with her left hand and pulled out a plastic container.

"Our mother was left-handed!" Trish said. "Me too. Used to drive Nana crazy. She tried to make me write with my right hand, but it never stuck. Did your parents do that to you?"

Billie shook her head and continued to unload food from her bag. "Anyway, I have to be careful about my diet. At places like this there's not much I can eat. I'll order a salad tonight to go with this stuff I brought from home."

"But that looks like pasta."

"It is. Organic, whole-wheat pasta with organic tomatoes, garlic, and olives. And I have some apple slices and roasted almonds."

"Hmmm." Trish picked up her menu, wondering about a person who would bring her own pasta to a place that probably served pasta. *So much for the honey ham at Christmas.* "Will, what are you in the mood for?"

Will shrugged. "We eat pizza all the time."

Trish felt her cheeks flush. She could feel the underarms of her linen top getting wet. She glanced at her chest and arms and was grateful to see that the sweat wasn't noticeable yet. "Not *all* the time."

Will stared at her. "You're right. Sometimes we have hamburgers or Chinese food."

"Sounds like my mother," Billie said "She's a champion orderer."

"Hey, maybe I'm *her* natural daughter." Trish laughed.

Billie gave her a stony gaze. "So what am I? Her *unnatural* daughter?"

"No! I didn't mean it like that." Trish's sternum started to burn. She looked back at her menu. What could she order now? She *was* a junk-food junkie, but Billie didn't need to know that just yet. She settled on a club sandwich and a side salad, no fries.

When the waitress came, Billie snubbed her nose at the ingredients in the house salad, as if iceberg lettuce was arsenic, and only ordered a glass of water with lemon.

Will slathered butter on some of the bread and Trish was about to join him until she noticed that Billie wasn't touching it. She pushed the bread basket toward Billie. "You want some?"

"I don't eat white bread. Just turns to sugar."

"Ha," Will said to Trish. "No wonder you love it!"

Smart-ass! He was really getting his revenge tonight. Luckily, the band started playing. Trish knew nada about music, but it sounded good to her. It was so exciting to be there with real live musicians. "It must be so cool to be married to a musician!"

Billie smiled in a way that made it seem anything but cool.

Trish waited a bit for her to speak, but then she realized Billie wasn't going to. She tried again to get a conversation going. There was so much she wanted to say, so much she wanted to know. Billie seemed reluctant to open up, so she decided to ask something easy. "Do you know what you're having yet?"

"No. Going to wait until the delivery room."

"Very retro of you."

"We're retro kind of people," Billie said, again with the wistful tone.

"I always wanted a little girl. Don't get me wrong, boys are great," Trish assured Will. "It's just . . . I had my boy. I thought it would be nice to have one of each, and I thought maybe a girl would stay closer to her mom, you know?"

"A son is a son 'til he takes a wife. A daughter's a daughter all of her life."

"Right."

"My mother used to say that to me."

"You guys are close, aren't you? I could tell by the way she acted when I showed up. She totally did not want me there."

Pride and something else flickered across Billie's face. "Why didn't you have more kids?" she asked.

Will pretended to be rearranging his place mat, but Trish knew his ears were pricked up so she gave the sanitized version. "Tommy was in the Marines and was often gone on duty, so dealing with one mostly on my own was plenty, but that is something I regret. Now I'll just have to wait for grandkids."

Will groaned.

"How do you like Denver?" Billie asked him.

"It's better now that I have a church home."

Trish made a see-what-I-mean face at Billie.

"I think it's healthy to put spirit at the center of your life," Billie said.

Will leaned in. "Where do you go to church?"

"I don't go to church."

"Then how do you put God at the center of your life?"

"Will. . . ." Trish warned.

"I meditate and pray. I try to be a good person. I listen, try to pay attention."

"But that's why you need a shepherd, someone to help you understand God's will."

Billie pinched her lips tight. "No, church is just not for me."

They sat in awkward silence for as long as Trish could take it, about a minute and a half. "So tell me about yourself," she urged. "I know what Nick does, but I don't know what you do."

"I teach Head Start."

"Is it fun, or do the kids drive you crazy?"

This time Billie's smile actually reached her eyes. "Both, actually."

The waitress brought their plates. Will poured about a gallon of ketchup on his cheeseburger and fries, embarrassing Trish no end. The salad seemed just fine to her, iceberg lettuce or not. Billie ate her cold healthy pasta.

After about an hour or so, the band took a break and Nick came over to the table.

CHILDREN OF THE WATERS | 163

"What are you doing here?" he asked Billie, clearly unhappy to see her.

"This is Trish and Will. They wanted to meet you," Billie said uneasily.

For one terrible moment, Trish thought Nick was mad at her for something, but when he looked at her and Will, she knew they weren't the source of his anger. "Yeah, hi. Billie, can I talk to you for a minute?"

What was going on?

Billie and Nick went into the entryway. Trish couldn't hear them, but she could see them through the glass doors. They were arguing. But about what?

Nick went back to the stage and after a few seconds Billie squared her shoulders and returned to the table.

"Everything okay?" Trish asked.

"Fine," she nodded, keeping herself tucked away.

So now Trish knew something about her sister: like their grandmother and Zenobia, she was a secret-keeper. How could a person whose very existence was kept a secret not be? But if Billie kept herself so hidden away from others, could she really know herself?

Trish stood in front of the rows of greeting cards that all seemed to have golf clubs, hammocks, or barbecue grills on the covers. She was buying a Father's Day card for Will to mail to his dad. *Why? I already know I'm crazy, but am I a masochist too? I must like pain. I married Tommy.*

On their very first Father's Day together Will was ten months old. She and Tommy made big deals of Mother's Day and Father's Day that year, though they had flown back to Aurora to spend Mother's Day weekend with Tommy's family, attempting to prove that his mother was the Best Mother in the Entire Universe.

But on Father's Day they stayed home. They were stationed in Georgia then. That morning, Trish made Tommy waffles, bacon, and eggs even though she had been up with the baby the whole night before. She gave him a nice Timex, a bottle of Eternity by Calvin Klein, and a bunch of other stuff, "stocking stuffers" even though it wasn't Christmas. Oh, and even before the big breakfast and all the presents she gave her hubby a blow job while Will howled in his bassinet.

They were renting a one-bedroom trailer at the time. It was ugly and cramped, but she couldn't have been happier. She was happy her whole pregnancy, and she had no postpartum depression. She was filled with wonder and gratitude that the two of them had created a child, and that child was going to have what she never did: a real family.

She picked up a card with a classic car on the cover and put it back, sighing guiltily. Had she tried hard enough? Maybe she should have stayed, looked the other way? Lots of women did. She picked up a card with a big-screen TV on the cover.

She and Tommy used to watch TV together. Mostly boy shows like *The X Files*, *Married with Children*, and *Star Trek: the Next Generation*. She watched the girly stuff (*Melrose Place*, *Party of Five*) on the little TV in the bedroom by herself. Six years later they were living in North Carolina in a real house and Tommy bought a giant TV and put it in the family room to create a "man room." He actually made Trish take a pledge. She had held up her hand and recited, "I will not stand in front of the TV. I will not speak while the game is on. I will not clean or change anything, no matter how much I might want to. This is Tommy's world, and sometimes he will let me live in it."

She had snickered the whole way through it. That was back when they laughed together. But then Tommy spent all his time at work or in the man room and Trish was at her job and busy with

Will. Somehow what had started out as funny ended up being part of what pulled them apart.

She picked up a card that had a cartoon drawing of a guy playing electric guitar and the words "Dad, you rock!" on the cover and was just about to head to the checkout when she spotted the religious cards. Certainly that's what Will would buy if he was here. But Will wasn't here. If he wanted to buy a religious card, he could shop for it himself.

She glanced at her watch. Time to go pick up Will and head to Billie's house for dinner.

"All I'm saying is that you didn't even try other churches before you got involved with this one!" Trish said. The evening was starting out all wrong. She, Billie, and Will were sitting at the dining room table, but it didn't look like Nick was going to be there. And from the minute they walked in Will had been picking at her about going back to church.

"If the first one you go to is cool witchu, why would you go to another one? Why fix it if it ain't broke?" Will shot back.

Trish gave an exasperated glance at Billie, looking for help, but Billie just shrugged. "I'm not sure I see what the problem is."

"Dude, your mom is right." Without warning Nick was standing in the kitchen doorway.

Billie gaped at him.

Trish was surprised too. She hadn't known Nick was even listening.

"What do you know about it?" Will asked.

"I was raised in a fundamentalist church."

"You *were*? I didn't know that!" Billie said.

"I guess we don't tell each other everything, do we?"

"Nick. . . ." Billie's eyes seemed to plead with him.

"I've seen those sisters who sit up with the big hats and praise God and then stab each other in the back. I've seen the ministers rollin' in Caddies while their congregation can't keep their lights on in their own houses."

Will shook his head. "Clear View ain't like that."

"I hope not. But you can never go wrong by thinking for yourself. What kind of God wouldn't want you to think for yourself?"

"That's all I'm trying to say!" Trish said, looking at Nick gratefully. Finally, someone was on her side! Maybe if Will wouldn't listen to her he'd listen to Nick. "Nick, aren't you having dinner with us?" she asked.

Billie froze; she seemed to be steeling herself for his answer.

Trish wondered, *Which was the right thing for him to say, yes or no?*

"Yeah," Nick said. "Okay."

Billie collapsed against the back of her chair. Yes was the right answer. So whatever was going on between them, it was Billie who was on the outs.

"We're having a mixed grill: chicken, zucchini, peppers, onions, and corn on the cob," Billie said.

Nick tried to swallow a grin. "I could smell it. I wasn't really feeling a PBJ."

"Come on, grab a plate and sit," Billie said.

Nick returned to the kitchen and came back with a plate and cutlery and sat in the empty chair across from Billie.

Trish passed the platter of grilled chicken to Nick. "So you were saying . . . ?"

Nick placed his napkin on his lap. "Just keep an open mind."

"Will's a musician too," Billie said.

"Yeah?" Nick said.

Will shrugged. "Not really."

"What do you play?"

"Guitar, but not in a long time."

While Trish and Billie were both sitting on the edges of their seats, Will seemed spectacularly uninterested in Nick. Trish knew it was because of Nick's stance on his church.

Trish willed Nick to keep talking, to keep trying to get through her son's thick skull. She was starting to have hope that she might have a good time after all. The food was good, if a little bland, and the dining room looked like a restaurant or something out of a magazine with the Christmas lights around the window and the candles on the table glowing brightly.

"Really, I'm just so jealous of your house," she said. "And you don't have to mow your yard."

"We have grass in the back," Billie said.

"Getting Will to mow is worse than pulling teeth."

Will frowned. "That's 'cause the yard is always full of dog poop."

"And whose job is it supposed to be to clean that up?"

"That's what I do for my day gig," Nick said.

"Clean up dog poop?" Will asked.

"I mow lawns."

"I should hire you to come do our yard. How much do you charge?"

"Somebody with a teenager in the house shouldn't be paying anybody to take care of their yard."

Will rolled his eyes, but Trish thought, *I'm loving this guy more and more*!

"Say man, you have a job lined up this summer?" Nick asked.

Will shook his head.

"I could use some help."

"You don't have to—" Billie said at the same time Trish said, "That'd be great!"

But Nick was only paying attention to Will.

"How much do you pay?" Will grumbled.

"Six an hour. Twenty hours a week."

"He'll take it!" Trish said.

"Will?" Nick raised his eyebrows.

Will looked from his mother to Nick. "Okay, I'll do it." He seemed suddenly more enthused.

"Good."

Wow, this guy is good! Trish thought. She had to badger Will incessantly to get him to do any chores, and now he was going to work twenty hours a week?! Obviously, Will needed a man around. "You know I was fourteen when I got my first job, scooping ice cream at Goodrich Dairy. And it wasn't just the summer either. I worked all through the school year," Trish said.

"Yeah, I know you worked for everything you got," Will retorted.

"I try to tell him how easy he has it," Trish said, rolling her eyes. "He has no idea."

"I was washing dishes at a soul-food joint when I was thirteen," Nick said.

Trish turned to Billie. "What about you? What was your first job?"

Billie shrugged uncomfortably. "Babysitting."

"I babysat too. I mean a job job?"

"My parents didn't want me to work while I was in school."

"What about summers?"

"I was in Jack and Jill. I volunteered at the Ronald McDonald House."

Nick chuckled and put his hand on Billie's. "Baby girl here was more fortunate than some."

"Nick, don't," Billie pleaded.

"I'm not saying anything," he said. "You do good work with your kids."

• • •

After that, the room seemed to settle in some way. Everyone seemed to relax. Even Juju strolled through the room on his way to the kitchen.

Billie filled Trish in on the swept yard. Nick chatted about his band. Will didn't say much, but he was no longer acting so damn surly. Trish wanted to pinch herself. This is something she would have never dreamed of in a million years, but she and Will were having dinner with her sister. It was a small miracle. Even better: she had an ally in Nick. She wasn't alone against Will and God. Nick was smart, funny, charming, and accomplished. *Bring it on, Pastor Bob and Reverend Eubanks,* she thought.

Nick opened a bottle of white wine to share with Trish. She was having a great time, but it seemed like Billie and Nick were enjoying themselves even more. More than once they seemed to share a private little joke. They brushed hands when Billie passed Nick the plate of vegetables for a second helping, and even Trish could see the lightning that crackled between them. Hell, Helen Keller would have seen it! Trish looked across from Billie to Nick. It seemed to be raining pheromones over each of their heads, and the storm between them seemed to be forgotten. Trish was happy for them. But she also felt a catch in her throat at the memory of Tommy and herself.

By the time the candles were burning low and Billie was serving bowls of tart raspberry sorbet, Trish had drunk two glasses of wine and was almost ready to start believing in God. When she scraped the last of the sorbet from her dish, she had to admit that it was time to go. It was nine o'clock and normally she'd be getting ready for bed. She was having such a good time she didn't want to leave. But she could tell that Billie and Nick wanted to be alone. "We better get going," she said.

"See you tomorrow morning?" Nick said to Will.

"Tomorrow?!" Will said. "But that's Friday. I thought we'd be starting on Monday?"

"Why put it off?"

"Do you work on the weekends?"

"Not usually. Usually I'm gigging on Saturday nights, and nobody wants to be bothered with me making so much noise on their lawn on a Sunday."

"What time do you want him here?" Trish asked.

"Seven?"

Will's eyebrows jumped to the sky. "Seven!"

"Seven it is," Trish said.

"Just a sec," Nick said. He dashed into the living room and returned with a CD that he handed to Trish. The Nick Campbell Quartet. How cool was that?

"Awesome! Thank you!"

"We're playing at Juneteenth next week. You should come."

"What's Juneteenth?"

"You never heard of Juneteenth?" Billie said, her voice high with surprise, as if Trish had just said that she didn't know what a shoe was.

Trish was starting to feel like life with her sister wasn't going to be what she had thought it would. She shook her head in ignorance and shrugged.

"Juneteenth celebrates the day when the slaves in Texas learned they were free," Billie said. "Two years *after* the Emancipation Proclamation took effect."

"Why was it two years later?" Will asked.

Billie chuckled cynically. "I guess they weren't in a big hurry to let all of us in on the news."

Will's face twisted and his hands curled into fists. More evidence. Now he could be angry about something that happened over 200 years ago. To somebody else.

They. Us. Just because of skin color, Will, Billie, and Nick were "us," and Trish was "them"?

"It's not like they had CNN and email back then," Nick said. "It probably took a while for *any* news to travel in the 1800s."

Trish looked gratefully at Nick. He really *was* on her side.

Billie frowned. "Yeah, that's it. The Confederates in Texas didn't get the memo."

"Well," Trish butted in. "We better get going."

She reached out to hug Billie good-bye. Billie kept her arms down, and leaned close enough that Trish could squeeze her forearms. It was another almost-hug, an ug.

In the car with her son, Trish tried to focus on the positive. She turned on the CD player and slid Nick's CD in. After a few minutes, she said, "They're good, aren't they?"

Will shrugged. "I guess."

"That's cool, yeah? A job hanging out with your *uncle.*" She put so much emphasis on the word uncle she about ground it into his skull.

He perked up. "Yeah, and I get to go to church."

"Uh, who said anything about church?"

"I'm not grounded anymore, right? I mean, if I can go to dinner with Billie and Nick and now I can go to work with Nick, I must not be. So I can go to church," he said with a devious smile.

Why the sneaky little shit, Trish thought. *He totally tricked me!* No wonder he had changed his mind so fast. She could say no, but that would just lead to a conversation about how she was trying to keep him away from church.

"Sure," she said, keeping her voice as neutral as possible. She wasn't about to let him know he had fooled her. She consoled herself by thinking that the influence of the church would be balanced by Nick. She wouldn't admit that the hopeful thought repeating in her mind was anything like a prayer.

CHAPTER 14

~~~~~~~~~~

Billie

Was she a fool or had Nick really been flirting with her at dinner? Billie's heart thumped with hope. Could it really be possible that somehow Trish and Will could bring Nick back to her? All through dinner he was looking at her and talking to her like he used to. And *damn* he looked good! Barefoot, in baggy jeans and a soft cloud-white T-shirt against the night of his skin. She lifted her hair off her neck, fanned herself with her rubber-gloved hand, and grinned, her face flushed. She was burning up, and it wasn't from the summer air or the hot water in the sink.

But her smile faltered when she recalled the end of the evening, when Trish and Will left and the spell seemed to break. Now she was in the kitchen alone washing the dishes and Nick was sitting outside on the front porch. Should she go to him? What would she say? More important, what would *he* say?

The front door opened and she held her breath. If anything was going to happen, it was now, when Nick went through the kitchen to get to the basement. She snatched off her rubber gloves and waited, her biceps clenching into hard little knots.

But a strange thing happened. Nick didn't head for the basement. He started to play the piano, something he hadn't done at home in ages. She leaned against the kitchen doorjamb and watched and listened. He wasn't playing any song yet, at least not that she recognized, just letting his fingers familiarize themselves with the keys. Still, it was a beautiful sound. The notes floated through the house like birds. Juju thought so too. He jumped on top of the piano to follow them. He loved for Nick to play piano. Usually he'd run back and forth trying to figure out where the sound was coming from. But today he seemed to be listening like Billie.

Eventually Nick's aimlessness drifted into a recognizable tune. Billie's eyes glistened. It was Stevie Wonder, just like he sang to her that first time. She went to Nick and sat next to him on the piano bench just as he started to sing, "There's something 'bout your love that makes me weak and knocks me off my feet."

She leaned against the familiar bulk of him, so solid and present. She watched his hands on the keyboard. There was a reason they called it tickling the ivories. He could play her body the same way, make her skin sing. When he was done the last note rang in the air for what felt like a long time. She took his right hand and kissed the inside of his palm. Then she kissed his cheek. He turned to her, pressed his mouth against hers, and let his long agile fingers run over her breasts and neck and through her hair. He smelled like home and tasted like raspberries and wine. He was every good dream she had ever had.

Breathing hard, she stood, took his hand—the same hand she had kissed, the same hand that just minutes ago was telling her he loved her with the song he played—and led them to their bedroom. Could it only have been days since Nick had last been here? It felt like eternity, but all thoughts of the past few weeks fell away as Nick slipped her sundress off her shoulders and kissed her breasts. When he slid her panties down her legs, the only thing that mattered was right here, right now.

When she removed his shirt, the results of his ribs-fries-and-cookies diet showed in his spreading love handles. She smiled and caressed his bare torso. The soft layer over the hard muscles made her feel as if she had gone back in time to when they first met, before he had her to cook healthy meals, before he said he was leaving her.

He took her hands, kissed the insides of both palms, and leaned her tenderly back onto the bed. Back she fell, back through time and space and emotion. And even though he was gentle, it was just like when she first met him: she fell hard.

When she woke the next morning, Nick was already out of bed. She heard the shower running and decided to fix him a hearty breakfast before he went to work.

She was in the kitchen stirring oatmeal when Nick came in soapy-smelling and dressed to cut grass in battered old shorts and a T-shirt.

"Good morning!" she sang.

"Hey," he replied softly.

She couldn't help notice that he wasn't nearly as chipper as she. "You want apples or blueberries in your oatmeal?"

"Uh, I'll just stop and get something while we're out," he said to his feet.

"These oats will stick to your ribs, keep you fueled up until lunchtime."

"Billie, I . . ."

Just then there was a knock on the front door and Nick almost broke his neck rushing to answer it. Billie heard his and Trish's voices. The door shut and it was quiet, except for the sound of footsteps toward the kitchen. Not Nick's.

"Nick left?" Billie asked when Trish entered the kitchen. She was trying to sound casual, but her voice quaked.

"Yeah," Trish said slowly. "He and Will are getting some Mickey Ds before they get started."

Crestfallen, Billie turned the burner off. "Great," she muttered. She should offer Trish some juice or tea or something, but now she wasn't feeling like company.

"How are you? You having morning sickness?" Trish asked shyly, almost fearfully.

Billie realized she had been curt. "No, not really." She was exhausted all the time. Her breasts felt swollen and tender, and the skin around her nipples had darkened. She also had to go to the bathroom a million times a day. Other than that, she hadn't noticed much difference. "Thanks for asking."

Trish smiled. "It's a boy. Or at least that's what they say. Girls are supposed to cause more morning sickness. But I was pretty sick with Will for the first trimester, so what do they know?"

A boy. Would that matter more to Nick to have a little person just like him? "I'm going for my first ultrasound this afternoon."

"That's so exciting!" Trish said. "I totally loved being pregnant. Especially the second trimester." Her eyes glazed and Billie was certain she was remembering being pregnant with Will. "Everything felt so rosy and hopeful, you know?"

Billie nodded. "I do know. Must be the hormones."

"You don't really believe it's only hormones?"

Billie was surprised that Trish was so perceptive. "No, I don't. I think it's the new life that makes you feel like anything is possible."

"I thought so."

Billie looked hard at Trish. She noticed that her eyes weren't truly blue; they were more a soft gray color. All the time that she had been telling herself there was nothing missing from her childhood, but that wasn't completely true. She had often felt like the odd one out growing up. The white sheep of the family. Was this why?

"So . . . is Nick meeting you at your appointment?"

The spell was broken. Billie was back to feeling disappointed about Nick. She dumped the half-cooked oatmeal down the drain into the garbage disposal. "No." She flicked the switch, hoping to mark the end of that line of questioning.

But after the disposal stopped grinding, Trish said, "It's not like much happens at those early appointments anyway. You like your doctor?"

Billie nodded.

"He specializes in high-risk pregnancies?"

"Yes, *she* does, but I really don't like to use the term high-risk."

"I just meant because of your lupus. . . ."

"I don't like to put thoughts of danger and fear into my mind or my baby's mind," Billie snapped. "You go in thinking you're high-risk, it's a self-fulfilling prophecy."

"Okay." Trish nodded, her smile dimmed. "Well, I better get going before I'm late." Obviously, she had felt the warmth between them disappear too.

"I'm sorry. I don't mean to be bitchy."

"Hormones." Trish's smile didn't hide that Billie had hurt her feelings. "Blame them whenever you can."

"I'm glad Will is working with Nick."

"Oh, me too," Trish gushed. "You've got a keeper with that one."

I hope so, Billie thought. She dried her hands and walked with Trish to the front door. She watched Trish get in her car and drive away, then she closed the door. Trish's words came back to her. *A keeper.* Would that be true? It had to be.

Focus on the positive. Nick and I made love *last night. That wasn't about being lonely or horny. That was* love. She let that thought fill her heart and calm the panicky feeling in her chest.

"See that flicker? That's the baby's heart beating. Next time, you'll be able to hear it," Dr. Fernandez said.

A tiny white spot flashed quickly on the screen. *Ambata's heart.* Billie covered her mouth with her hands, and tears slid down her cheeks. Trish said nothing much happens at the early appointments. She was so wrong! Nick should be here. If he saw this baby's heartbeat, boy or girl, there'd be no turning away. "It's so fast!"

"That's normal. They're like little hummingbirds. Everything looks good," Dr. Fernandez said, moving the ultrasound wand—a magic wand, Billie thought—around and tapping the computer keyboard. *Click, click, click.*

The sounds made Billie think of lyrics from one of the songs she and her students sang: *Give your hands a clap, clap, clap.* She imagined herself singing to Ambata, and wondered again what her baby would look like. Now she had to add Trish and Will into the equation. She watched the white flash of her baby's heart and wondered what would happen if Ambata would come out lighter than Billie. Would Nick still be able to bond with the baby? She knew what skin tone meant in this country—and in many other countries, for that matter.

Click, click. "I'm just taking some measurements, getting some pictures, and we'll be all done in a few minutes."

As she had told Trish, Billie really liked Dr. Fernandez. She was calm, with a take-charge quality that made Billie feel that she was in good hands, and she was cool with alternative treatments. Though she called acupuncture *complementary* to Western medicine and insisted that Billie not take any herbs while she was pregnant.

During the pregnancy Billie would see her once a month, Dr. Wu every week, and her rheumatologist once every three months. It was way more involvement with medical doctors than she'd had in the last several years and way more than she wanted, but for Ambata, for this chance, she'd do it.

They'd already taken Billie's blood pressure, which was a little higher than usual but still okay, weighed her, taken blood and urine samples, and quizzed her about symptoms. So the ultrasound was the end of this visit. She and Ambata had made it over their first hurdle.

Dr. Fernandez wrapped up and handed Billie some paper towels to wipe the gel off her stomach.

"This is good news, Billie. Lupus antibodies are still in your blood, but you're definitely still in remission. Your vitals are good." Dr. Hernandez printed out a photo of the fuzzy white against a black screen that was Billie's baby.

Billie sat up, starting to tear up again.

"We'll see you next month." Dr. Hernandez patted her on the back and left the room.

"Hear that, Ambata? It's all good," Billie said, grinning at her stomach as she hopped off the table.

Billie doused herself with lavender and neroli oils, stuck a single leaf of pennyroyal in her mojo bag, and stuck it in her pants pocket. Pennyroyal tea could bring on a woman's menstrual flow, so she was careful not to leave the herb in contact with her skin, but she needed it for strength.

She hadn't spoken with Nick that night or the next day. He came in late from his gig and stayed in the basement. Today was Father's Day, and it pained her even more that Nick had closed back in on himself.

On top of everything with Nick, she was going to see her parents for the first time since she had learned that she was adopted. They were meeting at a Rockies game. When major-league baseball first came to town more than a dozen years earlier, Zenobia had bought season tickets for the family on the Club Level as a gift for Herbert. This year, Billie and Jimmy had gone in on plane tickets for their parents to go to Kansas City to visit the Negro Leagues Baseball Museum.

Billie kissed the ultrasound photo of Ambata on the refrigerator and headed downtown to Coors Field.

It was an afternoon game. She was surprised at all the fans. Since the Rockies had gone to the World Series, attendance at the games had picked up. There were masses of people decked out in purple. Still, she easily spotted her tall, lanky brother and his wife waiting for her in front of the ballpark. Like most of the crowd, the three of them were all in purple. Herbert wouldn't have it any other way.

"Looking good, Billy Ray," Jimmy said.

"Feeling good, Lewis."

"Really?" he asked.

She shrugged. "I don't know yet. How are they?"

"Nervous."

"Definitely nervous," Yolanda added, handing Billie the Father's Day card to sign that would go with the gift from the three of them.

Billie's eyes filled as she thought about what to write, and settled on "I love you, Daddy." Just like that, her anger at being lied to began to dissolve. "Let's go up."

The Club Level had an elegant carpeted, glass-enclosed, air-conditioned concourse and food stations where you could get pasta, salads, and hand-carved sandwiches. The seats were outside, so Billie was slathered in sunscreen, and if no one was sitting behind her, she planned to open her parasol.

Her parents stopped talking and looked up as she, Jimmy, and Yolanda approached. This was the first time she had seen them since she heard the news. The tentative looks in their eyes, as if they expected her to yell at them, upset her. Those two faces had been the ones that looked at her over her crib in the mornings, the ones who sang her to sleep at night. They hadn't deliberately caused her pain, and she couldn't cause them any either.

Zenobia and Herbert, in matching Rockies baseball jerseys with the number of Herbert's favorite player, stood. Jimmy and Yolanda watched.

"I'm sorry," Billie said. "I'm really sorry." She hugged Herbert and then Zenobia like they were the sun and the moon. They had been her entire universe until she met Nick. They were the ones who educated her, fed her, clothed her, wiped away her tears, loved her. *Kept* her. She shared no blood with them, but they were her family. The connection between them was as deep and true as an ocean. Is blood thicker than water? Not if it meant her parents and Jimmy were less her kin than Trish was.

"You scared me," Herbert said. "You certainly had me going there for a minute."

"I'm sorry," Billie repeated. "But it threw me, you know?"

"Of course," Zenobia said. "We're sorry too. It was cowardly on my part."

Herbert started to speak, but she interrupted him. "No, it's true. Your father wanted to tell you long ago, but I always had some excuse, some reason the time wasn't right. But the real reason was that I was afraid you'd see us differently. You were never anything but our baby girl and I couldn't bear the idea that you might think of me as less than one hundred percent your mother because I'm not the one who gave birth to you. You are my child. . . ." Zenobia's voice cracked. "As much as James, you are my child, you understand?"

Billie nodded through her tears.

"Yeah, yeah," Jimmy said. " 'I love you. You love me. We're a happy family.' Are we done with the mushy stuff now? Some of us need a Rockies dog."

"Quit clowning!" Zenobia waved him off laughing, but she was clearly grateful to him for lightening things up.

You could order food and have it brought to you by waitstaff on the Club Level, but Herbert and Jimmy seemed to sense that Billie and Zenobia needed some time alone together so they went to get the snacks.

"Here." Billie handed her mother a small blue bottle. "Sandalwood and jasmine oils. Very spicy."

Zenobia dabbed a bit on her wrist and smelled it. "Now we're cooking with Crisco."

Billie smiled. "I saw the baby's heartbeat."

"Oh, Wilhelmina," Zenobia breathed, clutching Billie's hand.

"It was the most beautiful thing I've ever seen." She couldn't wait until she could hear the heartbeat, and feel her baby moving inside her.

"How's your health?"

"I'm fine. Still in remission."

"When we spoke about adopting a child, I had no idea the can of worms I was opening," Yolanda said. "Are you okay with the idea?"

"Jimmy says you're going to tell him he's adopted," Billie said.

"From the beginning." Yolanda glanced sympathetically at Zenobia. "I think things are different now. There's not the stigma like there used to be."

Billie hugged her sister-in-law. "I think it's a wonderful idea. Are you okay with me, you know, being pregnant?" Yolanda and Jimmy had been trying for years and hadn't been able to make happen what Billie had slipped into. She didn't want to make Yolanda feel insecure.

Her sister-in-law shrugged. "I'm hardly alone being an *infer*tile Myrtle. Even Angela Bassett used a surrogate."

Zenobia shook her head in amazement. "All the choices you all have these days."

"Have you met your birth sister?" Yolanda asked.

Zenobia grabbed her locket.

"Yeah. She kind of ambushed me." Billie wished she could say something that would take away her mother's concern, even though she still had concerns of her own. "It's different. You hear about people meeting their biological relatives and feeling this instant connection. I don't really."

Zenobia visibly relaxed.

Yolanda had a blizzard of questions: "What's she like? Has she told you about your birth mother? What about your birth father? Have you met the rest of her family?"

"You're really into this, aren't you?" Billie asked.

"You have no idea," Yolanda said.

"Oh, I think I do," Billie teased. "I don't feel connected to her, really, but. . . ." Billie wondered how to explain that something was going on, when she didn't even understand it herself. "I do with my nephew. He and I have the same name. Well, his is William and he goes by Will."

"My goodness," Zenobia said.

"Yes! See!" Billie said. "It's kind of a big coincidence, don't you think?"

"I've heard stuff like that happens a lot with adoptees," Yolanda said. "The connections can run deep even when you're separated."

"And you've met the boy too?" Zenobia asked, fingers back to playing with her locket.

"Mommy, he looks just like me. I think, on some level, we're connected. It's really something to have somebody finally look like me."

"*She* looks like you a little."

"We have the same birthmark," Billie explained to Yolanda.

"More than that," Zenobia added, playing with her necklace.

"She wants Nick to spend time with Will because he's having a hard time. She just got divorced, and he's all involved in this weird church."

"What weird church?" Zenobia asked.

"Clear View."

Zenobia nodded. "Uh-oh. No good is going to come of that. There's something crooked going on there, and it's just a matter of time before it all hits the fan."

Being a news anchor and a community leader, Zenobia always knew about stuff before other people. "Rumors are all over town," she said. "That Pastor Bob drives a Rolls-Royce. Come on now."

"Yeah, Trish said he wears a lot of bling. When are black folks going to wake up?"

"Black folks, white folks, Latinos, all kind of folks go to that church. How did her boy end up with them?"

"Friends from school. He's doing yard work with Nick."

Zenobia made a noise in her throat.

"Mommy, don't."

"Oh, don't be so sensitive. I didn't say anything."

"I know what that little sound means."

"I made the mistake of telling one of our producers about your reunion," Zenobia said, changing the subject quickly.

"Let me guess: she wants to do the story?"

"Are you kidding? She started salivating before I was done speaking. They want Sabrina Fisher to do the reporting. She's Korean and was adopted by a white American family. They're grooming her to replace me next year. It'll be their way of showing that the torch is being passed; they get to look diversity-minded at the same time they get rid of their middle-aged black anchorwoman.

"I have to admit, though, it's a dynamite story. I'm surprised they don't want to save it for sweeps. Are you interested?"

"I don't know. . . ." Billie furrowed her brow. "Do *you* want to do it?"

"Like I said, it's a great story. Think about it. Talk to Trish and let me know."

Herbert and Jimmy returned to their seats with trays of hot dogs, French fries, sodas, and bottles of microbrewed beers.

Billie half grimaced and half smiled. The Club Level offered much fancier (and healthier) fare than the rest of the park, but her family always went for the junk. Herbert believed baseball wasn't baseball without hot dogs and popcorn.

She, of course, had brought her own snacks: tamari-roasted almonds, organic strawberries, soy cheese, and whole-wheat crackers.

"Hey, before the game gets going, we should give you your present," Jimmy said.

Yolanda reached into her purse and pulled out the card and the small gift bag with the plane tickets.

"Kansas City?" Herbert asked, bemused.

"The Negro Leagues Baseball Museum," Jimmy answered.

"Really?" Herbert grinned like a little boy. "Satchel Paige! Thank you! I knew there was a reason I had children."

"Hardy har har," Billie said and hugged her father.

Then the game against the Arizona Diamondbacks began and everyone turned to it and their food. Billie didn't care much for baseball, but their seats gave them a beautiful view of the sun setting over the mountains.

Around the seventh-inning stretch when Yolanda and Jimmy went out for ice cream, Zenobia moved next to Billie and rubbed her back.

Billie felt lulled into asking her mother a question that had been bothering her since she learned she was adopted. "How am I supposed to know who I am now?" she asked, eyes closed, enjoying her mother's touch.

"How do any of us know who we are?"

"What do you mean? You're the most self-assured person I know."

"You think I know everything there is to know about myself?"

Billie opened her eyes. "Not all the time, but you always figure it out. When they told you they weren't renewing your contract, boom, you decided you would teach. Just like that. For all I know that's how you and Daddy adopted me. Just made up your minds one day and boom. I used to feel like I could do that. Now, everything seems different."

"I'm sixty years old," Zenobia said. "Keep living for thirty more years and you better believe things will get clearer."

Billie watched the sun sink below the mountains, wishing she had thirty more years before she knew what was going to happen between her and Nick.

CHAPTER 15

~~~~~~~~~~

Trish

This small group in the park was the big celebration of freedom? After reading online about Juneteenth, Trish had expected mobs of people, but there were maybe a hundred or so people milling around City Park.

She, Billie, and Will had only stepped out of her air-conditioned Subaru wagon moments ago, but already she was starting to sweat. She didn't mind. Sunshine poured down like melted butter. She wished she could lap it up. She was cold-blooded, like a lizard. Given the chance, she would happily lie on a rock and bake like a snake in the sun. She felt the wetness under her cotton T-shirt and around the waistband of her capris. They were new and already a little snug. She hadn't lost any weight since her pronouncement to Alicia. Between Will's escapades and finding out her sister was alive, she'd probably actually gained a couple of pounds.

Still, her mouth watered at the smells of barbecue, sizzling grease, and caramel popcorn. She knew they would be bad for her in all kinds of ways and that Billie wouldn't approve, but oh how she wanted a hot dog and bag of sweetened popcorn.

"Let me know when you get hungry," she said to Will.

"Just get something if you want. You ain't gotta wait for me."

He knew her too well.

Trish turned to her sister. She felt as if they had taken a giant step forward at dinner the other night.

Billie was wearing an ankle-length wraparound skirt with purples, reds, and blues in it, and a yellow long-sleeved tunic. She opened a pink parasol above her head. The look shouldn't have worked, but somehow, she pulled off wearing so many colors at once.

"Not much into the sun?" Trish asked.

"It can trigger a lupus flare."

"You have systemic lupus or discoid?"

"SLE," Billie said, looking surprised, using the abbreviation for systemic lupus erythematosus. "Most people don't even know there's a difference."

"Dogs get lupus too. So I know a little about it, at least discoid. I'm going to totally look like a prune when I'm fifty, but I love the sun."

"Wrinkles are one thing I don't really have to worry about. Black don't crack."

Billie spoke lightly, but still Trish stiffened. "You've got good genes on one side then. But being biracial—"

Billie also seemed to tense, speaking before Trish could finish. "I'm black. Not biracial. Not multicultural. Just black."

Trish wanted to keep things upbeat between them, but since Will was watching this exchange, she felt like she couldn't leave it alone. "Um, you're also white. You're looking right at the evidence."

"You and I might have come from the same womb biologically, but a *black* woman is my mother. My parents are black. My husband is black, and the child I'm carrying is black. End of story."

Not for Will. Not for me. That can't be the end of the story. "I'm not trying to take away the fact that black people raised you. Thank God for them. But if you're not half white, then where does that leave me?"

"I don't know."

"You don't know?"

"Not yet, no. I'm still . . . adjusting. Sorry, just being honest."

Adjusting. Trish was past adjusting. She wanted to know her sister. She wanted to hear about Billie and Nick's wedding. How they met. What her childhood was like. What it was like when she found out she was sick. What it's like having a brother. Her favorite movies and books. Everything.

They'd taken a giant step forward, but now here was a step back. She was disappointed, but at least Billie was talking to her. At least they were together. She asked a trivial question to change the subject. "Is that pumpkin pie in the summertime?"

"You've never seen bean pie before?" Billie replied of the orangish wedges wrapped in plastic.

Trish flinched at Billie's accusatory tone. "No. Is it sweet?"

Billie bobbed her head. "It's good. Probably too much sugar for me though. Try it. It's kind of like pumpkin pie."

So then it wasn't totally stupid of me to assume it was pumpkin, Trish thought, but shoved the idea to the back of her mind.

Will turned up his nose. "Isn't that what Muslim people eat?"

"I'm sure eating a piece of bean pie won't turn you into a Muslim," Billie responded.

"I didn't mean it like that!" Will said quickly, though he seemed embarrassed.

"Let's just do a lap around and check out everything before we decide," Trish said, trying to get them back on solid ground.

They walked by a few rows of African and African-American vendors selling incense, jewelry, photographs, paintings, gourd instruments, African drums, and plastic tubs of honey-colored shea butter.

Trish rarely felt so white. She and Tommy didn't see color. Unless they were around his family's disapproving eyes, she forgot all about race. With Will, she rarely thought of him as biracial. He was just her son. But around Billie, her white skin felt like a Klansman's robe. In his long denim shorts and T-shirt Will looked like the other boys loping around in small packs. He and Billie fit here, but Trish felt like she stood out like Daisy, three-legged at the dog park. She glanced around and noticed a couple of white women at the table next to them in weathered antiwar "Not in My Name" T-shirts. In this crowd of mostly black people did they feel their whiteness the way she did?

Billie stopped at a table that had a sign that read "Two bracelets for six dollars" so Trish and Will followed suit.

Billie picked up a bracelet made of small, multicolored beads. "How much is this?"

"Ten dollars," the skinny African man behind the table replied.

"Which are two for six dollars?" she asked.

"Which ones do you like?"

Billie pointed to a bracelet made of green glass beads.

"Ten dollars," the man said.

She pointed to another one made of cobalt-blue beads.

"Five dollars," he said.

She nodded her head, catching on, and started to walk away.

"No, wait. These are two for six," the man called. He pointed to two thin brass bracelets.

"We're going to look around," Billie answered.

"He was totally trying to screw you!" Trish whispered.

"Just bargaining. Trying to make a living like everybody else."

Billie seemed hell-bent on not agreeing with her today.

They passed a guy selling mix tapes. "Miss, buy for your son," he called, looking right at Billie.

"He's *my* son," Trish bristled.

The vendor didn't miss a beat. "Then you buy."

"You walked right into that one!" Billie laughed.

"That's okay, man," Will said as they kept walking.

They found Nick's band playing under one of three large tents. The music was instrumental jazz, and sounded great. But only a couple of people were dancing.

Billie headed out to the grass in front of the stage, swaying to the beat and waving at Nick. Trish followed.

The two women danced together, shyly and tentatively at first. Then Billie put her tote bag on the ground and began to twirl, a blur of yellow, purple, and pink. Trish too felt free to let the music take her. She lifted her arms over her head and closed her eyes. When she opened them Billie was doing a little bopping thing with her hips, and she joined her. By the end of the song, they were laughing and doing the bump. *Another step forward.*

Trish cheered wildly for the band, and Billie blew kisses to Nick. He tipped his head and blew a kiss back. When the next tune started, Trish wiped sweat off her brow. "I can't remember the last time I went dancing."

"Why don't you come to my dance class sometime?"

"Really?" Trish smiled. *Giant step forward.* "That'd be awesome." She looked around the small crowd. "Where's Will?"

"I saw him walk away with some kids."

"I guess it's not like I have to worry about him buying drugs or something. Hopefully, he's not asking people about their relationship with the Lord."

Billie laughed. "I'm starving. Let's eat."

Trish glanced at Billie's straw tote. "You brought your own, didn't you?"

"But I'll go with you while you get something."

They walked to one of the tents selling barbecue and Trish ordered a smoked turkey leg and a soda. They found an open table and sat down. Billie unloaded her bowl of leaves and grains.

"Appetizing," Trish teased.

"Don't knock it till you try it."

They dug into their food, but Trish kept looking around.

"He's fine. You need to get a life, my friend."

"Don't I know it. But right now I'm a little busy being a mom."

"You can't be a mom and have a life too?"

Trish snorted. "Let's see what you have to say about that after you have your baby." Juneteenth might be about freedom, but there was a reason there wasn't a holiday that celebrated mothers' freedom.

Billie rubbed her stomach, which was just beginning to bulge.

"Why wait till Will goes to college in two years before you have something you do that's for you?"

"If only I had a clue what that was." Trish took a bite of turkey leg. *Heaven.*

"What did you want to be when you were a kid?"

"A vet," she said, wiping her fingers with a paper napkin.

"Why not go back to school? Or have you ever thought about owning your own vet clinic or opening a doggie day-care or something like that?"

She sounded like Alicia. "Maybe when Will's in college."

"Trish, the boy is sixteen."

"I used to think he would need me less as a teenager, but now I think he might need me even more."

"He's gonna be fine. He *is* fine."

Trish nodded. They were both done eating. She had been fascinated by the paintings and sculptures, the jewelry and accessories. If she had some black culture around the house, that would be good for Will. "Let's go shopping."

• • •

Trish yawned like a cat as she stopped the car. She turned off the radio and sat there outside Billie's house. After ten hours of work, she was exhausted but excited to be spending time with her sister and to be dancing again.

She looked out the window. It was that golden time of year when 7:00 p.m. still holds possibility. The sun was starting to set, but it would be light for at least another hour. You could still work in your garden or play a game of tennis or a round of golf, not that Trish did any of those things. But she liked the idea of them. The long daylight was her favorite part of summer. She hated the early darkness of winter. Every year she wore black the day they turned the clocks back in the fall. And there was no better weather than Colorado in early summer. In North Carolina this time of year, it was already hot and clammy. Denver wouldn't see hot until next month, and clammy would never come. And when it did get hot here, she'd just take Will and the dogs and head up to the mountains. She hadn't been camping since she'd been married and was really looking forward to it.

But right now she was tired. Ten hours on her feet dealing with snarling, snapping, and hissing, and that was just the humans! People were such shits sometimes. It was so much easier to work directly with the pets, even the ones who were scared out of their wits and in terrible pain. At least when they snapped at you, you could understand why.

She sighed. Work wasn't the only thing that made her tired. She was also tired of Will. She hadn't ever imagined that a day would come when she'd admit to being tired of her own son, but here it was. Even when he was teething and when he went through the terrible twos, he wasn't this big of a pain in the butt.

She got out of her car and got her gym bag out of the trunk. She had no idea what a person even wore to an African dance class, and she was too embarrassed to ask Billie another politically in-correct question. She hoped yoga pants and a T-shirt would do. They would have to.

As she was walking up the sidewalk, she heard music coming from the backyard so instead of going to the front door, she went to the back.

It was Nick. He had a boom box going.

He jumped when he saw her. "Hi!" He sputtered and coughed.

"I'm here to meet Billie to go to her class tonight." She sniffed the air. Was that . . . ? She edged closer and noticed that Nick had put his right hand behind his back, but a stream of smoke was snaking its way in front of him. He was totally getting stoned!

She grinned. *Finally.* Expected behavior from a musician.

"Busted, huh?" Nick asked.

"The smoke kinda gave you away."

Nick brought the joint up to his lips and took a long toke. "When her cigarette smoke would get in my face when I was a kid, my mother would say 'smoke follows ugly.' "

"That's a mean thing for a mom to say."

"She was a mean woman."

"Is Billie here?"

"In a minute. She just ran over to the store."

Trish sat down in a wicker chair across from him.

He held the joint out to her.

She shook her head, laughing. "I haven't smoked pot in some-thing like seventeen or eighteen years. Right before I had Will." Thinking about Will at home reading his Bible made her stomach acid bubble.

"Hey back there," a voice called.

"Come on back," Nick yelled.

The old guy from across the street came through the gate and to the back porch. He was wearing plaid pants, a short-sleeved shirt, a white belt, and white shoes, and using a golf club as a cane.

Trish couldn't believe that Nick was sitting there with a doobie in his hand in front of this old guy. Wasn't he afraid he'd call the police?

"I been seein' you and seein' you around here. You and the boy," the man said.

"Fletcher, this is Billie's sister," Nick said.

The old guy slid his eyes back and forth between Nick and Trish, waiting for one of them to let him in on the joke. "No foolin'?"

Trish stood to shake Fletcher's hand. "My name is Trish. Nice to meet you."

"Fletcher is sorta the neighborhood watch," Nick said.

The old guy examined her. "You white?"

"Uh, yeah."

He addressed his next question to Nick. "Her daddy step out on Miss Zenobia?"

Nick laughed. "Naw, man."

"Billie's my birth sister," Trish said quickly, wishing Billie was there to hear her use the approved-of language.

"Oh! You mean you're in one of them classes about havin' babies with her?"

So much for correct terminology. "No. No. She's my real sister. We have the same mother. Different fathers."

Fletcher looked to Nick to explain.

"Billie was adopted," Nick said.

"You don't say." Fletcher studied Trish again and pointed to his cheek. "Yeah, I can see it. Y'all got the same mark." He shook his head as if he was still trying to absorb this news. "Back in my day how you got the mixed ones usually would be a white man creeping around the black girl, well, we used to be colored then. But you tellin' me your daddy was white and Billie's daddy was black?"

Trish nodded uncomfortably.

"You don't say," Fletcher repeated. "I done seen it all now. How you doin' on your supplies?" he asked Nick.

Nick held up the joint. "'s all good."

Fletcher nodded. "Well, okay then, I'ma get outcha way." He waved and ambled back through the gate.

"Was he asking you about your pot?"

Nick laughed. "Fletcher is my dope man."

Trish rolled her eyes. "Ha ha."

"I'm serious."

"That old guy sells pot?"

"Yep."

"Huh." *I bet he* has *seen it all.* Now Trish was the one ready to scratch her head.

Nick was about to extinguish the joint when Trish said, "Wait."

He looked at her.

"It's been a rough day." *Rough year,* and if old people were now buying and selling pot, who was she not to take a little toke?

He handed her the joint.

She inhaled the smoke into her lungs and immediately started coughing until her face turned purple.

Nick cracked up. He handed her a glass of lemonade, and took the joint, which went out.

She gulped it down. "That's what I get for trying to be one of the cool kids."

"Go slow, Sister-in-law."

Trish's heart warmed. "Sister-in-law" was the nicest thing anybody had said to her in ages. She liked Nick. "So what's going on with you and Billie?"

Nick relit the joint and took another hit.

"I can tell something is up," she prodded.

"She told you to ask me?"

"No. Trust me, that would be too much like being my sister."

He passed her the joint. "What's that mean?"

"When it comes to her personal life, her jaws are as tight as a pit bull's." Trish sucked a small cloud of smoke into her lungs. This time she didn't cough.

"Really? Girl told me her whole life story the day after we met."

"It's just me then."

"Give her time."

She handed Nick the now-tiny doobie. "You didn't answer my question."

He put his feet on the porch railing and crossed his long legs. "She knew I didn't want kids and she got pregnant anyway."

"Oh."

"Yeah, oh."

"But what can you do now? That baby is coming."

"Billie and me . . . we're not gonna make it."

"Why would you say something like that?"

Nick studied her.

The pot was kicking in. She was starting to feel really mellow from the music coming from the boom box radio. "You can tell me. I won't say anything to her."

Nick pulled his legs down from the railing, leaned over, and spoke to his bare feet. "I'm no good as a father."

Jitters? Was that all? Trish relaxed further. "Bah! You don't know that."

"Yes I do."

She waved her hand dismissively. "You're just nervous. We were as jumpy as your cat Juju right after Will was born, but—"

He looked back up at her. "No. What if I'm not good enough for her?"

"Billie must think you are if she was willing to make a baby with you."

"Billie sees what she wants to see."

"She loves you."

"Everything I touch turns to shit. No good comes from no good."

Trish narrowed her eyes. She could totally see what Nick's problem was. She thought about all the times she didn't call Tommy on his stuff. *It's time to call 'em like I see 'em. Maybe if I had with Tommy, things would be different.* "Know what I think? I think it's easier to be a bad guy than a chickenshit."

Nick looked stunned. "Damn. That was cold."

"If you're worried about fucking it up, just don't."

Nick grimaced. "Are you always this harsh or just when you're high?"

Trish considered. Had the pot loosened her tongue? She didn't usually talk to people like this, but she liked Nick. He was on her side with Will, and in a way Trish was closer to Nick than to Billie. She was only telling the truth because she didn't want him to blow it. But she also had to admit: boldness felt good. "Where do you get this shit? 'No good comes from no good.' 'Smoke follows ugly.' Is that all your mother? What did she do to you?"

"You mean when she wasn't running around with the pastor behind my father's back?"

"Your mother and the minister were having an affair?"

"And me, my sister, and his wife sang together in the choir."

"No!"

Nick chuckled ruefully. "Oh, yeah. Nobody pulls more than a black preacher."

Probably not just black ones. Trish could imagine Pastor Bob with his orange-skinned self chasing the women of Clear View. Sex *and* money. So that was why Nick was so down on the church. "How'd you know about it?"

"Man used to drop by some afternoons. Send me and my sister for ice cream or something. After a while, we put it together."

"Did your father know?"

"I always wondered about that. When he got liquored up on the weekends, he'd bitch about how we ruined his life. Like it was our fault his wife cheated on him."

And *that* explained why he was so down on having kids. Who wouldn't be with parents like that? "I was four when they told me my mother and Billie died and I would never see either of them again," Trish said. "My grandparents were cold people. My mother must have broken their hearts or maybe they were that way before she died, but either way there wasn't much love."

Nick listened intently.

"Love is everything. I don't know what I'd do if Tommy and I hadn't had Will. He's the best thing that ever happened to me. You and Billie found love. You have it! With your baby you'll have even more. More than you can ever imagine."

She didn't know if she had helped Nick, but something shifted inside her, and for one tiny little moment she didn't hate Tommy. There was no space for hatred because her heart was so full of gratitude. Tommy had given her Will, and no matter what else he had done, she'd always love him for that. "Don't ever give that up."

"The herb is kicking in."

Her smile spread slowly across her face. "I am feeling pretty mellow. Do people still say mellow?"

"Dunno." Nick's eyes were closed. He seemed to be feeling mellow too.

Trish heard a car come to a stop and a door close.

"There's your girl," Nick said.

"Billie! We're back here!" Trish yelled.

Nick jumped. "Damn, girl!"

"Sorry. Didn't mean to kill your buzz. Ha! Listen to me, 'kill your buzz.' I'm such a druggie!" *Man, it's fun being a druggie,* Trish thought. *Why did I ever give this up?*

"Mama?"

Trish sat up straight. *Oh, yeah. That's why.*

"What's up?" Billie asked, taking in the scene.

"You said you were going to be at a friend's!" Trish yelled at Will.

"Yeah, Nick and Billie."

"Be cool, Sister-in-law," Nick muttered.

"You didn't tell me Will was with Billie!" Trish screamed at Nick.

"I thought you knew."

Yeah, right! I'd be smoking a doobie knowing my son the Bible-thumper was going to walk up any second!

"You about ready to go?" Billie asked quickly.

But it was too late. Will went into the house, slamming the door behind him. Trish got up to follow him.

"Give him some space," Nick said.

"Come on. You can change at the studio," Billie said.

"No. I have to talk to him." Trish followed Will into the dining room, and Nick and Billie followed Trish.

"So this is why we left North Carolina?" Will demanded.

"Will. . . ." Trish said.

"At least Dad and I have some things in common. The Marines taught him duty, honor, values."

Trish wanted to scream, *Where were Tommy's values when he was fucking around on the mother of his child?!* "You think I have no values? No concepts of duty and honor?"

Will was quiet.

Sure. She had left his father, breaking her vow of "till death do we part," and she had been caught smoking pot. She was bad and Tommy was good. "Thanks a lot, Will."

"Everybody just cool out for a minute," Nick said.

They all turned to him.

"Sit down." Nick sat at the dining room table, and everyone followed.

"I'm sorry," he said.

Trish was shocked. *What did he have to be sorry about?*

"Will, man, you can't talk to your mother like that. She doesn't deserve it."

"How do you know?" Will mumbled sullenly.

"If you wanna be mad at somebody for getting high, be mad at me."

"No." Trish said.

Nick held up his hand. "And you're right."

"What?!" Billie asked.

"I don't need to be getting high," Nick said, looking only at Billie. "I quit."

Will looked suspiciously between Nick and Trish.

"I don't know what I was thinking," Trish said. "You know this isn't something I do all the time, right? This was the first time. . . . I was just . . . But there's no excuse. I'm a parent."

"Your mom wants me to be a role model for you, and I need to do a better job." Nick reached out his hand. "Accept my apology?"

Billie's eyes grew as round as dinner plates.

Trish held her breath. Will shook Nick's hand. He was obviously reluctant, but he shook it.

"Got anything to say to your mom?" Nick asked.

"Sorry," Will said.

Now it was Trish's turn to be surprised. "Thanks," she said to Will, but meaning it also for Nick.

Billie stood. "We better get going. We're gonna be late."

"You're going to be a fine father," Trish said.

Nick's face was a mixture of surprise and gratitude. Billie looked like the skies had opened up and puppies, roses, and hundred-dollar bills were raining down on them.

Trish always carried the letter from Nana with her, planning to tell Billie when the time was right, but the time never seemed right. Now though, Billie was clearly delighted with what had transpired at her house. She laughed and smiled all through dance class. And with good fortune and endorphins coursing through Trish's blood, she decided after class that now was the time. She waited for Billie to say goodbye to the drummers.

"Can we talk?" Trish asked after the drummers left.

"Absolutely," Billie said, wiping sweat from her brow. She looked beautiful. She definitely had that glow.

"I have something to show you. I found more than the picture when I found out about you." Trish retrieved the letter from her purse. "Our grandmother wrote this before she died. She wanted me to find you because she regretted the mistake she made."

Instantly, the happy look disappeared from Billie's eyes. Trish got a bad feeling, but still she handed her sister the letter.

Billie read it quickly. "No mistake was made." Her voice was like ice.

Trish's stomach started to gurgle. She waited for her sister to say something, but Billie just looked at her. Actually, she looked *through* her like she wasn't even there anymore.

"I'm so, so sorry," Trish said, acid creeping up her esophagus, trying to think of a way to erase this moment and go back to how things were during class. "I still can't believe it. It's so awful. So embarrassing. . . ."

Billie snorted. "This ain't much of a shock, if that's what you think."

Trish was stunned. "It's not?"

"Girl, please. I can put two and two together. Why else would they have kept you and not me?"

Trish started to say, Because I was older. Because one kid is a lot easier to raise than two. Because our mother died and they were distraught. But Nana had admitted to it. "It's just so unfair."

Billie opened the studio door. "Girl, wake up. Life's unfair."

The door swung closed with Billie on one side and Trish on the other. *One huge step back.*

CHAPTER 16

~~~~~~~~~

Billie

Billie tasted blood. She had literally bitten her tongue to keep from saying what came to mind. Thank God Cecilia wasn't in class tonight. Between her crazy ass and those racist grandparents. . . . But now that Trish was gone and Billie was back home on her porch, her eyes filled with tears. The words swam in front of her: *We didn't want to raise a black man's child.* Though she wasn't surprised, it sliced her to the bone to see what she had suspected laid out in black and white. Her own ancestors hadn't wanted her.

As she held a Kleenex to her tongue, she recalled telling Trish "Life's unfair" so casually. How she wished she really felt that way. But her sore tongue and thudding heart spoke the truth that her mind didn't want to admit.

She felt the way she did the first time she was called a nigger. She was twelve and had made friends with three other girls—two white and one East Indian—at her Catholic school. The green-eyed, dishwater-blonde Lisa was her best friend. Lisa liked her for who she was, not because she was a local celebrity's daughter. They shared secrets and had each other's back when it came to homework assignments, boys, parents, and other important aspects of preteen life.

Billie couldn't even remember what the beef was, but as is inevitable in groups of girls, something happened, the balance shifted, and alliances were formed. Lisa and the other white girl turned against Billie. Sharmila, the girl whose family was from India, apparently felt no choice but to join them.

First, Billie got the silent treatment. But the four of them shared a quad of desks in American History class, so they had to speak to each other one day. And when they did, Billie and Lisa got into it. Lisa spit out the "n word" and all the air went out of the room. There's a reason they call it a curse word. Her face turned red up to her hairline, showing that even she was ashamed by what she'd said. But she wasn't ashamed enough to apologize. She simply got up and left the room, the other girls in their group slinking guiltily behind her.

Billie was left at her desk with *nigger* hanging in the air like a bad smell. That's when she decided that no matter how nice a white girl acted, when the stuff came down, the line would be drawn, white would choose white, and she would be a nigger. *Forget them,* she had told herself then. She kept stepping, head held high.

And she would do the same today. Too little too late didn't even begin to touch how worthless Maxine's deathbed confession was. When it came time to face judgment, either in a courtroom or in heaven, even the worst racists suddenly saw the light. Tonight Billie would push her hurt away. She had a child coming into this world, and Nick had started to act like he wanted to be a father. Like Zenobia, she would not be so weak as to let an ignorant old bitch steal her joy. She wiped her tears with the back of her hand, took a deep cleansing breath, and went inside.

• • •

"Thank you for what you did for Will tonight," Billie said.

She and Nick were lying in bed, enjoying the cool night breeze over their bare sex-heated bodies. Nick hadn't moved his clothes back upstairs, but they were sleeping in the same bed again. Neither one asked what it meant. Billie was too afraid that if she pointed out to Nick that he seemed to be coming back to her he would change his mind. She imagined that he too was scared to acknowledge what was happening between them.

They were living in a peaceful limbo, each pretending that everything was normal. Most days Nick was gone doing yard work with Will and Billie puttered around the house. In the evenings she fixed dinner and they ate together. Afterward, Nick watched TV and she read or did yoga. Once Will brought his guitar over and played a little music with Nick. They didn't talk about the baby. They didn't talk about the future at all. But after tonight she felt a budding hope, and decided to directly face the issue.

"Nick, I'm sorry. This isn't the way I wanted it. I didn't mean for this. . . . But you can't leave me. You've got to be there for me. For us. You've got—"

He interrupted her. "Shhh. Hush."

Billie held her breath. She had already experienced one miracle in her life, overcoming lupus. Was she being greedy to hope for another?

"My mother . . . my father . . . ," Nick began speaking into the darkness. "Well, my parents were a trip. Mama was always on my father's case, always tearing him down. But every Sunday she had her ass up in a church where they believed men were 'the head of the house as Christ is the head of the church.' "

Nick paused. Billie had the feeling something important was coming. "The preacher was rollin' in a Cadillac. He was married.

Had kids. And he and my mother were fucking each other for years."

This was the most Nick had opened up about his family in all the years she had known him. She took his hand, but stayed quiet with the hope that he would keep talking.

"Every Saturday night my father would get drunk and tell pitiful stories about how he could have been a professional musician. How he should have left our asses and hit the road like his friends did who played with Miles Davis and Pat Metheny. He was pathetic.

"Then Mama would start in. 'Nick, you ain't nothin' and you wasn't never gone be nothin'. I don't know who you think you are. Best be happy cleanin' up that school 'cause that's all you gone do. Those white folks wasn't never gone hand out no music job to you, fool.' "

Billie couldn't even imagine what it felt like to hear your mother calling your father worthless, but she knew it must hurt doubly when you and your father share the same name.

"He was pathetic and now he's dead."

"It sounds like he tried to do right by you guys, though," she said. "I mean, it takes a big man to stay in the face of all that."

Nick drew in a sharp breath. "Billie?"

"Yes, sweetie?"

"What if I'm not big enough?"

She rolled on to her side, propped herself up on her elbow, and looked down at him. Light from the street fell across his face. "Why would you think that?"

He shook his head.

"Listen to me, you're not your father and I'm not your mother. This right here, what we have, is a new thing."

She lay back down and wrapped an arm around his torso. "A. Whole. New. Thang."

He shifted, putting his head against Billie's bare stomach and began to sing softly.

"Nicky's baby
Guess you better grow your little self down
Nicky's baby now
Guess you better grow your little self on down."

It was to the tune of "Mustang Sally," one of the million cheesy wedding-reception tunes that drove Nick crazy.

Billie started to laugh and cry at the same time.

"All you wanna do is ride inside of Billie
Ride baby ride
All you wanna do is ride inside of Billie
Ride baby ride."

He patted Billie's stomach for the drum part. Bam, bam, bam.

"But in a few months you're gonna put your tiny feet on the ground."

He kissed his way up her body to her face, where he met the tears streaming down her cheeks.

She felt as if she were in some alternative universe, one in which dreams come true. All that night, Nicky's baby played in her mind over and over again. Nick was back! And he wanted this baby too! She was getting everything she wanted. Her heart was so full. *I will be worthy of this blessing,* she promised God and whoever else was listening. *I will be a good wife, a good mother, a good daughter, and a good sister, even to Trish.* Especially to Trish, because Trish had brought her Will and Will had brought Nick back to her. But she wouldn't stop there. She would be more patient with her students and their parents. She would stop hating on Honking Harry and Republicans. She would even, swear to God, be kind to "triracial" Cecilia from her dance class.

. . .

To keep her promise of trying to be a good sister, Billie decided to visit Trish for the first time. Friday was Trish's day off from work. Nick and Will were busy cutting grass. Billie had nothing but time.

On a block of cookie-cutter houses, Trish's stood out: a stone Jack Russell terrier lifted its leg next to a juniper. Plywood shepherds and hounds lined the driveway. The mailbox was shaped like a dalmatian and painted white with black spots. The doormat had a paw-print design, and next to the front door was a sign made of sheet metal with a golden retriever above the word "Welcome."

The front door opened and Billie heard a cacophony of barking. Next she heard Trish's voice yelling at the dogs. Then Trish was coming through the door.

"You found it!"

Billie got out of the car. "Hard to miss," she said, with a big smile.

"I'll get the dogs on their leashes and we can get going. You take Daisy and Skipper and I'll take Little Buddy and Jigs—I mean Lucky."

"You don't know his name?"

"I planned to change it, but for some reason it won't stick."

"And Skipper and Little Buddy are . . . ?"

"Yep, named after *Gilligan's Island.* I watched way too much TV after school."

Billie found it very cute that unlike on the TV show, Skipper was the little dog and Little Buddy was the big one. Her heart warmed to Trish a little more.

Once everyone was arranged, they were off.

"We'll go to the dog park about a mile away if you're up for it."

As usual, Billie was decked out in long sleeves and long skirt, hat, and shades to ward off the sun. "I'm ready. I've got water and trail mix in my bag."

They strolled silently through the neighborhood. Billie was lulled by the sounds of birdsong, the *shush-shush-shush* of sprinklers, and the dogs' pants and jingling tags. They had to stop often for the dogs to sniff something or pee. Every now and then Trish would say "Leave it" or give some other command, and the dogs would obey. The sky was cornflower blue and the morning breeze was pleasant. But the temperatures would be above eighty before 10 a.m. They speeded up to a brisker pace, the dogs seemingly aware they were closer to the park. The mile went quickly.

"Maybe I should get a dog," Billie said when they arrived. "This was a great walk."

Nobody else was at the dog park yet. They closed the gate and let the dogs off their leashes.

"Dog is just god spelled backward," Trish said, watching the dogs with affection. "This is my church. No gods, just unconditional love, loyalty, and family. That's my idea of spirit, what gives me peace, makes me feel like everything is going to be okay."

"That's probably what most people get from their church," Billie said.

"This is when I'm supposed to say 'if church gives Will all that, then I'm for it,' right?"

"I'm not a church person, but there's a lot about religion and Christianity that's quite beautiful. I deeply admire Christians who really embody Christ's message, who believe in justice and nonviolence and love. Besides, he's only going to push harder as long as you give him something to push up against."

"That's what his father says."

"It's not like he's in a cult."

"What's the difference?"

"Clear View Church isn't going to kidnap him and take all his money."

"He doesn't have any money."

"They aren't trying to convince him to drink poison so he can go to heaven on a spaceship."

"No, not a spaceship, but he's all about going to heaven. And where is it? Up in the clouds somewhere? How can he be thinking about going to a place that nobody even knows where it is, but they all say they know it exists? That's craziness."

"You're not going to lose your son." Billie gently got to the heart of the matter.

"Yes, I am. In just two more years he's going to go to college, and once he's eighteen he can do what he wants."

"You're always going to be his mother."

"Thank you for saying that."

"You're welcome. Now you just have to believe it."

"I'm so glad you and Nick are around. He sure saved my ass the other night."

Billie again felt a surge of joy.

"But . . ." Trish hesitated. "Nick seems to think you'd be better off without him."

Billie's shoulder muscles clenched. "Why would you say that?"

"He told me when we were um . . . you know. . . ." She pretended to suck on a joint.

"He did?" Is talking with Trish what made Nick open up? If so, Billie owed her doubly.

"I think the responsibility of being a dad scares the hell out of him."

"Yeah, we talked about that. What did you say to him?"

Trish grinned sheepishly. "I told him I thought it was easier to be a badass than to admit that he was scared."

Billie evaluated the petite blonde. Again, she'd underestimated her. Trish was wise. "Thank you."

Trish did an "aw-shucks" shrug, trying to play it off, but Billie could tell she was pleased. "Husbands. Whaddya gonna do?"

"Nick's not my husband. At least not in the sense of a wedding. We're common-law."

"Why didn't you ever get married?"

Billie felt the familiar distrust, but Trish's blue eyes were as open as the sky. Maybe she too could open up. "I always said it was because we didn't need the law to validate our love, but the real reason is that I was always afraid that when it came down to it, he wouldn't go through with it."

They walked to a bench.

"Sit."

Billie sat quickly. "Jeez!"

"Sorry, bad habit, talking to people like I do animals," Trish said. "Will always, well used to always, walk around holding his crotch and I'd catch myself thinking 'leave it, leave it.' Same thing I say to my dogs to get them to not pick up a dead bird or something."

"I do the same thing. I almost talk to Nick like one of my students. In Head Start we sing all the time." Billie demonstrated: "Iiiii like the way that Trish is walking. She's getting her exercise."

"Hey, husbands and preschoolers probably aren't that far apart. Might work."

After an hour in the sun, they left the dog park and headed back to Trish's house. She was fixing them something to drink, and stopped to rub her breastbone.

"What's wrong?" Billie asked. "You do that a lot."

"Heartburn," Trish said, pouring milk into her coffee cup. "It's nothing."

Billie frowned. "Dairy upsets your pH balance, makes your body more acidic. It also causes inflammation."

"According to who?"

"Naturopaths, herbalists, nutritionists, lots of people."

"Anybody with a real degree?"

"Be threatened if you want. Keep your burning heart."

"No, I want to know. Your special diet really got your lupus into remission?"

"Really. I was sick as a dog. . . ." Billie looked down at three-legged Daisy, "No pun intended, and they couldn't do anything for me. The steroids made me gain weight. Girl, I was too through. I didn't get better until I took responsibility for my healing and looked at my condition from every angle: mind, body, and spirit."

"What else should I do?"

"Well, I'm not a naturopath, but I would say cut out alcohol, red meat, and sweets, and coffee should go too."

"Those are all my food groups! What's left?"

Billie smiled. "I used to love coffee ice cream and jamocha shakes from Arby's and frappaccinos. Put coffee and cream together and I was there."

"Omigod, Will and I are both crazy for coffee with lots of cream in it!"

"I see that. I gave all that up. It was worth it. I'd do it again in a heartbeat rather than go back to feeling like I used to. But I tell you what, I've been craving chocolate something fierce since I got pregnant."

"You want chocolate?" Trish brought a flat rectangular box out of the refrigerator. "Enstrom's Toffee?" she asked, opening the box.

Billie bit her lip.

"Just a little bite. Get that one. It's small."

Billie picked up a triangle of toffee covered in milk chocolate.

"One little piece can't hurt anything," Trish urged.

Billie popped it into her mouth. She closed her eyes and a slow smile spread across her face.

Trish ate a larger piece. "Good, huh?"

"Oh. My. God," Billie said.

"I know. Better than sex."

"I don't know if I'd go that far, but damn, that'll make you wannna hurt somebody."

"Another little piece?"

"You trying to turn me to the dark side?"

"You're eating for two. . . ."

"All right. One for mama, one for baby."

"And one more for auntie."

"Okay, seriously. Put that away!"

Trish laughed and put the box in the refrigerator. "We're safe."

"I tell you what. Next week I'll take you to one of my favorite restaurants. You'll see how good healthy food can be."

"Are we bonding? Cause it feels like we're bonding."

"Yes, we just may be."

CHAPTER 17

Trish

Bonding has its limits. People eat this stuff?

They were at Watercourse Foods, a vegetarian restaurant on 17th Avenue. The brunch menu seemed to consist mostly of buckwheat, quinoa, and tofu.

"So what's good?" Trish asked. There had to be *something* she could eat.

"Everything," Billie said with a smile. "Really, it's not so foreign. They put their foot in everything."

"Huh?"

"I thought your ex-husband was black. It means they really do a good job."

Why did black people turn everything around to the opposite? Bad was good. Sick was cool. And putting your foot in food meant you cooked it well.

"I'm sorry," Billie said. "I shouldn't tease you like that."

"Especially since I haven't had any coffee." Thanks to Billie, she was cutting back. She hadn't made coffee at home all week (though she had sneaked a couple of Starbucks lattes with Splenda) and had pitched out her white flour (not that she ever baked anything) and white sugar. She and Will were drinking tea with honey and having oatmeal or wheat toast with natural peanut butter for breakfast every day. It was a start, and to tell the truth, her stomach didn't bother her as much.

Her eyes landed on banana bread French toast. *Now* they were talking!

Billie ordered a Philly sandwich made out of seitan (satan?!) and hibiscus iced tea. Then she told her Zenobia's station wanted to do a story about them.

"Really? We'd be on TV?!"

"You'd want to do it?" Billie asked.

"Yeah, why not?" Trish asked. "It might help other people who've been in our shoes."

"I think Mommy wants us to do it."

"You never asked me anything about our mother. Aren't you curious?"

"A little. What do you remember about her?"

Trish smiled. "She taught me French. When I was four I could count to ten, say *merci, tres bien, je m'appelle* Trish, *Comment allez-vous?, au revoir,* and *avez-vous un bec?*"

"What's that last?"

"Do you have a lighter?"

Billie laughed. "Ain't no way my mother would have taught me how to ask for a lighter when I was four years old."

"Well, that's the difference between your two mothers. I wish Zenobia had adopted me too."

"She didn't need to, now did she?" Billie said with a tight smile.

Uh oh. Luckily, the waitress brought their food just then.

"Okay," Trish pointed at the beautiful food on her plate with her fork. "If *this* is healthy, I'm sold!" She took a bite—it was sweet and gooey and delicious.

The talk turned to children, which led to men.

"How long were you married?" Billie asked.

"We started going out when we were sixteen. We got married when we were eighteen. He's the only man I've ever been with."

"And you call me retro! I just hope you don't break your vibrator waiting for Will to grow up and leave the house."

"I don't have a vibrator."

"Tell me you didn't just say you don't have a vibrator?"

"What? Am I *supposed* to have one?"

"Hell, yes!" Billie slapped her thigh. "A grown-ass woman, especially a *single* grown-ass woman, is supposed to know how to take care of herself in the most fundamental way possible."

"You have a vibrator?" Trish whispered.

"Yes. I haven't used it much lately because Nick takes pretty good care of me. That's one problem we don't have." She smiled. "But yeah, of course I have one. Can I ask you a question? Do you masturbate?"

Roses bloomed in Trish's cheeks. "Hell's bells!" She could feel her face flush and was reminded of the night she had asked Will if he was using condoms. She wanted to go back to those good old days when the kid was the one being embarrassed about his sex life and the mom was left alone.

"It's good for you! Maybe if you did . . ."

"What? What if I did?"

"Maybe you'd lighten up a little."

"*I'd* lighten up a little?"

"Yes. You could stand to chill just a little bit."

"Omigod. I am so totally not the one who needs to lighten up!"

Billie cocked her head, black-girl style. "How do I need to lighten up?"

Trish sat up primly and pretended to be frowning over a menu.

"Well, I'd order the salad but it's not made from finely grown Corinthian organic gold-plated lettuce, so no way can it pass my precious lips."

"I'm disciplined about my diet for the sake of my health!"

"Whatever," Trish snorted.

"So, what? If I eat junk food, even if it makes me sick as a dog, I'll be a better person?"

"You can be a little rigid is all I'm saying, and it's hard for the rest of us to live up to your standards."

"You sound like Nick."

Trish just raised her eyebrows. Billie was so touchy. She didn't want to send her off the deep end.

"I don't mean to be judgmental," Billie said softly.

"I know. Forget I said anything. I don't know how we got on this anyway."

"I guess it's what I get for getting all up in your business."

Trish grinned. "That'll teach you."

As soon as the seed of the idea was planted, Trish couldn't stop thinking about it. The last time she had sex was over a year ago. It was like as long as she didn't think about it she was fine. But now Billie had put the idea into her head and her head had put it into her lower regions. She found herself staring at male clients and guys she saw running errands, wondering things about them she hadn't wondered about a man in a long time.

One evening after work she was in line at the grocery store and realized her cart only had cucumbers, zucchinis, summer sausages, and bananas. She was so mortified she dashed to her car, pulled out her cell phone, and called her sister.

"So remember that thing you said to me about getting . . . a . . . you know, when you were getting in my business?" Trish asked.

"I believe the word is vibrator. It won't make you a hussy to say it. Can Trish use her words?"

Trish blushed, grateful that Billie couldn't see her.

"Well, where would one find a vibrator?"

"Go 'head on with your bad self!" Billie chuckled. "Lots of places."

"Really?"

"Well, not at Target or Wal-Mart, but sure. You wanna go shopping?"

"You'd take me?"

"Why not? This is already the strangest relationship I've ever had in my life. Might as well go for broke."

The following evening they pulled into the Toy Party's parking lot. Next door was a sports bar. "I need a drink," Trish said.

"Come on, you're a big girl."

"This big girl needs a drink before she buys a you-know-what, okay?" It came out a little more forcefully than Trish had intended. She sounded borderline hysterical, which just proved to her that what she said was true.

Billie pursed her lips, but just nodded.

They went inside and got a table. "I wish you could have a drink with me."

Billie patted her stomach. "Not anytime soon."

A guy in a Rockies baseball shirt and jeans came to the table. "Whacanna getchu?"

Trish was trying to quickly look at the extensive drink menu, but all the choices overwhelmed her. "A margarita."

"What kind?"

"Surprise me."

"You serious?"

"Bring me the biggest, strongest one you have."

"You got it."

He turned to Billie. "For you?"

"Iced tea, please."

Even though she hadn't eaten since lunch, Trish declined to order any food. The waiter went to fetch their drinks.

Trish sighed and rubbed her chest.

"Why are you so nervous? It's no big deal," Billie said gently.

"I guess buying a you-know-what makes me think of everything that went wrong in my marriage. And how young I was then and how old I am now. It's pathetic."

"You're not old."

"Sometimes I *feel* old and used up."

"Even better that we're getting you something to play with."

The waiter set down a giant glass filled with slushy blue liquid. "Surprise," he said flatly. "You asked for big and strong."

Billie's and Trish's eyes widened. The drink had to be twenty ounces.

"What's in it?" Trish asked.

He handed Billie her iced tea. "Blue Curaçao, Cointreau, two kinds of tequila. Anything else?"

"If this doesn't do it, I'm in trouble," Trish said. The waiter left and Trish lifted her glass. "Courage!" she said, then took a long slurp on her straw. "Ow! Brain freeze!"

Billie rolled her eyes while Trish rubbed her forehead.

A couple, a white woman and a black man, came in and took the table next to them.

Trish leaned in and whispered. "Black women used to give me the stink eye so much when Tommy and I were together."

Billie didn't respond.

Feeling looser now that the alcohol had entered her bloodstream, Trish asked her sister one of the questions she had been dying to ask. "How do you feel about mixed marriages? You don't give people the stink eye, do you?"

"Not anymore," Billie said. "But I've seen black dudes with white women and hated on them."

"Why? I could never understand what my relationship had to do with strangers. Why would they care?"

"It's hard to have one of your own say you're not good enough."

"But how do you get that this guy is saying you're not good enough just because he's with her? Why can't he just be in love with her? Maybe his last girlfriend was black. Maybe his next one will be. Maybe his wife will be. Why does it have to be some big statement?"

"Everything we do is a choice, and when we make that choice, whether we want to or not, we're making a statement."

"Tommy didn't pick me because he hated black girls. His girlfriend now is black. He probably had sex with every color of the rainbow while we were married. He's an equal opportunity fucker." She cracked up at her own joke and slurped more of her drink.

There were a dozen TVs in the place and all of them were tuned to the Rockies game. "Why couldn't Will get into sports?" Trish mused. "Look at all those male role models."

"And you wouldn't complain when he came home scratching his balls and spitting?"

"He already scratches his balls. Though I have to say that that is one benefit of his going to church: he doesn't walk around holding his crotch anymore." Trish laughed. "I guess that's about what it takes for a man to forget his dick: divine intervention!"

This time Billie laughed with her. "Okay, girlfriend, I think you've had enough liquid courage for now."

Trish held up one finger and sucked the last of her drink down fast. "Aaah!" Trish paid the bill. "Whoa," she said, listing as she stood up.

"You okay?"

"Yeah. But I just realized I called my son a man. I must be drunk."

They left the sports bar and walked across the parking lot to the Toy Party. Before they walked through the door, Trish said, "Wait!" and put on her sunglasses. "Now I'm ready."

"You realize you're not Clark Kent? I can still tell who you are."

"They just make me feel better."

"You also realize that since it's evening, you actually stand out more with sunglasses on. *And* that if somebody in here recognizes you it's only because they were in here too?"

"I *said* they make me feel better."

Billie just shook her head and opened the door.

The Toy Party was so different from what Trish had expected. It was clean and brightly lit, and almost everything in it was the color of a Crayola crayon. Everything that wasn't flesh-colored, that is. Or black and red. But there were no skeevy-looking guys in trench coats and black socks. Everybody looked . . . well, normal.

"Let's go upstairs," Billie said.

As they were going up, they passed a wrinkly skinned, white-haired couple in matching black leather pants and jackets coming down the stairs. "Did you see them?" Trish asked to be sure she wasn't hallucinating.

Billie chuckled. "Hey, this is grown folks' business up in here. More power to 'em. Okay, so choose."

They were standing in front of a long wall of vibrators. Long ones. Short ones. Thick ones. Thin ones. Plastic purple ones. Pink-skin-colored strap-ons and brown-skin-colored strap-ons. Ones that looked just like penises and ones shaped like rocket ships.

Trish started giggling at the Wall of Vibrators shimmering in front of her. The margarita was most definitely kicking in. "There's so many!"

"I think there's more over there."

Trish had no idea there were this many vibrators in the world, let alone in one store in Denver, Colorado. She imagined the sound of billions of vibrators all buzzing at once. "I need one that doesn't make noise."

"Seems like other factors would be pretty important to consider too. You know. Size? Shape? Speed?" Billie wiggled her eyebrows.

"I'm a mom. A mom of a born-again kid. Who has already caught me tokin' on a doobie. The last thing I need is for Will to catch me with a vibrator. Talk about a buzzkill."

"Point taken."

They read package after package, trying to find one that promised discretion.

The descriptions were funny at first, but now the letters were starting to scramble in front of Trish's eyes and she was feeling a little dizzy. Maybe she should have had some food with her drink. "I don't feel so good. Let's just pick one and get outta here."

"This one says it's 'whisper quiet,'" Billie said, giggling and holding up a box with a turquoise rocket ship behind a plastic window.

"I'll take it."

They walked past bullwhips, leather panties, edible panties, tall vinyl boots, flavored lubricants, and XXX-rated videos, and Trish started to wonder whether if she had gone for this kind of thing when she was married, would Tommy have cheated on her with all those girls. Would her family still be together and her kid be healthy and normal? How's that for some fucking irony: if she had been more of a hoochie with her husband, maybe her child wouldn't be an insane Christian. Suddenly all her bitterness, hurt, and guilt and her slushy blue margarita came roaring up and out, splashing all over a pair of fluffy white handcuffs.

"Are you okay?" Billie asked when Trish was done.

Two frat-boy types in backward baseball caps turned their noses up and laughed.

"Like you've never seen a woman hurl in public before," Trish murmured. "Yeah, I'm okay." She looked at the formerly white handcuffs, which were now actually a kind of pretty shade of baby blue, if you could ignore the chunks and bile dripping off them. She cleaned her mouth with the back of one hand. "I own those now, right?"

"I believe that's the rule. You barf on 'em, you buy 'em."

CHAPTER 18

~~~~~~~~~~

Billie

"What you got going on here?" Billie asked, looking down at the unfinished puzzle on the table at Trish's house.

"Jigsaw, down!" Trish said to the black and white dog.

"What's up with you and jigsaw puzzles? You even named your dog Jigsaw."

"Only because Lucky wouldn't take. I told you."

"Told me what?"

"That's how I found you. First I started finding jigsaw pieces all over and then a client brings in this dog she rescued and said she was going to call him Jigsaw."

"No, I don't think I knew this. Plus, I don't get it."

"I kept telling myself it was all a coincidence, but Alicia, my co-worker, said that Nana was trying to talk to me." Trish explained about going to the cemetery for the first time and not finding a grave for Billie.

"My God."

"I didn't believe Alicia at first. I never felt Nana's spirit. Never felt our mother's spirit or Pawpaw's. I never believed in any of this."

"Really? I used to think my ancestors were always with me."

"Used to?"

Billie didn't feel right discussing the ancestors with Trish. "Let's put this bad boy together."

"Sorry, but I'm no help. I suck."

"How hard can it be?" She scrutinized the image on the box top and started shifting the pieces around. Then she looked again closely at the picture and rearranged the pieces some more. Within twenty minutes she had connected several parts of the puzzle. "I think this is part of the camel here in front of the pyramids," she said, looking at the picture on the box. "See the tip of red that's from the blanket the rider sits on?"

"I've looked at this damn thing a million times and it seems like all I ever saw was sand."

Billie shrugged.

"That's how Nana was. She could have put this thing together in her sleep."

Billie put the piece down and pushed the box away, the idea that she had something in common with the woman who gave her away slicing something open inside her. "I always knew I was different," she murmured. "I always felt like I didn't fit completely in my own family. I love them and I know they've always loved me, but somehow I knew something wasn't right."

Trish moved to the edge of her chair at Billie's confession.

"I always thought it was because my mother was color-struck."

"Color-struck?"

"Color-struck is admiring lighter-skin people. All the local TV people do their own makeup, did you know that? People think TV news is such a glamorous job, but they do their own hair and makeup. When Mommy started in the business, she had a hard time finding makeup that worked with her skin color. The white women shared their blushers and powders with each other, but they were no help for my mother's dark skin."

Billie didn't mean to ramble. But the thoughts were coming faster than she could process them. It was like that old *I Love Lucy* episode when the candies are coming too fast down the conveyor belt and Lucy shoves them in her mouth and shoves them down her dress trying to keep up. But Billie didn't want to stuff these thoughts deep inside. She didn't want to swallow her feelings. For one thing, they weren't sweet.

"Her mother wouldn't let her play in the sun because she was afraid she'd get 'too dark.' And I was so much lighter than either of them.

"But being light-skinned wasn't what I was feeling, or not just that. It was that I was adopted. That's what made me different."

The adoption fantasy is common among children. Most kids at one time or another have wondered if maybe their "real" parents—their famous, rich, loving, somehow-more-special parents—aren't out there somewhere. That's part of what made *Harry Potter* so popular. Here was a kid finally rescued by his true people.

For Billie, though, the idea wasn't a happy one. She never longed to be different from her parents. Quite the opposite. Every time some church lady or somebody at one of her parents' civic functions commented on the fine texture of her hair or the fairness of her skin her stomach clutched.

Suddenly, Billie felt exposed. She would think about all of this later, when she was alone. "You could make something with the pieces you found."

"Like what?" Trish asked. "None of the pieces fit together, and even if they did, I'm no good at puzzles."

Billie picked one of the pieces up and bounced it in her left palm. "You could glue them around a picture frame or you could make them into jewelry or something. Oh! I know. . . ." She took out her earrings and removed the wire hooks. "You have a needle?"

Trish fetched one.

Billie selected two puzzle pieces that were similar in size and colored rosy beige. With a little difficulty, she poked holes in each of them and connected the wire from her own dangly earrings to the puzzle pieces. "There. Earrings. Try them on."

"I can't believe how creative you are!" Trish stuck the wires through her ears. "How do they look?"

"Go see."

She dashed into the half bath off the hallway. "Oh, my dog! These are totally cool. You could sell these!" She walked back into the family room.

Billie grinned. "That's Zenobia in me. That woman could make a ball gown out of paper towels and ribbon." She had found herself again, at least the self she wanted to be—Zenobia and Herbert's daughter.

"You're very proud of your family, aren't you?" Trish asked shyly.

Billie nodded. There was so much there to be proud of. "My father's great-grandfather was born a slave and bought his freedom and his whole family's freedom and started a barbershop. We have a copy of his manumission papers."

"Manumission?"

"His letter saying that he was no longer a slave. You needed paperwork to prove you were free or slave catchers could get you and sell you back into slavery."

"Jesus Christ."

She took pleasure in shocking Trish. She wanted her to know what it truly meant to be black in this country. "One of my great-aunts worked with Madam C. J. Walker when she was just starting out."

"Okay, don't be mad at me, but I don't know who that is."

Billie wasn't mad. Just tired of white people knowing nothing about her people besides Martin Luther King, Jr. "She was the first female millionaire in this country, and she was a black woman. She got her start right here."

"Wow."

"We have gold miners, buffalo soldiers, doctors, teachers, and painters. Lots of people who were firsts. You know, the first African-American school board president, the first African-American dentist in a certain state, stuff like that."

"I can tell you a little about our mother's side of the family, but there's nobody particularly amazing there."

"Maybe sometime." Billie wasn't ready to know about slave-holding, Klan-belonging, plantation-owning ancestors, and surely there would be at least one. That was American history. There would also, hopefully, be some abolitionists and suffragettes, but she wasn't ready for them either. How could she pray to these people? How could they guide her? What would they know of her life? And on her birth father's side? Would she ever know who those folks were? Did she even want to know? "Are you curious about your father?" she asked Trish.

"I suppose."

"You never say anything about him."

"I guess I lived so long thinking that my family ended when you and Mom died in a car accident that didn't even happen that I got used to not having anyone. I had hoped that Tommy and I would make a family that someday somebody in the future would be able to trace back and feel proud about, but. . . . Well, that didn't happen."

"Sure it did. You have Will. He'll marry one day and give you grandbabies."

Trish smiled and grimaced at the same time.

"And it's not too late for you to have more kids."

Trish sputtered and sprayed diet soda through her nose. "Are you crazy?!"

"Lots of women have kids in their early forties."

"Yeah, but usually they didn't have kids in their twenties too. I can't even imagine running around behind a baby now. Besides, I believe the process still requires a man to be involved."

"That reminds me. Have you used your new friend yet?"

Trish looked down at the puzzle. A wicked grin spread across her face.

"That smile just told me everything I need to know."

Trish laughed, then leaned in and spoke in a low voice. "I have to tell you, I did it when Will was gone and still locked my bedroom door."

"But it was a good thing?"

"Oh. My. God."

Billie laughed too. "We'll have you with a real man pretty soon."

Trish slipped her hair behind her ears and touched her new earrings. "Maybe my new bling will get somebody's attention."

The two women continued to talk and laugh, and the puzzle stayed uncompleted in front of them.

What does it take to look your past in the face? Billie wondered as she stared at the three headstones. They were nothing fancy, flat against the ground, matching cold gray-blue mottled stone.

After hearing about Maxine's puzzles and talking about her adopted family's history, she felt compelled to go to the Kueppers's gravesites. She couldn't stop thinking that like the puzzle she'd worked on, there was something unfinished about her. If she confronted her past, maybe she could put an end to that feeling.

She stopped at Jocelyn's grave first, but it was Maxine and John whose graves called louder to her. Jocelyn might have kept her if she had lived. Jocelyn had not cared that her daughter was made with a black man. But Maxine and John might have drowned her in a bucket like a feral kitten for all she knew.

Maxine's own words rang again in her mind: we didn't want to raise a black man's child.

They didn't want me because of my skin color.

They didn't want me.

A rose was carved into the top of Maxine's headstone, and her name and the dates of her birth and death. But there was no "In loving memory" or "Forever in our hearts" added as on most of the tombstones around them.

"You waited cowardly until death took you before you admitted the truth," Billie said. "When I couldn't speak to you to your face. But luckily for us both I believe you can hear me. I believe you can see what's going on in this world. And I hope it pains you. I hope it hurts."

She turned to John's headstone, which had a cross on it.

Good Christian man that he was. "You must be having a fit down there," she said to him. "Not only did your daughter make a child with a black man, but so did both your granddaughters.

"I'm happy you didn't raise me. I thank God you never had a chance to make me feel like I was anything less than a gift. I have wonderful parents, and my grandparents, well, my grandparents were Disneyland and church and soul food and warm quilts and sunshine all mixed together. They were love and safety and acceptance. So I actually owe you both big-time."

This was the same cemetery her real grandparents were buried in. Aspen Hill had been an all-white cemetery until right before Grandpa Bailey died, and soon as they opened it up, black folks swarmed to it, happy that in death they would finally be treated as equals, delighting in the idea of all those white bones rolling in horror.

For Wilhelmina and Grandpa Bailey, Billie had brought roses from her yard. For Maxine and John, she had nothing. She was about to go back to her car to drive to her real grandparents' graves when she turned and placed a single yellow rose on Jocelyn's marker. And then because Jocelyn had wanted them to keep her, she gouged a pinch of grass and dirt from her grave and put it in her mojo bag before tucking it back into her bra. Dirt from a mother's grave was some of the strongest protection there was.

A few days later, Nick and Will had worked all day. Nick had headed off to play a private party and Will was hanging at the house until his mother got off work.

"My mother's been a member of her church for more than forty-five years and I've never heard her ask anybody about their relationship with God," Billie said.

"It says in the Bible—" Will started.

"I know what it says."

"*You've* read the Bible?"

She smiled to herself at his shock. "Most of it. There's a lot that's beautiful in the Bible. I particularly like the psalms; the Song of Songs is lovely."

"I wish you'd tell my mother that," Will said.

"I have."

"Then why is she still all weird about me going to church?"

"Maybe because *you* told her she's going to hell?"

"I was trying to tell her some stuff that would *keep her* from going to hell!"

"And you weren't messing with her just a little bit?"

"Nuh-uh!" He looked sideways at her. "I've been thinking it might be better for me to go live with my dad for a while."

"Really?" she answered casually. She could tell he was floating a big idea and was trying to be careful. And she knew why. "Your mom's not going to be too happy about that."

He rolled his eyes. "Tell me about it."

"What do you think will be different if you go live with your dad?"

"He's not like my mother. He doesn't have to control me twenty-four/seven. I'll be able to go to church."

"So it's not Clear View, specifically?"

"Well, I'll find another church with my same values. I wanna commit myself to something. I wanna get baptized. I know I need the Lord's strength to make it in this life. Plus, my dad. You and Nick are cool, a-ight, but I need . . ."

"A foundation."

"Yeah!"

He was so earnest. "I know how you feel. When I read that letter her grandmother wrote about giving me up for adoption because my father was black—"

"That's why they did it?"

"You didn't know that?"

Will shook his head. "See. I try to tell her that stuff like this happens all the time. Wonder what they'd think about me?"

"Good question."

"So you think it's a good idea for me to go live with my father?"

"I don't know. That's for you and your parents to decide. But I understand how you feel."

"Will you tell my mom that?"

"You need to tell her," Billie said. "Just say to her what you said to me."

"She doesn't hear it. If you think the Bible is beautiful, why aren't you a Christian?"

"I said I like *parts* of the Bible. There are other parts I don't like."

"Like what?"

"First of all, the Bible was written by men—"

"From what God told them."

"The Bible was written by men," she repeated, in full teacher mode. "Men who, because they were of their time and place, wrote from a perspective that I can't always get with. And, in addition, we can't be sure that what we think is the Bible now is actually what was written so long ago. There's a lot that was left out of the book for political reasons from the very beginning. And, on top of that, what was left *in* got translated from other languages. Jesus and what was written about him in the Bible are fascinating and moving, but there's so much more about him than most people know. Did you know he wasn't even born in December?"

"Whaddya mean?"

"Jesus was born in the springtime. The early Christians celebrated his birth in December because it was illegal and it was easier to hide their celebration around the celebration of the winter solstice. And did you know that Christians didn't even celebrate his birth for hundreds of years because they thought he was coming right back and the end times were imminent?"

Will looked confused and suspicious. "How do you know all this?"

"I studied religion in college."

"*You did?*"

"My degree is in early childhood education, but yes." She laughed. "Oh Will, Nephew, the world is so big." It was the first time she had called him that, and it felt good. She had a nephew. "There's so much to know. All I'm saying is, don't cut yourself off from it. You're too young to close yourself down this way."

She looked at her watch. They still had some time before Trish got off work. "Come on, I want to show you something."

"What?"

"Just come on."

She took Will to her parents' house.

"Mommy? Daddy? Anybody home?" she called after she let herself in. They waited in the Spanish-tiled foyer.

"Big house," Will murmured.

"My, isn't this a surprise?" Zenobia said, walking down the hallway from the kitchen. "My Lord," she said, looking at Will. She turned to Billie. "He looks like your child!"

Will shook her hand.

"Are you all here for dinner?"

"No, I want to show Will Daddy's office."

"Ah. He's in there. Has a baseball game on."

Billie nodded her head down the hallway and Will followed her. Herbert was sitting on the loveseat with his feet up on an ottoman watching a game. "Hiya, Pumpkin!"

"Daddy, this is my nephew, Will."

Herbert used the remote to put the TV on mute. "Hello, young man."

"Nice to meet you, sir," Will said politely.

"Daddy, can you show Will around your office?"

Herbert jumped up. The only thing he liked more than baseball was a teachable moment. He pointed at one of the pictures that lined the walls. "Do you know who that is?"

Will shook his head.

"Jackie Robinson. He integrated baseball. Before that he was in the Army and actually got court-martialed for standing up for the rights of black folks."

Will leaned in to stare at the photo. "Really?"

"Really."

"Tell him why you like Jackie Robinson so much," Billie said.

"He was cool as a cucumber," Herbert said.

"When Daddy was made dean, some of the alums and professors complained. One of their largest donors stopped giving money to the school. But he didn't let that stop him."

"We never can," Herbert said.

"I know who that is," Will said, pointing at a framed newspaper story about Tiger Woods.

"Yeah, Mommy was pissed when he claimed he was Cablinasian or whatever, but Daddy ain't mad at him," Billie said.

"What do you say you are?" Will asked.

"African American," she answered without hesitation.

"I used to say I was biracial. But now. . . ."

"One time some girls at Sunday school were calling me an oreo. See, when I was young we went to private school but we went to an all-black church. I 'talked white' and was light-skinned so they used to pick on me. I told Daddy."

"I don't remember this," Herbert said.

"We were in this room. You said, 'Do you think you're an oreo?' I said no. So you said, 'Then why do you care what those girls think?' "

This was the first time Billie had thought about that conversation in a long time. "It helped, what you said."

Herbert smiled with pleasure.

"But if you're part white—" Will asked.

"In this country, there's no middle ground."

"So I have to choose?"

"It's not about choice. The world is always going to see you and treat you as a black man. That's all there is to it. But there's nothing wrong with that! That's what I want you to know. That's why I brought you here. To be black is a beautiful, wonderful thing. You have a legacy to be very proud of."

Will held his hands up in surrender. "Okay, okay! I get it! I'm proud! I'm black!"

"I don't mean to come on too strong," Billie said with a laugh.

Will pointed to a certificate on the wall. "What's this?"

"That's an award for leadership the church gave me the last Men's Day."

"You go to church?"

Herbert glanced quickly at Billie before he answered. "I hear you do too?"

"Yes, sir."

"Good for you," Herbert said.

Will turned to Billie, confused. "So are you for church or against it then?"

"Neither one. I'm for you finding what works for you."

"Being a Christian works for me."

Zenobia poked her head in the doorway. "Poopsie, dinner just arrived. Billie, are you sure you won't join us? We have more than enough."

"No, I'd better call Trish and tell her I'm bringing Will home."

Will pulled out his cell. "I'll call her, but can we come back sometime?"

"Sure," Billie said.

"How'd I do?" Herbert whispered.

"Home run," Billie said, kissing her father's cheek.

Billie was downstairs in the laundry room folding clothes. A load of darks, things of hers and things of Nick's. She put one of his shirts to her face and inhaled the fresh smell. She used unscented, biodegradable detergent so the scent wasn't perfumey, just clean. Had she ever been any happier? Could life be any better than this?

She folded the shirt, stuck it on top of the stack in the wicker basket, and went upstairs to the bedroom to put the clothes away.

"Hey," Nick said nervously, quickly putting his hands behind his back.

"What's up?"

"Nothing." He surreptitiously slipped something into his sock drawer. "Just getting ready to go."

Tonight was his night to deejay on KUVO. He kissed her on the cheek. "What can I bring you from the great wide world?"

"I'm good."

"No pickles and ice cream?"

She shook her head. "Please, no."

He grinned that old Nick grin that she had loved. "All right. I'll see you soon. You going to listen?"

"Of course."

After he left, she kept wondering about what was in his drawer. She didn't have any of his socks in the wash so there was no reason to open his top drawer. It was probably nothing, anyway. Why stir up trouble when everything was finally, *finally*, going so well? She finished putting things away and took another load of dirty clothes downstairs.

Later, in the kitchen she turned on the radio and Nick's voice poured into the room.

"Good evening. Welcome to the Nick Campbell Hour. First up is a song for Billie. As Stevie Wonder said, 'Don't you worry 'bout a thing.' I'm gonna play 'Acknowledgment,' Part One of 'A Love Supreme.' "

Coltrane's tenor sax wailed, then the famous bass line played and the piano joined in. *Don't worry 'bout a thing.* Billie's mind went back to the sock drawer. She went over all the odd questions about his mail. How he'd been so upset when he found her downstairs among his things. She had to know.

She followed her questions back to the bedroom. Underneath a row of white sweat socks she found a square envelope addressed to Nick. She opened it. It was a graduation announcement for Nick Campbell III. Nick was Nick Campbell, Jr. Who was Nick Campbell III? Whoever he was he was graduating from a high school in Oakland, where Nick used to live, where he had just been for his father's funeral.

She sat on the bed and reread the announcement, certain that she had made some kind of mistake. But no. Nick seemed to have a child, a son.

This was crazy. How could Nick have a son? How could he have a son old enough to be graduating high school? Billie was stuck in a nightmare, but no matter how much she shook her head she couldn't wake up. She raced back to the kitchen and turned off the radio. *Don't worry 'bout a thing.*

She went to the living room and paced back and forth. Her Taurus energy was building strongly. He'd called *her* a liar when she told him she thought she'd be safe without the diaphragm. How was she going to wait hours until Nick returned? Maybe she didn't have to wait. The station was in Five Points, only a few minutes away.

The thought had no more entered her mind than she was slipping on her flip-flops and heading for the door.

Someone buzzed her in to the station and she headed back to where she knew Nick was recording. Through a window, she could see him standing behind the board speaking into the mic. She waited a few seconds until the on-air light above the door went out, then banged on the door.

He rushed over and opened it. "What's wrong?"

"What is this?" She held up the announcement.

"I don't know. What?" He sounded confused.

"It's a graduation announcement for somebody named after you."

"You went through my drawer?"

She was so angry she thought she would ignite from the heat inside her. "What. Is. This?"

"You just told me, so what is there to say?"

The list of things she wanted him to say was as long as her arm, but the list of things she *didn't* want him to say was even longer. "For starters, why didn't you tell me?"

"I was going to tell you, but then you got pregnant too. I should have—"

"You're a father?"

Nick nodded. "I saw him for the first time when I was home for the funeral."

"What do you mean for the first time? You didn't know about him?"

"Raynelle and I split up when she was pregnant."

"Is that when you moved to Denver? While she was pregnant?" Billie whispered, her hand on her belly. "You left a woman and a baby? And you called me a liar!"

"I didn't mean to hurt you."

That's what he'd said about her parents when she found out she was adopted and had a birth sister she never knew about. He had known then as he held her in his arms that he was lying to her too, that just as Trish had been a secret to her so was Nick Campbell III.

The fury of the bull was completely unleashed. She had so much adrenaline shooting through her veins she was going to have to fight and flee and then come back and fight some more to even begin to release it. "Before you left her, did you live in her basement too? Did you scrounge off her family?" *Did you tell her that you loved her?*

"Billie, don't. . . . It's not like that."

He had told her that he wasn't the man she thought he was and she had *argued* with him. *Lord help me,* she thought, *I disagreed with him.* Well, that stopped right now. "You were right Nick, absolutely right. You're not the man I thought you were."

"Let me explain." He glanced back at the board behind him. "You know I can't talk while I'm on the air."

"Now you want to talk?" she muttered, shaking her head. "It's too late." She rushed back to her car. She drove south on Downing for miles past their house before she realized she didn't know where she was going. She couldn't go to her parents. She couldn't face Zenobia and Herbert. Jimmy was out of town. She eased her

Toyota onto the highway, which would take her to Aurora, where Trish lived. Just as she was reaching for her cell to call her sister she remembered that it was plugged in to the charger in the bedroom.

She didn't remember the exact address, but she thought she could find it again. On the rare occasions she found herself out in the burbs, she always got a little turned around—the strip malls, quiet-colored houses, and cul-de-sacs looked the same to her. After a few wrong turns, she finally found herself on the right street in front of the house with all the dogs.

"Oh, hi!" Trish said when she opened her front door to find Billie there.

"Whoa." Billie fell back.

"What's wrong?"

"I just got a little dizzy. Give me a minute." She closed her eyes. "Breathe," she told herself. "Breathe."

"Come in!" Trish wrapped her arm around her and walked her into the family room.

Billie sat down on the sofa. She still felt light-headed.

"Should we call your doctor?"

"I just overdid it. Too much running around." *Too much truth about Nick.*

"Let me get you some water."

"Thanks."

Trish handed her a cold glass. "Has this happened before?"

Billie took a few sips. "No." Her head began to clear. "I'm okay."

"You don't look so good. Are you sure you're okay?"

Billie started to cry. "Actually, no." She told Trish what had happened.

Jigsaw put his head on Billie's knees and looked up at her with his wide-set eyes. His eyes said he knew about trouble. Billie rubbed his head. "This is something my cat doesn't do."

"He's usually skittish around people. But he likes you."

Billie petted him some more and he nudged his head against her leg. "I don't know how I'm going to face Nick tonight."

"Sleep here."

"I don't think so."

"Stay the night and maybe tomorrow morning things will seem different."

Billie arched to stretch the muscles in her lower back and rubbed her stomach. "Overnight we're going to go back in time and Nick's going to tell me about his son?"

"No, but after a good night's rest you'll be ready to talk to Nick, to hear what he has to say. I think you're too upset to see him now."

"I don't know. . . ."

"I totally insist. I'll call and leave a message to let Nick know where you are."

"Where's Will?"

"Bible study."

"Don't tell him anything about this."

"Of course not."

Billie followed Trish upstairs to the guest room.

Trish turned on the ceiling fan and Billie lay down on the bed. She was suddenly very tired, more tired than she'd been in a long time. She quickly went to sleep still dressed, stretched out on top of the covers.

That night she dreamed that she, Trish, and Will were being chased through the house by a serial killer. She was trying to save Trish and Will by barricading the door when she started bleeding from her vagina. She woke up breathing hard and sweating. She was having a miscarriage! She ran into the bathroom, almost tripping over Jigsaw, who had parked himself next to the bed. She pulled down her pants. There was no blood. Thank God! She sat on the toilet and cried. What was she going to do? What was she going to say to Nick?

It turned out that she had worried for nothing. The next morning when she went home, Nick was gone. She found a note on the dining room table that said simply "I'm sorry."

"In a report you'll see only on Channel Five, Sabrina Fisher talks to our own Zenobia Bailey-Cousins, her adopted daughter, and her daughter's birth sister," blond anchorman Dale Stevens announced into the camera. "It's a story of love, loss, race, and reunion."

"Here we go," Zenobia said.

Her parents and Trish and Will had gathered at Billie's house to watch the live broadcast of their story. Nick hadn't returned, and Billie hadn't heard from him.

Zenobia appeared on the television screen, sitting at her kitchen table flipping through a leather-bound album of brown-skinned folks. "The day we brought Billie home is engraved on my heart," she said.

Billie smiled at her mother, who was now dabbing her eyes.

"Mommy, don't start," Billie said, wiping a tear.

"You both have to stop," Trish said.

In a voice-over, Sabrina intoned importantly, "But Billie didn't know she was adopted. For this tale of two sisters has a dark heart."

Now the video showed Trish sitting at her own kitchen table with her own photo album filled with white faces, dogs rushing around her feet, wagging their tails and staring at the cameraman. "My grandparents told me my mother and sister died in a car accident," Trish said to the camera. "I was four and my immediate family was wiped out all at once. I don't think I ever felt safe again. I think after that I was always waiting for the other shoe to drop."

"Dear Lord," Billie said, her voice soft with commiseration.

What it would be like to have your whole immediate family taken from you in an instant and then find out that one of them was still out there? What would it be like to know that your own grandmother had lied to you about something so important?

On-screen Trish read from Maxine's letter, her voice shaking.

"It was in one of my grandmother's puzzle boxes," Trish said, wiping tears from her eyes. Then she explained how she kept finding puzzle pieces.

"She's going to get an Emmy for this story," Zenobia said, "an Emmy for my family's story and I'm being put out to pasture."

"Poopsie, hush," Herbert said tenderly.

Next on-screen, Trish was walking up the sidewalk to Billie's house.

"I don't believe it! Look!" Billie yelled.

On the television, there was Fletcher in the background across the street in his yard, watching the film crew in disguise in dark glasses and a hat.

"Well, Mommy, you sort of 'got him on the TV,' " Billie said with a laugh, amazed that she found something to laugh at.

On-screen, Trish and Billie sat on Billie's porch with Sabrina.

"What did you think when this woman, this white woman, came to you and told you she was your sister?" Sabrina asked.

In the video, Billie smiled sheepishly. "I wasn't exactly happy about it at first."

Trish said, "Who could blame you?"

You could, Billie thought.

"But now?" Sabrina asked, in that faux sincere way of television journalists, as if it was the world's most burning question.

"Now, I guess we'll see."

The screen showed Billie and Trish talking on the porch as

Sabrina's voice-over ended the story. "Now the two sisters go forward, to work through personal and societal history, hoping to finally put together the pieces of the puzzle."

It was over. And it wasn't bad. Will and Herbert applauded. Billie and Trish stared at each other. Everything about their story was public now. Trish reached over and squeezed Billie's hand, and Billie squeezed back.

"Wow, powerful stuff," the blond anchorman said to his twenty-something female coanchor.

Billie was looking for the remote to turn off the TV when the female coanchor said perkily, "Next up, in another exclusive, the pastor of Clear View Church and his staff face charges of fraud."

Everyone froze.

"You didn't know about this?" Billie asked her mother.

Zenobia shook her head.

They waited anxiously while the station went to a commercial break.

Will looked like he had lost Santa Claus, the Easter Bunny, his first love, and his best friend all at once. "Oh, Buddy," Trish said. "I'm sorry—"

"We don't know anything yet," he said. "We don't know. We don't know."

But then soon enough the news was back on and they did know. The story unfolded like a cheap paperback, full of theft and deceit allegedly involving all the top officers of the church.

When the report was over, Billie clicked off the TV.

"They were stealing people's houses," Will repeated in shock. "Old people. Poor people. Taking their life insurance. Pastor Bob has two fucking Rolls-Royces."

Nobody scolded his language.

"Reverend Eubanks has a Caddy and a Hummer."

"I knew it!" Trish exploded angrily. "I knew something wasn't right about that church!"

Will's eyes were full. He grabbed his backpack and headed for the door.

"Oh, I'm so sorry, Will," Trish said, following him.

He didn't turn around.

"Will?"

He went through the door, down the stairs, and jogged down the street.

"Where's he going?"

"Give him some space," Billie said.

Trish shook her head. "He didn't even cry when we told him we were getting a divorce. Or at least not that he let us see. This is really bad."

"Men don't like crying in front of people," Herbert said kindly.

"I shouldn't have said 'I knew it,' but it just popped out. It was like rubbing his nose in it. What a fucking disaster. I could kill those bastards!"

Trish called him on his phone, but he didn't answer it.

"He'll be okay," Billie said. "Let him have a little time to sort things through."

"I don't know what to do. I should go home. I should be there when he gets home. But what if he comes back here?"

"I'll bring him straight home."

"If he calls—"

"I'll tell him to call you. I promise."

CHAPTER 19

~~~~~~~~~~~

Trish

Trish sped home and charged through the garage into the kitchen. "Will! Will, are you here?"

The dogs ran around and barked in glee that she was home. She ran up the stairs and all of them except Skipper raced behind her.

It was crazy to think that Will would beat her home, but she had to look. She threw open the door to his bedroom. Of course it was dark and empty. Her chest threatened to crack open at the sight of Henrietta, the stuffed snake coiled on his pillow.

The dogs panted and wagged their tails. "Guys, I think I fucked up big-time." She called him. Straight to voice mail again. "Okay, so he doesn't want to talk right now. Maybe Billie is right." She checked the time. It was 6:30. If he wasn't home in an hour, she'd call again.

It was the longest fucking hour of her life. Every second

ticked by like it was dragging a two-ton boulder behind it. At 7:30 she was standing on the sidewalk outside the house looking up and down the street, acid bubbling in her stomach, sweat making her bra and T-shirt sticky against her skin. No Will. She called his number again. "Will, call me, okay? I'm totally freaking out."

She called Billie.

"How is he?" Billie answered.

Trish gulped. "So that means he's not there."

"It's only been a little over an hour," Billie said soothingly.

"I don't even know how much money he had on him. What if he doesn't have enough to get home?"

"He'll call you if he needs a ride. What about his friends?"

Who would Will call? Josh used to be his best friend, but he hadn't talked to him since he had joined that freaking church.

"Maybe his girl, Makeesha?"

"Yeah. Yeah. Makeesha. I'll try her."

"Let me know when you hear from him, okay? And take some deep cleansing breaths."

Trish ran into the house, looked on the family room phone's caller ID, and found Makeesha's number. She dialed and it rang and rang. Finally on the sixth ring a breathy girl's voice said hello.

"Oh, thank God! Makeesha, have you seen Will?"

"Who is this?"

"His mother. Have you seen him?"

"Oh, I'm sorry Mrs. Taylor. But I haven't seen him. Why are you looking for him? What's wrong?"

"You haven't heard about your pastor?"

"Yes, but nothing's been proven. These are just things that people are saying because they don't like what our church stands for."

Was she insane?

"Besides, only God is perfect, so if Pastor Bob did get tempted, this is only a test of faith for our church to stay on the right path."

She *was* insane. "Makeesha, if you hear from Will tell him to call home, okay?"

"Yes, ma'am."

Trish hung up the phone. *Please God, who I don't even believe in, don't let Will call that girl and get sucked deeper into this bullshit. A test of faith?!*

She called his cell phone again and left another message saying she was out looking for him and for him to call her on her cell. She left a note on the kitchen counter and dashed back to her car to go back to Billie's neighborhood.

It was getting dark. Will was a big boy, not a little kid, but still her heart skittered around in her chest at the idea of him out somewhere by himself when he was wounded enough to cry. She massaged her sternum. For the first time in a long time, acid had backed up into her chest. She drove slowly up and down the streets of Billie's neighborhood, feeling oppressed by the downtown skyscrapers she could see through the rows of brick houses and old trees, much taller than the ones in the suburb in which she lived. The urban landscape that looked hip and cool during the day felt menacing as night fell. Even though some blocks were made up of Victorian mansions with wrought-iron fences around the lots and expensive cars with ski racks on their roofs parked in front, there was enough graffiti, trash in the gutters, and men hanging out on stoops and corners that she could tell this was not a good place for a kid to be alone. *He could get shot in a drive-by or beat up by drug dealers,* she thought as she drove by City Park. She didn't like feeling this way, but it was true. They didn't have gang wars in her neighborhood. She called home and Will's cell every fifteen minutes. By nine o'clock the sky was like ink. Will had never pulled a stunt like this. Never. Not even when he was little and got in trouble. He had always been a good boy. Always worried about her feelings. Trish pulled the car over and tried home and Will's phone one more time. When she got no answer, she snapped her phone closed and put her head on her steering wheel. *Where the hell was he?*

She was just about to restart the car when her phone rang. Her heart jumped like a retriever ready to play fetch. "Will?"

"Mama?"

"Jes—" she caught herself before she took the Lord's name in vain and alienated her son forever. "Where are you? I've been losing my shit! You wanna give me a heart attack?"

"I have something to tell you."

She sucked in her breath. "Where are you? I'll come get you."

"I'm getting ready to go to Charlotte."

"What?!"

"I'm at the bus station. The bus is about to leave. I talked to Dad. I just wanted you to know."

"You stay exactly where you are, do you understand me? I'm on my way to pick you up."

"I gotta go. The bus is leaving."

"Will, don't you—"

"I'll call when I get there. Don't worry."

"Will!"

"Bye, Mama." The line went dead.

She called his phone back, but of course he didn't answer. She dialed Tommy.

"What the fuck?!" she screamed when he answered.

"Trish, calm down."

"Calm down?! My son is on a bus going across the country by himself. Does he even have any money?"

"He has money. He'll be okay."

"Did you talk him into this?"

"No! He called me all upset and said he needed to get outta Dodge. He told me about what happened at his church. He's humiliated, Trish. You were right and he was wrong. He needed to get away."

She tried to collect herself. "How long is he . . . are you planning on him staying?"

When Tommy didn't answer right away, Trish knew something was wrong. "Tommy, you better start talking or I'm going straight to the airport and I'm going to get on a plane so fast—"

"We thought it might be a good idea for him to stay the school year."

"No fucking way!"

"Trish, Tamia and I are getting married. Right before Christmas. Will can be here for the wedding. I asked him to be my best man."

"Okay, so fine. I'll fly him down for your wedding." She didn't add, *to the bitch from hell.*

"It's done."

"Like hell!"

Tommy sighed and Trish wanted to reach through the phone and smash his face in.

"We have joint custody," he said bluntly. "Will is sixteen and coming here by his own choice. You want to sue me? I'll take my chances in court on that one."

She had never hated her ex more than she did right that second. "Fuck you, Tommy."

"I'll call you when he gets here."

She closed the phone with a loud click and threw it on the passenger seat, raising a small cloud of dust and dog hair. "Fuck! Fuck! Fuck!" She punched the steering wheel.

The phone rang again.

Will had come to his senses! She picked it up breathlessly. "Will?"

"It's Billie. And I guess you just answered my question. Still no word from him?"

Trish opened her mouth to answer, but the sound that came out sounded more like a mournful hound baying at the moon.

"It's okay. I'm sure he's just—"

"No!" Trish sobbed, desperately sucking air between each word. "He's. On. His. Way. To. Charlotte!" She sobbed and gulped her way through the whole story.

"Where are you?"

"In. My. Car."

"But where?"

"Somewhere. By. City. Park."

"Come over. It'll be okay. We'll figure it out. Just drive slowly and come back over."

"O. Kay."

CHAPTER 20

〜〜〜〜〜〜〜〜〜〜〜

Billie

Billie handed Trish a glass of cranberry juice with a slice of lime.

"Don't suppose you have anything stronger?" Trish asked with a grim smile. The blood vessels in her eyes had grown large and angry, and her hand trembled as she accepted the glass.

"No, that was Nick's department." Billie took a sip from her own glass of juice. She hadn't been feeling well since the day she had found out about Nick's child. She still couldn't believe he had packed up and taken off like that. As angry as she had been, she had never imagined that he could do something like that.

"We are one sorry-ass pair, aren't we?" Trish asked.

Billie set her glass on the coffee table and lit a fat lavender-scented candle. Nick had left. She still felt a little shaky from seeing her life on TV. And now this. They needed some calming up in here quick. "You still have your boy. He'll always be your son."

"Oh, you bet your ass I do. There's no way I'm letting him stay in North Carolina with Tommy and the woman he was fucking when he was married to me."

"Listen, I know this is painful, but maybe it's for the best."

Trish's face was swollen from crying. Now furious scarlet blotches bloomed on her cheeks, matching the birthmark already there.

"I mean just for a little while. I think Will needed this, no matter what happened with the church. He needs a father figure and with Nick who-knows-where, it makes sense that he would want his father."

"But . . . how could you say he should *leave* me?"

"Will told me he was thinking it might be a good idea for him to go live with his father for a while."

"And you didn't tell me?" Trish breathed.

"He said he was going to talk to you about it."

Trish set her untouched juice on the coffee table and folded her arms. "Exactly when did you and my son discuss all this?"

"The day I took him to visit my father. We were talking about faith and what it's like having your world rocked. I told him how I felt when I saw that letter from your grandmother and—"

"Wait. You told Will why they put you up for adoption?" Trish asked.

"I didn't know you hadn't."

Trish stood up. "Oh, fucking hell. You knew he was confused about stuff like this! I can't believe you. After I was there for you when you found out about Nick. You're *my* sister, not just Will's aunt. You're supposed to be on my side."

"Your side? When did this get to be about sides?"

"When Will told you all this, what did you tell him? Did you tell him he should go?"

"No. But I told him I understood how he could be confused about his identity."

"What the fuck am I supposed to do without my son? We just got here. He hasn't even really given it a chance. I can't move back to Charlotte. I never knew my dad, and the last thing on earth I would have ever thought is that my son would be without his dad. But I also lost my mother. . . . I don't want that for him either. I want—"

"I thought being a parent meant it wasn't about what *you* want anymore? It's supposed to be about what's right for your child."

Trish glared at Billie. "You wait until you pop that kid out and then tell me I should let my kid go away!"

"Don't take this out on me. All I did was empathize with a boy, almost a man actually, who's very confused about who he is. He got treated like a black man and he didn't know what to do, how to handle that. I'm sorry, but that's not something you can help him with."

"Cut the lecture about what a stupid white girl I am. I'm so over the whole subject."

Now Billie's hackles were up. Her long hair had come undone and her loose curls bounced wildly around her face. "You're the one who married a black man and had a son with him. This is what comes with it. Deal."

"Where is this coming from? Is it because of the letter?"

"Hell, yes! Why should I claim them when they didn't claim me?"

"What about claiming me? Where does that leave me with Will? He's not a part of me at all? Doesn't biology have anything to do with it?"

"It has *everything* to do with it. In this country one drop of black blood means you're black."

"But I'm not the one who gave you away. They kept me, but gave you up. But *it wasn't me*. I hate our grandparents for what they did."

"Don't call those people my grandparents," Billie snapped. "My grandparents were Mr. and Mrs. Cousins and Mr. and Mrs. Bailey."

"And so were Maxine and John Kuepper! Even though they fucked it up royally, they are your blood and so am I! So can you just stop playing the race card?"

"No, you didn't just say that!"

"Yes I did. You act like it's a big fucking contest. All of us get beat up by life sometimes, not just black people. My husband, my *black* husband, I might add, cheated on me. I'm white and I'm a victim, so put that in your pipe and smoke it!"

Billie thought of Cecilia and all the white girls she went to high school with, of being called a nigger at the drop of a hat. She thought of her parents and the racist bullshit they'd swallowed to get ahead. There were actually death threats against Zenobia the first few months she was an anchor. She thought of the ancestors, who she knew at this moment she was still a part of no matter what, who had been stolen from their homes, sold away from their families, beaten, tortured, cheated, raped, and murdered. Their anger was her anger. Their wounds were her wounds. Her hands went on her hips and this time, she let loose. "You are outta your fuckin' mind if you really think that your ole funky husband sleeping around on you is anywhere near the same as four hundred years of oppression!"

"Grrr!" Trish growled with frustration.

"Let me ask you this: what did you think when those security guards handcuffed your son but not the other boys?"

"That it was unfair!"

"Unfair? Unfair? Unfair is when you get picked last for dodge-ball because none of the kids like the way you dress. What happened to your son was so much deeper than unfair!"

"Okay, you win! You win! You get to be the most abused and the most loved at the same time. Happy?"

"Most loved?! I'm supposed to be happy now? The Klan ain't burning a cross in my yard, so I'm supposed to be happy?"

"Face it, mixed-race people are the hottest thing going! Barack Obama, Halle Berry, Alicia Keys! What have you got to complain about? How has your life been so bad? Hell, your parents were better than the ones who raised me! I already told you I was jealous."

"That's right! And I saw what it cost them to do everything they did for me. It damn sure wasn't for free. And if you think that Obama or any of them or me don't have to pay a price, you've lost your natural mind. All that talk about 'transcending race'! Jesus Christ! You don't remember the death threats? The man has to have extra Secret Service protection! Didn't you see the shirts with his name and pictures of monkeys on them? Don't you remember how many white folks refused to vote for the man simply because he's black?"

"God, you don't even hug me. You ug me."

"*What?*"

Trish grabbed two handfuls of her hair. "Are you *ever* going to stop being so goddamn worried about skin color and just be my sister?"

Billie stood up. "That's what I was trying to do!" Forget Trish with her neediness and incessant whining. Forget the blood between them. She was just like her damn grandparents. Their betrayal roared back from the place she had tried to hide it from herself, and with it came hurt from bone memory. She suddenly wondered how many millions of black folks had felt the same way she did every single day and tried to pretend like they didn't. Because who wants to be mad all the damn time? Who wants to let stupid people get to them? Family unity be damned. She stood up with every intention of telling Trish to get out, but her anger was replaced suddenly with panic at the strange sensation she felt. It was something she hadn't felt in months. Something that shouldn't be there. Heavy dampness between her legs.

"What's wrong?" Trish asked, her eyes anxiously searching Billie's face.

Billie didn't answer. She rushed to the bathroom and closed the door. Her breath came shallowly, and her heart was ping-ponging against her breastbone.

Please God. Please God.

She pulled down her jeans and underwear and saw it, bright red, the color of warning lights and stop signs. Blood. "No, no, no." She began to sob.

Trish knocked on the door. "Are you okay?"

Billie sank to the floor.

"Billie?" Trish cracked open the door and peeked inside. "Oh, no! Oh shit! We have to get you to the hospital."

The ER waiting room was cruelly filled with mothers and children. But Billie tried to keep calm. Lots of women spotted early in pregnancy. Some blood didn't have to mean the end. She pushed away the memory of dreaming about miscarrying, and the way she'd been feeling off lately.

"You okay?" Trish asked her for the tenth time since they had arrived. "Can I get you anything?"

Billie smiled tightly and held up her hand. She couldn't talk. Talking would make her scared, and she couldn't be scared right now. She needed to stay positive. If she got upset, if she gave in to the waves of panic and sadness that wanted to drown her, she would lose everything. She needed to stay loose to counter the tightening she was beginning to feel in her pelvis. Billie knew how Will felt earlier when he kept saying "We don't know anything yet." Until they said the words, there was still hope. Right now there was still a chance. She took a deep breath. Then another. *Good. Calm. Easy.*

Finally a nurse called her name. She jumped up and followed her into the darkened exam room.

"You're having some spotting?"

Billie nodded. "I have lupus. Is this because of lupus?"

The nurse smiled kindly. She was a heavyset black woman, and when she smiled, her face added another chin to the two that were already there. "Baby, let's see what the doctor says. Just relax." The nurse took her blood pressure and her temperature and drew blood, all the while Billie kept herself from screaming *Just tell me if I'm losing my baby!*

"Here." The nurse handed her a long paper blanket. "You can keep your top on, but take off everything below the waist. The doctor will be in in a few minutes, okay?"

After the nurse left, Billie took off her jeans and her underwear—there was a crimson streak in the middle of the sanitary pad—laid the paper over her legs and sat on more paper covering the table. Cold, stale air blasted her from the vent above.

The doctor came in, a white guy. He looked like he was eighteen years old in his little tie and white coat. His face was flushed pink, and his shaggy brown bangs were too long.

Billie wondered how many pregnant women he had ever seen. How many of them were losing their babies?

"I'm Dr. Summer," he said, extending his hand. Billie shook it, thinking how crazy it was to be shaking someone's hand when the world was coming to an end.

"How are you?" he asked, shaking his hair out of his eyes.

"Scared."

"Well, try to hang in there and let's see what's going on. When was your last ultrasound?"

She couldn't think. "I can't remember. A month ago? I'm supposed to have another appointment this week. I'm supposed to hear the heartbeat."

"Can you lie back? I'm going to do a couple of things. Take some pictures from the top and then we're going to do a vaginal ultrasound as well."

Billie lowered herself onto the table, shivering. The room was freezing.

The doctor spread cold goop on her belly, pulled the computer cart around, waved the magic wand over her, and started clicking the keyboard, just like Dr. Fernandez had done last time.

"It's really cold in here." Billie's whole body shivered.

"I'm sorry." *Click, click, click.* "We're almost there."

She closed her eyes and said the tiniest of prayers, just *Please.*

"Okay. Now this part is kind of awkward." Dr. Summer pulled out what looked a lot like the sex toys she and Trish had giggled over. "I'm going to ask you to insert this into your vagina. If you like, I can call for a female nurse or tech to be present while we do this part of the exam."

Billie didn't want to wait. She bent her knees, opened her quaking legs, and inserted the probe.

"Now, I need you to be still for just a few seconds, okay?" he asked gently. He was good at this; maybe he wasn't as young as he looked. Or, she thought, with a catch in her throat, maybe he had been raised by a good mother.

"I really have to use the bathroom," Billie said to the ceiling. They had made her drink glasses of water so her bladder would be full for this internal exam.

"I know this is uncomfortable. Just hang in with me for a little bit, okay?"

There was no sound but the clicking of the computer keyboard.

"Okay, we're all done. Why don't you get dressed, use the restroom, and we can talk in a minute."

Billie wanted to say just tell me now, and she wanted to never hear the results at all. The doctor left and she hurriedly pulled her jeans on and ran to the bathroom. She relieved herself, washed her hands, and dressed. The bleeding hadn't stopped, but it seemed no heavier than earlier. *Please let that be a good sign.*

But back in the exam room, the fluorescent lights were on, and she could tell by the look on Dr. Summer's face that it was over. She slid down into a chair.

"Ms. Cousins, these measurements show a fetal sac that's only eight weeks."

Relief washed over her. "So, we just estimated wrong?" Her mind was too scrambled to do the math, but she clung to the idea that somehow she wasn't as far along as she had thought. Bleeding that early in a pregnancy would be less dangerous. This could all just be some weird mistake.

Dr. Summer sat on the little wheeled stool again, took Billie's hand, and looked directly into her eyes. "I'm sorry, but the pregnancy stopped around four weeks ago. It's just taken your body a while to release it. That happens sometimes."

He kept looking at her and saying things, but Billie didn't hear a word. It was like she was underwater. She was trying hard to figure out what was going on, trying to remember how to use her words. That's what she always told her students: use your words.

"I'm really sorry," the doctor was saying when Billie was able to hear again.

"But no. That can't be. I saw it flicker, the baby's heart. It was a hummingbird."

"I'm sorry. But there's no longer a heartbeat. Like I said, the pregnancy ended about four weeks ago. Probably very soon after your ultrasound."

The pregnancy had stopped. She wasn't pregnant anymore. Ambata was dead. Had been dead inside her for four weeks. "But my lupus is still in remission," she murmured. "What did I do? How did this happen?"

"We'll see if your blood work shows any increase in antibodies, but it may not have anything to do with your condition. Miscarriage is actually pretty common. Most women go on to have healthy pregnancies afterward."

"Most women."

Dr. Summer stood. "You'll want to think about whether you want a D and C or if you want to let things . . . progress naturally. Talk to your ob-gyn about it."

Naturally. "I want to go home," Billie said.

He stood. "Of course. Also, you might have a lupus flare-up now, between the stress and the changes in your body, so you should schedule an appointment with your rheumatologist."

"Will you turn the light back off?"

"Sure." He hit the light switch, leaving Billie in the dark.

CHAPTER 21

~~~~~~~

Trish

"You look like shit," Alicia said.

Trish looked at her, aghast. She didn't think Alicia's lady-like lips could form dirty words. "Since when do you cuss?" she asked, pouring herself a huge mug of coffee even though it was bad for her. It was seven a.m. and she had a long day ahead.

Alicia knew what had happened with Will and Billie. "There's no other word for how you look. You getting any sleep?"

"Sleep? What's sleep?" Trish hadn't been this sleep-deprived since Will was an infant.

"Why don't you take something?"

Trish yawned and slumped against the kitchen counter. "I can't. What if Will calls and I'm so drugged up I don't hear the phone?"

"*Mija*, why would Will be calling you in the middle of the night?"

"That's just the thing. I don't know. I don't know anything that's going on down there. There could be a fire or a burglary or anything and I wouldn't know it. I wouldn't be there to protect him."

Too chicken to talk to her, Will had sent her an email and a couple of text messages begging her to let him stay in North Carolina. As much as she wanted to hear his voice, Trish was kind of glad he hadn't called. She was so angry and hurt that she was sure she'd only do more damage if they talked right now.

"He's sixteen, not six. And he's with his father."

Trish groaned. "I can't do anything right lately. My son hates me. My sister hates me."

Alicia's dark eyes softened. "You know you didn't make your sister lose her baby. These things just happen. It's terrible, but it's true."

"You weren't there. It was ugly."

Alicia reached in her pocket and offered Trish a Hershey's Kiss.

Thanks to Billie, Trish had actually been able to cut back some on the sweets. She declined.

"Tums?" Alicia offered next.

Trish realized that even as upset as she felt right now the fire in her chest was extinguished. She shook her head.

Alicia held up two patient file folders. "You want the vomiting cat or the poodle that licks his testicles too much?"

"The ball-licker." It was probably just allergies. Trish would weigh the dog and take his temp. Then the doc would go in and look at his genitals and tell her to take some blood just in case and prescribe some cream and a special diet. She'd spend twenty minutes with the dog and the doc would spend five. Yet she'd only make about $6 for her time and the doctor would make about $40. Just one more thing about her life that sucked.

She entered one of the exam rooms. The client with the dog was pregnant, reminding her of her sister. Trish hadn't spoken to Billie since she had taken her to the hospital. Every time she picked up the phone to call, she hung up because she didn't know what to say.

She should have listened to Zenobia when she warned her that it wasn't a good idea for Billie to meet her while she was pregnant. If Trish had never barged into her life, she might still be pregnant. She couldn't stop hearing herself shouting at Billie. What could she say? *I'm sorry I yelled at you and made you lose your baby.* Sorry could never be enough.

Trish turned to the ball-licker. Poor boy. She willed herself to stop worrying about Will and Billie and to concentrate on work. The last patient of the day was a Lhasa apso named Serena, who was owned by Mrs. Clarkson, a small round barrel of a black woman who demanded the very best for her little Serena. Trish was unsure of Mrs. Clarkson's age, but the way she spoke and carried herself made Trish believe she was at least in her sixties, maybe even older. Serena was old too, thirteen, and had come in for her geriatric checkup and grooming session.

When Serena's exam was all done and she was washed, dried, brushed, and fluffed, they were at the front desk to check out.

"You want another case of the senior pet canned food?" Alicia asked Mrs. Clarkson.

"Someone will help me out?" Mrs. Clarkson asked, looking pointedly at Trish.

"You bet," Trish replied.

"Then yes and one of the five-pound bags of the dry food too."

When Trish came back from the supply room with the dog food, Mrs. Clarkson was waiting.

Donna, one of the women in the cleaning crew, had come in and she and Alicia were talking and laughing in Spanish.

Mrs. Clarkson rolled her eyes, and as soon as they were outside she said, "They're in America now. Why can't they speak American?"

Trish was exhausted, and normally she would want Mrs. Clarkson and Serena to be all loaded into their Chrysler Le Baron and on their way so she could go home and pass out, but the idea of being in the house all by herself depressed her, so she spoke to delay the inevitable. "I think most people do learn English after they come here."

"No, they don't," Mrs. Clarkson said, securing Serena into her doggie car seat. "Or why would they need all that 'dial one for English' mess? It's a shame! I never let my children speak anything but proper English—none of that Ebonics foolishness—and both my children are professionals."

Trish loaded the dog food into the trunk.

"These people won't get anywhere speaking that Mexican, and they want to take the rest of the country down with them!"

These people. Mrs. Clarkson sounded like her grandfather. Maybe Billie was right. Maybe there was no way to get past race in this country because here she was again. The thought made her queasy, but instead of ignoring the remark or changing the subject she decided that Billie might also be right about talking about it.

"I don't mean to be disrespectful, but surely you have experienced racism?"

Mrs. Clarkson nodded somberly.

"Then how could you talk about people of another race like that?"

"Because, child, it's not remotely the same thing. My people were dragged here, beaten, and tortured, treated worse than animals. *They* sneak over here and take what they can, take jobs away from people born and raised here who still can't get ahead."

They, they, they! Trish was so sick of people dividing themselves that she wanted to throw her head back and howl at the moon. "There is no them, there's only us. Only one race. The human race."

Mrs. Clarkson opened her car door and climbed inside. "You keep thinking that," she said and drove away.

I will, Trish thought. *I will keep thinking that because that's our only hope.*

Later that night, after Trish had fed and walked the dogs, she retrieved her jigsaw puzzle from the drawer. She hadn't looked at it in weeks. She dumped all the pieces on the family room coffee table. Absentmindedly, she turned the pieces over, grouping them by color, as her grandmother had done and as she had seen Billie do. *This is what we do to ourselves,* she thought, *separate ourselves into our little groups.* She had tried so hard not to become like her grandparents. But was she really any different? She thought of how hurt Will had been because of those stupid security guards. Josh and Eric were wearing baggy jeans and hoodies and had probably been holding their dicks too. If Josh and Eric had been brown-skinned they would have been in handcuffs too.

After she had most of the puzzle sorted, she tried putting a few pieces together. On her third attempt, she was surprised when one piece snapped into place with another. A little later another few pieces fit together. She kept working, the whole time thinking about Will, Billie, Mrs. Clarkson, and her grandparents. Alicia was right: she hadn't found any more puzzle pieces since she and Billie had met. At four a.m. she was done. On the table was a complete picture of a litter of happy puppies lolling in grass.

"Hey, what do ya know?"

At the sound of her voice, Jigsaw's tail thumped against the carpet. "I guess you're keeping your name, aren't you?"

She couldn't deny what her grandparents had done and how it had affected her and Billie. All of that had come back to bite them in the butt. The only thing to do now was to decide where to go from here. Trish wasn't going to be a victim anymore. She didn't want to be someone who everybody left behind.

It was six a.m. in Charlotte. Will would be asleep, but she could leave a message on his cell. She hit number one on the speed dial and got Will's voice mail. "I love you," she said. "I will always love you no matter what you do. There's nothing you could do to ever change that. So if being with your father is what you need to do now, then I totally accept that. I just want you to be happy."

She hung up the phone and thought about how to help her sister. What could she do? She was beginning to see how a god might come in handy. Once you start thinking you're wrong about one thing, you can see how you might be wrong about everything else too. "Okay, God or whoever you are or might be. My son and my sister believe in you, and I believe in them, so I'll give this a shot. Please help me find something to say or do that can help Billie."

She sat quietly until something—God? Her own common sense?—told her to do what she knew how to do. She went to the computer, typed "miscarriage" into the search engine, and got more than six million hits. She narrowed her scope by adding "advice" to find ideas about how to help someone cope.

An article about how Japanese people grieve miscarried, aborted, or stillborn children caught her eye. Some Buddhists in Japan believe that life forms in primordial waters and that if a fetus or young child dies its soul simply goes back into those waters until it is reborn. Trish could see how it would comfort grieving parents to believe that their child wasn't gone forever. She read on and learned that these children even had a sort of patron saint who watched over them.

She was excited. She knew instinctively that Billie would like this idea. Pink early morning light was shining through the curtains when Trish stopped reading. She printed out the pages. She would take the article and one other thing to her sister.

CHAPTER 22

~~~~~~~

Billie

For a week she lay in bed—her stomach cramping, Ambata falling from her in clots—getting up only to change pads and wash herself. Each day she woke up feeling less pregnant. When she rolled over, her breasts felt a little lighter, her abdomen and pelvis less occupied.

Today, Billie felt morning tugging at her, but she couldn't wake up and for once she was grateful for fatigue. All she wanted to do was sleep. Sleep was a relief. When she was asleep she didn't have to think about all that she had lost. Though sometimes she dreamed of rivers of blood and someone in her dreams was always lost. She would wake up crying and even that wasn't as bad as being awake, because at least she could tell herself it was just a dream. When she was awake there was no such comfort.

Zenobia and Herbert tried to take care of her. They

brought treats from the health-food store: rich, garlicky hummus, organic strawberries, fresh-squeezed orange juice, and dark chocolate bars filled with lavender or blueberries, laying them on the end table next to her bed like mama and papa birds. Zenobia even made chicken soup in one of her virgin pots.

Billie couldn't take any of it. Food curdled in her stomach. The only thing she could handle was iced green tea, which Zenobia made for her by the gallon.

Jimmy, Yolanda, even Katie, her assistant teacher, had all stopped by. Their concern made it worse. Made her remember that she had brought this on herself, on Ambata. Because she had done everything wrong. This was her fault. She almost laughed when she thought about it. They had been worried about her body, but it was her spirit that had done her in. It wasn't her flesh that was weak, but her ego. You have to take responsibility for what and how you put things out into the universe. If you're not careful, if your intentions aren't one hundred percent clean and clear, wishes that you send out can get mixed up and land at your feet completely different than the way you planned.

Herbert marched into the room, opened the blinds, and cranked the windows open. "Billie, Pumpkin, why don't you get up and come out on the porch? It's a nice day out there."

She thought of the night she had told Nick she was pregnant. She had urged him to open the windows and let in the fresh air.

Herbert looked around. "What happened to your altar?"

"I didn't want it anymore."

"Why not?"

"Daddy, I'm tired. You're asking too many questions."

He sat on the bed and put the back of his hand against Billie's forehead. "You feel hot. Have you taken your temperature?"

Billie shook her head.

"How long have you had a fever? Do your joints hurt?"

Herbert knew the signs of a lupus flare-up as well as or better than Billie. After Billie was diagnosed, her parents had done so much research they could have written a book on the subject.

"Everything hurts," Billie answered, it just dawning on her that her joints *did* hurt. Her hands and wrists ached and were so weak she could barely hold a glass of tea or open or close the bathroom door. But that didn't matter.

"You need to go to the rheumatologist and get this under control before it gets worse."

How could things get any worse?

Zenobia walked in. "Poopsie, why don't you bring her some applesauce?"

Herbert left and Zenobia sat next to Billie. She leaned close to touch her forehead to Billie's. The scents of jasmine and sandalwood rose off Zenobia's skin. "I know how you feel. I've lost three children. I *know* how you feel, but your life is not over. You have to be strong now."

Billie started to cry. Her mother might understand the loss, but she couldn't know what it was like to do it to yourself. This pregnancy was doomed from the beginning. The way it happened was all wrong. You don't wish to bring a baby into this world with a father who doesn't want it. It was like the ancestors had warned: this is what happens when you try to control things that are not yours to control.

Zenobia hugged Billie. "It's okay to cry, baby. You go ahead and get it out, but you have to take care of yourself. You've barely eaten in days. I'm going to call Iseman and tell him you need to get back on your medication."

Billie pulled away. She took a tissue out of her pajama pocket and mopped her eyes. "No. I'm not taking that shit again." The steroids made her feel puffy and disgusting, and if she wasn't very careful they could make her blood sugar go up. The other drugs made her nauseous and even more sensitive to the sun. What kind of cures were these when they just made you feel a different kind of bad?

"Wilhelmina. . . ."

"I'm not. I won't put that toxic shit into my body."

"Then Dr. Wu? Will you go see her?"

Acupuncture hadn't stopped her from miscarrying. She had been so cocky. Just knew that everything she was doing was going to make her pregnancy go well. What was the point? Would it be so bad to slip away like her baby had done? "I just want to go back to sleep, Mommy. Can't you let me rest?"

Herbert returned with three ibuprofen, a glass of water, and a bowl of something. "Take these."

"Daddy," Billie whined.

"That wasn't a request."

Billie downed the red pills from her father's palm.

"Now, have some of this."

He handed her a dish of applesauce. He'd sprinkled a little cinnamon on top, the way he used to when she was a kid. Zenobia was always gone in the mornings before Billie and Jimmy woke, and it was Herbert who would make breakfast and get them ready for school.

Holding the bowl and spoon hurt her fingers, but the cool pureed fruit felt good in her mouth and reminded her of all those mornings with her father and brother. In spite of herself, she started to feel a little better.

Her parents waited until she finished.

"Good girl." Herbert kissed her on top of her head and took the bowl back to the kitchen.

Zenobia reached for her locket, but this time instead of pulling on the chain she opened it and leaned over to show Billie. Inside the golden heart were two small black-and-white photos of Billie and Jimmy as infants.

"I didn't carry you in my body, but I have carried you with me every day since the day we got you," Zenobia said, her usually strong voice cracking. "It breaks my heart that you lost your baby. But it would *kill* me if something happened to you. Do you understand me?"

Billie knew it was true and didn't want to cause her mother any more pain. She nodded, tears spilling over the rims of her eyes.

"Good." Zenobia closed her locket and pulled herself back together. "Then I'm making an appointment for you to see Dr. Wu. If you don't, I'll call Iseman. You hear me?"

Billie nodded again, rolled over, and went back to sleep.

She thought she was dreaming when she opened her eyes a little later and saw Nick sitting beside her on the bed.

"Baby," he said.

She closed her eyes. She didn't want the dream to be over. She had missed him so.

"I'm so sorry," he said, caressing her cheek.

At his touch, she jumped. She sat up, blinking her eyes in disbelief. "You're really here?"

He nodded.

She realized he had been touching the rash on her face. This was the first time in a long time that she'd had the telltale butterfly-shaped rash over the bridge of her nose, each cheek a wing. "The baby died."

"I know. I'm sorry."

"You didn't want him." Her voice was flint. She didn't want Nick's pity. Besides, it was a lie. There was plenty of blame to go around. She had screwed up, but Nick had too. He'd lied to her about having a child. He'd walked away when she needed him.

"I didn't want to fail him. Or you."

She eyed him warily. "How could you keep such a secret from me?"

Nick searched the wall behind her for an answer. "I don't know. I don't think I really knew what was going on. I saw myself in Will when I was a young dude. But when you found out, it hit me: I'm not that boy anymore. I'm grown. I don't have to act like I did when I was young and dumb. I'm a man."

Billie wasn't ready to stop being mad at him yet. "A man doesn't lie about having a child and sure doesn't leave him," she said with derision.

"I know. That's why I went back to Oakland."

Billie's mouth dropped open.

"I'm making things right with Nicky. As best I can."

Suddenly, Billie was frightened. She was livid at him for disappearing on her and the baby, but the idea of Nick being gone forever was something she hadn't allowed herself to really believe would happen. "You're moving back there?"

"I'm trying to get Nicky to visit on one of his breaks from school. He's going to college."

So while she had lost a child, Nick had gained one. All of a sudden she was exhausted again. Too tired to be relieved or angry. Too tired to feel anything.

Nick climbed into bed next to her, his back against the headboard and his long legs stretched out in front of him. He took her hand. He didn't speak, but she knew what he was saying. He was planning to stay. At one time she would have been so happy. Now? They certainly couldn't act like nothing had ever happened. Could they start over? Like so many things lately, that was a question Billie didn't have the answer to.

CHAPTER 23

~~~~~~~~~~~~~~~

Trish

The windows were open, and cool air wafted through the bedroom. *August in Denver was so beautiful it almost made the ferocious heat and dryness of July worth it,* Trish thought. Zenobia had let her in and told her that Billie's lupus had returned, although the rash on Billie's face would have told her all she needed to know.

Billie was sitting up in bed.

"I'm so sorry." It came out in a whisper. Trish cleared her throat and started again more forcefully. She wanted Billie to hear her. She wanted Billie to believe her. "I'm so, so sorry. I never in a million years would have done anything to cause you any pain, to cause this."

Billie looked mystified. "You thought this was your fault? It's not your fault. The pregnancy ended weeks ago."

"What do you mean?"

Billie explained what the doctor had told her. "It was over

before we argued. Before Nick left. You didn't do it. I did. This is my fault."

Here Trish had been blaming herself and Billie had been doing the same. How totally ridiculous it seemed now. What a waste of time. She could have been here at her sister's side since the day it had happened if she hadn't been so afraid that she was to blame.

She started to wonder what else she might have missed carrying a heart full of blame. Being so mad at Tommy and her grandparents. Being so mad at herself about the divorce and beating herself to a pulp believing that she was a bad mother.

She sat down on the bed next to Billie. "Did they say what caused it?"

"Just one of those things," she said bitterly. "But it was me. I should have never gotten pregnant."

"Oh, honey, you know what I think? I think shit just happens. Bad shit and good shit. To everybody. It's just life. How are you?"

"Sad," Billie said so simply that it pierced Trish's heart.

"I found something I think might help. Have you had any kind of service for the baby?"

For the first time since Trish arrived, Billie seemed to perk up. "Service?"

"A memorial. In Japan they believe in this Buddhist divinity called *Jizo* who protects and cares for children, especially ones who have been aborted or miscarried. Japanese parents do these ceremonies called *mizuko kuyo*.

"*Mizuko* means 'children of the waters.' The idea is that life happens on a continuum. A fetus isn't fully a baby, but it's more than just a clump of cells."

"What I lost was more than just a clump of cells."

"Exactly, and they honor that."

She handed Billie one of the articles she had printed out about the Jizo shrines where parents leave clothes, toys, candies, flowers, and other gifts for their "water children."

Billie read quickly, then set the article on the bed and looked out the window. After a time she took a deep breath, pulled back the covers, and eased off the bed. She looked like she was in great pain. She went to the dresser and brought back a crocheted baby cap. It was sea-foam green. "I made this for Ambata."

Trish rubbed her hand over the fabric. She imagined the small, soft head this hat was supposed to cradle and flashed on when Will was a newborn. What if she had never had him? "Ambata would have liked it."

Billie nodded, tears streaming down her cheeks.

Trish stood up next to her sister. "The next thing I want to give you is silly, I know, but I want you to have it."

Billie used her sleeve to dry her eyes. "A spoon?"

"From Vegas, of all places. Our mom gave it to me. It's tacky, but I guess it's what she had to give. When I was little I thought it was beautiful. I was going to give it to you when you came home from the hospital."

Billie's eyes grew large with acknowledgment, almost recognition, as if some part of her finally remembered the small girl who had held her close, whispering all the plans she had for them.

Yes, Trish thought. *It's me. Your sister.*

"It's lovely. Thank you."

"You know, I don't think we need a statue of Jizo to do like they do in the article."

"Give me a minute?"

Trish went back into the living room. "She's getting up."

Nick looked shocked. "What'd you say to her?"

She told him, Zenobia, and Herbert about the *mizuko kuyo* tradition.

A few minutes later, Billie came out dressed for the sun in a long-sleeved T-shirt and sweatpants. She was moving slowly. Trish's heart just about broke at the sight of the teensy hat in Billie's hands, and she noticed Zenobia's eyes well up.

Nick went to Billie and took her elbow to help her. "I'm so sorry," he said.

"I know. I want to have a service for Ambata," Billie said.

"Whatever you want," he answered.

"Let's go outside."

Billie collected her hat and shades, and they all went out the backdoor into the yard next to the koi pond.

It didn't seem like a day for a funeral. The sun was warm, the sky an optimistic, true blue, and above them the old tree stretched like a green canopy, blessing them with its shade.

Billie slowly crouched down, Nick helping her, until they both knelt in the grass. Trish, Zenobia, and Herbert stood behind them. Billie floated the tiny cap on the water, and the fish rose to the top of the pond to meet her.

For a few heartrending moments the trickling water of the pond filter and the sound of her own heart beating were the only sounds Trish heard. Then the cap grew heavy with water and sank to the bottom, and Billie released a low moan and started to slump. Nick held her, steadied her, and the next sound was Zenobia's voice.

"Father and Mother God, please watch over Ambata."

Father and Mother God? Trish had never heard anyone pray that way.

"We know that he or she is with you now and that there is no better place to be, but we miss this little baby. We miss all this baby was going to be."

Billie sobbed. Trish reached for Zenobia's hand, thinking the older woman would falter at her daughter's cries. Zenobia took her hand and squeezed it, but her voice stayed strong and even. They used to call Walter Cronkite "the voice of God," but Zenobia's voice, half lace and half steel, would be the one Trish would want to listen to for eternity.

"Father and Mother, please let Billie and Nick know in their deepest hearts that you have a plan for each of us, even if we don't always understand it. Because we don't understand this one, God. This one is hard for us.

"So please keep Billie and Nick close to you and send them comfort and peace in their hour of need. Send them courage and strength to know how to move forward from this."

Zenobia looked pointedly at Herbert.

Herbert put his hands on Nick's shoulders and bowed his head. "Thank you, God, for the blessing of family. As we grieve our losses, we don't want to ignore all that you have given us. I've been hard on Nick."

Nick put his head in his hands and his shoulders began to shake.

"Too hard. And I'm sorry for that. I want to thank you now for bringing Nick into this family."

Trish mopped her wet eyes, imagining what it'd feel like to have a fatherly hand on your shoulder at a time like this.

Herbert kept his hands on Nick's shoulders, but he turned to look at Trish.

"Thank you for uniting us with the rest of Billie's family. They are reminders that wonderful blessings can come from loss. Help us remember that now. Amen."

"Amen," Trish murmured, a simple word that could never express all that filled her. Being born like a star inside the galaxy of her heart was a new knowledge of what it meant to belong to a family.

The blessing hung in the air until the silence was broken by someone honking a car horn incessantly in front of the house.

"Well, I left my Kleenex in my bag," Zenobia said. "I suggest we go back inside before I start blowing my nose on my sleeve."

Everyone laughed harder than necessary, grateful for a break from their sorrow.

Nick stood and grasped Herbert quickly and awkwardly, patting him on the back.

Then Trish hugged Billie and Billie wrapped her arms around her sister and squeezed tight.

"That wasn't an ug!" Trish exclaimed.

"An ug?" Zenobia asked.

"Long story," Billie answered.

They all headed back to the house. Just as Trish was stepping into the house, Zenobia turned around to Trish and whispered, "Thank you."

"You're welcome," Trish mouthed back.

The night before Will came home, Trish had a dream. She was in the house she grew up in. Nana was there. Surprisingly, the TV wasn't on.

"Why aren't you watching TV?"

"Who has time for TV?" Nana said. "I've got things to do."

"Like what?"

"Life."

Nana picked up her jigsaw puzzle box like it was a purse, and kissed Trish on the cheek, right on her birthmark, something she hadn't done Trish's whole life. Then she walked out the door.

Trish woke up and immediately turned the TV off. She jumped out of bed, ran down to the family room, and went on the computer to send for brochures for Colorado State University and the University of Colorado. She was going to get her bachelor's degree and go to vet school. Maybe she'd be out by the time Alicia opened her clinic and they could be partners, or maybe she'd strike out on her own. Either way she was going to get a life. Time was short.

• • •

"You're so tall!" she exclaimed. It wasn't possible that Will had really grown in only a couple of weeks. But it also didn't seem likely that he was this grown-up before he left. Had she not noticed?

After he got her message, he called and agreed to come back home to talk about what would happen next. That morning, he cleaned the backyard and mowed the grass. Unasked.

"I'm only five-seven. Dad says he kept growing until he was nineteen."

"I'm sorry, Will. I'm sorry everything became such a mess. But you know your father and I did what we thought was the best thing. I can't take it back and make it right. It was what we needed to do. I tried living for other people and it doesn't work." She shrugged. "I'm glad we're not teaching you that living a lie is better than the truth, but ending our relationship totally had nothing to do with you—"

"I know. He cheated on you."

Trish's jaw dropped.

"He told me."

She flapped her mouth open and shut like a guppy, but no sound came out.

"He said he was sorry."

"Yeah, well. . . ." She nodded, then shook her head, trying to snap out of the shock. "Anyway. . . ."

"I'm sorry about everything too."

"Are you going to church down there?"

"Not yet. Have you heard anything more about Pastor Bob?"

"You really want to know?"

"Yeah. I need to hear it."

"He's missing. They think he's somewhere in South America."

"Pussy," Will spit.

"Language!" Trish tried not to let on that her heart gladdened. She hated the word, but at least he sounded more like the boy she remembered.

"Sorry," he said.

"More people have come forward. There's going to at least be a federal civil lawsuit. The attorney general is investigating, and there may be criminal charges."

"Reverend Eubanks?"

"Makeesha didn't tell you any of this?"

"I haven't talked to her."

"Well, he was fired, and he's cooperating with the attorney general."

"So he's telling the truth. That's good. Christ died for our sins, and if we repent we can be forgiven. I really do believe that."

He did. She could read his faith in his eyes. His belief wasn't a passing fad like popping his collar up or wearing his do-rag. "Listen, if you want to go to church, you should."

Will looked surprised and wary.

"I mean it. These guys are dicks—"

Will grinned and lifted his eyebrows.

"I know. But they are. Just like those guys at the mall. Don't let them take away something that means that much to you. If you didn't let *me* stop you, why let them?"

"You really won't care if I go to church?"

He had the same look on his face as he did when he was four and insisted on jumping into the deep end of their apartment complex swimming pool. After diving in to get him three times, Tommy warned him if he did it again he was going to sink or swim on his own. That stopped him for about a second. In he went and dog-paddled his way to the ledge with a big shit-eating grin. What had she been thinking, assuming that he didn't know what he wanted? Will had been born determined.

"Just be more careful this time. Let your dad check out the churches with you."

"Tamia wants me to visit her church."

"Ah."

"You're really letting me stay with Dad?"

"If that's what you want," she said even though she wasn't sure she was ready for that to be what he wanted.

"Not forever. Just until I figure some stuff out."

"I thought it would be easier than this. Especially for your generation. I thought by now, with so many interracial relationships and so many mixed people it would be no big deal. It really shouldn't be a big deal."

"For the most part for kids my age it ain't no thing. Nobody even trips about race. But the security guards made me feel different because of who I am, and they made me feel like I was worse than Josh and Eric."

"But you're not!"

"I know that. But not everybody does. And that's just a fact. So I thought I needed to be black, whatever that means. Seriously, are you black because of your skin color? Are you black because of how you talk or how you dress?"

"You're part of me and you're part of your dad, and no matter what label you decide to give yourself you'll always be part of both of us."

"Yeah, labels, Dude. I don't want one at all. I just wanna be me."

"So what's stopping you?" Trish smiled. It felt like things were almost back to normal. Yes, her son would be leaving to go back to live with his dad for a while, but they were back to a place where she was just a mom and he was just a kid and she could help. "Did I tell you I was going back to school?"

CHAPTER 24

～～～～～

Billie

"Pick whatever you want. We're here for you," Trish said. They were in Idaho Springs, in the Rocky Mountains about an hour west of Denver at a natural hot springs resort.

"I'm not an invalid," Billie protested. "I'm better, really."

She saw Dr. Wu three times a week. She drank raspberry leaf and nettle tea to help rebuild her strength and restore her system's balance. After only two weeks of the needles and Dr. Wu's herbs, she felt strong enough to start doing yoga again, slowly and just for ten minutes at a time, but it felt good to be up and about. And the rash on her face was disappearing.

"Just tell the nice lady whether you want to go in the caves or to a private bath," Trish insisted.

"You told me not to be so controlling, so I'm trying not to be controlling."

"But this time it's okay for you to choose. Just tell me your opinion."

"I don't care, really. Whatever you want. I'm too tired for this."

"You guys sound just like me and my sister," the woman said. "We can turn anything into a chance to argue."

Billie remembered telling Will the story of those girls who had picked on her as a child. How she thought she had learned not to care what other people think, but that wasn't true. She had cared that Fletcher would see a white girl coming to her house. She had worried about what her parents thought of Nick. She had even worried what Nick would think if the baby had come out paler than she. She had worried what Trish would think that she and Nick weren't married. Maybe it was time to truly learn her father's lesson and stop caring so much what other people thought.

"I know just what you mean," she said to the receptionist. "My sister here drives me a little crazy too."

The woman looked from Billie to Trish and back again, then rolled her eyes. "Well, no wonder. Let me make some suggestions? Cause if we wait around for two sisters to make up their minds, we'll be here all day."

There it was. No big crisis. Nothing racist. No questions. Just a minute to figure it out.

She and Trish were sisters, not just because they were born to the same woman. Just as lack of shared DNA didn't make Zenobia, Herbert, and Jimmy any less her family, sharing DNA wasn't what made Trish her sister. Trish had been there for her when she lost her baby. Trish brought her the comfort of knowing that Ambata was still out there somehow, still waiting to be born into this life either through Billie or through some other woman.

The receptionist suggested the caves and massages, and they agreed. They went down the stairs into the locker room. Billie started to undress.

"Okay, let's just get this out of the way," Trish said. "I'm fat. I know it. But I'm strong and I walk my dogs every day. And I have lost a little weight."

Billie was startled. "You're not fat!"

Trish snorted.

"Don't do that to yourself. You might be a little rounder than you want, but you're fine."

"I have stretch marks up the wazoo."

"You had a son." Billie said softly. "And, as you said, you're strong. You're healthy. Don't do that to yourself, okay?"

They locked eyes.

"Okay."

They undressed, stowed their things, wrapped towels around themselves, and went through a long hallway into the geothermal caves. Trish opened the door and a blast of moist heat hit Billie, immediately soothing her.

"Holy shit! This really is a cave," Trish whispered. She touched the hard rocky surface where walls should have been.

It was dark, like a womb, miner's lamps emitting just enough light for safety. The first sunken pool was occupied by a trio of older Japanese ladies.

By the time they reached the next pool, sweat was starting to bead on Billie's upper lip. She removed her towel and walked slowly down into the steaming black waters until it reached to her neck and cradled her body. There was no reflection but the light shining on top of the water. The water wasn't black itself. It just looked murky in the dark belly of the pool. But this water, filled with iron, calcium, magnesium, zinc, and other minerals, felt different, silkier than the water at home. Almost instantly her skin felt softer and she was beginning to feel the pain in her bones ease. Every cell in her body seemed to say "Ahh."

Trish followed her into the water. She had been in the sun a lot this summer; her arms and hands and face were about the same light brown as Billie's, while her torso was white as chalk. Her hay-colored hair was up in a loose ponytail, and with the flush in her cheeks she reminded Billie of a ripe peach.

Billie wished she could make Trish see herself as she saw her just then: round, feminine. *White girls and their bodies,* she started to tsk-tsk, but stopped herself. For a few seconds she hadn't seen Trish as a white girl at all, just as a woman, as her sister. "This was a good idea," she said instead.

They sat and let the steam and hot water cleanse and purify, healing their bodies, minds, and spirits.

After an hour's soak, it was time for Billie's massage.

"What do you want to focus on?" Anna, the massage therapist, asked. "Do you have any problem areas I should know about?"

"I just lost a baby," Billie said. She was lying stomach down, her face in the headrest off the edge of the massage table. The massage room was small and cozy. "And I'm trying to come out of a lupus flare."

"Oh, I'm so sorry." Anna touched Billie's bare shoulder. "Sounds like some stress relief would be good?"

"That would be great," Billie said to the floor. She could see pink light coming from the Christmas lights strung on the plant in the corner and Anna's polished toenails, also pink. Native American flutes and drums played softly from a CD in the background.

Her body felt pleasantly heavy from the long soak. Anna's hands were strong, and when she kneaded the muscles in Billie's neck and shoulders, Billie felt her regrets and sorrows begin to rise through her skin and into Anna's fingers. Then Anna started to work on her lower back, and she felt her solar plexus tighten, but as Anna rubbed, the knots began to give. Billie felt herself opening all the way up to her chest, her heart chakra. At first it scared her and she clenched, trying to stop it. Opening up was dangerous. The pain would come again. But then she remembered a quote from Audre Lorde's *The Cancer Journals:* "I must let this pain flow through me and pass on." The only way out of the sadness was through it. She stopped fighting and let her body unleash all the hurt it had been holding.

"You want to stop for a while?" Anna murmured, as Billie wept.

"No."

Anna handed her a tissue. "Good. It's good to let it out."

Billie blew her nose and they continued.

"Just breathe it out. Let it all go," Anna said softly.

Salty tears flowed down Billie's cheeks and soaked into the terrycloth fabric around the headrest. She let herself cry for the loss of her baby, and for the mistake she had made by not talking with Nick about a baby before she got pregnant. For how she had almost turned Trish away, for all the lost years she had missed with her sister.

She remembered how she had injured her parents with her silence when she first found out she was adopted, and she cried for the mother who had raised her and for the mother she never knew. For as much as she loved and was grateful for her parents, surely there was a little part of her infant self that missed her original mother.

Anna pressed and pulled her aching body, murmuring, "Let it go. Let it go," until Billie was completely cried out.

When the massage was over, Anna mixed a bucket of sea kelp and clay with water and spread it on Billie's face, arms, and legs with a paintbrush. Then she wrapped Billie in sheets and blankets as if she were a caterpillar in a cocoon, and turned the heat lamp on above her.

"Comfortable? I'll be back in half an hour."

As the mud tightened over her skin, Billie breathed more deeply than she had in days. With her steady breathing, the mud, and the heat lamp, all four elements—earth, water, fire, and air—were brought together to help heal her. She settled into them, gave herself over to them.

Afterward, her joints feeling looser than they had in days, she waited outside on the deck for Trish. Below, the Soda Creek whooshed over river rocks and boulders. Up here in the Rockies the air was pleasantly cool and fresh. Potted plants and wildflowers along the creek below danced in the breeze. Billie was as relaxed as she had ever been and knew she'd go back to sleep on the drive back home. She was sleepy, but in a good way. Now sleep was about rest, not escape.

Soon Trish stumbled outside, blinking in the sunlight. "*Wow, do I feel good!*"

"Me too."

"I'm like a giant noodle."

As they walked to the car, the wind grew stronger. Red, yellow, and pink flower petals pirouetted in the air like ballerinas, landing softly on the gravel around them.

Billie climbed into the car and buckled her seat belt. Just as she was closing her eyes, she felt warmth build in her, and a familiar voice said, "*Rest yourself, Daughter.*" She smiled with gratitude. Whoever these ancestors were, they were back. She obeyed them and let sleep claim her.

She woke when she felt the car come to a stop. She looked around. They were still in Idaho Springs, at a stop sign in front of a row of tiny Victorian houses painted in cheerful pastels, like Easter eggs. Pine-covered mountains rose on either side of them, the highest peaks covered in snow, even in late summer.

"I have to let him go, don't I?" Trish asked.

"I think so," Billie answered, knowing Trish meant Will.

Trish took a deep breath. "How?"

Billie looked into her eyes. One day she would tell Trish that she knew how hard it was to let go of a child. A child she had never even held. She could only imagine how hard it must be to let go of one that you had loved and protected for sixteen years. But if she said all that right now, she'd cry all the way home and she wanted to do as the ancestors had recommended. She wanted a rest from her grief.

"The same way mothers have been letting go of children since the beginning of time. With tears. And with help from your sister."

Trish smiled a small, sad smile. She spoke, looking straight ahead, "You asked me before what I thought when I saw Will in the mall handcuffed by the security guards. . . ."

Billie waited.

"I thought, 'He's not like that.' I thought, 'He's one of the good ones.' And I always thought that about Tommy too. Like it was okay that he was black because he wasn't like all those other black people.

"But what does that even mean? He's not a thief or a crackhead?" she asked, still not looking at Billie. "And I was relieved, I was, when I met you and you were so . . . like me. Not foreign somehow. Ugh, I'm so disgusted with myself."

Billie didn't reply. Trish seemed to be working things out as she spoke. Billie could almost hear the realizations clicking together in Trish's mind.

"I think, maybe on some level, I knew about your race when I was little, you know? Maybe I overheard something? And I wonder if maybe that's not why I ended up with a black man and maybe that's why I had Will. Like I could make up for the past, like I could have the life that our mother was denied. . . ."

Finally, Trish looked at her sister. "Listen, I'm not asking on behalf of all white people for you to speak for all black people. I don't want you to absolve us for generations of prejudice, but can *you* forgive *me*?"

Billie searched her sister's face. She saw contrition and the beginnings of understanding. "When you first told me about Will and his thing with church, I thought you were overreacting," she replied. " 'Silly white girl,' I believe is what came to mind."

Trish's expression was a mixture of hurt and knowledge; a suspicion confirmed.

"But you were right about Clear View. Your intuition was speaking to you, and you were being wise to listen. I was wrong about you."

Trish's eyes welled, but she blinked back the tears and kept them from falling.

Billie looked out the windshield at the road ahead of them. "Through the ages, white people used skin color to divide us and we bought into it. House slaves versus field slaves. In South Africa the 'colored' versus the black. My own mother even envied me my skin color because it would give me a little step up that she wouldn't have."

"Jesus." Trish let out a long breath.

"It just seems to me that if I don't claim my blackness then I'm falling into that same trap. I'm playing a game I don't want to play."

"Do you think you might be able to claim me without feeling like you're rejecting your mother?"

Billie turned to look at Trish. It was true. That was the choice she felt in her heart, and she would never reject her parents. But maybe there was a way to have both. She realized she had been holding her own breath, so she exhaled too. "I had a dream right before you came to my house that first time," she said. "My grandmother Wilhelmina and an elderly white lady came to me and told me they believed in Ambata; the name means 'to connect' in Kiswahili. At the time, I thought they were symbols of the crone trying to tell me something about the baby. But it was our grandmothers, and they were talking about connection."

"Wait, Nana was speaking *Swahili*?!"

"I guess she wanted to get my attention."

"To tell you she wanted us to connect?"

Billie nodded, hoping Trish would see that she wanted to be done fighting too.

"And your adopted grandmother was in on it too? What, you think the two of them met in the afterlife and cooked up a plan?"

Billie shrugged and nodded. Stranger things had happened.

"Well, that's damn fucking amazing," Trish said.

"It most certainly is." Billie felt lighter than she had in weeks. The weight of being angry at herself about losing the baby, the weight of holding back her heart from Trish, the weight of worrying about Nick were gone.

But the lightness of her heart didn't extend to her eyelids, which felt heavy again. "I'm just going to close my eyes for a bit."

"Have at it."

Billie felt the car start to move again and they were on their way.

She slept sixteen hours straight that night. The next day, after she ate a large bowl of oatmeal with blueberries and cinnamon and two mugs of green tea, she went into her bedroom and pulled the small table out of the closet. She covered it with the white table-cloth and got the photos of her family out of her drawer and returned them to their rightful places. She looked at the faces staring out at her, hope in the eyes of the young, and lifetimes of joy, pain, betrayal, and redemption etched in the faces of the old. All of them beautiful.

Free men, former slaves, miners, farmers, doctors, artists, teachers, soldiers, singers, builders, preachers. They *were* her ancestors. They were part of the people who had loved her and raised her, therefore they were part of her. She even included the photo of the Cheyenne girl, who had represented the Native American blood she had been told she carried. Now the girl would symbolize the link between all peoples. After all, everybody came from that first mother who walked out of Africa and populated the earth.

But something was still not quite right. She got the picture of her birth mother, Trish, and herself when she was an infant and added it to the table. There. She smiled at the faces of her family, known and unknown, related by blood and related by spirit.

Next, she retrieved Maxine's letter, set it in the blue bowl, and lit it with a match. After she watched the paper turn from white to black to ash, she lit a sage smudge stick and went through the house clearing the air with smoke.

Two days later Nick moved back into the house.

Billie lay on her back, looking into the eyes of the man she loved. This was the first time since she lost the baby that they would make love. Her diaphragm was securely in place. Until she and Nick agreed, she wouldn't be taking any more chances on creating another baby. No matter what the calendar said.

Nick was propped up on his right elbow looking down at her. He slipped his left hand under the cover, gently circling his fingertips over her breasts and torso.

Full, Billie thought as he brushed the ribs under her left breast. *My heart is full.*

Then his hand landed on her belly, and the word that came to her was *empty.* She moved his hand back to her heart.

"I still want to have a baby."

He sighed. "I know, but I can't watch you go through another miscarriage. I couldn't take that."

An idea had been working its way around inside Billie for a few days. But was this really the time to bring it up? She held her breath for a second. *Say it,* the ancestors told her. *Just spit it out.*

"What would you think about adopting?" she blurted in a rush of air.

Nick traced his finger down the center of her body, following her breastbone to her navel to the wild triangle of hair between her legs. She inhaled sharply.

"That's a thought," he said.

"Really?"

He kissed her. "Let's see where life takes us."

They made love gently. Nick had never left her heart, and she welcomed him back into her body.

Afterward, they lay quietly together until Nick's stomach started to growl.

"Be right back," Billie said. She recalled Trish's smile when she told her about using the vibrator. If Trish could lighten up, so could she. She went to the kitchen and returned to bed with two bowls and two spoons.

"What's this?" Nick took the bowl she handed him. "Ice cream?!"

"I'm having fruit salad." Her spoon was tiny; the mouth of it could barely hold one piece of fruit at a time, but she felt happy using it.

CHAPTER 25

Trish

"You keep in touch with your mama or I'ma come down there and whup some namesake behind. Hear me?" Billie said to Will.

"Yes, ma'am," Will answered.

They were in the terminal at Denver International Airport and Will was heading to live with his father for the school year. Trish had shipped boxes of video games, CDs, comic books, and sneakers back to North Carolina. All Will was taking was a roller suitcase and a backpack. Henrietta would stay on his bed in Colorado waiting, like Trish, for his return.

Nick and Will did a man-hug: chest bump and pat on the back. "Take it easy, Nephew," Nick said.

"God bless you, Uncle."

Trish couldn't believe it was really happening. Will was leaving. But she had agreed to it, had determined that it was the right thing to do. "I'll see you at Christmastime," she said to him, the quiver in her voice betraying her uncertainty.

"I love you, Mama."

That's when the water in her eyes spilled over. "I'm so proud of you and love you so much!"

Will awkwardly hugged her to him, which only made her cry harder.

"Don't cry. C'mon. It'll be okay," he murmured.

Trish struggled to pull herself together, but the cat was out of the bag about how she felt. Mopping her eyes, she said, "You're still underage. I could get a pass and come with you to the gate."

"I'm good. I'll call you when I land."

Trish clutched his shirt. "You'll keep in touch, right? You won't make me have to track you down?"

"I'll email you and call you."

Nick looked at his watch. "Hate to say it, but you better go. That security line is long."

"Yeah. You don't want to miss your flight," Billie added.

Trish looked down at her hand grasping her son. One by one she loosened her fingers. She watched him, a piece of herself, walk away. When he was out of sight, she grabbed her stomach and doubled over. "I can't . . . I can't breathe. I don't think I can do this. I don't think—"

Billie gripped her arms and pulled her up straight. Then she leaned in and put her forehead next to Trish's, their faces almost touching, the splotches on their cheeks the mirror image of each other. "Yes, you can. You can do this. I'm right here with you. You *can* do this."

Billie took a deep breath and Trish mimicked her, inhaling and exhaling until the sound of their breathing was louder than the memory of Will's goodbye.

When Trish was breathing steadily, Billie pulled back. "Want some lavender oil? It'll help you relax."

"Can't hurt," Trish said, accepting the small bottle. She dabbed lavender oil on her wrists and rubbed some behind her ears. "Maybe I should dump the whole thing over my head. Shit, what the hell am I going to do with myself?"

"You're going to school to become a vet."

The lavender smelled good, but didn't affect her emotions. She was starting to panic again. "I don't start classes until next semester, five whole months from now."

Billie linked one arm through Trish's arm and one through Nick's and started walking. "Well, right now we're going to the health-food store and then you're coming over for dinner at our house. Jimmy and Yolanda and Mommy and Daddy are coming too. Tomorrow, you'll be busy at work. And Monday you're bringing Jigsaw to my class."

Billie had read that sometimes kids felt more comfortable reading out loud to a dog. Billie's students weren't old enough to read yet, but she had asked Trish to bring Jigsaw over for story time once a week.

"That's the foreseeable future that we have all planned out," Billie said. "We'll tackle the rest as it comes."

"We?" The word circled Trish like a life preserver and pulled her to the surface.

"We."

She remembered the comfort Nick had offered that night on his porch. "Say, Nick, you wouldn't happen to be able to hook me up tonight, would you?" she asked.

"I could probably get my boy Paul to come over to meet you for dinner," Nick replied. "He's a drummer."

"No!" Trish's whole face turned the color of her birthmark. "I was talking about . . . you know . . . what you get from your neighbor. . . ."

Nick laughed. "Sister-in-law, I can hook you up with both."

She shook her head. "Not tonight."

"But one day," Billie said.

Trish could almost see it: Billie, Nick, their baby, Will, Zenobia, Herbert, Jimmy, Yolanda, and their child all together. And a man for Trish to love as much as Billie loved Nick. A family. "One day."

"I'll take you over to Fletcher's," Nick said. "But I won't be lighting up with you. I'm still trying to chill on that a little bit for a while."

"Yeah, maybe I'd better cool it too. Don't want Zenobia to think I'm a junkie."

They stopped in front of the reflecting pool that travelers use as a wishing well. The fountains weren't on, so the water was still. Trish looked down and could see the copper and silver wishes of hundreds of travelers shimmering at the bottom. She made out her reflection on the water's surface. Then Billie's face appeared on the water next to hers.

We.

All day she had been consumed with what she was losing, but look what she had gained. She realized that in some way Billie had been with her all along. She'd named Will after her, after all. If Billie had always been with her, then Will didn't have to be right there to be with her. She'd let him go, but she wasn't losing him.

She stared at her image in the water. She looked the same, but how much had changed in so little time.

She thought of Nana. If her spirit had managed to bring Trish back together with her sister, then somewhere along the way Nana had experienced a shift too. Maybe by the time Trish was in high school and had met Tommy, Nana *really* did feel remorseful for what she had done.

Someone tossed a coin into the water, and Trish and Billie's reflections dissipated in the ripples and then came back together.

Maybe it was like the information I found about the Japanese Bud-dhists. Maybe we were all mizuko, *all unformed beings, always in a state of becoming,* Trish mused. *Everybody is a work in progress.*

She felt Billie take her hand. Then, at the same time, the two faces in the water smiled and turned away to go home.

ACKNOWLEDGMENTS

As always, I will start by acknowledging my family; they are where I started. This time I add someone new to the mix: my half sister, Charlene, who I'm just getting to know after all these years. I owe a great debt to my sister-in-law, Suzanne Brice and her birth sister, Carolyn Kay Meyeraan, to my friend Amber Batson for inspiring the starting point of this story, and to Kathy Mackechney and the folks at Colorado Adoptees in Search for sharing their stories of relinquishment, adoption, and reunion.

I'm grateful to Brenda Sasa and S.R. for educating me about what it's like to have lupus. Billie isn't meant to represent either person, but I hope I did justice to the insights they provided.

Victoria Sanders and Benee Knauer, my go-to girls: A bazillion thanks for everything! Caron K, thanks for your help with Lifetime and movie rights for *Orange Mint and Honey*. I'm grateful to Melody Guy, my editor, for your patience, thoughtful insights, and kindness. Melody, you are a gem! Thank you also to Porscha Burke, Jane von Mehren, Dreu Pennington-McNeil, Shona McCarthy, and to everyone at Random House for your hard work on my behalf.

I'd like to thank my Lighthouse Writers Workshop teacher Bill Henderson and master-novel classmates for helping me figure out my story. Muchas smooches to Marisol Simon, the best beta reader a writer could ask for, and to Rob Simon, for the infamous web video.

Thank you Denver Literary Ladies Luncheon. And my gratitude to all my writer buddies: Lisa Kenney, Ellen Oh, Olufunke Grace Bankole, Tayari Jones, Lady Lee, Judy Merrill Larsen, Karen Simpson, Karen Carter, Larramie, J. D. Mason, Gina Black, Shauna Roberts, Shon Bacon, ReadersRooms.com, the Girlfriends Cyber Circuit, Bernice McFadden, Lori Tharps, Kim Reid, Amy MacKinnon, Therese Fowler, Donna Hill, Bonnie Glover, Donna Grant and Virginia DeBerry, and many others for your advice, encouragement, support, and friendship! The Internet is a wonderful thing.

My sincere thanks to booksellers and librarians everywhere! People who love books are my favorite people in the world. Also, I say a hearty thank-you to Patrik Henry Bass and the *Essence* Book Club, Carol Mackey and the Black Expressions Book Club, Pat Houser and members of the Go on Girl! Book Club, Yasmin Coleman and the APOOO Book Club, Tee C. Royal and the RAWSISTAZ Book Club, Troy Johnson and AALBC.com, and all the book groups who read my work and invite me to participate in your discussions in person or over the phone. You all make or break a book, so I'm honored to have your support and very grateful to you!

Last, but nowhere near least, my love to Dirk and to the Dicksons for making me feel like a beloved member of their family, and love to my women friends, sisters all.

Children of the Waters

CARLEEN BRICE

A Reader's Guide

A Conversation with Carleen Brice

Random House Reader's Circle: Carleen, it's a pleasure getting the chance to sit with you and talk all things books, now that you're a seasoned and award-winning novelist! Perhaps the best place to start would be to ask how you feel about the success of your first novel. *Orange Mint and Honey* earned the First Fiction Award from the Black Caucus of the American Library Association and debut novel honors from the African American Literary Book Club. It was an *Essence* book club pick, and there's been interest from Hollywood—and of course, admiration from readers everywhere. Did you have any idea that this would happen?

Carleen Brice: I hoped, of course, for good things to come, but it's pretty surreal when it happens. When they called my name at the awards for the African American Literary Book Club, and people at my table—who I had just met that night—screamed for me, it was amazing. The whole process has been incredible. I'm overjoyed and honored that my work has received so much attention. But the best thing has been reader response—I'm so grateful to the people who've taken the time to email me or write reviews online.

RHRC: Can you tell us a bit about your visits to individual book clubs to discuss *Orange Mint and Honey?* How did that come about? How did you find the experience?

CB: Book clubs contact me through my website, www.carleenbrice .com, or approach me at events and whenever I can, I make it a point to attend in person or via phone. It's wonderful to hear the discussions firsthand. When you're writing about your characters, it's just you and them in a room. It's really fun to see other people relate to them and treat them like they're real—feeling sorry for them or getting mad at them—just like I did when I was writing.

At first people are a little shy because the author is right there, but eventually they loosen up (the drinks served at book clubs might have a little to do with that!) and start saying how they really feel about the characters and the plot. I encourage that honesty (though so far it's easy to do because nobody has hated it). It's fun to hear one person say "I thought it was wrong for them to act out in the church the way they did." And then someone else say, "I understand it. If I was Shay I would have been hollering too!" It makes me feel like I did my job when some of the group is siding with Shay and some of the group is siding with Nona, which happens at every single book club.

RHRC: Did any of the early feedback you received about *Orange Mint and Honey* impact the way you wrote this novel (which, by the way, is simply stunning)?

CB: Thank you! I wouldn't say the feedback impacted how I write. I feel like I learned a lot writing my first novel, but writing this book was a completely different thing so I don't know how much was applied to it. My goals were the same: to make people think and feel and for them to be entertained. It was inspiring to see that people responded so well to my first novel. It gave me hope that readers are interested in the same kind of characters and stories that I am.

RHRC: *Children of the Waters* touches on so many issues—chronic illness, family secrets, interracial relationships, challenging pregnancies, holistic healing, self-esteem. How did you come to write this novel? Did any characters or storylines jump out at you above any others?

CB: Well, the nugget of the story—the relationship with Trish and Billie—is based on a true story. One of my sisters-in-law is biracial and her family put her up for adoption and kept her older sister who is white. In real life she was adopted by a white family, so when her white birth sister found her, race wasn't much of an issue. (And unlike Billie she was actually immediately very close with her birth sister.) There was also a young woman who worked for me years ago who discovered at a young age that her birth mother was Native American. Those two stories fascinated me.

And truth be told I have a half sister who I've never met, and yet here I've written two books with characters who are half sisters. We've recently been in touch and I hope we'll meet one day soon.

As far as interracial relationships go, my husband is white. One brother was married to a biracial woman and all his in-laws were white. My other brother is married to a Latina. Our family is, like many, many families in this country, quite a mixed bag.

I'm fascinated by reconciliation and how the past affects us even if we don't think it does. So family secrets and dynamics are something I'm just naturally drawn to.

RHRC: All of your characters have so many layers—especially Billie, whose ability to self-heal, reverence for her ancestors, and fulfilling love life are so expertly combined into one fierce package. Can you tell us a bit about how you came to put her together?

What would you like most for readers to come away with in their understanding of this amazing woman?

CB: My husband says Billie is me. That's not completely true, but I believe my ancestors are with me, and I'm into holistic healing. Billie and Trish are both combinations of myself and other women I know, and my family. My family is all through this book! I have a couple of aunties who are different parts of Zenobia. Herbert and Fletcher are different parts of one of my grandfathers. Billie's love for them is definitely my love for my family coming through. So I start with those basics and then characters become themselves. It's funny how once you give a character a name and a little history, you start to know the rest of what works for them.

RHRC: Why did you select lupus as Billie's illness?

CB: I have a friend who was diagnosed with lupus, and it's a disease that affects a lot of women in this country. I'm happy to shed a little light on it.

RHRC: Admittedly, Nick just might be our favorite character—although his irritable mood in the early chapters did kind of get under our skin. There was obviously so much more to this man than meets the eye. And in the love scene with Billie, where she thought he was moving back upstairs, he just about took our breath away! May we ask where you drew your inspiration from for Nick—and if he's based on a real life character, does he have any real life brothers?!

CB: That's so funny! I'm sure there are plenty of Nicks out there in real life.

RHRC: More seriously, *Children of the Waters* brings to the forefront so many questions about black male identity, from Nick's familial challenges to Tommy's distant parenting approach and

Will's struggles with being reared by a white woman. What type of dialogue are you hoping to encourage with these intense characters and scenarios?

CB: I like writing about people who are like the people I know and see in real life. I like Nick because he's flawed and human, and yet very romantic and a good guy. I'm interested in helping the world see that Barack Obama isn't the only good black man. There are many. And what about Fletcher—he just might be *my* favorite character!

RHRC: Now, we know you're no stranger to discussions of race with regards to literature. In your blog welcomewhitefolks .blogspot.com, you host a forum for discussing how books by black authors are marketed, sold, and appreciated by non-black audiences. What made you begin this blog and what types of feedback have you received?

CB: My blog is an answer to a call to action a writer posted on readersrooms.com (a site about African American fiction). Shon Bacon and novelist Bernice McFadden were discussing writers starting a grassroots effort similar to President Obama's campaign to reach a wider audience. I semi-jokingly said, "We should start a holiday called Buy a Book by Somebody Black and Give It to Somebody White," and one thing led to another.

The feedback has been overwhelmingly positive. Most people get it. However, anytime you start talking about race in this country, things can get dicey. Some blacks and whites have been offended by the blog. Some don't understand why it's necessary, or disagree about how I'm choosing to talk about these issues, and that's their right. But the best response has been emails from white readers asking me for suggestions of books to read, and a white editor who works in New York City publishing blogging about racism in publishing. I feel like my blog readers and I are shining a light on an issue in a way that will hopefully benefit writers, publishers, and readers.

RHRC: What do you think needs to happen in order for up-and-coming black authors to rise to a level of visibility like the Toni Morrisons and Maya Angelous of the world?

CB: Well, I suggested in one article that booksellers make their African American fiction sections smell like cookies; shower customers with confetti every time they enter the section; and let the champagne punch flow like a river. But that's probably not realistic!

I think it will take a concerted effort on the part of readers to shop outside their comfort zones. I think people will need to stop assuming that just because black people are on the cover, the book is *only* for black readers.

Through my site I've discovered that most white readers don't even know that African American fiction exists. And some black readers are turned off by urban fiction, therefore they avoid the section. I'm trying to help get the attention of all those readers to let them know about the enjoyable, well-written, high-quality fiction (literary and commercial) shelved in the Af Am section. I know the audience is out there of people of all races who will find that many, many black writers write fiction that is universal. We've just got to find them and encourage them.

RHRC: You mention the 2008 Democratic National Convention in this novel. Can you share with us some of your experiences around this moment—especially as a Denver resident—and whether or not you think there's an "Obama Effect" on all things black, including fiction?

CB: Right in my own backyard and I didn't see any of it in person! I was sick during the convention and standing in lines and walking for miles from where you parked to the convention sights just wasn't an option. So my experience was much like the rest of the country's—staring at a television through tears of joy. But I did have one "celebrity moment." I watched Joe Biden's speech in Lou Gossett Jr.'s hotel room! Mr. Gossett is a promoter of my first non-fiction book, so while he was in town we got to finally meet in person. Afterward, while I was waiting for the valet to get my car at his hotel, a young woman asked me to share a taxi with her. I explained I was waiting for my car and going home, but later heard her talking about a hip party she was going to where Kanye West was supposed to perform. I wish I could have forgotten about my car and hopped in the taxi with her, but I would have been asleep hours before Kanye came on stage! Sad, but true.

I'm hoping and praying for an Obama effect. I'm hoping all those white folks who put race aside and voted in their own best interests will do the same in their personal lives. Vote their own best interests in book stores and be exposed to some really good books regardless of the race of the writers or characters. We'll see. . . .

RHRC: And for fun—where did you *ever* come up with names Cymfonee and A'Lexus?! How on earth do you think of this stuff? (And more important, can you tell us about your writing process, how you find inspiration, what keeps you motivated, and how you find the discipline to finish a novel?)

CB: I'm glad you liked them! They were fun to come up with. I volunteer at a Head Start and I see lots of interesting names, so I had some good inspiration.

My writing process involves lots of coffee, tears, prayers, and walks. It used to involve lots of cookies, but I'm trying to tempt my muse with healthier options these days. I also keep track of my daily word counts in a notebook and I love to see the numbers add up (sort of like going on a diet, in reverse).

Writing a book in much like starting a relationship. At the beginning it's all hearts and flowers and you're madly in love with your story. Your story can do no wrong. Until it does. (For me, this is around page 100.) Then you start to notice what a jerk your story really is and start secretly thinking you can do better. You may even start cheating and work on another story on the side. Whether you give in to temptation or not, this is the moment you have to ask yourself why you thought your story was worth it in the first place. You remind yourself of why you wanted to tell this story and how important it is to you, and, you hope, how important it'll be to others. Then you stop winking at other stories and focus on this one. You do this over and over and over until publication do you part.

RHRC: We've already discussed your blog (well, *one* of them—how do you have the time?!), and you're also active on Facebook and Twitter. How are you finding the experience of all the social networking online? Do you think all of these Internet tools are really useful to writers—or even necessary—and in what way?

CB: I love online networking. I really do. When you're writing at home in your pajamas, the social networks online are like your water cooler and break room. And online friends have been enormously supportive of me and my work. It's great to "meet" people with shared values or opinions and help each other out. I love promoting other authors and the good karma has come back to me 100 percent.

But it's time-consuming, and really easy to hang out on Facebook rather than get work done. But writers are always going to find a way to procrastinate—at least I will! So it might as well be a way that promotes my work and allows me to gain great information and friendships.

RHRC: Well, thank you very much for your time, Carleen. We're true fans, and we count ourselves lucky to work with you and to help share your work more widely. We wish you the best in all you do—and hope to read more from you soon!

QUESTIONS AND TOPICS FOR DISCUSSION

1. On p. 230, Billie puts dirt from her mother's grave in her mojo bag, noting that, "Dirt from a mother's grave was some of the strongest protection there was." Why do you think that is? What protective elements would you put in your mojo bag?

2. Do you agree with Trish in keeping Will out of church while he was grounded?

3. Was Will justified in being angry with the mall security guard who picked him up for shoplifting?

4. Was Billie unrealistic in how she expected Nick to react to the news of her pregnancy? Do you think she purposefully tried to get pregnant against his will?

5. How would you gauge Trish's decision to visit Billie, despite Zenobia asking her not to out of concern for Billie's illness and the health of the baby? Would you say Trish's actions were selfish? How could her visit have benefited Billie? In Trish's shoes, would

you have visited Billie immediately, or would you have respected Zenobia's wishes and waited until after the pregnancy?

6. How did you feel about Billie's visit to her mother and grand-parents' burial site? Did you think her harsh words to her grand-parents were warranted? Did it seem hypocritical of her to speak to her true maternal ancestors in that way after she so reverenced her other ancestors?

7. Why do you think Zenobia and Herbert chose to keep Billie's adoption a secret? Do you feel that adopted children should al-ways be informed about their natural parentage?

8. What do you think Tommy's role is in Will's life? And do you think he's more important to Will, or to Trish, and why?

9. Why do you think it took so long—until meeting Billie, really—for Will to find a connection to his African American heritage? Why didn't he learn about black history earlier? Do you think Trish's desires to see the world through a colorblind lens helped or harmed him in the end?

10. How would you compare or contrast Will and Billie with re-gard to how they construct their ethnic identities? Billie's sense of identity was shaken when she learned of her mixed-race her-itage. In what way does Will, when he is accused of shoplifting, also have to face startling truths about his ethnicity?

11. Billie sums up the way she was treated by black girls on p. 234 by saying, "I 'talked white' and was light-skinned so they used to pick on me." What does "talking white" mean? Have you experi-enced being called (or calling someone else) an oreo? What im-pact did that experience have on your idea of race and skin color?

12. Does the information she found justify Billie's searching through Nick's things on p. 236? Have you ever snooped through a loved one's belongings and had your suspicions confirmed? How did you feel afterward, and were you able to forgive or be forgiven?

13. Did you sense anything fishy going on at Clear View Church? Was the clergy's outward showing of wealth suspicious to you? What did you think was at work within that church? Why do you think it was attractive to Will?

14. On p. 255, Trish says to Billie, "Face it, mixed-race people are the hottest thing going! Barack Obama, Halle Berry, Alicia Keys! What have you got to complain about? How has your life been so bad?" Is what Trish said true? How do you perceive people of biracial parentage? Are they more privileged than their single-race peers?

15. On p. 282 Will says, "Are you black because of your skin color? Are you black because of how you talk or how you dress?" How would you answer him? What does make a black person black and a white person white in America? Do you think that race is more of a social construct or a biological one?

ABOUT THE AUTHOR

CARLEEN BRICE is the author of the *Essence* Book Club pick *Orange Mint and Honey, Walk Tall: Affirmations for People of Color,* and *Lead Me Home: An African American's Guide Through the Grief Journey.* She also edited the anthology *Age Ain't Nothing but a Number: Black Women Explore Midlife.* She lives in Denver with her musician husband and two cats. You can visit her online at www.carleenbrice.com and www.pajamagardener.blogspot.com, where she blogs about writing, gardening, and other topics that strike her mind or boggle her fancy.